THE UNICORN QUEST
FIRE IN THE STAR

Also by Kamilla Benko

The Unicorn Quest
Secret in the Stone
✳
Frozen II: Forest of Shadows

THE UNICORN QUEST
FIRE IN THE STAR

KAMILLA BENKO

BLOOMSBURY
CHILDREN'S BOOKS
NEW YORK LONDON OXFORD NEW DELHI SYDNEY

BLOOMSBURY CHILDREN'S BOOKS
Bloomsbury Publishing Inc., part of Bloomsbury Publishing Plc
1385 Broadway, New York, NY 10018

BLOOMSBURY, BLOOMSBURY CHILDREN'S BOOKS, and the Diana logo
are trademarks of Bloomsbury Publishing Plc

First published in the United States of America in February 2020
by Bloomsbury Children's Books

Bloomsbury books may be purchased for business or promotional use. For information
on bulk purchases please contact Macmillan Corporate and Premium Sales Department at
specialmarkets@macmillan.com

Library of Congress Cataloging-in-Publication Data
Names: Benko, Kamilla, author.
Title: Fire in the star / by Kamilla Benko.
Description: New York : Bloomsbury Children's Books, 2020. | Series: [Unicorn quest ; v. 3]
Summary: When Claire discovers that "only a queen can defeat a queen," she knows
she must steal and reforge the ancient Crown of Arden to stand a chance against
the darkness that threatens the world and her family.
Identifiers: LCCN 2019053842 (print) • LCCN 2019053843 (e-book)
ISBN 978-1-68119-249-9 (hardback) • ISBN 978-1-68119-250-5 (e-book)
Subjects: CYAC: Sisters—Fiction. | Magic—Fiction. | Adventure and adventurers—
Fiction. | Unicorns—Fiction. | Fantasy.
Classification: LCC PZ7.1.B4537 Fir 2020 (print) | LCC PZ7.1.B4537 (e-book) |
DDC [Fic]—dc23
LC record available at https://lccn.loc.gov/2019053842

Book design by Amanda Bartlett
Typeset by Westchester Publishing Services
Printed and bound in the U.S.A. by Berryville Graphics Inc., Berryville, Virginia
2 4 6 8 10 9 7 5 3 1

All papers used by Bloomsbury Publishing Plc are natural, recyclable products made
from wood grown in well-managed forests. The manufacturing processes conform
to the environmental regulations of the country of origin.

To find out more about our authors and books visit www.bloomsbury.com
and sign up for our newsletters.

For Andrej,
I'm glad we're on this quest together

THE UNICORN QUEST
FIRE IN THE STAR

THE TRAVELER'S SONG

The horn may sound
And faces may fade
But follow the edge on the blade.

The sails may rip
And signs be misread
But follow the needle in the thread.

Lands may be lost
And worlds may be found
But follow the moss on the ground.

The way may be long
And the path may be hard
But follow the fire in the star.

Your feet may fail
And your eyes grow dark
But follow the beat of my heart.

And I'll meet you there,
In the space between,
For the unicorn
Was always
me.

—S. A. M.

CHAPTER
1

Claire Martinson was doing something either incredibly brave or incredibly foolish—and deep down, she suspected it was the second. Because if she were actually brave, her heart probably wouldn't be pounding in her throat and her palms wouldn't be slick with sweat.

A hundred feet below her, the sea chopped at the wooden hull of the *Thread Cutter*, sending Claire's world swaying. She wasn't *un*comfortable with heights necessarily, but being huddled at the highest point of the ship, with only a few wooden slabs to stop her from tumbling into the gray water, left her feeling exposed. Still, it wasn't the height of her perch that set her pulse racing.

Bracing herself against the mast, Claire carefully sifted through some of the contents of her traveling pack: a blanket, a bundle of seed cakes, a tiny pink marble, and a water-stained map.

Normal enough.

But what wasn't normal—at least for a rising sixth grader to have—was the slender spyglass that gleamed from within the bag's belly, nestled next to a gauzy handkerchief that shimmered like the Milky Way.

And, of course, the arrow in her hand.

A Lode Arrow, to be specific. One that would take her exactly where she pointed it. Exactly where she needed to be . . . hopefully.

Staring down at the weapon, Claire wondered for the thousandth time if she was making the right choice. If the stone was properly attached to the arrow. If the bow she'd cobbled together would give her the spring she so desperately needed. That Arden so desperately needed. That Sophie needed.

"Mind the rigging!"

Claire looked up just in time to see the tail end of a rope whir upward as the crew on deck used pulleys to unpack barrels and crates from the anchored ship. From the vantage point of the crow's nest, the ropes moved around in a hypnotic ballet of twists and spirals, some just sweeping past one another while others swung into solid knots that might never be undone . . . knots like the one Claire had found herself in.

All their fates—Claire's, Sophie's, Arden's—were tangled together, and Claire didn't know the exact moment in time the knot had formed.

Had the threads first begun to weave together when her older sister, Sophie, asked Claire to follow her up the ladder in Great-Aunt Diana's fireplace and they clambered into Arden? Or did they have the chance, even then, to avoid becoming snarled in a legend? Maybe the binds tightened when Sophie threw herself between Claire and an arrow, almost fatally injuring herself, or the moment Claire freed the last unicorn from the rock.

Or perhaps their lives would have always been tangled with Arden's, no matter their choices.

Because they hadn't been the only Martinsons to discover Arden. The first had been Great-Aunt Diana, who had fallen so in love with it that she had decided to change her name to Nadia and stay in Arden permanently, leading everyone else to presume she was dead.

Which had led to Dad inheriting Windemere Manor and all its contents.

Which had led to a family summer spent cataloging the house's more interesting collections and the discovery of double doors that opened into a gallery with a fireplace on the far end.

But it was also possible that the threads stretched back even *further* than Great-Aunt Diana/Nadia. After all, Claire and Sophie and Aunt Nadia weren't just visitors *to* Arden— they were protectors *of* Arden—princesses, specifically, as they were all the descendants of a long-ago prince who had tunneled his way to another world to escape his older sister, the unicorn-hunting queen Estelle d'Astora, nearly three hundred Arden years ago.

Claire shivered. The garnet tunic had been warm enough when she packed it a week ago, but the wind had picked up, bringing with it the taste of cold and a distant rumble of thunder, as well as a brand-new worry: How long would she stay invisible if it started to rain?

She was not invisible in the way grown-ups sometimes used to describe Claire and other kids like her who were good at being quiet and remaining unnoticed, but in the *truest* sense of the word. Because even though Claire could feel the arrow's slight weight on her palm, it still appeared to be floating in midair. She was *actually* invisible—but for how much longer?

At the beginning of her journey, she had needed to tilt her head and squint to see the outline of her body, but now, as she looked, she only needed to half squint to make out her chewed fingernails.

The Invis-Ability dye was definitely wearing off.

In Arden, the four guilds knew how to coax magic out from the basic building blocks of craft. Spinners knew how to spin and sew fabric in just the right way to make a cape fly, while a Forger could polish a mirror so shiny that it could reflect the future. There were also Gemmers, like Claire, who, if they were inclined, could carve entire armies from the sides of mountains. And finally, there were Tillers, those who could whisper sunlight from leaves or brew herbs into a dye that could paint something—or someone—the color of invisibility.

And it was *this* that had most interested Claire as she had stood in Woven Root's colorful market and watched a teenage Spinner and Tiller dye countless pairs of boots for the hidden village's assembling army. She'd offered to help them clean up, but instead of dumping out the cauldron, she'd stored it away, waiting until everyone was asleep before she carefully painted herself—clothes, pack, skin, and all—with the leftover Invis-Ability. It had all gone according to plan.

Sort of.

Maybe it was because it wasn't a fresh batch of dye—or because she wasn't a Tiller who could convince the herbs in the concoction to work at their highest potential—or maybe it was because she simply wasn't as absorbent as fabric—but the results had been mixed: Claire really wasn't so much *invisible* as she was *camouflaged*. In dim light, she vanished completely away. But if she stood within reach of a lantern's glow, she could see herself as clear as ever. So long as she kept to the shadows and away from the noon sun, she would be invisible enough—she hoped.

And so, in the gloom of predawn, with her bottomless Hollow Pack filled with magical objects and Gemmer tools as well as a twig-looking pencil, Claire had slipped through the Camouflora and out of Woven Root.

It had been surprisingly easy. Everyone had been so focused on what might be coming for them on the other side of the veil that no one bothered to check who might be leaving. After all, no one would be reckless enough to leave, not with all of

Arden now searching for the illegal village of alchemists—those few people who believed that magic shouldn't be separated by guild and worked to jumble talents together.

But one person *would* have been reckless enough. And that's exactly why Claire had to leave first.

It was Claire's turn to do the right thing—to save Sophie.

Her sister, Sophie, was many things. She was reckless, willing to explore fireplaces and forbidden chambers. She was brave, grappling with magic and evil queens. She was Claire's best friend.

And she was turning into a unicorn.

Claire had to figure out how to undo this, how to make sure Sophie remained human so that no one would hunt her sister.

And she knew this much: the key to Sophie's safety lay somewhere on the edge of the Sparkling Sea, in the knowledge of a magical creature known as a Spyden. Claire didn't know too much about them (she hadn't wanted to ask too many questions, in case it caught the attention of her friend Nett's endless curiosity), only that they could spin answers from the air and patch any problem. And that they lived somewhere near Needle Pointe, the only permanent community of Spinners, located on the other side of Constellation Range, where the Rhona River emptied into the Sparkling Sea. In this small bay, the Spinners' sails could catch the hint of stories on the wind and easily move their narrowboats inland.

With the spyglass, Invis-Ability, and a little bit of luck,

Claire had managed to scoot undetected onto a cargo raft of a Spinner fleet. And luckier still, the raft had contained crates of the autumn's harvest. She'd tucked herself in under the carrots until this afternoon, when the river picked up the scent of salt and gulls shrieked overhead, and she knew: they had reached the sea.

At first, Claire had been grateful for the heavy blanket of clouds from the brewing storm. It had made the afternoon gray enough for her Invis-Ability to be effective. She'd slipped off the raft and into the main harbor, a small forest of bobbing ships' masts. She'd selected the largest ship, the *Thread Cutter*, and had scrambled to this highest point, where she now needed to . . .

Well.

Claire's semi-visible fingers gripped the arrow harder, and she tried to swallow her heart back down to where it belonged. She must choose: either test the arrow—or leave the crow's nest and find someplace safe to hide until she was ready.

But instead of making up her mind, Claire reached for the spyglass.

She just needed one more look at where to aim. She knew from experience that a Lode Arrow could take her miles high and miles across in only a few short seconds if she shot it properly. But she had only used one once before, not on purpose, and that arrow had been crafted by the commander of the Wraith Watch, a man with many years of Gemmer experience. This arrow, however, Claire had crafted herself, using the lessons she'd learned at Stonehaven. It wasn't really sharp, but her fingers had tingled as they always did when she created something using her own Gemmer magic.

Holding the spyglass to her eye, Claire braced for the eddy of colors that would immediately bring on a headache. She shifted slightly, and there it was, drilled into a cliff face, thousands of feet above the water: a single black hole. The mouth of a cave marked on one of Aquila Malchain's maps as *Spyden's Lair*.

A raindrop plopped on her head.

Uh-oh.

Claire froze, waiting to find out if more drops would come, but it seemed to be the only one.

Hurry! her mind urged. *Shoot before you're caught!*

But her hand seemed to have other ideas, and without meaning to, Claire turned away, the spyglass still held to her eye. Change was coming over Arden. Trees had lost their leaves, and the world was a palette of fawn brown and dove gray. She found the frothy white ribbon of the Rhona and began to follow it north, through a gorge in the mountains, toward where she'd last known Woven Root to camp. She didn't think they would have moved yet—

A brilliant light flared across Claire's vision, followed by a giant *BOOM* . . . and the applause of a million raindrops hitting the wooden deck.

She'd waited too long to make this decision!

Claire couldn't shoot the arrow in the middle of a

thunderstorm, but she also couldn't stay *here*, at the tallest point of the ship, while lightning zagged across the sky and rain threatened to wash off the last of her Invis-Ability dye.

After shoving her spyglass and arrow into the Hollow Pack, she quickly grabbed her bow and slung it over her shoulder. Maybe she was wrong. Maybe the invisibility *would* stick—

"*Hey!*"

Claire looked down to see a Spinner on the deck pointing up at her. She glanced at her arm, where she could see streaks of pink skin as the invisibility dye streamed off.

"Slug soot!" she cursed. If she wasn't already completely and utterly visible, she would be soon. Which left her no choice.

With the shouts of Spinners climbing up the ropes toward her loud in her ears, Claire again grabbed the arrow from her pack and set it to her bowstring. She scrambled up to the top of the wooden rail, balancing precariously over the angry sea.

Lightning flashed. Thunder cracked.

Claire shot the arrow.

CHAPTER
2

The wind snatched the scream from Claire's mouth as everything turned gray and blue, cold and wet. She hurtled through the storm.

Her Lode Arrow was working!

The Gemmer-ness in her blood clung magnetically to her transportation, making sure her fingers were stuck to the arrow's shaft so that she wouldn't accidentally let go. It wasn't like flying, because even though she was arching forward, she was also sinking down toward the sea's churning swells. The storm's winds buffeted her about, pulling her off course. She wasn't going to make it to Spyden's Lair—she was barely going to clear the mast of a looming ship!

Desperately, Claire hiked up her feet, leather boots narrowly missing the wide-eyed expression of a Spinner in another crow's nest as the wind shoved her on again.

She just needed to clear the sharp outcropping of spindly rocks called the Needles that jutted out of the water, protecting the bay. If she could land beyond them, they would temporarily conceal Claire from Needle Pointe's harbor, and she didn't think anyone would dare sail out to investigate until the storm passed.

But if she landed in front of the rocks, a nosy Spinner searching for a story might risk the wind anyway. And if she managed to make it to the rocks but not *over* them . . . Well, there was a reason why the town was called Needle *Pointe*.

The rocks came close . . .

Closer . . .

Closest!

Claire's toes skimmed the outcrop, and she kicked down, giving her and the arrow one more slight lift to miss the rocks—before splashing down into the sea on the other side.

Silence engulfed her. The water smothered the roar of wind and thunder.

Without the sun, all she could see was midnight blue, except when a flicker of lightning illuminated the seascape below her: swaying shadows of seaweed, glimmers of fish and intricately shaped rocks, the color of apples, that twisted delicate branches upward like the fanciest of candelabras. It was an underwater forest that loomed larger as the Lode Arrow dragged Claire along with it.

It would not stop until it hit a target.

Claire unwrapped her fist, but still the Lode Arrow stuck to her palm. She couldn't break away from her magical transportation, and now, she realized, it was delivering her to their final destination—the bottom of the sea.

She screamed.

Lacy bubbles streamed from her mouth and floated upward to sky and air, to where Claire could not follow.

Let go! a familiar voice shouted in her mind's ear. *For goodness' sake, stop being a baby and let go already!*

Claire had heard that phrase so many times before, in the exact same tone. When the family had gone ice-skating and she'd clung to Sophie's gloved hand even as she spilled onto the ice, pulling her big sister down with her—

On the monkey bars, when a much littler Claire had hung there, tears dripping down her cheeks because she was too scared to swing herself across—

After she'd lost the fire-safety poster contest to Brittany, and she'd spent a week accusing her classmate of copying the winning poster from the year before.

Let it go, Claire!

Salt stung her eyes. Salt lashed her tongue.

Claire kicked, trying to propel herself and the arrow back up, but the strength of the stone tip pulled them down.

She was helpless.

Panic settled in her chest, burning her lungs—or maybe that was the lack of air. What had she been thinking? She closed her eyes. Gemmers shouldn't play games with water! They knew how to nudge the potential of rock, but rocks *sank*.

Something hard scraped across her arms.

Claire's eyes flew open. She was now hurtling through the rock forest, the red branches grazing her as she dove past. And it should have hurt, but instead of feeling pain, she felt only the overwhelming sense of . . . of *welcome*.

There was no other word for it. It wasn't as clear as a "hello" or even a handshake, but it was definitely a greeting. Each time a little branch touched her arm or leg, she sensed a salutation. Like if the rock had a tail, it would be wagging it. As if the rock were *alive*.

And it was.

Because the stone forest wasn't stone at all. It was coral.

Coral, Claire knew from her fifth-grade unit on the ocean, looked like rock but was actually an animal. An animal that was intimately acquainted with stone, just as Claire was herself. It seemed to know this and had recognized Claire as a friend.

And as she felt the coral's hello, she became aware of a welcoming song in the water all around her, the tiny notes cradling her and carving away the panic for one single instant. And into that space, a memory came to her in startling, water-clear detail:

✳

Late-afternoon sunlight streamed into Starscrape Citadel's classroom as the apprentices settled around their millstone desks, craning their necks and whispering excitedly to one another. Bowls of brightly colored powders lined the front table, looking like ground sidewalk chalk. Some were a rich mustard, others a rusty red, while one pewter pot held a blue so dark that it could have been a piece of crushed midnight.

The classroom door opened, but instead of Scholar Pumus, Grandmaster Carnelian strode in, his ram's head cane beating a staccato clip as he wound his way among them.

"Wake up, apprentices," he grumbled as he moved to the front of the workroom.

The students sat up straighter. "Good afternoon, Grandmaster," they chorused.

"Scholar Pumus is needed today to work on the Grand Hall's gargoyles. The last storm did significant damage to the pipes. He's asked that I show you a bit of my specialty: glass."

Claire cocked her head, frowning.

"Claire, do you have a question?"

Claire's ears burned red. The grandmaster never seemed to miss a beat. "Uh, I was just wondering . . . what does glass have to do with rocks?"

The titters that flitted through the classroom were all Claire needed to know that she'd asked a silly question.

Carnelian stood at the front, glaring at his charges until they quieted. "Apprentice Claire has asked an excellent question," he said. "One that we should all review. Who would like to help answer her?"

Zuli's hand slowly rose into the air, and when Carnelian nodded at her, she spoke. "Glass is melted sand," she explained. "And sand is comprised of rocks that have been beaten by the elements, like wind or water, until they turned into small grains."

"Well said." Carnelian nodded. "Glass is my favorite form of rock. Mountains might be tall and mighty, but they're young. Sand grains, though, they are the ancient mountains. They've traveled the world, the oceans, the air. They've taken so much but withstood so much, too. Nothing, in my opinion, holds our history better than glass. It's fragile, yet it protects. With glass, you can even paint light . . ." He held a prism up to a sun shaft, and suddenly rainbows swirled around the workroom.

The class let out a collective breath of wonder, Claire among them.

"What are you waiting for?" Carnelian said, dropping the prism into his pocket. "To the front!"

❋

Claire now knew who sang those tiny notes of welcome. They were the greetings from the millions upon millions of sand grains that floated in the sea's endless waters. Claire was surrounded by possibility—so long as she didn't pass out.

A jolt shot up her arm as the Lode Arrow hit the seabed, sending up a billowing cloud of sand, and with it came another memory: a family vacation, not so long ago, when Sophie had just started getting embarrassed about playing make-believe in public. But on this trip, a rare one for the Martinson family, whose vacations usually consisted of a week camping in a state park, Sophie had played make-believe with a vengeance. There had been Experience after Experience: from the secret messages in every bottle to the cracking paint in their vacation rental that

Sophie claimed was actually a coded treasure map. Sophie even had, for one morning, played dolphins with Claire, and they'd spent the entire afternoon building sand châteaus and mermaid tails.

The memory gave her an idea.

With her one free hand, Claire grabbed at the sand on the seafloor. It disintegrated into a blurry cloud around her. But she kept the memory of playing in the sand with Sophie close.

Using her artist's eye, she spotted the curve of a fin in the murky sand, the same way she would have spotted a sheep in summer clouds. She moved her hand wildly back and forth, thinking about all the times she and Sophie had scraped wet sand into a pail and turned it upside down, followed by the nervous anticipation of lifting the bucket away to reveal either a slender turret or a crumbling mess.

Sand *liked* to cling together. Each little grain had once been a part of something large, of something more than itself.

Whenever you feel small, Mom always used to say to her, *just remember that we are all part of something much bigger, even if you can't always see it.*

Claire called to the bits of sand that had come from the coral, from the living stone, and asked them to remember what it had been like to be a part of a giant animal.

From some of the grains, she caught a whisper of snow and pine. This was the sand that had once been the mighty shoulders of Constellation Range.

Stick together! Claire pleaded. *Ignore the water that separates you!*

And meanwhile, she would try to ignore the burning sensation in her chest and the black dots creeping into her vision. She squeezed her eyes shut, not wanting to see the end coming.

She was running out of time.

Were her fingers tingling? She couldn't tell. They were numb from the cold of the water. Her heartbeat seemed to be slowing, and she feebly waved a hand, urging the sand to remember its capability to traverse the currents, its ability to shift and change and adapt . . .

Then: something hit her hand—the one stuck to the arrow.

Claire's eyes flew open as a great sandy beast rushed at the arrow again.

And it was either the rough scrape of sand against her skin or her utter shock at the grin of the newly sculpted Sand Dolphin, but in that moment, the connection between her palm and the Lode Arrow broke.

Claire was free.

But she was also out of air and out of time. She was too weak.

The Hollow Pack on her shoulders shackled her down, and the magic—the great, tremendous magic she'd just crafted—had wrung her out like a sponge. Reaching the surface was impossible.

There was a nudge again, this time at the small of her back, as the Sand Dolphin pushed her up with its nose. In a swirl of bubbles, it was suddenly in front of her, its backfin between her fingers. With the last drop of her strength, Claire closed her fingers around the fin and clung.

With the power of a geyser, the Sand Dolphin shot upward. And even though Claire could feel grains of sand slipping away as it pulled her up through a dozen feet of water, she still held on.

They burst from the water! For one soaring moment, the salt water and raindrops were one and the same, and Claire was a part of it all—sea and sky, water and rock and breath.

The Sand Dolphin neatly tucked itself in for the dive. They hit the surface, and the Sand Dolphin disintegrated on impact.

The grains twirled around Claire's arms and legs, as if to say they'd had fun and they should do it again sometime. One more gentle nudge, and she realized the sand had swept her close to a beach on the far side of the Needles, hidden from the Spinners' town. A few yards later, she was able to touch the bottom.

She dragged herself through the water and waded onto the pebbled beach, where she promptly collapsed, taking hungry gulps of air, feasting on it. She hardly noticed the rain that still poured down, even though the thunder was diminishing in the distance.

In fact, Claire hardly noticed anything at all, until the creak of a door reached her ears, and she realized she was not alone.

CHAPTER
3

Claire struggled to sit up, her waterlogged tunic clinging uncomfortably to her. As she pushed herself onto her forearms, she clearly saw the pink of her skin. The Invis-Ability had completely washed away, leaving her as exposed as a shell-less snail. In fact, with the rain clouds still thick over the setting sun, all color seemed to have vanished as well.

And maybe that was why she hadn't immediately noticed the little gray house perched precariously on a rock jutting into the hidden bay. It was more of a squat tower, really, with beach stones haphazardly stacked on top of one another like Dad's stack of overflowing books. A tiny staircase of driftwood wrapped around it, leading to a landing a few feet above the still agitated waves—and an opened door.

Claire scanned the pebbly beach she'd washed up on. She

didn't see anyone. All there seemed to be was this house, her Hollow Pack flung a few feet away from her, and the sharp rock wall that shielded her from the eyes and ships of Needle Pointe.

Which meant that whoever had opened the door must still be inside the house, watching her. Could it be a Spyden?

Claire tried not to be afraid. After all, finding a Spyden was why she'd come all this way. To save Sophie.

On that night on the Sorrowful Plains, which seemed so long ago now, Sophie had been pierced by a Royalist's arrow, and the unicorn Claire had released from Unicorn Rock had healed Sophie. Or so they thought. It turned out, however, that the unicorn had *changed* Sophie instead, setting her on the path to becoming one of its own kind: a unicorn.

But *why*—that Claire still did not understand. Or *how*.

Would Claire wake up one morning to find that her human sister was completely gone, replaced by the creature of starfire she'd only glimpsed once before? Or would it be a slow and gradual change, with all of Sophie's hair turning creamy white first, and then . . . what—a delicate crystal horn protruding from her forehead?

Claire shook her own head, wincing at the thought. She knew lots of girls who wouldn't mind becoming a unicorn. She'd been to plenty of unicorn-themed birthday parties in the past, and even her own Language Arts folder had a picture of a unicorn galloping in the moonlight. But that was just it: uni-corns belonged on invitations, on cupcakes, and in magical worlds—*not* in her family.

And Queen Estelle believed that the only place unicorns belonged was on a shelf—as a hunting trophy. Unicorns were creatures of pure magic, and unicorn artifacts crafted from their manes, their tails, their hides, could make guild magic stronger.

Sophie, as far as Claire knew, was the last unicorn in Arden. The unicorn Claire had freed from the rock seemed to have vanished into thin air. Which meant that all of Queen Estelle's focus would now be on hunting Sophie so that she could drain the last of the unicorns' magic for herself and regain the throne . . .

Unless Claire could find a way to keep Sophie human—and safe.

Which meant she had to be brave—had to seek out a Spyden and ask it the right questions.

"Helupf?" Claire coughed. Her mouth, which had only minutes before practically swallowed the entire sea, was now as dry as chalk. Dragging herself to her knees, her tunic squelching uncomfortably, she felt for the smallest outside pocket in her Hollow Pack and pulled out her pencil. It was slightly damp, but luckily it hadn't snapped in two. Pencils were hard to find in Arden, which was why Claire had held onto it, even though it came with memories of Terra.

Scholar Terra had been the Martinson sisters' first defender at Starscrape Citadel and their biggest advocate. She'd taught Claire how to coax the magic from stone on purpose, had believed Claire's wild story of calling a unicorn from stone, and gifted her with Charlotte Sagebrush's famous pencil. Around Terra and her mass of curly black hair, glittering rings, and magical spectacles that seemed to always cut through to truth, Claire had felt that maybe she'd found a place in Arden where she belonged. Terra was a friend—until Claire learned that her name wasn't Terra at all but Estelle. *Queen* Estelle. And the only reason she'd helped Claire was because she needed a Gemmer princess of Arden to call the last unicorn to her.

In Arden, one always had to be ready, and so Claire kept the pencil in her hand as she called out again, "Hello?"

Her voice was barely a scratch, but there was a response this time: the sound of many footsteps behind her.

Claire twisted around and tried to scramble to her feet, but her legs felt about as sturdy as sea-foam. And so she stayed where she was, on her bum, her Hollow Pack now too far away to nab anything useful from it. And though there were rocks all around, she was so tired. So, so, so tired.

The footsteps stopped. And then . . .

"You look like a pretzel."

No. Water must still be in her ears, because Claire was definitely, one hundred percent hearing things. Because that voice—Claire knew it as well as her own.

She snapped around to see the figure of a girl emerging from behind a few boulders lying on the beach. And though the girl wore a long black gown edged in lace and a funny tall cone hat with a gossamer veil that quivered as she jogged over, Claire recognized the wide, wild grin beneath it.

"Sophie?"

"Of course it's me!" Sophie said. "Who else would you be expecting?"

The answer was practically anyone else, ranging anywhere from an angry Royalist, to a suspicious Spinner, to Rudolph the red-nosed reindeer. When Claire left Woven Root a week ago, Sophie had been curled up and fast asleep in their tent. There was no way she could have traveled here this fast, ahead of Claire, without Claire even knowing.

. . . Could she?

"B-but—" Claire spluttered. "When did you— What did you— *How?*"

"I came by cloak," Sophie said, shooting Claire an older-sisters-always-know look as she came to a stop next to her. "Obviously."

Claire tried to close her gaping mouth. Sure, she knew Sophie was a Spinner. They had all only recently discovered it: that Sophie could pluck the chords of potential within fabric so that they could snag the wind's currents and fly. She just didn't realize how quickly Sophie had mastered her new ability. It had taken Claire *weeks* to even spark a ruby.

Sophie reached down to pull Claire to her feet, and even though Claire's legs were wobbly, she remained standing. Her knees seemed to have locked in shock. She still couldn't believe this. Sophie was supposed to be in Woven Root, where it was *safe*. And yet here she was, always one step ahead of Claire—*and never listening to her.*

"I told you to stay in Woven Root!" Claire said, her voice shaking. She couldn't tell if it was from exhaustion, or anger, or something else entirely. Her emotions seemed to bleed into one another, like splattered paint.

First there was fear: that her sister wasn't behind the protective secret curtain of Woven Root.

Then annoyance. She should have *known* better than to think Sophie would ever let her do anything by herself. That Sophie would ever trust Claire enough to take care of something on her own.

Finally—and worst of all—relief. She wouldn't have to do this all herself. And for some reason, the relief made her even angrier.

"You shouldn't be here," Claire stated, twisting the pencil into her hair.

Sophie held out her hands, her expression wounded. "Did I do something wrong? I was just trying to look out for you!"

"But you don't need to!" Claire yelled, too tired to rein in her fury. All that sneaking, the nights spent pressed under carrots, the slippery climb up the crow's nest, the lightning, the near-drowning—it had all been for *nothing* if Sophie was not safe.

"Shh," Sophie said, her eyes growing wide. "The Spyden might hear you."

Claire wanted to stamp her feet. "How do you know about that, too?"

"I just . . ." Sophie sighed. "I *sense* these things."

It was as if Sophie's sigh had blown out Claire's anger.

Because it was gone as suddenly as it had appeared, leaving Claire feeling hollow and alone.

Sense these things—because her sister was an almost unicorn. Was that what she meant?

"But what about all this?" Claire asked, pointing to Sophie's strange outfit. She looked like she belonged in an old oil painting and not at all like she should be on a beach.

"Hey, let's get you inside," Sophie said, gently brushing a wayward curl off Claire's forehead. "You're shivering. I can tell you everything once you're dry."

"Okay but . . . have you actually seen any Spydens?" Claire asked, eyeing the strange house and the open door warily.

"Don't worry—it's safe. I'll explain everything. I promise. But now that the sun has set, we should, you know . . ." Sophie didn't have to say anything more, because Claire knew what would happen when the sun set: the wraiths would begin to stir.

No one knew where Arden's hordes of wraiths had come from, but they had started to appear around the same time the unicorns had begun to go extinct. They were creatures of coldness and shadow, their forms skeleton-like but horrifically elongated, with odd swinging gaits, and they could wield fear like sharp claws. According to Arden lore, Queen Estelle was supposed to be able to defeat them. The legend had been kind of right. Because while Queen Estelle might be able to defeat them, she had no reason to: the creatures of terror obeyed her every command.

Claire quietly watched Sophie bend down and sling Claire's

Hollow Pack over her shoulder. And when she felt her big sister wrap an arm around *her* shoulder, Claire let herself sink in. This was how they always were, and maybe this was how they would always be.

Together.

They skirted the scalloped edge of the sea and made their way up the driftwood stairs and to the open door.

A strange smell tickled Claire's nose as she stepped inside, but she brushed it away like a crumb and took in her surroundings. It was dark, except for a few embers that glowed in the small black stove at the far side of the room and provided enough light to see. It wasn't as cozy as Aquila Malchain's gold-and-blue-painted cottage, nor was it as airy as Claire's tent in Woven Root, but it was clean, and the spare wooden furniture had a certain elegance to it.

The only thing that hinted at luxury was a dusty tapestry that hung over a spinning wheel. Claire wondered if a spinning wheel could turn straw into gold here, but there was no straw in sight, just a basket of lumpy wool and a blue sleeve.

A jolt of electricity shot through her spine.

Stepping away from Sophie, Claire hurried over to the basket. A *royal*-blue cloak—just like what Royalists wore—lay there like a deflated balloon.

"Who lives here?" Claire asked. She looked wildly about the room, half expecting Mira Fray to appear from the shadows. Fray was one of the Royalists who had captured Claire and Sophie in the Drowning Fortress two weeks ago. The Royalists were members of a secret society, one that was often laughed at for their belief that the stone monoliths on the Sorrowful Plains had truly been the living forms of the last queen and the last unicorn. They had worked for years to try to free the queen from the stone she'd been transformed into, believing she'd bring about a better day for Arden. Now they'd succeeded and were her most loyal followers, aside from the wraiths.

Sophie shook her head. "Nobody, as far as I can tell. A Spinner probably lived here once, but look." She pointed to a corner of the ceiling, where Claire could just make out a colony of cobwebs. "I think it's been a while."

Claire shuddered slightly. She was still worried about the Spydens. Though she had intentionally set out to find one, she knew they had to be wary—Spydens were known to be tricky. They could easily weave you into a dangerous web of half-truths if you weren't careful.

But Sophie didn't seem concerned about any Spydens bursting through the door and claiming this musty old house. And she didn't even seem, come to think of it, all that surprised that Claire had found her. Or that she had found Claire.

Claire looked around at the modest home. "Did Nett mention this place to you?" she asked. "Did he come with you?"

Sophie shrugged and walked over to the stove to stir a pot that bubbled on top. From behind, with her face turned away, she looked kind of like a fairy-tale witch. "Nett?" Sophie spoke his name like a question.

Claire felt a sigh well up inside her but pushed it down.

Even here, miles and worlds away from home, Sophie liked to tease her. Well, two could play at that game.

"You remember Nettle Green—my height, black hair, know-it-all? The foster brother of Sena Steele, the tall redhead who likes to stab things."

"He didn't want to come with me," Sophie said. "Neither did Sena," she added.

"Really? They stayed in Woven Root?" Claire guessed it made sense, but still, she was disappointed. She thought they would have wanted to come, after all they'd been through together. But she supposed the knowledge that Sena's parents weren't dead had changed the Forger girl's goals. The second-to-last time Claire had seen her (the *last*, last time, she'd been asleep in a hammock hung next to Sophie's), Sena had been poring over her parents' notes and journals, trying to figure out their experiments at the seams of the world, with an eager Nett practically standing on his chair with excitement.

"You need to change out of those wet clothes," Sophie said, always in her role as bossy big sister. "Maybe put on that cloak."

Claire let out a strangled yelp. No way was she going to put on something that strongly resembled a Royalist cloak!

Sophie, oddly, didn't seem bothered by it. Even though it was the Royalists who had almost succeeded in killing her.

"Or," Sophie continued, "there are some dresses in there." She pointed to a freestanding wardrobe in an adjoining bedroom.

"What is *up* with you?" Claire asked as she shuffled over to the wardrobe, then opened it to reveal five or six black gowns, all identical to Sophie's, along with matching pointy hats. At least now it was clear where Sophie had gotten her strange outfit. Typical Sophie. She *would* play dress-up, even in this unusual situation.

"Nothing," Sophie said from the main room. "Why?"

"Oh, I don't know, it's just—you're acting like you own this place, like you've been here for ages, like you've been expecting me, even though you couldn't have been exactly sure of where I'd gone."

"I guess I just know you better than you think, Claire," she said. But not *Clairina*, like she usually called her. Something was off with Sophie, and it was making Claire feel itchy and frustrated, but it was hard to put her finger on what was wrong, especially as she was still dripping wet and exhausted from her journey.

After peeling off her wet tunic, Claire pulled on a dress. It was way too big for her and pooled around her feet like melted wax around a candle. But it was dry, at least. And warm.

Next, she took the pencil out and squeezed the salt water from her damp braid, making a face at the strange texture of her hair. Next to Mom and Dad, Claire missed her shampoo and detangling spray above all else. She debated undoing the french braid she had coaxed Sena into doing before she snuck away, but she was too tired to deal with the snarls that would come as a result. Maybe she would just— Wait, what was that?

Claire stopped squeezing the end of her braid and gripped

her pencil as though it were a staff from Gemmer practice. She thought she'd heard someone say something, a word, maybe, or a sniffle, low and mournful. A quick glance over her shoulder told her Sophie was still in the kitchen.

Then it came again, quiet, almost like a hush. *"Help."*

A chill moved through her.

Someone else was in the house.

CHAPTER
4

Tentatively, Claire walked over and untied the gauzy white curtain that covered a small square window. Peering out, all she could see was the darkness of the night sky and the even more velvety darkness that was the sea. So close to the water, it almost sounded like the sea itself was breathing as it inhaled and exhaled its way onto the shore.

Understanding broke with sudden clarity. She wasn't hearing someone crying at all—it was just the sound of the waves sighing against the rocks.

There was a flutter out of the corner of her eye. The curtain swayed, even though there was no hint of a breeze. Odd.

Claire trailed the long drop of gauze to the top of the window, where the fabric was heavily draped to resemble linked crescent moons. It was a grand style, one that would have been a better fit at the opera house Mom had once taken her to rather than this bare little cottage.

"Soup's ready!" Sophie called. Tucking the pencil back into her braid, Claire left the strange bedroom just in time to see Sophie ladling broth into a clay bowl with unexpected ease. Though perhaps it shouldn't have been unexpected, as Sophie had, after all, spent weeks at Stonehaven working in the Citadel's kitchens while Claire had been taking magic lessons.

"Sophie, are you *sure* you haven't seen anyone else around? Or heard anything?" Maybe she was being paranoid; maybe it was just the whisper of the sea, but . . . "I swear I heard someone calling for help a minute ago."

Sophie laughed, a distant, forced laugh that sounded more like a noise a tired Mom would make at the end of a day teaching her college courses. Not like a real Sophie laugh, wild and free. "Oh, Claire," was all she said.

Sitting down at the table, Claire kept her eyes on her sister, looking for a sign that Sophie was becoming a unicorn. But as far as Claire could tell, there wasn't any change at all. In fact, the opposite seemed to have happened.

She stared at Sophie's hair, currently out of its signature ponytail in order to fit beneath the cone hat. There was no streak of white in it like the last time Claire had seen Sophie. Perhaps it had grown out . . . ?

As she watched, Sophie sprinkled something into the small bowl. There was still that strange smell that lingered in the air, as if something was rotten. Fish, probably, as they were so close to the sea. She hoped it wasn't Sophie's soup.

Smiling proudly, Sophie walked over and set the bowl in front of Claire. Claire fought to keep her features neutral. The bowlful in front of her looked more like damp green yarn than anything that could be called food.

"Seaweed goulash," Sophie said. "Eat up. You need to be well fed when we go to the Spyden's Lair tomorrow."

"If we can even get up into those caves and find it," Claire muttered as she hesitantly accepted the spoon Sophie handed her. "It's really high up. I'm not even sure what we should do when we find it."

"What was your plan?"

"I have a snippet of Spyden silk in the pack," Claire said. "Supposedly it's really rare, and I had the feeling from Cotton," she said, referencing the teenage Tiller in Woven Root who had helped her and Sophie, "that it was stolen. I thought maybe the Spyden might want it back in exchange for some solutions. But maybe it won't be special enough." Claire paused. She hadn't really thought it out beyond that.

Sophie blinked at her, her brown eyes looking black in the red glow of the stove. "What do you know about Spydens?" she asked.

"Not much," Claire admitted. "And you?"

"I know that they are very old and that there are very few left. I know that they are skilled in the same way spiders are and that they can weave anything: maps, castles, and even different forms. And that they like to follow the rules."

"Rules?" Claire repeated. "But I don't know about any rules."

"Manners," Sophie clarified. "But don't worry. Go on, eat. It'll make you feel better. And you'll hurt my feelings if you don't at least try."

Claire stared at her sister again. "It'll hurt your feelings?"

"Yes!"

"You are being. So. *Weird*. I don't like it."

"You'll like starving less—I can guarantee that," Sophie said, but she didn't break out in the usual grin she'd make when teasing Claire.

Something was definitely wrong, and unease moved through Claire. She didn't like this feeling. She didn't like it *at all*.

Reluctantly, Claire pulled the bowl closer to her. She'd tried liver pâté before—how bad could this be? Taking a deep breath, she twirled her spoon, wrapping some seaweed around it. Before she could rethink it, she gulped it down.

The texture was like noodles boiled a little too long, but the taste was similar to crushed walnuts. In fact, if she could ignore what she was eating, Claire would have said it was pretty good. Or maybe it was good only because she was so hungry.

Which was why it took Claire a few minutes to notice that even though Sophie had sat down, she hadn't put a bowl in front of herself. Instead, she'd pulled out a pair of knitting needles from somewhere and had begun to knit.

Click-clack. Click-clack.

"Aren't you going to eat?" Claire asked.

"Later," Sophie said, not even bothering to look down at

her hands while her fingers flew across the yarn, tightening soft loops.

"I didn't know you knew how to knit," Claire said.

"Really, Claire, I'm a Spinner—how do you keep forgetting?" *Click-clack. Click-clack.* "Now, tell me, how did *you* get here? And what question are you going to request of the Spyden?"

Request of the Spyden? First there was the cooking and the knitting and now this fancy vocabulary? Claire felt her frown deepen, but still, she answered her sister's question. "I'm going to ask what happened to the unicorn of Unicorn Rock. And if he can put you back to normal."

Sophie tilted her head. "But that doesn't sound like the question you actually want to ask."

Claire crossed her arms. She was exhausted and anxious and didn't have any patience left to deal with Sophie's airs of fake mystery. "Yes it is."

Click-clack. Click-clack. Sophie's knitting needles tapped faster, a beautiful, shimmering blanket slowly billowing from beneath them. Claire couldn't believe how rapidly Sophie had learned her magic skill.

"No," Sophie said, "it sounds like a question hiding a question. What do you *really* want to know, Claire Elaina Martinson?"

It was like Sophie's question was a hook, and Claire's answer was the slippery secret that had gotten caught. Because without wanting to, without really thinking about it, she blurted,

"How do I make sure everything stays the same?" Question after question tumbled out, piling on top of one another so quickly, Claire felt like they might crush her. "What's it going to be like when we go home? Will it ever be the same again? And not just before Arden but *before* before, when you weren't sick at all. When we could just—"

Her voice cracked. She didn't even know what she was about to say—just what? Just be sisters? Just be kids? Just *not* be a princess and unicorn of Arden? The number and power of her questions overwhelmed Claire.

It's all too much.

She buried her face in her hands. And again, she tasted salt at the corner of her mouth as tears trailed down.

"Hey, now," Sophie said softly. She patted Claire's shoulder, her long black sleeve brushing against her cheek. "It's going to be fine. I've taken care of it."

Claire looked up, startled. "What?" she demanded. "How?"

"Nothing, I just meant, tomorrow we'll find the Spyden. It'll be an Expedition!"

"Experience," Claire said, but her voice felt jumbled in her throat. In fact, all her thoughts were becoming soft and tangled, like yarn.

"What was that?" Sophie's face appeared above hers, and again, Claire thought it was funny how black her eyes looked, when they were typically a vibrant brown. Something was off; something didn't feel right. It was as though her sister *wasn't actually her sister.*

Claire knew she should be alarmed at the thoughts plodding through her mind, but . . . she was so tired.

"You don't call them 'Expeditions,'" Claire mumbled. "You call them 'Experiences.'"

The *click-clack* of the needles stopped.

"You're falling asleep," Sophie said. Something as soft as the underside of a cloud drifted across Claire and settled over her. It was warm and silky, conforming to her shape. Was Sophie tucking her in with the blanket she'd just knitted?

Her eyelids drooped lower, but she could see Sophie standing over her. For some reason, her head was so heavy now, she could barely lift it.

The transparent veil on Sophie's hat dipped and floated down, covering Claire's face. It was hard to breathe under it. She thought about tugging it off her face, but her arms felt heavy, as though they'd been filled with warm water. She was scared, but her fear was fuzzy like the edges of dreams. Or nightmares. This was not normal. Sophie was not normal.

And then the strangest thought: the person in front of her was not Sophie at all.

As soon as Claire thought it, she saw a dark shadow cross over Sophie's face. And as she watched, it grew . . . and grew . . .

The shadow wasn't crossing—it was *splitting* Sophie's face.

Two long and hairy spider legs burst from Sophie's head, the conical hat falling on either side of her neck like a banana peel.

Claire screamed—or tried to, but her throat wasn't working! With a horrible rip, Sophie's black gown burst open, revealing more legs wrapped around rows upon rows of glittering eyes. The legs hit the floor, and the newly appeared spider lurched forward, pulling itself out of Sophie's black gown.

But Sophie *wasn't* Sophie.

And the blanket wrapped around Claire was no blanket at all.

It was a web woven just for her.

CHAPTER
5

The giant spider's legs *click-clack*ed like knitting needles as they scuttled toward Claire. She tried to scream, but the seaweed seemed to have strangled her vocal cords. Like a black wave, the spider loomed above her, a wall of fur and eyes and legs—then plunged.

For the second time that day, Claire felt the world around her sway. This time, though, it wasn't the rocking of the sea's waves; it was the spider wrapping her up the same way Mom wrapped up lunchtime sandwiches.

She told her legs to kick! But the blanket stuck, keeping her stiff and still.

"Stay calm, Claire," the spider said, no longer speaking in Sophie's voice but in a voice that rasped and clicked. "You don't want the silk to be too loose, or else you won't be fresh for later.

Stay still, and all will be well." There was a pause, and then the spider added, "Maybe not well for you but definitely for me. I haven't had Gemmer in ages."

Gemmer. The word cut through Claire's tangled panic like a pair of scissors. Yes—she *was* a Gemmer. She was not helpless! She just needed a plan. She needed to *think*. But being rolled across the floor by a giant spider—her back, sides, and stomach thumping hard against the floor with each turn—was scrambling all her thoughts.

Her fear grew sharper as the blanket wrapped tighter and tighter. Pain rumbled through her. She was going to be one giant bruise . . . if she even managed to survive being treated like a washrag across the flagstone floor.

Wait. An idea whirled past her, and Claire grasped at it. Flag*stone* floor.

The silk wrapping around her was nothing like the smooth polishing rags Claire had used in Starscrape Citadel to call forth light from gems. But it wasn't light she needed. She needed *heat*.

She stopped straining and let herself and the silk be rolled. And as the world turned and her body connected with the floor again and again, Claire thought of Mom lighting the coals under the grill. Of blistering summer sand under her bare feet. Of rock striking rock, releasing a shower of embers.

And as she rolled, she felt a hum. It trickled through her bones, and she felt the rock's answering song. Though she was exhausted—exhausted from running, exhausted from almost drowning, exhausted from worrying—the rock was not. Magic was always in the material, and stone did not tire and it did not forget. It remembered heat at its beginning, when the world's weight formed it.

Claire smelled singed hair, and a second later, a high-pitched screech filled the cottage as the room finally stopped spinning.

"You *foul* Gemmer!" the spider spat, but Claire could barely hear its angry *clack* over the sound of its eight feet stamping the floor as it tried to avoid the stones that were now as hot as summer sand.

Flinging herself in the opposite direction, Claire unrolled as fast as she could. The silk blanket clung to her, resisting, but at last, she was free! Lurching to her feet, she glanced around the room just quickly enough to see that the spider had sprawled onto the ground, its eight legs akimbo beneath it . . . but for how long? Claire sprinted for the door.

She was ten feet away. Then three. One . . . She reached out, fingers straining for the handle.

"Helmmmmppfff meefff!"

Claire stumbled to a stop. There it was again, that same mournful cry she'd heard in the tiny bedroom. The sound that she'd decided was just the sea slapping against the shore. But now she was certain: that was an entirely *human* voice. And she could make out all the words: *Help me.*

Claire whirled around. The bedroom door was open, and she could see straight into it . . . but it wasn't the same as she'd left it. The great curtains, which had hung so elegantly, were now shredded. And in the middle of the room, next to the wardrobe of black dresses, stood a ghost.

Claire gasped. No, not a ghost. Though tattered white gauze clung to the tiny figure, binding their arms and ankles, Claire could tell by the sparkle of brown eyes and flush of cheeks that the person was very much alive.

"Helpfff!" The person moaned, taking a hop forward before toppling to the ground in a nest of tattered spider silk . . . just as the spider finally got its first foot back from underneath it.

There was no time for a plan. Claire ran!

"I'm here!" she said, falling to her knees as she grabbed for her Hollow Pack, thankful that she'd left it in this room. She tugged open the smallest outside pocket and pulled out the bronze circle inside it: a Kompass, a Forger object crafted so that she and Sophie could always find their friend Aquila. But Forgers liked to put an edge on everything. Sliding her thumb over a hidden mechanism, Claire clicked open a small blade.

"Stay still," she told the wild brown eyes that moved back and forth above the silk that obscured their nose and mouth. The figure looked like a strange butterfly, stuck within its cocoon. As carefully as she could, Claire sliced through the threads, making a slit in the wrappings that was big enough that she could begin to rip the web away. The feet emerged first, and then as soon as hands were free, they reached for the material wrapped around their mouth, clawing at it. *"Mmmph!"*

"One second," Claire whispered, reaching for the Kompass's blade again. "Don't worry; you're almost fre— *Aah!*"

Fire exploded across Claire's shoulder as the spider, all its legs finally gathered beneath it, had at last lunged—and sank two fangs into her skin. Bright bursts of color erupted across Claire's vision as the venom shrieked its way through her veins. She could no longer see what had happened to the person she'd been trying to free from the web.

She dropped to the floor as the spider released her. "Meddle-some human!" the spider sneered. "Venom always makes for a funny aftertaste. I'll have to wait until your blood is fresh again."

But Claire wasn't going to wait around for any spider. She rolled to the side, trying to avoid its feet. The pain was already receding, but she wasn't sure her legs would support her. Curl-ing into a ball, Claire tensed—

"No!" a clear, entirely human voice yelled. "Ariadne of Silk Web Fleet, I command you: do not eat!"

Claire turned her head. A young girl, her cloak still covered in swaths of web, stood in front of the spider. So *this* was the person who had been trapped, who had been crying for help. In her hand, she clutched the soup ladle, even though her head barely came up to the spider's knees. Claire squeezed her eyes shut. She didn't want to see the spider's fangs sink into the girl. But no scream burst forth—no shout of pain. Instead, she heard an annoyed *click-clack*.

"That," the spider said, "is an amateur's rhyme."

Claire's eyes flew open just as the girl crossed her brown arms. "But it *does* rhyme," the girl retorted. "And I've called you by your true name. So by the rules—*manners*—of your own kind, you must *stand down*, and you know it!"

A sound like chalk between teeth ground across Claire's ears, and it took Claire a moment to realize it was the spider's laughter. "Foolish Spinner, you know this can't end well for you."

"Away, great spider," the girl countered. "Er . . . go stand by the fire!"

Dazed, Claire pulled herself up. And the giant spider—*Spyden*, Claire finally realized—stood on the far side of the room, its massive bulk almost completely hiding the stove. It clicked its pincers when it saw Claire staring at it. Claire's stomach rolled.

"What—?"

"Shh!" The girl's hand slapped over Claire's mouth. "If you're within earshot of an unmasked Spyden, don't ask a question until you're sure it's the only question in the world you want answered!" The girl rattled off her words so fast that Claire could hardly keep up. "Spydens are tricky—they know the answer to almost anything! They're able to catch story threads on the wind and spin patches that will mend any problem. But there are *rules*. An unmasked Spyden can be controlled by rhymes and is obligated to truthfully answer *one* question you ask—only one. But if you ask a second question, it's allowed to attack, no matter the rhyming command. I hope you understand."

Claire didn't. She didn't understand *anything*.

One second her sister was here, and then she wasn't. Spydens weren't helpful creatures after all but giant, hungry *were* spiders. And somehow this Spinner girl was here . . . and helping her?

Still, Claire nodded, and the girl removed her hand from Claire's mouth. Then the girl turned her attention back to the Spyden, lifting the ladle that the fake Sophie had used only minutes ago to spoon soup into Claire's bowl.

Slowly, Claire dragged her eyes away from the girl and to the Spyden, who had done just as the girl had asked and was standing as if frozen near the fire. Her stomach twisted at the sight of its bristly, too-long legs and eyes. *So* many eyes. Large ones, small ones, but all orbs of inky blackness, so it was impossible to tell where the Spyden was looking, except for the creeping feeling that skittered across Claire's shoulders that told her it was very much watching her.

"Just to be clear," Claire said to the girl, "I can only ask one thing." Even though her voice was squeaky, she was careful to keep her words flat and unmarked by a question.

"Yes. But Mama says asking a Spyden is just asking for trouble." She began to criss-cross her braids over her ears, forming makeshift earmuffs out of her thick hair. A second later, Claire knew why.

"Are you really going to believe a duplicitous-tongued Spinnerling," the Spyden clacked at Claire, "or me, whom you have sought out? Ask all the questions you would like. I know how to make you the richest person in the world—or the most beautiful. I know the easiest way for you to go home. I know where unicorns can be found."

Claire stayed silent, her panic-drenched brain racing, trying to keep up. One question—but which? Technically, Claire already knew where more unicorns could be found: in the moontear necklace that now hung around Queen Estelle's neck. But would even unicorns be enough? Last time a unicorn had helped Claire and Sophie, it changed Sophie. She needed to ask a question that would fix everything.

Fix . . . *everything*. Claire tried to think. Three hundred years ago, Queen Estelle led the Gemmers into war against the other guilds, and in her quest for power, she'd called for a unicorn hunt. Arden legend said that killing a unicorn would make its slayer immortal, but that had not been true. However, unicorns *were* beings of pure magic, and they made all magic greater, all things possible, and while a living unicorn was the most powerful of all, a hair, a hide, or a horn of a unicorn worked just as well . . . and could be controlled.

The only useful unicorn is a dead unicorn, Estelle had sneered at Claire. Estelle wanted the last unicorn. And while there was a chance a second unicorn might still be out there, roaming the fields and mountains of Arden, there was definitely at least one unicorn—she just happened to still be a human girl. Hopefully. But as long as Queen Estelle was looking for a unicorn, Sophie would be in danger.

And it wasn't just Sophie. *Arden* would be in danger—and the land was already suffering.

The great domed roof of Starscrape Citadel loomed in her mind, its sleekly polished marble distracting from the crumbling ramparts and the ruined village in its shadow. The once gleaming copper of chimera, now green and weathered by the elements, standing frozen in fields.

The memory of watching Forgers march in their city, training to fight because of a rumor crafted by the queen; children left orphaned by wraiths who stalked and turned Arden's night into something to fear; a pile of charred unicorn artifacts, a sad shadow of the living creature Claire had seen only once. All of them orchestrated by Queen Estelle's hand.

But Arden was more than what Queen Estelle had made it to be. It was *more* than suspicious guilds and haunting wraiths and dead unicorns.

There were fireflies that glowed in the swamps. Halls lit by diamondlight and song. Feasts beneath bright lanterns where alchemists shared both stories and talents and whispered of a better and stronger Arden, just beneath the surface.

And there was Nett.

Sena.

Aunt Nadia.

Anvil and Aquila and Zuli and Lapis and Cotton. The freckled scribe in Greenwood who scratched notes at her trial. The Forger inspector who asked for her papers. The Spinner trader who led horses down the river. And all the many people Claire had seen in her travels—and all the ones she hadn't seen.

All of them at risk. *All* of them in danger.

A new question seared through her, begging to be asked.

But how could Claire ask it? Because there was Sophie—a girl, a sister, a heart who wished so hard that it could contain moonlight and an infinite amount of possibility. And then there was Arden.

To save an entire world . . . or to save her sister.

Claire. Sophie's voice again echoed in her mind. *Ask the question.*

But which—?

Claire.

"Well? Hurry up!" The girl she had rescued had lifted an earmuff braid up for a second to scold Claire, then she scooted it back in place.

Forcing herself to look directly at the Spyden's fathomless eyes, Claire cast her words and hoped she'd chosen right. "The queen will destroy Arden; how can she be defeated?"

The pincers clicked. "Only a queen can defeat a queen."

Claire held her breath, waiting for the Spyden to continue, for details and a plan to come spinning out, the solution to all their problems, but no more words followed.

Wait. That was it?

That was the answer that the great Spyden had spun from threads of air? Claire's blood heated.

"That's not an answer!" she exploded, frustration pushing away any nausea she felt looking at the hairy forest of legs. "You're supposed to give answers! You're supposed to tell *how. How* do I—?"

There was a clatter, and Claire looked at the floor to see

the ladle had been thrown between them. "Stop talking!" the other girl shouted frantically. "We need to get out of here. And, um . . ." She scrunched up her face, then quickly spun a new rhyme. "Spyden, your feet shall stay on the floor. You will not follow us out the door!"

Claire hurried to where she'd left her Hollow Pack, then raced toward the exit.

"Faster!" the girl called from the cottage's stoop. "Come on!"

"Free me," the Spyden sighed, its rasp threaded with melancholy. "I know so many things, and I have no one to share it all with. I know how to spin miniature worlds, weave stone, hide your deepest secret so it can never be found. So many things, but no one ever asks . . ."

Claire almost felt bad for the giant spider. Almost. But strands of spiderweb still stuck to her boots. "Maybe if you didn't go around wrapping people up for dinner, they would ask a question," she said, trying to scoot around the Spyden's bulk. There was not enough room to pass by without brushing against the spider's bristles. The creepy-crawly sensation that had been limited to her shoulders burst across her arms, but now she was only a step away from the threshold.

"If only someone asked," the Spyden continued, as though it hadn't heard her at all, "I could tell the person how to stop change. How to prevent a transformation of a girl into a unicorn so that she could be by your side forever. I have seen many a great transformation in my time . . ."

Claire hesitated. "I don't believe you," she said faintly.

The Spyden swelled. "I was there when the guilds and unicorns first forged the Crown of Arden and made Anders king! I was there when—"

But Claire had stopped listening.

Forged a crown . . . and *made Anders king*.

Only a queen can defeat a queen . . . That's what the Spyden had said.

Could Claire *make* a queen? Crown someone new, someone who could defeat Estelle?

The image of a woman with white fluffy hair and kind eyes herding chimera ahead of her through Woven Root's camp flashed through Claire's mind: Aunt Diana. Known there as Mayor Nadia.

Claire was a Gemmer princess, but her aunt was the eldest Martinson in Arden, which meant that by those rules, she was next in line to the throne.

What if Claire helped her aunt become the new queen? Would she save Arden and defeat Estelle?

But if she was wrong . . .

Claire paused a moment, wondering how to shape her question so it *wasn't* a question. She pulled the pencil from her hair once more and gripped it like some sort of royal scepter, then carefully stated: "Queens are made. They are *crowned*. I can defeat the queen by *creating* a new queen of Arden who can defeat her."

All the Spyden's eyes opened at once. "You tricked me!"

It was just the confirmation she needed. Triumph surged

through Claire. She gripped the straps of her Hollow Pack tighter and strode out onto the stoop. "You wanted to eat me."

"Miserable human," the Spyden spat. "You stand no chance! The queen of wraiths will rule you all!"

Her stomach clenched. What would Sophie do?

"Have a nice night," Claire said and slammed the door shut.

CHAPTER 6

Claire half stepped, half tumbled down the slippery wooden steps and crunched onto the beach outside the Spyden's home. Night had descended around them; the ocean roiled darkly in the distance. She breathed in sharply. Everything hurt. Not the sharp pain of a kick but the ache of the stomach flu all over her body, as though elbows and knees could throw up, too.

"Come on!" the girl said, tugging on Claire's overlong sleeve. She had let her hair unwind, and it was no longer forming earmuffs around her ears. "I don't know how long the Spyden has to listen to commands. We need to move!"

Claire couldn't agree more.

They ran.

Pebbles sprayed up, stinging her ankles, as they darted across the beach. She gasped for breath. The air, thick with damp and salt, didn't seem to hold enough oxygen for her lungs. In the dark, there was no way to tell the land from the sea, and so it wasn't until she heard the slap of her boots hitting water and felt cold seep into her socks that Claire knew she'd reached the end of the curved beach.

Her stride faltered, and at last, she stopped. They were as far away from the Spyden's cottage and its sticky words as they could be without swimming into open water or scaling up the rocky mountainside. Neither of which was an option. Not in the dark, anyway.

Letting her pack slip off her shoulder, Claire sank onto the beach after it. The storm had blown away the clouds, and brilliant stars outlined the jagged peaks of the Needles. The sharp peaks reminded her of teeth, and the bite in her shoulder began to smart. She put her head between her knees and inhaled deeply. What she'd just seen—what had just *happened*—was too terrible to think about head-on. She could only just glance at it, in quick snatches.

Claire heard the scrape of pebbles, and she looked up just in time to see the younger girl flop onto the beach next to her.

"Threads' *end*," the girl said with feeling and lay back flat on the beach. Tattered strips of cobwebs still clung to her, and the white silk fluttered in the dark with each great gulp of air. She looked like a strange sea creature that had been rejected from the water.

Claire's heart still raced, but her thoughts ran quicker. *Could* the girl actually be some sort of sea monster? In Arden, the world had a tendency to shift and change. Friends turned into enemies. Rocks became evil queens. And a sister could stand in front of her one moment and be replaced by a giant, human-eating spider the next. Taking a deep breath, she tried to pull herself together. After all, sudden changes could also happen in the world of Windemere Manor, too. One moment, Sophie had been fine and healthy, just like any other seventh grader, and the next . . . she wasn't.

As her eyes adjusted to the night, Claire could begin to make out the features of her partner in escape. She was shorter than Claire, though her hair was twice as long. It fell almost to her tailbone in a curtain of braids, loops, and twists. And even in the dark, Claire could see pops of canary yellow and bright pink where thread had been woven into her hair.

There could be no doubt about it: the girl was a Spinner.

Worry squeezed Claire. She wasn't sure what to do next. On the one hand, she should leave now, before this little Spinner got a good look at her and realized Claire did not belong. That she was a Gemmer. But on the other hand . . . Claire couldn't just *leave*. Especially when the girl appeared so *young*.

"Hey," Claire whispered, keeping her voice low and soothing as she scooted a couple of inches closer. "What's your name? Are you all right?"

The girl sat up and gazed at Claire with wide eyes. For a second, Claire was scared the girl would burst into tears, but in the next second, she let out a whoop of what could only be called delight.

"All right?" The girl flung her hands out wide, as though to embrace Claire, the beach, the entire world. "This has been the best night *ever*! Kay is never going to *believe* what we did! Needle's eye, *I* barely believe what we did! Can *you* believe what we did?"

It was what Mom would have called a rhetorical question, because the girl didn't wait for Claire to answer. "We escaped an unmasked Spyden! And look!" She thrust her hand under Claire's nose. A swath of silk clung to her palm. "There's so much of it!" She glanced at Claire, and her eyes widened even more. "And there's so much on you! Do you mind?"

And before Claire could respond, the girl had reached out and yanked. A sound like Velcro ripped across the water as a long strip came reluctantly away from Claire, as though the sticky strands were sad to let go of her warmth.

Claire's stomach churned. "Take it all," she croaked out. Raising a hand to her head, she checked her own single braid and shuddered. It, too, was sticky, and she knew it would be a long, *long* time before she was sure she was web-free.

"Oh my words!" The girl clasped her hands over her heart. "Thank you! Thank you! Tha—!" She stopped pulling the web on Claire's shoulder. "I'm sorry; I don't even know your name!"

"It's Elaina," Claire said, sharing her middle name. In times like these, better to be safe than sorry, even if the girl in front of her seemed as harmless as a puppy. "Who are you?"

"Lyric," the girl said, sticking out her hand to shake before noticing a bit of web still stuck to her palm. "Blech, this stuff is gross, isn't it?" She waved her hand, and the silk undulated like a worm.

Claire's stomach flipped. "What happened to you, Lyric? How long were you trapped?"

Lyric pursed her lips and looked up at the night sky. "Judging by the constellations, either exactly a year or just since this afternoon," she said at last. "I'm guessing this afternoon. I don't think I would have been very . . . *fresh* if it had been a whole year I was wrapped up. You know what I mean?" She shook her head in disbelief. "I can't believe it was only yesterday that I ruined my entire future!"

Claire sat back on her ankles, bemused. Lyric couldn't seem to sit still. Even when the girl spoke, her hands moved faster than her lips, each word accented by its own hand flourish.

"Ruined?" Claire asked politely, recognizing Lyric's pause as an invitation to pry. It was a tactic Sophie used when she was trying to get her parents' attention: say something big and dramatic and wait for people to ask more.

"I completely *knotted* my audition yesterday," Lyric continued, "and now I'll *never* be sent to court!"

"Audition? Court?" Claire repeated. When Claire first arrived in Arden, every other word from her friends' mouths had sounded alien and strange. But she'd been in Arden for nearly three months now, and it had been a while since she'd felt so discombobulated. "Aren't you a bit small to go on trial? How old are you?"

"I'm eight and three-quarters," Lyric said indignantly, lifting her chin up to be half an inch taller. "And not court as in trial but court as in *royal* court. You know, Queen Estelle's new court."

. . .

   . . .

      . . .

Claire's heart stopped. Her lungs did, too. And though she could still hear the rush of the ocean and the rasp of the pebbles shifting beneath Lyric, her ears couldn't have been working. Because what Lyric had just said, well, no one *knew* Queen Estelle had returned. No one except for Claire, Sophie, their friends, Woven Root, and the—

Claire's thoughts broke off.

For the first time, she looked at Lyric. *Really* looked at the girl she'd rescued. And now, away from the red glow of the cottage's stove, without the tattered strips of gauzy web coating her clothes, and with Claire's eyes fully adjusted to the moon's thin light, she saw not only the yellow thread in Lyric's hair and the white of her smile but the blue of her torn cloak.

And not just any blue.

It was the same blue Claire had seen that terrible, horrible night an arrow had pierced her sister. The same blue she'd spied through a crack in a secret passage of Starscrape Citadel. The same blue she'd seen in the damp cells of Drowning Fortress.

Royalist blue.

But—Lyric was so *young*! And wearing it in the open! The Royalists were usually much older and stayed secretive.

"Lyric," Claire said, her voice sounding weirdly hollow to her own ears, "when you say 'Queen Estelle,' I mean . . ." She smiled hesitantly. "Are you talking about *the* Queen Estelle? The one from made-up tales and poems?"

"Where have *you* been?" Lyric asked. Her hand hesitated above the next strand of silk she'd been about to collect, and she peered at Claire. "Your fleet must have been in a *really* remote run of the Taryn to not have heard the news! The monoliths weren't destroyed by Forgers or Gemmers like we all thought at first. No—Estelle's *actually* returned! For real! Historian Fray confirmed it for all of us!" Lyric's voice took on a tone of amazement. "The Royalists weren't just a group of foolish dreamers. They were *right*!"

Claire's heart began to pound again, twice as loudly and twice as fast. So it was all out in the open now. Estelle was no longer in hiding . . . which meant she must have grown even more powerful since Claire had last met her.

Keep calm. Sophie's voice cut through Claire's frantic thoughts. *Don't give yourself away!*

"Have you actually seen her?" Claire asked, pretending this was all brand-new information to her. "The queen, I mean?"

Lyric sighed deeply. "No, not yet. But Historian Fray arrived a couple weeks ago with a message from the queen. Her Majesty has invited the guilds to join her at Hilltop Palace for the Starfell holiday, and asked that they bring with them all their unicorn artifacts and their quarter of the Crown of Arden."

Crown of Arden? The little triumph Claire had pulled from the Spyden turned into dismay. She knew she needed to *make* a queen, and she'd thought that it would be easy enough. After all, to be a queen, one needed only a crown, and Claire had made plenty of crowns before, out of both construction paper and flowers. But the way Lyric had said the words "Crown of Arden" with such importance—and knowing that Estelle wanted it—Claire began to suspect she couldn't just make *a* crown but would need to find *the* crown.

She wanted to interrupt, to test her theory, to ask any of the thousands of questions that had exploded within her, but Lyric kept talking.

"Not everyone can go to the re-coronation, of course, though a handful of Spinners will be attending so that they can perform for Her Majesty, and yesterday . . ." For the first time, the girl faltered. "Yesterday, I was cut from the troupe. Which is why I *had* to see the Spyden, to ask if there was a way I could get another chance, but"—Lyric stared meaningfully at the ball of web now collected in her palms—"that didn't really go according to plan, either."

She sighed, and the sound was surprisingly heavy from someone so small. "I know I'm not the best dancer, but I don't *want* to be a dancer—I want to be the youngest Historian ever! And the only way for that to happen is if I get a chance to witness this incredible moment! I want to *see* history being made as the guilds crown Estelle our queen for all time, and then"—Lyric's voice took on a dreamy quality—"magic will flourish, the unicorns will return, and the wraiths will be vanquished, once and for all!"

Claire's breath came fast and shallow, but Lyric continued to talk, oblivious to what her words were doing to Claire.

"I'm still trying to decide what I'll call my historical account," Lyric rambled on, "but I've already chosen my historian's name! Lyric the Lyrical, Youngest Historian of the Last Queen, Teller of Tales Both Dreadful and Glorious, and Master Witness for the Crown!" She raised an eyebrow in Claire's direction and said, rather smugly, "It's good, don't you think?"

But Claire could hardly get her lungs to suck in oxygen, let alone think.

"Well?" Lyric asked, demanding an answer to her question.

Claire nodded. "Yeah, it's good. Sorry, this is just . . ." She trailed off. *Just terrible.* But she didn't say the last part aloud.

Lyric frowned. "I really can't believe this is the first time you're hearing about all this," she said. "Grandmaster Bobbin sent word up and down the rivers and sea for all fleets to return to Needle Pointe for preparation." She tilted her head. "What fleet did you say you belonged to again?"

Claire hadn't said. Most names in Arden usually reflected the guild, but Claire didn't know the first thing about Spinning! Panic darted through her, startling away any words that could have helped. "It's . . . I'm with—"

But she was spared having to answer as Lyric gasped and clapped her hand over her mouth. "Oh, Elaina," Lyric said, "I think your thoughts have been *Gathered*."

Claire blinked. "I— What?"

"It's what Spydens *do*." Lyric's hands fluttered in concern. "They can pull out memories so they have them for themselves. But not to worry!" she added hastily. "Your memories will grow back in time. Or, at least, they should."

Nausea swept through Claire. "But I thought they gave answers?"

"They do that, too," Lyric confirmed as she took a bit of gauze off Claire and began to wrap it neatly around her hand in a figure eight. "Back when magic was still strong and the Guild War was just beginning, the Gemmers crafted all these terrible stone wyverns and the Tillers and Forgers teamed up together to craft the very first chimera. Spinners wanted their own war creatures. Some of them became convinced that the only way they could protect themselves was to integrate their skills with those of *true* spiders. But they made a huge mistake."

Lyric cheerfully dropped the wet web onto the beach. And after selecting another scrap, she began to collect again. "Instead of their humanity controlling their arachnidity," she continued, "it was the other way around. The creatures grew as large as men and women, and human knowledge helped them do spidery things even better. The beasts figured out how to knit themselves a human skin in which to hide."

Spyden silk all collected, Lyric sat back on her heels and stared at Claire. "Patches, *none* of this is familiar to you, is it?" She tilted her head and frowned. "We should get you to Needle Pointe."

Claire froze. The absolute last thing she wanted to do was

go to Needle Pointe, especially now if all the Spinners were Royalists. Someone there was sure to recognize her and alert the queen. "I don't think that's a good idea," she said quickly. "It's too dark to see a path. We might fall. Besides, what about the wraiths?"

"They won't bother us—not here, anyway," Lyric said. "Historian Fray said that the queen has already ensured the wraiths will leave Needle Pointe alone forever! And don't worry about light—I got this." Lyric reached into her cloak pocket and produced a ball of yarn. "My B.P.S.: Ball of Positioning String," Lyric said proudly, and began to fiddle with it. In the dark, Claire couldn't exactly see what Lyric was doing, but Claire thought that maybe she was tying the yarn to her finger in a complicated knot.

"Mama got it for my birthday, since I'm always getting lost. Though I have to admit, I've been struggling in my String Theory Class. Heads up!"

The ball of string whistled past Claire's head to land with a soft *thump* somewhere in the darkness. Lyric twisted the string on her finger. A second later, a golden glimmer began to shoot along the string, lighting up the darkness. It led to the ball of yarn, which was now bouncing up a nearly invisible path cut into the cliffs: a safe way over the Needles and down to the city and its bay on the other side.

"You see?" Lyric said brightly. "It'll be as easy as a cross-stitch to get back. And don't worry. You can stay with my family until your memories grow back. I bet your family is in the city now. It might take a day or two to locate them—it's been so crowded the last few days with everyone gathering for Starfell—but we'll find where you belong!"

But that was exactly the problem. Claire did not *want* to be found. Even the thought of Estelle finding her sent a tremor through her bones. The queen would probably try to use Claire as bait to lure out Sophie, and then—

"Hey, you're shivering," Lyric said. "Take this."

Lyric pressed something soft and thick into her hands, and Claire looked down to see she was holding a Royalist cloak. It took everything within her not to toss it into the water and let the tides drag it down to the coral forest hidden far below.

"That's yours, isn't it?" Lyric asked. "I grabbed it from the Spyden's basket before I ran out."

The coldness edged away from Claire as a realization suddenly struck her: Lyric was so free with her because even though she didn't think Claire—or Elaina, as was the case—remembered anything, she assumed that Claire was a fellow Royalist.

Lyric began to follow the glowing string. "We should get going. It'll take us all night to get back."

Only a queen can defeat a queen, the Spyden had said. And if anyone knew how to make a queen, it would be this mysterious, secretive society that had spent hundreds of years researching the royal family. There might be Queen Estelle, Mira Fray, and Royalists in the city, but there could also be answers.

"Are you coming?" Lyric called back.

Claire had to defeat the queen. To keep Arden—*and* Sophie—safe.

She whirled the cloak over her shoulders, and this time when it touched her skin, she didn't shudder. As soon as she saved Arden, she could start saving Sophie, and then they could go home, where the biggest worry they had was who would get to choose the next song in the car.

"Coming!" Claire replied. But as she followed Lyric and her glowing string up the twisting path, the Royalist cloak around her shoulders felt as heavy as a lie and twice as dangerous.

CHAPTER
7

By the time Claire and Lyric had trudged the rocky path from the beach to Needle Pointe the sun had started to rise, but the morning fog had not yet burned away. It rolled in from the water, adding iridescence to the newly hoisted sails of the ships. In this light, they looked more like butterfly wings than simple sheets.

Right before the narrow path merged with the main road, Lyric paused to rewind the B.P.S. while Claire studied the layout of the Spinners' only permanent town. It was a city of crescents; the water from the harbor was carefully guided into a series of circular canals that, even from this vantage point, Claire could tell were crowded with Spinner narrowboats. The Rhona River hugged the city before running out into the sea, making the entire settlement one little island. As far as she could tell, there were no walls or gates or inspectors, but still—she knew Arden had ways of dealing with unexpected guests.

Her hand drifted to the pencil wedged securely behind her ear, and the weight of her Hollow Pack on her shoulder was a friendly one. She wasn't powerless the same way she'd been when she first climbed up the chimney-well and stepped into Arden. After all, Claire knew how to polish a gem just right so that it could remember how to glow. But even though she knew she wasn't helpless, she didn't exactly feel *not helpless*, either. And she wouldn't—not until she managed to find out more about this "Crown of Arden." But to be able to do that, she had to make sure she wouldn't be caught as soon as she stepped foot inside the city limits.

"Lyric," Claire said, interrupting the girl's current monologue on what kind of gown Queen Estelle would most likely wear to her coronation, "what exactly are we telling the inspectors about me again?"

"Oh, don't worry about *them*," Lyric said, waving an airy hand, and Claire suspected that she had never been interrogated on the waterways before. Because if she had, she would certainly know that to *not worry* was impossible. "We just need to stick to The Story, and everything will be all right."

The Story, as Lyric put it, was one she'd happily pulled together as they'd followed the glowing B.P.S. It involved a dastardly shipwreck, lost papers, and a daring, dashing Lyric who'd discovered Claire on the beach when Lyric had slipped out to collect early-morning sea urchins. For dye, of course.

Tragically, upon finding Claire's unconscious body, she'd lost her entire morning's catch.

It made Claire's head spin.

"What will we tell your mom, though?" Claire asked. "If you've been gone since yesterday morning, she'll know you've been missing for an entire night!"

"Ah, yes, well." Lyric's expression turned guilty. "I kind of, sorta told her that I was staying overnight with Velvetina so we could get in some more studying. But like I said"—again that airy wave—"everything will be all right!"

"LYRIC WEFT, IS THAT YOU?"

Claire jumped at the unexpected sound and whirled around, but no one was there. That made sense, though, because the voice hadn't come from behind her but from above. Squinting up, she saw a cluster of metal cups hanging in the olive tree above her. Thin red threads had been tied to them, and Claire traced their path all the way down to the rooftops of Needle Pointe before they disappeared.

"Patches and rags," Lyric muttered before cupping her hands around her mouth. "IT IS, SCHOLAR SYLVESTER, AND I'VE BROUGHT A FRIEND."

Claire stared curiously at the cups. She'd once tried to do something similar with Sophie, when Sophie was upset that Mom and Dad wouldn't be getting her a cell phone even though she was about to start middle school. She'd been Claire's age then, and Claire had been nine—just entering the fourth grade and excited when Sophie told her they could make their own set of cell phones, so long as they had tin cans and a piece of string. She said she'd seen it on an old TV show once. But though they had both tried, neither of them ever heard so much as a peep.

"WHAT WAS THAT?" the voice said, and Claire had the sense that whoever was on the other end of the string must be sitting in the harbor, if not completely submerged under the salt water. "YOU WANT TO PLAY PRETEND?"

"NO," Lyric shouted back. "I SAID, 'I BROUGHT A FRIEND'!"

"I'M GLAD YOU KNOW YOU'LL NEED TO MAKE AMENDS," the voice, Sylvester, said. "YOUR MOTHER IS FURIOUS."

It was funny to watch the undertones of pink drain from Lyric's face. Her hand dropped from her mouth. *"Patches,"* she repeated and broke into a run while Scholar Sylvester crackled, "LANGUAGE!" at her back.

"Lyric!" Claire called, chasing after her. "Slow down!"

"Can't!" Lyric huffed back. "If Mama knows—and of course she does! I can't believe I forgot about the Snitch Stitches!"

"Snitch Stitches?" Claire asked. She wished Lyric would slow down. The Royalist cloak was thick and just a little too long, so that it flapped behind her like an obnoxious tail.

"Needle Pointe can hear anything at any time, so long as there's a Snitch Stitch about—but don't worry! They're only around the perimeter of the city," Lyric added, correctly interpreting Claire's look. "It's just best not to say anything too private." She winced. "Like our cover stories—oh, Mama is going to *murder* me!"

The two girls sprinted down the road. As Lyric had predicted, the inspectors at either end of the suspension bridge that allowed pedestrian access into the city did not bother to stop them. In fact, Claire was pretty sure she saw an inspector shake his head sympathetically when Lyric yelped out their names. It seemed the Spinner girl was well known to the inspectors . . . as was her mother's temper.

It was still early enough that the streets were relatively empty, and it was easy to keep up the sprint. "If we can just get back to Tina's," Lyric was saying as they crossed the first canal, "then maybe—"

"Lyric Calliope Weft." A voice rang out over the waterways.

Lyric stumbled to a stop. "Here we go," she whispered. Taking a deep breath, she plastered a smile on her face and twirled around. "Hi, Mama! What are you doing up so early?"

Claire turned just as a woman in a ruffled pink apron marched up behind them. She was a tall woman, with the same thick black hair as her daughter, though hers was twisted into a series of tight knots across her head, while one skinny braid hung down over her left shoulder. The freed braid swung like a pendulum, and it took Claire a second to realize why: Lyric's mother was practically quaking with fury.

"Where in thread's end did you disappear to?" Lyric's mother's voice was like a teakettle's hiss before it screamed.

Without thinking, Claire took one step back.

"Don't!" Mistress Weft said as her daughter opened her mouth to reply. "Not one word from you! Can you *imagine* the terror I've been through? First, finding out you weren't at the Hares' house. Then being told by the Watch that they couldn't go looking for my daughter because a *Forger* with a golden spyglass *attacked* the *Thread Cutter's* crow's nest! What do you have to say for yourself?"

Lyric opened her mouth and closed it again, looking uncertain as to whether she was allowed to answer. By now, Claire was aware of a small group of Spinners watching from behind their shutters and a pair of boys laughing from a narrowboat. Poor Lyric. But there was nothing she could do to help—even if she did bristle a bit at the news of a "Forger attack." Claire hadn't attacked anyone!

"The *truth*, Lyric—and I mean it!" her mother snapped.

"I'm sorry, Mama," Lyric said, sniffling a little bit. "I made a mistake—but I'm free now! Elaina saved me!" It seemed all of Lyric's stories had gone out the window at the sight of her mother's ruffled fury.

"Saved?" Mistress Weft's eyebrows shot up, and she looked suspiciously at her daughter. "Saved from what?"

Lyric shifted guiltily, then reached into her cloak pocket to pull out a swab of web. Even seeing it sent a shiver of prickles across Claire as she remembered the sticky warmth wrapping around her ribs and coating her nose.

Mistress Weft gaped. "Did you go to the Spyden?"

Lyric cringed, but she nodded and didn't run. Which was rather courageous, Claire thought, especially taking into consideration the rising color on Mistress Weft's brown cheeks. For a moment, Claire thought the woman might actually explode. Instead, Mistress Weft took a deep breath, seeming to pull in her words like wool on a spindle, before she turned her attention to Claire. "And you saved her?"

Uncertain, Claire nodded. Suddenly, her world was a haze of pink frills as Mistress Weft gathered Claire and hugged her tight. "Thank you," she said into Claire's hair. Lyric's mother smelled a bit of lavender, reminding Claire of her own mother, who liked to make sure there was at least one jar of lavender bubble bath in the closet.

"And what about your parents?" Mistress Weft asked. "Where are they?"

Claire threw a frantic look at Lyric, who quickly stepped in. "The Spyden Gathered all her thoughts, Mama. She doesn't remember much of anything."

"You poor dear!" Mistress Weft said, giving Claire one last squeeze before letting go. When she didn't look like she might explode, her face was as open as a sunflower and just as pleasant. There was also something familiar about Lyric's mother—something about the way her eyes crinkled or her nose—that made Claire wonder if she'd met Mistress Weft before. Lyric, too, for that matter, but Claire knew that was impossible.

"Come, you must be hungry," Mistress Weft continued, "Let's get you comfortable while we figure out which fleet you belong to—and a suitable punishment for Lyric."

Lyric gulped.

Claire followed mother and daughter through the city.

Bright townhouses edged the canals like lace on a collar. But though the colors were beautiful, Claire couldn't help but notice the odd tilt of many of the buildings that maybe a Tiller could have helped straighten out, and the crumbling corners of the stone bridges that could do with a Gemmer's touch. After a few more steps, three more bridges, and a turn or two, they at last arrived in front of a bright-yellow door of a stately home.

"This way," Mistress Weft said quietly, lighting a lamp and sending the apartment into a blaze of color. Everywhere Claire looked, there was fabric: on the wall, beneath her feet, above her head, where the ceiling was draped in gauzy strips of pink, drawing out from the center like a tent's pavilion. There were even barrels outlining the room's perimeters, each filled to the top with Royalist-blue yarn. Claire's stomach turned. There was enough yarn in them for a hundred new cloaks. A hundred new people who believed Queen Estelle's lies.

"Have a seat," Mistress Weft said warmly, pointing to a rickety kitchen table. "Lyric—can you go get some of your sister's clothes for Elaina to change into? Then come help me in the kitchen. You, though, poor little knot," Mistress Weft said as she caught Claire covering a yawn, "go lie down and get some rest. We'll call you when breakfast is ready."

Soon enough, Claire had dropped her Hollow Pack in the corner of the bedroom, tugged off the strangely witchy Spyden's dress, and pulled on a new outfit, which, though a bit big, was the most comfortable thing she'd worn in weeks. The wide-legged trousers, embroidered with silver galaxies, swished around her legs like a skirt, and the scarlet sweater was as warm as her puffiest winter coat but felt as thin as moth's wings. Ignoring the blanket on Lyric's sister's bed (it would be a while before Claire wanted to wrap herself up in *anything*), Claire flopped over the covers of the large canopy bed, and quickly fell asleep.

A few hours later, Lyric came in to wake her and help her detangle her curls until Mistress Weft called for them. Breakfast—or brunch, rather, as Mistress Weft had let her sleep a couple of hours more—was ready.

Between bites of thick oatmeal and nibbles of honey-drizzled toast, Lyric and her mother tried to piece together a story from Claire's vague answers. It wasn't hard to keep her replies short. Any time Claire paused, Lyric would barrel in, coming up with fifty different possibilities. So long as Claire remained quiet, Lyric would create Claire's cover story for her without even realizing it.

The only time Claire didn't manage to keep her expression of vague confusion was when Lyric went off on a tangent, describing in excruciating detail what everyone had worn the day Historian Fray arrived with the good news.

"Tina wore her gown that looks like an upside-down rose, but it just could *not* compare to the color of the prince's doublet!"

Claire took a bite of toast. "What prince?"

The only prince she knew of was her many-times-great-grandfather Martin, or the Lost Prince, as he was known in Arden. Most historians in Arden believed that Prince Martin was killed in battle against the Forgers and Tillers. But the truth was that the prince, horrified by his older sister's actions, had fled to an entirely different world.

"Ha! You're funny," Lyric was saying. She shook her head, smiling like Claire had made some sort of joke. "Prince Thorn, obviously— Ew, Elaina!"

Claire covered her mouth too late to stop the spray of soggy crumbs across the embroidered tablecloth.

Mistress Weft appeared with a damp dishrag in hand. "Is something wrong, dear?"

Mortified, Claire took a hasty sip of orange juice and cleared her throat. Maybe the Spyden had actually done something to Claire's mind, because she thought that Lyric had just said *Prince Thorn.*

"Who?" she asked again when she was sure she had stopped coughing. It *couldn't* be the same person.

Lyric's eyes widened. "You've forgotten about Prince Thorn, too?" She clasped her hands to her heart. "He's *only* the reason why Queen Estelle returned! He's her great-something-grandnephew, who managed to wake her from Queen Rock with his tremendous magic!" Her face took on a solemn expression. "He's the most powerful Spinner of all time, to be able to unravel the queen from *stone.* Her Majesty has named him her heir."

The kitchen suddenly felt cramped. Even Claire's skin felt too tight, as though it were too small for her body.

Thorn Barley had once been her friend—and Sophie and

Sena and Nett's friend—until he'd betrayed them all, leading them astray while he secretly went to release Estelle from Queen Rock. He'd been born without magic, or so they had thought. But in actuality, he was a Spinner born into the Tiller guild, destined to never learn where his true talents lay so long as interaction between guilds remained illegal. But with Queen Estelle's return, he'd met Mira Fray and learned he could spin. And so, when he'd next seen Claire and her friends, he'd tried to capture them and bring them to the Royalists. Later, however, Sophie had claimed that Thorn helped them escape from their cell underneath the Drowning Fortress. Though when it came to Thorn, Claire suspected her older sister could be a bit biased.

Claire suddenly understood why everything felt too small. Nothing was big enough to contain the burning-red feeling that was clawing out of her, setting fire to her blood.

Claire was *angry*.

How could he? How *dare* he!

And yet, Lyric was still going on and on about the great new prince of Arden. "I've actually seen him before, you know. He visited Needle Pointe a few times with Mira Fray."

"And is Prince Thorn"—the words felt like ashes in Claire's mouth—"still here?"

Lyric looked mournful. "No, he left a little bit ago, but he'll be at Hilltop Palace for Starfell. Queen Estelle is going to crown him, too."

There it was—the opening she needed! "Crown," she repeated, pushing aside her anger and making her eyes as wide as possible, the same way Sophie would when she was trying to look extra innocent. "When you said 'crown,' I think—I'm not sure, but I *almost* had a memory. It felt familiar."

Not a lie. Crowns were familiar to Claire. She'd worn them at Halloween parties and for history class, when she'd had to give a speech as King George III. And once, she and Sophie had gone through an inordinate amount of construction paper to make a crown for their uncle's new puppy, Sir Beast, who just kept chewing them up.

Lyric beamed. "Yay! See? I *told* you Gathering shouldn't last too long. Maybe you did know about the queen's coronation! This makes me think your family probably was planning to spend Starfell at Hilltop Palace."

"Maybe!" Claire nodded quickly. And though she was curious about what this *Starfell* was that Lyric continued to mention, she kept her question focused: "Can you tell me more about the . . . what did you call it? The Crown of Arden?"

"Lyric can tell you lots about it," Mistress Weft said as she hung up her dishrag and moved toward the spinning wheel at the far side of the room. Settling on her stool, Mistress Weft looked at her daughter with pride. "Lyric is one of only two preambles selected to attend Queen Estelle's re-coronation. Which is why," she said, arching an eyebrow at Lyric, "I've decided that your ten months of detangling my yarn barrels can begin *after* Starfell, so that you may use all your extra hours for practice."

"Oh, uh, thanks," Lyric said, and Mistress Weft smiled before bending over her work. As soon as her mother's attention was elsewhere, Lyric shot a Look at Claire. Claire didn't need to know the girl well to understand what that meant: *Don't say a word about the failed audition.*

Claire nodded ever so slightly, and Lyric relaxed, though her gesticulations seemed a little more frantic than usual as she dove into the history of Arden's crown.

"The Crown of Arden is *more* than just a crown. It's said to be the very *first* instance of jumbled magic in all of history. Woven, grown, sculpted, and forged from starfire, then blessed by unicorns, the crown was created to protect Anders d'Astora, a Tiller who'd been chosen by everyone to challenge a terrible evil that threatened the world. An evil *so* terrible that even the Spinner historians were too scared to record what it was, so that its name has been lost to time. But what we *do* know, is that Anders was victorious!" She brandished her sticky bun as though it were a sword. "With the crown's help, King Anders the First saved Arden."

"But how?" Claire asked. "Wouldn't a sword or something have been more useful?"

Lyric shook her head. "The crown is rumored to have a mysterious ability to connect the monarch to the land, giving the wearer immeasurable power."

Oh, no.

"What kind of immeasurable power?" Claire asked, the bits of toast feeling like boulders in her stomach. Estelle already had an arsenal of unicorn artifacts, and if she got ahold of this crown . . . she would be unstoppable.

"Oh, all sorts of things!" Lyric said around a mouthful of

sticky bun, finally having managed to take a bite. "Some legends say that Anders was able to make mountains walk and rivers knot up, but he's not the only d'Astora who managed such incredible feats. Estelle herself is said to have created the Petrified Forest! The Crown of Arden is *the* most powerful object ever crafted, which is why, when the Guild War ended, it was decided that it would be hacked into four tines—"

"Tines?" Claire interrupted.

Lyric nodded. "Yes, that's what the point on a crown is called: tine. Rhymes with 'line.' Anyway, the Crown of Arden had four: the Spinners' Love Knot Tine, the Forgers' Hammer Tine, the Tillers' Oak Leaf Tine, and the Gemmers' Stone Tine. It was decided that each guild would guard its own piece—a symbol that each guild would from now on be in charge of its own destiny." Lyric gave a slight flourish of her hand and bowed her head. "The end!"

"Well told," Mistress Weft said kindly. "But the tale isn't done."

Lyric's eyes widened. "Oh, you're right!" she said. Beaming, she turned to Claire. "I forgot, because *this* history hasn't ended! Queen Estelle has invited each of the four guilds to Hilltop Palace to celebrate this year's Starfell—"

"Starfell?" Claire interrupted again.

Lyric blinked, startled. "You—you don't even remember *Starfell*?"

Claire bit her lip. Maybe Zuli or Lapis had mentioned it in passing, but when she was at Stonehaven, Claire had other things on her mind. She shook her head.

"It's *only* the biggest holiday of the year!" Lyric flung out a hand so wildly she almost took out the honey pot. "It's a ginormous meteor shower that marks the end of the traveling season and the beginning of winter. We usually start the evening with a special dance and then spend the night bundled up with friends and families on rooftops, eating and drinking, while we watch the stars until they fade. Mama, Kay, and I usually go over to Tina's house."

"This year will be different though," Mistress Weft said, momentarily pausing the wheel to collect more blue yarn from her basket.

"What do you mean?" Lyric asked.

Mistress Weft glanced sharply at her daughter. "Both you and Kay will be spending Starfell at Hilltop Palace, performing for the queen's re-coronation . . . won't you?"

"Oh right, that, yes, of course!" Lyric said quickly. She turned away from her mother's shrewd gaze and looked at Claire. "The guilds will present their tines to Queen Estelle that evening." The girl's eyes practically shone like stars themselves. "Then the crown will be reforged, and Arden will be like it was in the days of yore, when magic was strong!"

A hole seemed to be digging itself in Claire's stomach. For all Lyric's talk of a perfect, sparkly past, Claire knew it had not been like that for every guild, especially the Forgers, who'd toiled under horrendous and dangerous conditions for the Gemmers and Spinners.

"And do you think that *all* the guilds will give her their piece?" Claire asked.

"We are unsure," Mistress Weft admitted from her corner. "The Spinners have already decided to support her, and we can't imagine the Gemmers would go against one of their own. But as for the Tiller and Forger guilds . . ." She paused in her spinning. "The future is never certain."

Claire bit her lip. So much of life was uncertain—so much of it new and strange, but now, at least, she knew one thing for sure: she needed to collect the tines of Arden—and she needed to get them before Estelle did, if she were to have any chance of crowning Nadia queen. But first . . .

"So the Spinners—I mean, *we*," Claire quickly corrected herself, "have a quarter of the crown. Where do we keep it?"

"Come on, I'll show you." Lyric shoved away her breakfast plate and sprang up. "We're going to be late anyway!" She leaped to the door and picked up a box of woven ribbons waiting beside it.

"Don't forget your cloaks," Mistress Weft called. "It's getting cold."

"Wait, where are we going?" Claire asked, getting up and clearing her dishes to the great tin sink.

"The Historium, obviously." Lyric whirled on her Royalist cloak. "It's where the Love Knot Tine is displayed!"

Lyric was already out the door as Claire called after her, "But what are we late for?" She'd have to keep up to find out.

CHAPTER
8

$\mathcal{T}$he sun had fully risen, along with the rest of the city. Voices called out greetings from the narrowboats as Lyric hurried Claire alongside the canals and over bridges. Claire had read about cities in her own world where streets were made of water, but she hadn't been able to picture it until now. She marveled as a boat floated right up to the door of a townhouse for a boy and his little sister to clamber into as easily as Claire and Sophie did into their parents' car.

If she'd had all the time in the world, Claire would have loved to spend a day on a bridge and dedicate an entire after-noon to capturing the shifting colors of the river that linked the city together. And she could have spent at least a *week* trying to draw the Spinners, who were of all different shapes and sizes—literally. Some of the women bustled around in square-shaped skirts that were as wide as park benches, while the men wore thick overcoats with enormously puffy sleeves.

And the hair! Wherever Claire looked, there was a different style. Some pulled their hair into elaborate knots on top of their heads, while others let it flow in a waterfall of braids and threads. And the few men who happened to be bald all had the thickest, longest beards Claire had ever seen.

"Watch it!" a Spinner snapped as Claire, studying a woman's hair sculpted to look like a swan, accidentally stepped on her long train.

"Sorry," Claire mumbled and tried to move out of the way, only to bump into another Spinner, this one with arms full of scrolls. He glared at her without changing his pace, the scrolls' colorful tags wagging at her like an admonishing finger.

Claire hurried to follow Lyric through the crowded streets, trying not to get too distracted by the massive ribbons fluttering from the boats' decks in the harbor, their flags crisscrossing the sky like a giant's game of cat's cradle.

Needle Pointe was, as Sophie would say, *spectacular*. Claire wished Sophie were here to see— No. Claire stopped that thought in its tracks.

She did not wish Sophie were here at all, not in the slightest! Sophie needed to stay safe in Woven Root until Claire had managed to gather all four pieces of Arden's crown.

"Gather"? Claire could practically imagine Sophie's snort (a habit she'd picked up from Sena) at her plan. *Is that the new word for "steal"?*

What would you do? Claire thought back at the little voice in her head, which was sounding more and more like Sophie with each passing day.

The voice was silent. Because Claire's plan was exactly something Sophie *would* do. Sophie would let Lyric lead her straight to the Love Knot Tine, and then once she'd figured out how to steal it, she'd flee before anyone could catch her. It was a terrible plan, a dangerous plan, a Sophie-like plan. And therefore, it must be the right plan, even if her blood ran cold whenever Claire thought about the last time a valuable object had been stolen from a guild. The Unicorn Harp. Sena had taken it with all the best intentions, and she'd almost been killed for it.

"Look out!" There was a yank on Claire's sleeve, and Lyric pulled her away from the swinging tail end of a rolled-up carpet slung across the shoulder of a tired-looking Spinner. If it had connected with Claire, she definitely would have fallen into the canal.

"Thanks," Claire said, feeling a little breathless. Making a splash in front of everyone wouldn't have been the best way to start her new plan. Needle Pointe was crowded—more crowded than any of the other places Claire had visited in Arden, and with each passing minute, more and more narrowboats floated into the canals.

"Lyric," Claire asked, curious, "how will they fit more boats here for Starfell next month?"

"Next month?" Lyric looked puzzled. "Elaina—Starfell isn't next month; it's three sunsets from now."

Claire stumbled to a halt.

"What?" She looked around wildly. There were still leaves on some trees. "But you said—I thought the star shower marked the beginning of winter! It's not even that cold yet!"

"Speak for yourself." Lyric shrugged. "It's always chilly on the river ways."

"But," Claire said, her voice beginning to edge on frantic, "that means Estelle is going to be crowned in just *three* days!" Her chest tightened. That wasn't even enough time for a watercolor to properly dry!

"I know," Lyric squealed with excitement, and she broke into a quick jog, as though by moving faster, she could make Starfell arrive even sooner. Claire, however, felt rooted to the spot.

She would never be able to collect all four tines in three days.

Deep breaths, the Sophie voice in her mind instructed. *Don't give up—you're already close to the Love Knot Tine, and it's not even noon.*

Claire breathed, and focused. Estelle had demanded that all the guilds meet with her, which must mean she needed all four tines for the crown to be as potent as it was in the old tales. If Claire could prevent just a *single* tine from getting to Hilltop Palace, maybe she could delay the coronation until sometime after Starfell, buying herself and Nadia the days they needed to gather the other three.

You mean, the Sophie voice teased, *steal*.

"Come on, Elaina, don't get lost," Lyric called over her shoulder. The box of ribbons she was carrying bounced in her arms.

The closer they got to the city center, the larger the crowds became. An excited hum seemed to thread throughout Needle Pointe, the sounds of laughter and excitement amplified by the waterways. Spinners kept breaking out into bursts of song, and from far off, Claire could hear the notes of a violin dance down the canal while the snapping of flags kept time.

"Almost there!" Lyric said, hurrying Claire over one last bridge and around a final turn—

Claire gasped.

In the center of the plaza stood the most beautiful building Claire had ever seen. It was made of swooping arches and stately columns that rose over the crowd like a giant wedding cake. The many long, low stone steps leading up to it looked like a fancy serving tray, which only added to the confectionary effect.

So this was the Historium.

It must be a museum, the kind that looked as grand as a castle, and Claire's heartbeat ticked up as she imagined all the wonders that must be contained within. She always loved field trips to museums, loved wandering through massive, echoing halls, hearing the soothing click of heels against marble floors, and staring at the artwork made by visionaries long since dead and gone. In her world, it was the closest she had ever felt to magic.

Hundreds of tiered balconies trimmed the outside of the building, and as they got closer, she saw that from each one dangled a crescent banner, with the same symbol repeating again and again: a single star suspended over a white crown against a field of Royalist blue.

No need to wonder whose seal it was, though. Lyric squealed in delight again: "They put the queen's banners up!" She looked at Claire proudly. "When Grandmaster Bobbin heard about Her Majesty's return, he had all the preambles practice our embroidery on the banners so that we would have them in time for Starfell." Lyric shielded her eyes from the sun and scanned the tiers. "I think that one there is the one I did!"

"How can you tell?"

Lyric waved an unconcerned hand. "I accidentally added a fifth point to the crown, but who's counting? Come on!" She took the stone steps two at a time, and Claire hurried to keep up. But with each step that took her nearer to the Historium, the more certain she grew that her plan was a terrible one. Maybe she should just tell everyone the truth as soon as possible. Dad always said the truth would set her free, but what if the Spinners didn't *want* to listen to the truth? Everywhere she looked, from the banner-wrapped building to all the blue cloaks on the streets, she saw how excited the Spinners were for Queen Estelle's return.

When they reached the top of the steps, instead of leading them through the grand arched doors of the museum, Lyric slipped around the corner to a side entrance. Stopping, she pulled out a key. "My sister, Kay, is a stage assistant," Lyric explained, fitting it in the lock. "She was asking Mama to come drop off so many things that the director finally gave Mama her own key so she wouldn't have to stand out here so long and be questioned by the Wraith Watch. They're usually here to guard the Love Knot Tine, but after the Forger attack yesterday, I think they've all been sent to the city's perimeters instead." She gave the door a push. "Welcome to the Historium!"

All the museums Claire had ever been to—with the exception of a children's museum the Martinsons visited every couple of years—had been quiet places, somewhere between a church and a library.

Needle Pointe's Historium was anything but.

Claire jumped at the roar of noise that greeted them as Lyric ushered her inside.

"Mind the ropes!"

"Where's my hat?" a boy dressed in a green jerkin and tall boots called as he rushed through the hall. "I'm on in ten minutes!"

"Did you ask Roberto?" a woman called as she hustled, arms full of long gowns, toward another door. "Dancers, don't forget to give me your props when the number is up!"

Claire blinked. "Where—?"

But she was interrupted as a Spinner wearing a wig of gray curls and drawn-on wrinkles hobbled by and exclaimed, "Patches, Lyric! Where have you been? Your sister has been looking for you!"

"Sorry, Bard," Lyric said and nodded down to the box in her hand. "But I have the spare ribbons. Where should I put them?"

From somewhere down the chaotic halls came a bellowing. Bard winced. "Probably best to head to the stage directly. They started rehearsal already and . . . uh, the director has been a bit . . ." He trailed off as the bellow grew louder. "Touchy," he finished.

Before Claire could quite wrap her mind around the conversation, Lyric had nodded and broken into a jog.

"Lyric?" Claire panted, slightly out of breath. "Why didn't you say the Historium was a theater? I thought it was going to be a museum!"

"What's the difference?" Lyric asked, opening yet another door and walking behind a set of pulleys and ropes. "Performance is how we remember our history. Why should the past be confined to books and objects? Besides, it's more fun this way!"

She swooshed Claire into an auditorium of plush red seats and pushed her into one just as the conductor lifted his hands and the curtain raised. Dancers, all in shimmering silks and holding fluttering ribbons, twirled onto the stage.

Claire's breath caught. She'd seen a few ballet recitals before—they were impossible to avoid if Sophie Martinson was your older sister—but these dancers were as different from the intermediate Tuesday afternoon class as a puddle was from a lake. This wasn't even like the professional ballet the Martinson family had decided to see a few years ago over winter break.

Those dancers had only *seemed* to fly across the stage, but in Arden . . . Claire leaned in her seat, squinting at the stage.

"Lyric," Claire whispered, wondering if she were seeing things. "Their slippers—they're not touching the ground!"

"Of course not," Lyric whispered back. "Because they're not *slip*pers; they're *Fly*ers, which, you know, fly."

How wonderful! And practical. Claire wished she could show the footwear to Grandmaster Carnelian of Stonehaven. If the Gemmers had some of these shoes, it would be so much easier for them to fix the crumbling gargoyles that lined the Citadel's soaring domed roof—and much less dangerous.

The sounds of violins and harps reached inside and soothed her, and for a moment, Claire let herself get lost in the melody and movement. Each costume was an incandescent white, the color reminding her of a soap bubble when the sunlight caught its curve. With each kick and grand leap, the dancers sparkled. As the music gathered force, the twirls became tighter and the ribbons arced higher, looking like liquid moons. It was beautiful. It was magical. It was—

"Stop! Stop! Stop!"

Claire jumped in her seat as a tall, thin man unfolded himself from where he'd been sitting in the front row. Like all the other Spinners, he, too, seemed to take his clothing seriously. Bedecked in a fine suit of orange brocade and with his Royalist cloak tossed jauntily over a single shoulder, he looked a bit like an off-kilter sun setting against a navy sky. But unlike the other Spinners, his white-blond hair was wild. It stuck up in all directions. Here and there, Claire could see some dangling threads as well as an unraveling braid or two, as though nervous fingers had been tugging at their ends.

"You look like a bunch of *popcorn*!" the man exclaimed. "And not beautifully falling stars!" Striding up onto the stage, he plucked a streamer from a stunned dancer and, with a flick of his wrist, sent it shimmying into the air. With another flick, the ribbon shifted direction, shuttling back and forth like a fish swimming upstream.

"Watch carefully," he instructed, and with a final flick, he let go of the streamer—but this time, it did not float back down. Instead it stayed suspended, twisting itself into the shape of a star.

"*That* is how all your ribbons should look on the eight count," the man said. "But you're all a beat too early!" He reached up a long arm and tugged the ribbon. The star immediately undid itself and folded itself neatly in his palm. Letting out a great sigh, the man rubbed his temples. "Let's review again *why* the Starfell Dance of Ribbons is so important. Can anybody—?" But he hadn't even formed his full question when a forest of hands shot up in the air. Claire bit back a smile. The kids of Needle Pointe, it seemed, didn't have a shy bone in their bodies. The Spinners really *were* a guild of Sophies.

The director nodded to a girl with hair as black as Lyric's who promptly said, "Because it's tradition. The Dance of Ribbons is always performed on Starfell."

"Yes, but *why*?" the director asked. "Why *this* dance at *this* time? Anybody?"

Only one hand went up, and the person didn't wait to be called upon. "I know, Director!"

Claire glanced toward her left while the rest of the dancers and the director turned around to look out over the seats in the auditorium.

"Is that you, Weft?" the director asked, scanning the dark shadows in the theater.

Beside Claire, Lyric slowly stood up. "It's me."

The director fixed a tough eye on her. "I thought you were cut from auditions already."

Lyric hung her head. "I was, but . . . I still know the answer, sir."

"Go on, then."

For once, Lyric was quiet, and Claire recognized the slight quake in her knees. "You got this," Claire whispered quietly. "He's no Spyden."

There was a slight uptick of her lips, and then Lyric spoke. "The dancers, they're supposed to represent the shooting stars. And the ribbons in their hands are meant to remind the audience of unicorn manes and tails. There are songs about unicorns galloping up the mountains during Starfell, as though they were racing the stars themselves. The light of the shower would turn their manes and tails all silvery. That's why we dance with silver ribbons and decorate Needle Pointe with them around Starfell."

"Very good," the director said, and Lyric beamed widely as he turned back to address the dancers on the stage. "You can hit your steps perfectly, but if you don't know the meaning behind what you do, then the motion is worthless. When you dance, I want you to think about how these steps connect us to the past and how the Dance of Ribbons was created to remember something of great value."

His voice lowered and took on a wistful tone, and he flicked his wrist. The silver ribbon again raised effortlessly into the air. This time, it did not fold itself into a star but arced up, flowing into the outline of an arched neck, a pricked ear, and a spiral horn. The ribbon whipped along faster and faster, tracing the outline of a silver unicorn onto the air.

"Which is why," the director said with a final flick, and the unicorn neatly folded itself up, "you must *concentrate*! You are the ones selected to perform for Her Majesty's coronation. When the queen sees you dance, she will select the best of you to join her court. And if you're chosen, you will bear witness to one of the greatest days in Arden's history: the return of the unicorns."

His words sent a trill of excitement flapping around the room. Dancers lifted their heads, smoothed out their costumes, and set their jaws as they all prepared to rehearse again, for such an opportunity, for such an honor.

"And we have mere hours to whip you into shape!" the director shouted, his voice snapping everyone into position. The silver ribbon fell down into his palm. "We only have three sunsets until Starfell, so I advise you to take position again and remember, for all that's spun and silken, don't forget to keep your toes pointed!"

As the dancers hustled into their places, it felt as though one of their ribbons had cut itself loose, only to wrap around Claire's ribs.

Three days. *Three days* to gather each of the four guilds' tines, reforge the circle, crown Nadia, and then, after all that, defeat the queen . . . and save Sophie.

It seemed impossible.

It *was* impossible.

But Arden was a land built on the impossible, and it could hold at least one more. Maybe. Probably. *Hopefully.*

"Lyric," Claire whispered. "Can you take me to the Love Knot Tine now?"

Lyric nodded, but she looked longingly at the stage. "It's just out these doors, in the lobby."

"The lobby?" Claire was surprised. Lobbies usually made her think of movie theaters, where on special occasions Dad would stand in line to get a small bag of popcorn for the family to share. Those places were usually a bit sticky from spilled soda drinks and dropped candies. She couldn't imagine a crown's point being stored someplace like that. But then again, she hadn't expected it to be in a theater, either.

"Yeah." Lyric nodded. Keeping her voice low, she quickly explained, "After the Guild Treaty, the Spinner grandmaster in charge of Needle Pointe decided to display the Love Knot

Tine in the most public place possible: the Historium's lobby. That way, we are all responsible for its safekeeping. The more eyes on it, the better!"

"Right," Claire said, keeping her voice light even though it felt like her body was sinking into the ground.

Still thinking of it as gathering? Sophie's voice sounded cheerfully in her mind. And even though the voice belonged to Claire . . . Claire had nothing to say.

Lyric carefully slipped out from her seat, and Claire followed. Trying to be as quiet as possible, they began to scurry up the aisle to the large domed doors at the back of the theater.

"Weft!" The director's voice boomed over them. "Where do you think you're going?"

Lyric stopped in her tracks. "I . . . Excuse me, Director?"

"You've missed a day and a half of practice. If you want to be an understudy for Claudia"—he nodded in the direction of one of the younger dancers, who didn't throw ribbons but scattered silk flowers across the stage—"you had better get your Flyers on and get up here."

Lyric gasped. For the first time, she was truly speechless. She didn't move.

The director frowned. "Unless, of course, you don't *want* to travel to Hilltop Palace?"

"Congratulations!" Claire said, trying to conceal the eagerness in her voice. She was happy for Lyric, really, but also it would be *much* easier to observe the protective measures around the Love Knot Tine if she didn't have to worry about what she'd say to Lyric. She liked the younger girl and didn't want to get her in any trouble. "Go on up there!"

"But," Lyric whispered back, "the tine! Your memory!"

Claire gave her a gentle push. "I'll be fine."

Lyric didn't need to be told twice. She bounded up to the stage and disappeared into the wings. As the musicians again struck the first note, Claire turned her back on the stage and began to walk up the dark aisle.

It was time to steal a crown.

CHAPTER
9

Tapestries covered the lobby's walls, and the carpet was so thick, Claire felt as if she were wading through wet sand. But though the lobby was beautiful, full of intricate and lush details, her eyes were drawn to a single spot. Two grand staircases curved down to the first floor, and in the center, like a charm on a necklace, was the Spinners' Love Knot Tine.

At least . . . Claire thought it must be the Love Knot Tine. It was hard to tell.

Thick walls of glass surrounded all sides of it, distorting and warping its shape so that all she could make out from it was something vaguely crescent-shaped. It didn't help, either, that the glass had been carefully cut and polished so that it sparkled with the intensity of the sun.

Claire hastily drew her eyes away and checked to make sure

she was truly alone. It seemed that she was and that Lyric's theory was correct: the Wraith Watch was on high alert on the edges of the city instead of inside. Still, she was cautious stepping forward. In a world where everyone could manipulate magic in the material, anything could sound an alarm. Anything could be a defense. She scanned the ceiling. There were no obvious nets waiting to drop down from above, and the carpet under her feet seemed disinclined to wrap her up like a burrito.

That left only the red velvet rope, cordoning off a six-foot circle around the pedestal.

That definitely looked dangerous. Using the toe of her other foot, Claire slipped off a boot and tossed it inside.

Nothing happened. She'd have to risk it. Holding up the velvet rope, she quickly ducked underneath.

Again, nothing happened. Still, two minutes passed before Claire felt comfortable enough to slip her boot back on and step forward.

Now she was close enough to see that the vault wasn't just a typical glass box balanced on a podium like how so many artifacts were displayed in museums at home. The neck of the podium had been cleverly crafted to look like the trunk of a tree, its branches arching up and over to form the protective box around the tine.

It took Claire one more step to realize that the podium didn't just look like a tree—it *was* a tree. Glass roots sank into the carpet, disappearing into the foundations of the

Historium. And the glass wasn't glass at all but thick, clear diamond: a Diamond Tree Vault.

Her breath caught. This diamond tree was jumbled magic, clearly of both Gemmer and Tiller craft. Which meant at least some members of the Tiller guild had joined the queen's Royalists. She knew of at least one Tiller who'd already joined the queen's army: Francis. He was Nett's grandfather and Sena's guardian after she'd been exiled from the Forger guild. And he'd been Claire's friend. Or so she'd thought. In truth, he'd been a Royalist, and he'd figured out who Claire and Sophie truly were—and had betrayed them both.

The betrayal still stung. Even now, when she thought about it, Claire had a hard time breathing. In fact, she felt weirdly out of breath, and her vision blurred.

She caught a glimpse of the crown piece, though it was difficult to make out through the beveled glass casing. It wasn't gold, like Claire had expected, or even silver. It was black. But the black of a raven's wing, or eyes, or a starlit sky. The strange metal had been twisted into a point, with a hollow spot at its base meant for a stone, or perhaps a moontear.

As if the sight of it had strangled her, she suddenly sank to her knees, gasping for breath. The sweater she'd borrowed from Lyric's older sister had been too large for her just minutes ago, but now it was so small, Claire could see her wrists. But though the sweater was shrinking, it wasn't tearing. It was clinging to Claire, squeezing her. Black dots swarmed at the edge of her vision, and she felt like she was drowning all over again.

"Elaina—Elaina!" Lyric's voice reached her as if from afar.

Hands gripped under her armpits, and her legs burned slightly as she was dragged across the carpet. And then, suddenly, she could breathe! The sweater around her loosened, and the sleeves dropped back to where they should be. She lay on her back, letting her rib cage expand and contract, while a circle of faces looked curiously down at her, including one very angry face with wild white-blond hair.

"How *dare* you disturb rehearsal!" the director exclaimed. "You know better than to go inside a Smother-Ring! You are hereby *banned* from the coronation celebration! No, banned from the entire Historium!"

"Director," Lyric said timidly, "she actually doesn't know—"

The director whirled on her. "What do you mean?"

But before Lyric could reply, another one of the dancers—a boy with a long chin and even longer nose—gasped. "Oh, is that the girl whose thoughts have been Gathered? The one found washed up on the beach?"

"I heard it was the harbor, actually," said another dancer, her many braids and twists pulled into a high ponytail on the top of her head. It bobbed and swayed like a question mark.

"Lyric was there!" the boy said. "Lyric's the one who found her—my little brother said he heard her mother yelling at her this morning."

Claire was surprised, but she knew she shouldn't be. In a city of professional storytellers, *of course* news of the girl with lost memories would spread quickly. Which meant that soon, Mira Fray and the queen would learn of it, too.

"Enough!" the director snapped. "You." He pointed at

Lyric. "Explain." Lyric stepped forward and quickly rattled off The Story, and Claire tried her hardest to look as though she had lived through it. When Lyric was done, the director's eyebrows had lowered so much that Claire thought they might slip off his nose. "Historian Fray warned of two dangerous girls who have been flouting the Guild Treaty and causing havoc for our queen. How can you be sure this is not one of them?"

Claire's heart caught in her throat. He had already guessed her identity!

"She's a Royalist, sir," Lyric jumped in, and Claire's heart inched back down. "She had her cloak on when I found her. And it's not just any cloak—it was woven by Historian Fray herself and marked with the queen's own seal. I checked the tag."

Claire tried to keep her face blank. She hadn't realized that! With so many Royalists now in Arden, she hadn't thought to check to see *whose* cloak she might have been wearing. If it was one woven by Fray herself, then that meant it probably belonged to one of the Original Royalists on official queen's business. Which meant someone before her had gone to the Spyden with questions—someone who worked directly for the queen.

She didn't know what it meant, but the thought unsettled her.

"Hmm," the Director said, weighing Lyric's words. He looked around at the circle, which had grown to include not only dancers but other stage assistants. "Journeyman Weft," the director said to someone Claire couldn't quite see. "Is what your sister says true?"

A young woman—maybe sixteen—stepped forward, her long black hair neatly looped into thin braids, then twisted into a knot on the top of her head. She wore a floating canary-yellow dress, and in her hand she held a notebook with one page marked by a feathered quill sticking out of it.

Suddenly, Claire realized why Lyric's smile had seemed familiar and where she'd seen Mistress Weft's dark eyes before. And she realized that Lyric wasn't saying *Kay* but *K*. A single initial. A nickname for a sister named—

"Kleo," Lyric said, looking relieved.

She was indeed the same Spinner who'd helped Nett and Sena and her escape the Fyrton inspectors when Claire first journeyed up the river. Kleo, who'd spent afternoons with Thorn and Sophie in Fray's floating library, sharing stories about unicorns, their histories and their magic.

Kleo, who knew *exactly* who Claire was.

"Yes, sir," Kleo confirmed to the director, "that's what our mother told me as well on the Hearing Thread." Her brown eyes took Claire in, and there was not a spark of recognition within them. Could it be possible that Kleo didn't recognize her?

"If that's the case, perhaps she should be at the infirmary instead," the director said. "Especially if she can't remember the warnings for a Smother-Ring."

"No!" Claire blurted out. If she were sent to a hospital, there would be no way she could steal the tine by Starfell. "I mean," she backtracked quickly, "I feel better when I'm here, in the Historium, sir. I have a feeling my—my parents—" She tripped over the words. "They will come searching for me here."

"And why, exactly, did you go close to the podium?"

For once, the words were right there on the tip of her tongue. "To see the Love Knot Tine," she said. "Because of the queen's seal in my cloak, I thought that maybe seeing it with my own eyes would help jog the memory of when I received my cloak."

"And did it work?"

"Uh, no, not exactly," Claire said. "I can't really see it that well through the glass. But maybe if it was opened?" she suggested hopefully. She held her breath as the director gave her a piercing look.

"I don't think that's wise, even if it were possible," he said at last. "If you had come a month ago, you would have seen the crown clearly, no vault grown around it. But as it is, the vault is newly set, and can only be opened by the queen's hand."

The director sighed and rubbed his temples. "This is much too distracting," he said. "I think it would be best to send for Grandmaster Bobbin and make this his problem—"

"I'll look after her."

Claire turned her head and saw, to her surprise, that Kleo had spoken up. "I need an extra pair of hands if the sets are to be ready in time for the coronation."

There was one more beat of silence, and then the director let out his breath. "Very well, then. Elaina can assist until her parents come to claim her, but if you disturb my rehearsal again," he warned, "you will face much more than a Smother-Ring—I guarantee that."

Claire could manage only a shallow nod as the director shepherded his flock of dancers and Lyric back to the stage, leaving Claire alone with Kleo.

Suddenly, it felt like she was in the Smother-Ring all over again. Was Kleo going to summon Fray? Would she tell on her? But it seemed the older girl truly didn't recognize her, because she gave Claire a friendly smile. "Follow me, Elaina. I need some help polishing the shoes for act three."

Claire's heartbeat began to return to its normal rate. Maybe everything wasn't lost after all. Maybe she would be able to figure out a way to break the tine free. She thought about what the director had said: only Queen Estelle's hand could open the lock. If she were a Gemmer master or even a Gemmer journeyman, maybe she would have been able to sculpt a hand that looked like Queen Estelle's or find a statue of her and animate it just enough to open the glass box. But Claire had only been able to chisel a rather misshapen boat from pumice rock back at the Citadel.

With magical ideas from her days of Gemmer school still swirling through her head, she allowed Kleo to whisk her into a massive prop closet somewhere behind the main stage. Pairs of magical dance shoes roosted on shelves like plump pigeons. *Sophie would love all these*, Claire thought, gazing up at them in awe. *Mom too.*

But as soon as the door clicked closed, Kleo whirled around and pulled on a string. A light flickered on, and Claire's stomach dropped at the look of fury in Kleo's eyes. "What are you doing here, Claire?"

CHAPTER
10

So. Kleo *did* remember her.

Slug soot.

"I'm—I'm here because . . . because—" Because her sister was not just her sister anymore. Because a queen was looking to kill her, and Sophie would never, ever be safe in this world or any other world, so long as Estelle still had power. Because Arden was dying. But she couldn't say any of that. "Because—"

"You're going to tell on me, is that it?" Kleo asked, her skirts rustling as she paced a tiny line in the closet.

"What?" Claire shook her head. "No—why would I do that? I thought *you* were going to tell on *me*!"

"Because if Mira—or Queen Estelle!—found out I *helped* you and let you escape, I would be . . . My family, it just can't . . ." The Spinner trailed off, then sank onto the floor of the closet with a loud groan, settling in between a pair of red cowboy boots that looked startlingly out of place and some leather sandals that looked not unlike Dad's favorite pair. "I figured it all out, you know," Kleo mumbled into her hands. "When Historian Fray came and told us of the queen's return, we all began to study what the Royalists have known for years. 'A great unicorn treasure—*a place where fire meets water*.'"

When Kleo looked back up, Claire realized it wasn't fury in her eyes at all but fear.

Kleo took a ragged breath and went on. "Mira Fray says she is looking for two girls—two sisters—who tried to steal the moontears away from her, but . . . I *knew* Sophie. I *saw* her wearing the necklace long before the queen's return. She didn't steal it from anyone. Why would Fray lie? What else is she hiding?"

Claire opened her mouth, but Kleo held up her hand. "Don't tell me. The less I know, the better." She stared fixedly at a pair of tap shoes as though they might have the answer. Finally, she looked up. "This is what's going to happen. You'll stay with me today so I can keep an eye on you and make sure no one asks you too many questions."

"You're not going to turn me in?" Claire asked, hope rising within her.

"I'm not," Kleo said, though her eyes were worried. "I can't risk getting my family in trouble. I'll help you as long as you make sure Lyric doesn't find out who you really are and you leave first thing in the morning. Do we have a deal?"

The morning. That left only a few short hours in which to figure out how to steal—gather, really—the Love Knot Tine. It wasn't enough time!

"Actually," Claire said slowly, "I need to stay here just a little bit longer. I need to . . ." But she stopped talking, as Kleo shook her head.

"No," Kleo said. "You can't. It's not just about me—it's also about *you*. It's too dangerous for you to be in Needle Pointe. All these shoes and ribbons and dresses, they look pretty, but they can be downright dangerous. If you're not a Spinner, you could get hurt. Badly." She pointed at the red cowboy boots. "Do you know what those are?"

Claire glanced down. "Boots?"

"They're Seven League Boots. Take a single step with them, and you'll suddenly find yourself seven leagues away from where you started."

Claire stared at them with new interest. "What's so bad about that?"

"Do you know how many buildings and trees are between here and seven leagues? If you're not careful, you could splatter into a wall. There are Method Mules in here that if you slip them on, they can turn you into the previous owner—they're popular for actors getting into character, and sometimes they *never* come off. And it's not just shoes." Kleo waved her arms. "There's an entire closet here named the War-Drobe, filled with dresses that if you put them on, they will set you on fire, and feathered boas that take after the snake they were named for. A trained Spinner can recognize what is a crafted object and what is just a usual set of underwear, but if you're not trained—and not a Spinner—then everything here is dangerous. So—do we have a deal?"

Her mouth dry, Claire nodded.

Kleo sighed and glanced around. "Now. Where to put you?" She tapped her feathered quill nervously against her lips. "How are you with a needle and thread?"

"I can make friendship bracelets?"

"I don't know what those are," Kleo said with a shake of her head that sent her inky-black hair bouncing. "What else can you do?"

Claire could do lots of things. She could make gems glow and clay explode and unicorns come out of rocks, but she didn't think that was going to help her case with Kleo.

"I can draw," Claire offered.

Kleo brightened. "Great! You can work on some traveling backdrops that we'll need once Queen Estelle is in court. Most Spinners prefer to be in the spotlight, not painting back-grounds. So they'll hardly notice you."

Claire didn't mind being behind the scenes. In fact, she preferred it. The only time she had stood alone on a stage was last year, when her fifth-grade teacher had asked her to read out loud the opening remarks at the elementary school gradu-ation ceremony. All week long, Claire had been plagued with nightmares: What if she tripped? What if she messed up? What if everyone laughed at her? The seventh time Claire asked the same question, Sophie had let out an exasperated sigh and said to just imagine everyone in their pajamas.

"How's that supposed to help?" Claire had asked.

Sophie had shrugged lazily from where she'd been lounging across the old floral armchair. "No idea. I don't get stage fright! It's just what I've heard you're supposed to tell people."

And when the moment finally arrived and Claire had to walk to the podium, she'd looked out into the auditorium and seen . . . nothing. The lights had been too bright. So instead of picturing the crowd in their pj's, she just imagined she was talking only to Sophie. That was what got her through it.

Afterward, Sophie had said, "See, it was easy, wasn't it?"

Claire had looked at her sister, wondering what it would be like if being brave came as naturally for her as it did for her sister.

But, looking back on it now, she *had* been brave, hadn't she? She'd done the thing she'd been terrified of.

The memory gave Claire confidence as she followed Kleo through a side door leading them up onto the stage, behind the backdrop curtains, where all the sets were in various phases of construction. Colorful chaos ruled backstage, and Claire and Kleo had to dodge bolts of fabric and assistants dashing around until they reached the far corner of a wing. From here, Claire could be left alone and still watch all that was happening. Near her, a group of younger girls including Lyric giggled as bits of ribbon twisted around their legs like friendly cats and boys made silly faces at one another as they stretched, warming up their muscles.

Onstage, through a series of side curtains, Claire could see the older kids rehearsing, raising their legs high above their heads before dipping down again, always in perfect unison. Though she couldn't see the musicians in the orchestra pit that sat in front of the stage, she could make out the tops of their heads and a conductor's wand waving in rhythm.

Making sure Claire had all she needed, Kleo left, promising to come back soon.

Claire picked up a brush and looked at the paints. There was a jar of cerulean, the same color as the water in Needle Pointe's bay, and another jar brimming with an iridescent white. It reminded her of Mom's mother-of-pearl earrings and . . .

A shot of light across a midnight plain.

A glimmering streak in a dark ponytail.

Sophie—becoming a unicorn.

Claire shook her head, trying to clear her mind of the memory, and set the paintbrush down. She wasn't ready to draw anything permanent yet. She tugged the pencil out of her hair, sat down on the floor with her back against the wall, and sketched a silver line across a scrap of parchment that had been left for her to test out the paints. And as she moved across the wild blankness of the page, confidence swept over her, and she began to feel calmer. This was something she *knew* how to do.

Letting her pencil fly across the page, Claire began to draw without setting out to sketch anything in particular. Her mind was filled with sharp points and jagged edges. Sketching was the best way of smoothing them out to make sense of what was happening. It was how she'd spent most of the nights when Sophie was away in the hospital and their home felt particularly empty.

She drew a zig and then a zag and finally another zig. It could be the top of a mountain range or . . . She added a few lines and began to shade it in: a crown.

Claire felt prickly with frustration. She was *so close* to it. Well, to the first part of it, anyway. The Love Knot Tine was only a few yards away, resting out there in the lobby for anyone to see, and yet it felt as far away as the moon.

She drew another line, thick and heavy—as heavy as the crown must be to wear. Claire could hardly tolerate a headband, the way it pushed on her temples, so she could only imagine how heavy a metal crown must feel.

She added a few more lines to her drawing, her pencil speeding along faster than her thoughts. Usually, magic was in the material, and Claire helped guide it out, but now it almost seemed as though the pencil were dragging *her* forward, and she let the image, whatever it was, spill onto the paper. A story unspooled within her that felt like a forgotten memory:

✳

"I don't want to wear it," the princess complained. "It's heavy, and it makes my head hurt." Plus, it was noisy. Whenever she was around the crown, she could hear the hum of the meteorite it had been forged from.

"My sweet star, you're never going to have to wear it." Her mother, a woman with a sparkling veil pinned to a small tiara nestled in her hair, dropped a kiss on the girl's forehead. "That's your brother's burden to bear."

The girl gazed at the crown, her gray eyes solemn. The crown was wrought of starfire—meteorite—and sparkled in the dim light of the throne room. "I'm glad," the girl said emphatically. It seemed impossible that this heavy thing would one day fit her brother's head. His baby skull still felt squishy in parts. She felt bad for him. After all, how could one ride a unicorn and melt into the morning with something as heavy as the crown weighing one down? As princess and not the heir, she had to wear only a thin circlet of silver while riding about with Papa.

The woman laughed, the smile lines around her eyes crinkling. "Is someone thinking about a unicorn ride?"

The girl dipped her head shyly, embarrassed but also happy that her mother understood. Queen Elaina always did—that's why much of the kingdom knew her as Elaina the Compassionate.

"Come, Estelle," her mother said, holding out her hand. "Let us check on the garden pond! Shall we see if the swans aren't bullying the poor goslings?"

Princess Estelle slipped her hand into her pocket to pull out the bit of cranberry scone she'd saved from breakfast. Even though it was her favorite pastry, she was worried about the nest of baby geese that had hatched a little too late in the summer.

"Great minds think alike," Queen Elaina said as she reached into her pocket and pulled out a matching scone. Estelle grinned up at her mother just as a horn sounded from the ramparts. How strange. Usually the horn trilled only when her father was spotted on the road, returning to the castle. But Estelle had seen her father just that morning, head bent over the many papers in his study. Which meant that the horn wasn't calling out a welcome; it was warning them of—

"An attack," her mother breathed out. Footsteps sounded down the corridor as her mother grabbed her hand, knocking the scone to the floor. "We must move fast," her mother said as she pulled her to the door. "The Forgers are here."

"My scone!" Estelle protested.

"We won't be visiting the goslings today after all, I'm afraid," her mother said. "You must be brave, my gem." Estelle felt tears prick her eyes, but she stayed silent. Just as they exited the throne room, she ducked her head under her arm. The crown winked at her in the torchlight, the moontears inlaid into each of its four points glimmering like stars set in a dark, black night.

✳

Something bright was shining in Claire's eyes. "Elaina, wake up!"

Claire opened her eyes to see Lyric standing over her, tugging her arm. The Historium seemed to have emptied, and now only a few straggler dancers remained, squeezing in one last practice. Claire hadn't realized she'd fallen asleep, and she must have been out for at least a few hours for everyone to have gone home. The last thing she remembered was the smooth way the image beneath her pencil's tip had blossomed across the page, along with a story . . . or maybe it *was* a dream?

Claire gave her hands a little shake. She'd fallen asleep on them, and they tingled a bit. The sketch was smooshed against her face, and she peeled it off. Even though it was a little smudged, the illustration was still clear. She'd sketched a princess and a queen standing in an unfamiliar throne room. Both their backs were toward the viewer, but a crown was on full display. It was a rough sketch, but she could just make out four little symbols, one on each of the crown's four points, beneath the moontear settings: a hammer, an oak leaf, a love knot, and a gemstone.

Claire studied it. Sometimes scenes came tumbling out of her. And when they did, it always felt a little like magic. As though the pencil had taken control of her fingers. Her eyes shifted to the edge of the page, where she'd drawn a border of geese. She followed their flight down to the corner of the page and paused.

Her fourth-grade art teacher had made a big deal about signing all their pieces with an Artist Signature, which she'd always pronounced with a capital *A* and a capital *S*. Claire usually marked her art with clear block letters: *C. Martinson*. This time, she'd signed her sketch with something that looked more like a scribble, though she could make out a capital letter *E*, complete with curlicues.

She wondered—had she written *E* for her fake name, Elaina, or *E* for Estelle? She shook her head. That made no sense. She'd let herself get too carried away by her imagination.

"Lyric, did you find her? Oh, there you are!" Kleo's voice came from above, and Claire hastily scrunched the sketch into her pocket. She didn't need Kleo or any of the Royalist Spinners to see that she'd drawn a crown. She didn't want them getting suspicious of her intentions.

"I'm s-sorry," Claire sputtered. "I haven't slept in—"

"That's fine," Kleo said, cutting her off. "It's time for you and Lyric to head home."

"Wait," Lyric said with a frown. "Are you not coming back with us? You promised you'd go over the steps with me!"

"I'm sorry, L," Kleo said, and her eyes shifted to Claire for just a moment. Unease trickled through Claire. "I promise I'll help you when I can, but something's come up."

Lyric crossed her arms, and her eyes flashed. "What's come up that's more important than keeping your promise?"

"We just got a message written in the queen's hand," Kleo said, offering her own to pull Claire to her feet. As she stood, Claire felt something rough slip into her palm. A note. Claire's fingers closed around it as Kleo continued. "His Royal Highness has been asked to escort the Diamond Tree Vault and the tine within it to Hilltop Palace."

Now Kleo was looking directly at Claire. "Prince Thorn will be here at dawn."

CHAPTER
11

Supper was a simple affair that night. Sharp cheese with grapes and an apple tart that smelled delicious, though Claire couldn't manage anything more than a few bites. Kleo's note, though now just soft ash in the Wefts' stove, seemed to have burned a hole in Claire's stomach.

At first bells, Claire was to leave the Wefts' townhouse, and by second bells, she should be on the Weaver's Bridge, meeting up with Kleo and the narrowboat she'd arranged to slip Claire far away from Thorn's bright-blue eyes—and the Love Knot Tine . . . unless she could find a way to break it free in just few short hours.

Grown-ups always complained about time, but before now, Claire had thought she had too much of it. Long classes about even longer division would drag on for what seemed like days, and boring summer afternoons weeding the garden felt like an eternity. But now . . . Claire would give anything for those lengthy moments. In Arden, she could feel time slipping past her, rushing her recklessly forward like rivers nearing a waterfall.

The faster it flowed, the closer she was to disaster.

The closer she came to losing Sophie forever.

"Elaina?"

Someone tapped Claire's shoulder, and she looked up to see Mistress Weft gazing down at her, a worry line between her brows. "I was wondering if I could take your plate, dear," she said, and from her tone, Claire had the feeling this wasn't the first time she'd asked.

"I can do it," Claire said quickly, scooting back the wicker chair. She reached for the other empty plates on the table. "Where should I put these?"

"The sink is just fine," Mistress Weft said, gesturing to the dishes already stacked there. "We'll deal with it in the morning." Mistress Weft glanced at the pile of wool that still needed to be spun before her eyes slid to Lyric, who'd excused herself earlier and was again practicing the steps in front of the fireplace.

As she watched, Lyric rose onto her toes, executing a crisp pirouette. She spun faster and faster, looking for all the world like a top, when suddenly—

Thump.

She was sprawled on the wooden floor.

"Lyric, dear, are you all right?" Mistress Weft asked, setting down the spindle she'd just picked up.

Lyric sat there, seemingly surprised. "Of course I'm not! How can I be? I don't know the steps. And Kleo—she promised—argggh!"

Lyric leaped to her feet and ran toward the stairs. Claire knew that in any other, non-Spinner household, they would be hearing the stomp of her feet up the stairs, but the cushy carpet completely muted the sound. It was too bad, really, Claire thought sympathetically. Sometimes, the loud declaration of a stomped foot was helpful in getting rid of anger. The sound meant that she was here, and she was important, and she should be paid attention to. That's what Mom had explained when Sophie had started getting particularly moody and was slamming doors on a near weekly basis.

"Sorry you had to see that," Mistress Weft said. "I'll go and check on her."

But Claire again saw how the woman's eyes sized up the amount of wool still left to be tamed.

"I'll go," Claire said, quickly placing the plates in the sink and wiping her hands on a nearby towel. Sometimes when people were upset, they wanted to be left alone, but from the expression in Lyric's eyes . . . Claire thought that maybe just the opposite was happening.

And if she was really going to run away tonight, she'd at least have to say good-bye to Lyric first.

Claire climbed the stairs and stopped in Kleo's room to

grab something from her Hollow Pack before she tapped on Lyric's bedroom door. "Lyric? Can I come in?"

There was no response, which Claire took as a good sign. She let herself through.

Lyric had flopped onto her bed and was staring wide-eyed up at her canopy, while her braids and loops hung over the mattress's edge, nearly brushing the floor.

"What do you want?" Lyric asked. She didn't sound mad, only glum.

"I just wanted to see how you were." Claire replied with the truth. "And to say, I think you looked really good during practice. I think you have a chance."

Lyric sighed, and the sound wrapped around the room. "I don't know about that. Maybe if Kleo were here to help . . ." She rolled onto her belly and looked at Claire. "She left us earlier than she had to, you know. She had an entire summer she could have spent with Mama and me before she started on her journeyman trials. She has her whole life to be a historian!"

Claire was confused. "But you're also rushing away to something," she pointed out. "You want to go be a part of the queen's court."

"So I can see Kleo!" Lyric said, flopping again into the pillows. "She was Historian Fray's former apprentice. Historian Fray will make sure she's at court. She'll probably be the youngest royal recorder and I'll just be . . . silly little Lyric, stuck at home."

Though Lyric's story was different from Claire's, the

words were familiar to her. There had been so many times—even before the ladder—that Sophie had gone off and left her.

"She's just spreading her wings," Claire said, repeating what Mom had often said to her about Sophie.

Lyric snorted, and Claire remembered how useless those words had first sounded to her. What had *actually* cheered her up was when Mom said that she could invite her friend Catherine over, and they'd spent a fun afternoon together, watching movies that Sophie would have called babyish. There were no screens in Arden, but that didn't mean she and Lyric couldn't do something fun. Claire reached into her pocket and pulled out what she'd stopped to collect from her room: a bit of chalk.

"Hand me your Flyers?" Claire said, and when Lyric looked at her, startled, Claire just smiled and shook her head. "It's a surprise. Trust me."

With the chalk, Claire began to draw lightly on the underside of her dance shoe. A comfortable silence settled over the room, but with Lyric around, the quiet never lasted long.

"I'm sorry," she said unexpectedly from her pile of pillows.

"For what?"

"For your thoughts getting Gathered. If I hadn't been caught, you wouldn't have had to turn around to rescue me."

"True," Claire admitted, and paused her sketch. "But then I wouldn't have known how to ask the Spyden my question."

"Do you remember what you asked?" Lyric said, sitting up. "Are your memories coming back?"

"Uh, no," Claire said, trying not to feel too bad about

deceiving Lyric. Because technically they *weren't* coming back. She'd always had them.

Again she began to draw, and the images flowed, as if they'd always meant to exist . . .

"Oh, wow!" Lyric grabbed the shoes from Claire moments later. "It's beautiful!" She held the soles out so Claire could examine her own handiwork. Two unicorns now pranced on the bottom of Lyric's Flyers. One reared up, his horn piercing a crescent moon Claire had just managed to fit in the corner, while the other unicorn jumped over a curtained stage.

"When my sister had a dance recital, she'd always ask me to draw something lucky on the soles for her before she went out to perform," Claire explained. "And the chalk should stop you from slipping again." It wasn't Gemmer magic, though chalk was made from crushed stone—just something useful she'd learned at Sophie's dance classes as she'd watched the students rub the dust onto their slippers. Okay, maybe she'd done a *little* Gemmering, just to make sure the chalk would stick longer than usual and hold its design, but that was it.

Claire glanced away from her drawings to smile at Lyric, but the girl was already throwing herself at Claire for a hug. "Elaina!" she squealed excitedly. "Your memories, they're coming back! You remember you have a sister!"

Claire smiled. It couldn't hurt to say the total truth for once. "I do." She settled comfortably against the pillows and watched as Lyric tried out her newly chalked shoes. "And I miss her."

Claire knew she would miss Lyric, too, as she watched the

younger girl, inspired, begin to practice her dance moves on her own. But Claire couldn't risk telling her the plan. An uncomfortable thought brushed against her. Was this how Sophie felt all those times she'd chosen to leave Claire in the dark? If it was . . . well, Claire *still* didn't like it, but maybe she understood her older sister just a little bit more.

Claire was about to say good night, instead of good-bye, and head to Kleo's empty room to pack when her eyes settled on a pile of books stacked up next to Lyric's bed: *Royal Compendium*, *Histories of Arden's Queens and Kings*, *Journals of Majesty*. And last but not least, *The Crown and Its Making*.

No wonder Lyric had been able to answer the director's question! She'd been doing her homework, throwing her heart and soul into becoming an expert on the d'Astora family. That was another thing about Lyric that made Claire think about Sophie. Sophie, too, would become invested in a certain topic or era and become an expert on everything about it. So far, Claire had been a part of Experiences involving Greek gods, Shakespeare's plays, and right before she went into the hospital, Jane Goodall and other naturalists.

"Can I see your books?" Claire asked.

Lyric nodded, too out of breath from her deep knee bends to respond.

Flipping *The Crown and Its Making* to its index, Claire scanned the topics for something that could be helpful. She thought "The Breaking of the Crown" might hold something useful, but the pages there, written by a Spinner historian named Alice the Acute, contained only information Claire already knew: that the Spinners had chosen to display their portion of the crown proudly, while the other three guilds were more secretive about what had been done to their tines: if they had been hidden, destroyed, or maybe even lost.

She flipped the pages again—and froze.

It was a simple drawing, done in ink and charcoal. It didn't prance across the page, but Claire had seen it before and not only seen it—but *drawn* it: a queen and princess, their backs toward the viewer, stared upon the Crown of Arden.

"Hey, Lyric?" Claire called, and the girl came over. Claire pointed to the sketch. "What is this?"

"Oh, I love it, don't you?" Lyric said. "This is supposedly a sketch that Queen Estelle drew—well, Princess Estelle, actually. This is just a copy—I think the original might have gotten destroyed in the great flood, about one hundred and fifty years after the war."

"Do you mind if I borrow this?" Claire asked, already shutting the book and clutching it to her chest. Lyric nodded, and Claire hurried to the guest room and closed the door. She went to her cloak pocket and pulled out the sketch she'd done, along with the pink marble she'd found in Woven Root. Carefully, she flipped open the book and placed her sketch next to it. With barely a thought, she polished the pink marble to a glow so that she could see the details more carefully.

Claire's breath caught. Her sketch was exactly the same as the one in the book, right down to the border of geese. But *how*, if Claire had never seen this image before? Nervously, she nibbled on the end of her pencil.

The pencil.

Claire pulled it away from her lips.

Letter stone was rare in Arden, and pencils were treasured. This was the only pencil she'd seen in Arden. Legend was that it had belonged to Charlotte Sagebrush, who'd created Arden's first alphabet. Claire wasn't sure if that was true or not, but she knew for sure who had been its owner before her: Scholar Terra. Otherwise known as Queen Estelle d'Astora.

What if Queen Estelle had had this pencil since she was a little girl? It was a rare enough treasure to be fit for a royal gift.

Her fingers traced the drawing she'd done that afternoon. Rocks held the memory of the earth—isn't that what she'd learned in Arden? They contained imprints of all the creatures that had once swum in the seas and walked on the land. Claire had even witnessed for herself how a stone forest could keep the echoes of a unicorn hunt. If petrified wood could do all that, why couldn't the letter stone in her hand remember what it had been asked to draw before?

Wonder swept through Claire. Her sketch was not *her* sketch at all but an echo of the queen's sketches, done so long ago. The pencil had somehow recognized the crown Claire had been drawing, and its memory of that moment had been released. That dream within Claire, that almost memory, *was* a memory, but not Claire's. It had belonged to Princess Estelle.

Claire's eyes darted to the corner of the page, and excitement began to course through her. She knew how to open the Diamond Tree Vault!

A slight gasp came from over her shoulder. Claire had been so absorbed in her thoughts that she hadn't even been aware of Lyric opening the door to the guest room.

"Elaina," Lyric said, taking a step closer. "What's that?"

Confused, Claire glanced back at the girl. Lyric's eyebrows had risen into twin arcs above very round eyes that were staring at the pink marble that sat forgotten . . . and glowing. Claire slapped her hand over it, but it was too late.

"Elaina," Lyric whispered, "are you a Gemmer?"

CHAPTER
12

"What?" Claire asked a little too quickly. "Why would you say that?" The marble pressing into her hand hurt, but Claire ignored the pain as she tried to roll the stone without Lyric realizing what she was doing. She could feel the marble protest slightly against her skin, but a quiet hum shot through her, extinguishing the light just as Lyric reached her.

"Let me see that," Lyric demanded. Claire let her fingers fall open to reveal nothing but an ordinary marble; the only extraordinary thing about it was its pretty pink color. "Oh," Lyric said. "What happened to the light?"

Claire licked her lips, her mouth suddenly dry. Sophie would never have let herself get caught! And even if she had, she would have had a quick story at the tip of her tongue. But all Claire could manage was to repeat whatever word Lyric said last. "Light?"

"Do you think this is a hint of who your family is?" Lyric asked, excitement threading through her voice. "I wonder if it holds a clue to what happened to you! Do you think you could be a Gemmer and not a Spinner? Elaina, I bet you're someone really important to the queen! You need to meet with her to figure out who you are! Maybe you could even be—"

"Lyric." Claire hurried to cut off whatever story was running through Lyric's extravagant imagination. "It's just a marble, see? It's not glowing." And then she bit her lip but silently added, *Not anymore.*

"But I saw it!" Lyric said. "I know I did." She prodded the marble with her littlest finger, and Claire hastily wrapped her hand around it again.

"It's my good luck marble!" Claire said brightly. "I use it as a paperweight . . ." But her voice trailed off as Lyric's eyes fixed on hers. Claire flinched. They weren't accusing, exactly, more . . . more *wounded.*

"Elaina," Lyric said slowly, "if you forgot your memories, how can you be sure your name *is* Elaina? Or that you are a Spinner?"

Claire flinched again. With all her heart, she wanted to tell Lyric the truth of who she was: Claire Martinson, rising sixth grader, a Gemmer princess, Sophie's little sister.

But.

The ribbons on Lyric's nightgown were Royalist blue. And Claire had promised Kleo to leave *her* little sister out of this. It was better for Lyric not to know. Safer. Yet Claire's lies were becoming tangled, and each new one sat angrily on her chest, as if to say, *You've created us—what do you want to do with us?* She was so tired of them. And she missed having a sister nearby.

And so she decided to tell Lyric the truth.

Kind of.

"I'm not entirely sure," Claire admitted. "But," she hurried to add, "I know that I want magic to return to Arden. That unicorns should run free. And that I am your friend."

Claire watched as Lyric took in this information. She could practically see the strands of a narrative weaving in front of her, and Claire wondered what kind of stories Lyric might write down one day. Kleo wanted to be a historian, to record fact, but Claire suspected that maybe Lyric would be a novelist, spinning stories that contained the kind of truths that could be seen only in glimpses.

Suddenly, Claire felt arms wrap around her waist, and she glanced down to see the mermaid-like braids and twists of Lyric's hair. "Thanks for my shoes," Lyric said softly. And then, so quietly that Claire could barely hear: "Thanks for saving me."

And then she was gone.

It was easy to slip quietly through the hallway of the Wefts' home. The thick carpets muffled even the heaviest of footsteps.

Seeing, however, was another matter.

"Ow!" Claire let out a gasp of pain as she ran into the edge of a table. She clapped her hands over her mouth as tears pricked her eyes. Had anyone heard her? One second passed, then another. There was no creak of an upstairs door or a concerned call from Mistress Weft. Her breath slowly returned to normal.

Picking up the pace, Claire moved forward, keeping her hand outstretched and careful not to rustle the Hollow Pack. Ten feet . . . five feet . . . Her hand grasped the doorknob, and then she was out in the fresh air, always slightly tinged with salt.

Though the hour was late, a few Spinners still strolled the streets, admiring the Starfell ribbons and enjoying cups of warm nectar as they ambled by, arm in arm. And while one or two Spinners kept an eye on the shadowy patches, most of them moved loosely, taking their time to stop and stare up at the moon without fear of a wraith's attack. With the queen's promise of protection, it seemed many of them wanted to explore the night.

None seemed to take notice of a girl quietly making her way toward the Historium. She would steal the tine and make it to the Weaver's Bridge with enough time to meet Kleo and safely escape.

Or she'd fail, and . . .

No, she couldn't think about *that* possibility.

After hours, the theater was as quiet as it was large—an eerie contrast to the afternoon's flurry of noise and color. The smell of smoke hung heavy on the air, and for a moment, Claire imagined Gemglows in the sockets of the stone wall, perfectly lighting up the tapestries of the greatest historians Arden had ever known. She could almost imagine Nett's face there, brown eyes smiling, hair tufts and all, beaming down from the walls. The first Tiller in more than three hundred years to be honored in the Spinner Historium.

She had entered through the back door, which she knew would be open, as earlier she'd left a pebble carefully wedged in its crease so that it wouldn't seal closed. Now she tiptoed past the dressing stalls, letting the pale pink of the marble's light shine over the shoe closet and the practice rooms, before she at last reached the lobby. There the Love Knot Tine stood on its diamond-tree pedestal. The diamond branches hadn't stirred since she'd seen them last. They still grew up and over the tine, weaving themselves into a thick, seamless box. An unbreakable box.

Claire slipped off the Hollow Pack and pulled out a pair of scissors she'd bought from Woven Root's Exhibition's Row. Carefully, she closed the blades around the rope and began to cut. As the blades flashed before her, she recalled what Sena had told her about the history of scissors in Arden—that they were once used to ward off Spinner weavings during the Guild War. Queen Estelle had wreaked havoc while on the throne, but according to Lyric, tensions among the guilds stretched from before even her reign. Claire wondered if it were possible for Arden to ever change.

The rope snapped and her muscles tensed, ready to run if an alarm sounded, but the theater remained quiet. One hurdle down, a hundred to go. She approached the vault.

This time, she breathed normally. Or at least as normally as possible when one is conducting a heist. The diamond vault glittered in her marble's light, each of its thousands of facets cut to blinding perfection. It was like looking at an eclipse.

As quietly as she could, Claire set the pink marble on the floor, and the vault's glitter dimmed. It still sparkled, but this time it was bearable.

Claire pulled out the pencil and studied it. Charlotte Sagebrush's pencil always looked more like a twig than a yellow pencil, but tonight, it looked even more twiglike, with a tiny spot of green that resembled a new leaf. Rubbing her thumb over it, Claire tried to brush the speck off, but it remained. She squinted, and slowly a smile crept across her face. The green spot was, in fact, a tiny sprouting leaf. No matter how many times Claire used it, the pencil would never become a stub. It would always be just the right fit.

"I hope that's a lucky leaf," Claire whispered to it. "Because I could use the help."

The transportation Kleo had arranged for her would leave in just a few minutes. She needed to be far, *far* away by dawn. Far away from the so-called prince. Far away from an empty Diamond Tree Vault.

Taking a deep breath, she placed the pencil's point on the diamond and scrawled the first thing that came to mind: *Open up.*

Nothing happened. The pencil didn't even leave a mark.

Claiiirrre, Sophie's voice groaned. *Relax.*

Shh, Claire mentally shot back, but she felt her shoulders slump. There'd been no hum of magic when she'd moved the pencil. How had she released the echo-sketch before? Claire's foot tapped nervously. She'd been thinking about the crown and how heavy it might be to wear . . . a thought she might have shared with a younger Princess Estelle.

Again, she placed the pencil's tip on the box. But she didn't move her hand. Instead, she tried to settle into the memory the pencil had shared. Of the weight of the petticoats around Estelle's ankles. Of the way the crown had winked at her, humming a quiet song.

Claire's pencil, held by her hand, began to move across the diamond box. This time, instead of sliding off, the tip sank into the diamond, leaving in its wake an orange gleam of molten diamond and an extravagant *O*. Followed by a swooping *P* and then the curlicue *E*, just like the signature at the bottom of her sketch—*Estelle's* signature, as she'd realized in Kleo's old bedroom.

These were not Claire's own round, straight letters but were flowing, full of flourishes and impossible to mimic: Estelle's handwriting. Or, as Kleo had referred to it: *written in the queen's hand.*

With a final swoop, the pencil scrawled an old-fashioned *N*. The four letters, all glowing bright orange, burned for a moment on the vault and then slowly sank into diamond. Tiny chimes suddenly filled the air as the diamond branches began to move, unlocking one by one. And then it opened, unfurling like a tulip to reveal a black seed: the Spinners' Love Knot Tine.

There wasn't time to admire it. Claire grabbed the quarter of the Crown of Arden—and gasped.

She stared at the sharp point, barren of its moontear. Even though the piece of crown looked like all the other sketches she'd seen and matched the crown in the pencil's memory, it didn't *sing*.

The tine felt dull under her fingertips. And . . . not heavy, like Estelle had described.

It felt . . . *wrong*.

She stared at the point as the horrible truth sank in:

This Spinners' Love Knot Tine . . . it was a fake.

Disappointment slammed into Claire, and she swayed. What now? She'd lost so much time here—and for what? Who had the *real* Love Knot Tine?

"Halt! Who goes there?"

Slug soot and rust and *patches*! She wasn't alone in the Historium!

Claire whipped her hand away from the vault and turned away. In the dim light of the lobby, she could make out three figures coming toward her, one of them dressed in Wraith Watch white and the other two in Royalist-blue cloaks.

"It's m-me, me?" she stammered, taking a step back from the podium. "Elaina? I'm a friend of the Weft family? I accidentally left something here earlier today?" She tried to make her sentences sound commanding, but they all sounded like questions.

"Your name isn't Elaina," a new voice said.

Claire's heart stopped. A tall boy with bright-blue eyes, sandy hair, and overlarge ears stepped into the light of her marble.

Thorn Barley had arrived.

She was out of options, out of lies, and out of time.

Claire turned—and ran.

She sprinted into the auditorium, flung herself onto the stage, and disappeared into the wings. Pounding down the twisting hallways behind the Historium's stage, Claire ran faster than she ever imagined she could. The footsteps were coming closer! But she was running out of breath.

She reached for a nearby door, and flung it open. She had only a moment to see that it was the same closet Kleo had pulled her into before the door swung shut, locking her in total darkness. Scrambling on her hands and knees, Claire made her way toward the corner, trying to be as quiet as possible. But even with care, a few shoes thumped to the ground. At last, her fingertips found what they had been looking for. As quickly as she could, Claire tugged on the red cowboy boots that Kleo had called "Seven League Boots." The boots that could get her seven leagues from here in a single step . . . or splatter her completely.

It would be her last resort.

As soon as her heel sank into the last one, she heard footsteps and muffled voices outside the door.

"Which way, Your Highness?"

"Take the left corridor," Thorn said, his voice commanding. "Oscar, you go right."

"Are you sure?" one of the guards asked. "She might have gone into a closet."

"No," Thorn said. "I definitely saw her pass this section."

Claire held her breath as the footsteps passed by. It was too soon for relief, but she hoped that maybe, just possibly, she was going to get out of this. She stood up but stayed crouched as she hooked a finger in the back of a boot, ready to take them off. There was still enough time. If she ran, she could make it to the narrowboat Kleo had arranged for her. There, she could figure out her next steps—and try to figure out what had happened to the *real* Love Knot Tine.

The closet door cracked open, and light fell on her. Claire looked up from the boots to see Thorn's eyes widen. "It *is* you," he gasped. "How—?"

But Claire didn't hear the rest of his sentence.

She'd already taken a step.

CHAPTER
13

Once, not so very long ago, shortly after the Martinson family arrived at Windemere Manor, Dad had pulled out the cleaning sprays and Mom had tossed the girls a few rags. Before all Aunt Diana's treasures and artifacts could be organized and packed up for the estate sale at the end of summer, the mansion itself needed a good scrub.

Carpets were rolled up and suds splashed out of buckets as the family tackled the grime. But it wasn't too long before sponges and rags lay abandoned on the windowsills while Sophie and Claire, socks on their feet, took turns running and skidding down the long corridor.

"I'm practicing for the Olympics!" Sophie had called as she'd swooshed past their disapproving parents.

"We're drying the floors!" Claire had added in the split second before she'd crashed into an old pirate's chest.

That's what the Seven League Boots felt like, as if that split second of pitching forward had been extended into an eternity.

One second, Claire was in the shoe closet, and in the next, the world was yanked out from beneath her, sending her toppling forward, past Thorn and through the door—and straight toward the stone wall of the Historium.

Claire threw out a hand. Maybe if she hit the blocks just right, the stone would—she wasn't sure—turn soft? Become sand? Or, more likely, she thought to herself, her finger bones would be the first to shatter, the sound of their snapping a prelude to the crunching of her ribs, and spine, and skull.

She didn't want the last image she saw to be of the Spinners' Historium, so Claire squeezed her eyes shut and let her memory flash backward to Sophie, leaning over to help her up from the floor while Mom and Dad flicked soapy water at them, sending bits of white foam high into the air.

"Not fair!" Sophie had shrieked as she raced outside and onto the manor's sprawling yard. "You're taller than us!"

"And you're younger! You should be able to run faster!" Mom had said before overturning a bucket of clean water over both their heads.

The memory continued—but *how*? Claire should have hit the wall already! She should be in smithereens! Slowly she opened her eyes. Her mouth dropped open as she saw that not only had she somehow maneuvered around the wall, but that she was now speeding through the Historium's front doors, mercifully left open by Thorn and the guards. But though she was racing through Needle Pointe's narrow and twisty streets, Claire didn't so much as bump an elbow or scrape a knee, and townhouses and bridges were seemingly whisked away a split second before she would have crash-landed into them.

It was the weirdest sensation. Even though Claire *knew* she was moving—even though wind whipped against her, blowing her braids back and pulling her cloak—she felt as though she were staying absolutely still. As though she were a needle in a sewing machine, staying in one place but still crossing yards of fabric as hands twisted and tugged the material beneath. And like the needle, Claire bobbled and lurched, feeling at every moment that she would somehow fall flat on her face. But she never did. Instead, the boots whisked her out of Needle Pointe and into the wilds of Arden.

Trees and narrowboats and meadows swept by her toes so fast that they looked like stretched shadows. As Claire skidded across the landscape, her arms windmilling at her sides, a jolt of laughter leaped from her, surprising herself and a herd of sleeping cattle, which thundered into a stampede at the sound. But she wasn't in any danger. They were already gone, yanked away before hooves could trample her. An orange-streaked shadow swept by, probably a lantern-lit village. Giddily, Claire wondered if anyone looking out their windows could see her, and if they did, what they thought she might be: a fleeing deer, a touchable breeze, the friendly passing of a ghost.

A whisper from a unicorn.

Slowly the streaks around her shortened and started to take

solid shape again. The world was slowing down, and at last, the earth itself seemed to rise up just a bit to reach the sole of her cowboy boot.

In a single step, she had traveled seven leagues. Which, Claire supposed, was something more than a mile, but she wasn't really sure. Breathlessly, she looked around.

There was no sign of Needle Pointe, or its ships, or even its towering cliffs. Now, the tallest thing she could see was a row of squat fruit trees. She'd exchanged a bustling port city for an orchard, and instead of salt, there was only the sweet fragrance of crushed apples.

Dizzy from the rush and slightly discombobulated, Claire brushed her finger against the pencil still woven fast in her hair and felt the soft bump of the leaf. It must have been a lucky sprout. Only sheer luck could have stopped her from splattering into anything. And only sheer luck could have set her down in a corner of an isolated orchard and not in the center of a busy village square, or worse—smack-dab in the middle of a Royalist meeting. But how long would the luck hold? Her next step could send her to the bottom of a lake. She needed to think. She needed to plan. She needed to know what had happened to the Love Knot Tine . . . Did Estelle already have it?

Being sure to keep her boots' soles firmly planted in place, Claire let herself topple back into the grass . . . except the grass didn't *feel* like grass. Grass was soft and ticklish, but what she'd sat on was something both hard and squishy.

Something that yelped, "Ow!"

Hands pushed at Claire, and she rolled off into a harvesting cart's dirt path. Scooting on her backside and hands, Claire scrambled from the soft mound as it slowly pulled itself into a seated position. Suddenly, she realized it wasn't just the wind that had been pulling on her cloak earlier: Thorn Barley had followed her.

Claire leaped to her feet, boots still on.

"Wait!" Thorn said, struggling to stand up, his long blue coat getting in the way. "Don't move! You'll hurt yourself without me guiding the Seven League Boots!"

So. It hadn't been a lucky leaf that had saved her. It had been one lying, traitorous, fake prince. Anger simmered in her chest. Thorn had claimed a lot of things before. He'd claimed he would show them a shortcut through a mountain. He'd claimed that Mira Fray wanted to help. He'd claimed he was Claire and Sophie's friend.

But he'd tried to lock them up anyway.

"Sorry if I don't believe you," Claire said and lifted her foot.

"Please," Thorn cried. "I need to talk to you! It's about the queen—and the unicorn!"

Claire froze, foot still in the air. She couldn't move forward or backward. She was stuck yet unbalanced, like a dandelion seed teetering on the edge of the stalk. She'd needed to find out what had happened to the real Love Knot Tine and collect the three other tines, all before Starfell—but.

What did Thorn know about the unicorn?

What did he know about *Sophie*?

Claire swayed, and Thorn moved toward her.

"Stay back," Claire ordered. "If you get any closer, I *will* put my foot down. What about unicorns?"

Thorn nodded quickly. "I will, only, just . . . please sit down. I'm not kidding about the boots."

Claire would rather wobble on one leg than trust Thorn, but she couldn't risk accidentally putting her foot down before she found out what he knew. And so, for the second time that night, Claire let herself tumble back onto the ground. Her hand squished down into a rotten apple, but she didn't care.

"Tell me," she demanded, crossing her legs but leaving her red cowboy boots on.

For a moment, Thorn stood silent, looking just as he always did: blue eyes bright beneath sandy hair, with ears that stuck out just a little too much, though he did appear taller than when she'd last seen him a few weeks ago. A growth spurt might have accounted for the new hollows in his cheeks, or maybe that was due to the thin circlet of gold that flashed in his hair.

"When we were at the Drowning Fortress," Thorn began slowly, "Sophie said something about the queen, something I didn't believe." He stumbled over the words, and his eyes remained fixed on the distance somewhere over Claire's shoulders. "Do you remember?"

Claire frowned. "You said you had something to tell me, Thorn. Not the other way around." She was surprised at how cold her voice sounded, but if she let herself unfreeze even a little, her own question would escape, the one she wanted to scream to the entire orchard: *Does Queen Estelle already have Sophie?*

"Right, sorry." Thorn ducked his head, and his hair fell forward to cast a shadow across his cheek. "I overheard something. Something the queen didn't want me to hear, but she has this—this *plan* to save Arden. And it's . . . it's *horrific*," he finished with a hush.

The only useful unicorn is a dead unicorn. Claire shivered as Estelle's words seemed to creep across her skin. The last time she'd seen the queen, Claire had been trapped with her friends in an underground treasury while the queen bedecked herself in unicorn artifacts. Some of the objects had been made of mane and tail, but the others . . . the others had been hewn of horn and hoof, sinew and leather. Things that could be harvested only from a unicorn that was . . .

An image of Sophie, soaking wet and laughing as she ran after their mother on the front lawn of Windemere Manor, flashed across her mind. Claire couldn't bring herself to finish her thought.

"Thorn," Claire said, taking a deep breath. "What do you know?"

Thorn looked up at the sickle moon. It was even thinner tonight and would disappear entirely in just a few evenings. Its points, though, were sharp, and when Thorn looked back at her, it seemed as though the moon had sliced his soul in two. "Queen Estelle says that to get rid of the wraiths—she's ordered me to . . ." He gulped. "She needs a unicorn's heart."

Claire's own heart beat once. Twice, then stopped entirely.

"And does she have it?" she asked, her voice sounding very far away. "The heart? The unicorn? Sophie?"

"No," Thorn said, shaking his head quickly. "She's still looking for a unicorn, but—" He looked at her quizzically. "Why do you think she has Sophie? Is Sophie missing again?"

"Sophie's fine," Claire said over the pulsing in her ears. Her heartbeat had returned with a rush.

Queen Estelle hadn't told him who Sophie was. *What* Sophie was. That was good. The fewer people who knew, the better.

Still, as she looked at Thorn, a bit of apple mush dripping down his linen shirt, she was confused. "Why are you telling me the queen's plans now?" she asked. "When we told you the queen was not what the legends said, you didn't believe us!"

"That's just it." His fingernails clinked against the circlet as he ran a frustrated hand through his hair. "I *didn't* believe you, so why would other Royalists believe what I'm saying? You are one of the only people who might believe me—and help me."

"Help?" Claire asked. "Help you do what?"

Thorn lifted his chin. "Stop the queen."

Old Claire would have believed him. There, in the moonlight of an apple orchard, in his long blue coat, tall boots, whip coiled at his hip and a circlet of gold around his brow, he looked like a prince from a fairy tale. One who knew exactly how to storm the castle and defeat the dragon, or in this case, the queen. But Claire wasn't that girl anymore. And even though she wished she could trust his words—words that would make everything so much easier—she couldn't.

At least not yet.

"What about your magic, Thorn?" Claire asked as she slowly uncrossed her legs. If he was really just stalling, trying to give his fellow Royalists time to locate them, she'd be ready. If he uncoiled the rope at his hip, she'd be ready. "Aren't you afraid if you defeat the queen," she prodded, "you'll lose your magic?"

A shadow flitted across his face, and she could see his lips turn down ever so slightly. "Yes," he admitted. "And so will everyone who got their magic after the queen woke." His breath caught. "My grand always dreamed of the day Queen Estelle would return, but she wouldn't have wanted it this way. Not if it costs us our unicorns." His voice strengthened. "I would rather have no magic than live in a world without the chance of it."

A cold wind blew by, rattling the autumn leaves, lifeless and brown, around her feet. Claire took a breath as she considered his words. Thorn had lied, yes, but he'd also helped Sophie, Sena, and Nett escape from the Drowning Fortress. And he'd directed the other Royalists in the Historium away from her. And because of him, she hadn't become a Claire-shaped smear across one of Needle Pointe's townhouses.

Claire slipped a hand into her cloak's pocket and felt the curve of her pink marble. "Thorn, do you know what happened to Unicorn Rock?" she asked.

He shook his head. "It was already destroyed by the time I got there."

"And did you ever wonder if maybe Sophie and I beat you to the Sorrowful Plains?"

Though it was dark, she could practically feel the heat coming from his cheeks at the mention of his lie. He'd told them they could take a shortcut through Mount Rouge, when in truth, he'd hoped the twisting miners' tunnels and cave-ins would slow them down. "I just—I never really thought—"

As he sputtered into the night, Claire pulled out her marble. With a quick brush against her sleeve, she set it aglow. Light pulsed in her palm, looking as though she'd fished a tiny pink star from the ocean of sky.

Thorn's eyes bugged out. "*Claire!* You're a Gemmer?"

"Did you know a wyvern lives in Mount Rouge?" Claire answered his question with a question. "I asked her for help, and she guided us out."

"Guided you out?" Thorn repeated incredulously.

"Well," Claire said, thinking a moment more, "we actually rode her out."

"You—you rode a wyvern." He shook his head. But though the tone of his voice was disbelieving, the expression in his eyes as he stared at the glowing marble was one of a hungering hope.

"I found my magic before you even got to the Sorrowful Plains. Before you woke Estelle," Claire said and wrapped her fingers around the marble. Light streamed out from around her knuckles, sending rays of pink light to dance across Thorn's tunic. "You've *always* had magic, Thorn. Estelle can't take it away from you."

Claire wasn't a natural storyteller like Sophie or a trained one like Kleo or even an enthusiastic one like Lyric, but she'd gone over the events of that night so many times that the words came easily: the hours in the Petrified Forest, the truth behind the hunter, and Prince Martin's great gamble to flee with the Great Unicorn Treasure until Arden was safe for unicorns again.

As she spoke, Thorn began to look like he had more in common with an empty seashell than a fourteen-year-old boy. And when she was done, he, too, was sitting on the grass, his head bent to his knees.

He didn't say anything for a long time, but finally, he spoke. "Ever since I was a sprout, I've been a burden. First to my grand, then to the rest of Greenwood. I was a lackie who was only good for shoveling straw for the horses. But then everything changed for me. I was Historian Fray's assistant. I'm the one who woke Queen Estelle. Now I'm a *prince*!" His breath hitched. In the moonlight, he looked vulnerable. Fragile.

"All I wanted," Thorn whispered, and Claire couldn't be sure if he was speaking to her or not, "was to prove to everyone that I could be a hero—even if I didn't have magic. That they had misjudged me. That I . . . that I *matter*."

In the last word, there was enough sorrow that Claire could feel its weight. Like the moon, it tugged on her own currents of emotion, stretching and pulling them into a different shape.

She recognized the loneliness in Thorn's voice. It had clung to her both in Windemere's halls and in Stonehaven's corridors. Claire looked at the pink marble in her palm. She had changed so much since she'd climbed up that chimney . . . Why couldn't Thorn change, too?

Pulling her feet in closer, Claire first removed one boot and then the other. Then she took off the Hollow Pack and reached into its limitless belly. Wiggling her hand around, she felt what she thought was a squishy package of oatmeal mix and then the smooth, thin metal of the ReflecTent before her fingers finally brushed against something sticky. She grasped it tightly in her palm, a tiny grin playing on her face.

"Hey, Thorn," she called softly over to where he still had his head buried in his knees. "What do you know about Spydens?"

CHAPTER
14

The next morning, Claire woke to a crinkling tap on the outside of the ReflecTent.

"Hey, are you awake?" Thorn called softly. Blearily, she opened her eyes to see a Thorn-shaped shadow outlined on her tent by the newly risen sun. The shadow raised a hand and tapped again. "Claire?"

"I'm awake," Claire mumbled and, stifling a yawn, she pulled herself up. She had tried to stay awake to help Thorn, really she had, but after two nights of almost no sleep, the world had gone fuzzy around the edges. Thorn had been the one to pull the ReflecTent out of the pack and tell her to rest. Claire had been too groggy to argue.

Claire yawned again. "Everything all right?"

"It's done," Thorn said simply.

Any trace of sleepiness immediately vanished. As quickly as she could, Claire crawled out of her sleeping bag and out from the tent. There was a chill to the air, and frost laced the ground. Claire reached back to grab the Royalist cloak and wrapped it around her shoulders before hurrying to Thorn's side under an apple tree. In his hands, he held what looked like two lumpy, loosely knitted ski hats.

"It's not my best knitting," Thorn said apologetically as he handed one to Claire. "I'm calling it a Make-a-Face." From far away, the hat had looked navy, but up close, she could see it was a hodgepodge of color: pinks blending into yellows, which quickly swirled into a shocking green. But threaded throughout all the colors, there was a shimmering iridescence, like sunlight on spider silk.

Or, more accurately, Spyden silk.

"Will they work?" Claire asked, sticking a pinkie through a dropped stitch.

Thorn looked worried, but he nodded. "As long as we keep the anchor objects in our pockets, we should look just like the Malchains."

Nerves settled heavily on Claire's chest. That was the plan—*her* plan.

The Love Knot Tine was missing, which meant one of two things: either it had been smuggled out of Needle Pointe and was far away from Estelle . . . or Estelle already had it in her grasp.

Thorn, unfortunately, hadn't known.

"Sorry," Thorn had said after she'd explained everything last night, "even though I'm her heir, Her Majesty treats me like a little preamble. But just so you know, Queen Estelle already has the Stone Tine with her, I've seen her wearing it, and both the Spinners and Tillers have promised to present their tines on Starfell."

"The Tillers, too?!"

Thorn nodded. "We got their message right before I left for Needle Pointe. The Forger Guild hasn't decided yet, though!" he'd added hastily as dismay twisted Claire's face. "If you tell the Forgers everything you just told me, I bet they would give the Hammer Tine to Nadia and help crown your aunt."

But Claire doubted the grandmasters would believe her. As Thorn had just pointed out, even in Arden with all its enchantment, grown-ups were still grown-ups. They would never take a kid like Claire seriously . . . but Anvil and Aquila Malchain, famed treasure hunters, were another matter.

It was the Spyden silk that had given Claire the idea.

If a Spyden could weave itself disguises from silk, maybe a Spinner like Thorn could, too. Thorn hadn't been so sure (after all, he wasn't part spider), but he thought that if they each held an object that belonged to the person they were trying to illusion themselves into, maybe it would work.

Luckily for Claire, many of the contents in her pack—like the RefleçTent, her map, and a few clothes—once belonged to the Malchains. And the famous cousins didn't need their belongings at the moment.

When Claire and Sophie had escaped from Stonehaven, they had tracked Anvil and Aquila to a dusty cottage. But Queen Estelle had found them first. She'd frozen their blood into rubies and left the cousins to stand in the cottage forever. But after Nadia rescued Claire and Sophie from the Drowning Fortress, they'd finally trusted the mayor enough to tell her about the Malchains' awful fate. Nadia had immediately sent Woven Root scouts to collect them, and now they were standing safely in their own tent, with a whole cohort of alchemists attempting to turn their blood back into liquid once more.

Now, Claire reached into her pack and handed Anvil's Kompass to Thorn before slipping Aquila's compact mirror of polished silver into her trouser pocket. She looked at Thorn expectantly. "On the count of three?" she asked.

"I'll go first," Thorn interjected. "I don't think anything should go wrong, but in case I messed something up, better for a Spinner to handle it." And before Claire could protest, Thorn slipped the hat over his head.

Nothing happened. Five full minutes passed before Thorn finally pulled it off with a frustrated sigh. "I don't get it," he said. "It *feels* like the threads want to work, but it's like they're, I don't know, too tired to stand up. As though . . ." He trailed off, blue eyes somber.

"As though what?" Claire prompted.

"As though the magic in Arden really *is* dying."

But magic wasn't fragile in all parts of Arden. Claire had

seen powerful magic before. Big magic. *Wondrous* magic. Woven trees that could hide an entire village. Sewn packs that could contain as much potential as a seed and be just as light. The shining flanks of copper chimera as they galloped, pranced, and snorted in the sun. In Woven Root, one could still find the powerful magic that most believed was lost to the past.

"I have an idea," Claire said, and hurried to the Rhona, which curved calmly through the orchard. Kneeling on the bank, she reached into the water. It was icy cold, numbing her fingers, but she scooped up a bit of river sand. Remembering how she'd once shaped it into a dolphin, she began to rub the sand into the hats Thorn had knitted, letting the wet grains bury themselves in the yarn.

"What are you doing?" Thorn asked, crouching down next to her.

"Where I come from, artists use strips of linen coated with plaster to make molds of people's faces for masks or whatever," Claire explained, tugging his hat away from him. She scooped grit onto it. "And plaster is basically just fancy sand. When it hardens, it helps the cloth keep its shape, making a perfect copy."

Claire brought her wet hands to her lips and blew warm breath on them. Her fingers were cold, but she was pretty sure she could feel a slight hum in her bones.

"Here," she said, handing the soggy hat back to him. He flinched away.

She frowned. "What's wrong?"

Thorn's mouth turned up slightly at the edges, and his forehead wrinkled in embarrassment, but Claire could see a tiny bit of fear in his eyes.

"If it works, I mean—that's jumble magic!"

"So?" Claire asked, confused. "Royalists use jumble magic, like the Diamond Tree Vault."

"True," Thorn admitted. "But that's because Queen Estelle ordered it, and she's, you know, a legendary ancient queen . . ." His voice faded away.

Claire pulled her hair into a tight bun at the nape of her neck. There was no time to deal with Thorn's prejudice now, but Claire knew that if Aunt Nadia ever did become the ruling queen of Arden, the guilds would have a lot of adjusting to do. "Ready?" she asked. When Thorn nodded, she began to count. "One, two, three!"

They pulled the hats on. This time, she didn't have to wonder if the magic was working.

Something cool and slimy seemed to drip down her face, as if she'd cracked a raw egg against her head. The feeling spread as the fabric clung to her, tucking itself over her mouth and under her nose . . . and then over her nose. For a moment she felt like she couldn't breathe! But then the Make-a-Face seemed to know what it had done, and there was a soft tickle as the fabric inched away from her nostrils. Claire inhaled deeply.

The fabric began to dry, and as it did, the mask grew heavy, making it hard to wiggle her eyebrows or wrinkle her nose. And then the squelching stopped. The fabric lay still.

Tentatively, she raised a hand to her cheek. Smooth, warm skin met her fingertips but . . . Claire frowned as she felt the planes of her face. Her nose felt shorter, and her cheeks felt as round as apples.

"Claire?" a deep voice rumbled, and she turned to see Anvil. Or, actually, a not-*quite* Anvil.

It was Anvil's eyes, dark as coal, that looked at her, but the expression of amazement—something about the way the eyebrows twisted—seemed very much like Thorn. Claire whooped. "You look like—" She stopped, her hands flying to her throat.

"Are you all right?" Thorn asked, hurrying over to her.

"Yes," Claire whispered, but she heard again what had so startled her: Aquila's voice, dry as fire but just as warm, coming from her lips. She cleared her throat and spoke louder. "Even my voice is different!" She plunged her hand into her trousers and pulled out the little silver mirror. With a click, she flipped it open.

Bright-blue eyes above pink-apple cheeks stared back at her, while steel-gray hair wisped over her forehead. Wonder filled Claire. She looked exactly like Aquila—down to the little scar on her cheek that hinted that this sweet-looking grandmother might be able to swing an ax as easily as she could bake a pie. Though there was still something a little soft around the chin to be properly *Aquila*, and when she smiled, something seemed off. While the hats had made them look like the Malchains, in reality they were only as much the Malchains as a photograph of them would have been.

Gray hair and rosy pink cheeks weren't what made Aquila *Aquila*.

Claire was relieved. She was still *her*, even if she looked like the famous Forger. She guessed it was because even though clothes could make you feel and look different, they didn't actually change who you were. The Make-a-Face was more of an illusion, really, than an actual transformation.

She clicked the mirror closed and put it back in her pocket before turning to face Thorn, who was using his new height to pick one of the few apples left on a tree.

"You're going to need to stand a little straighter," she told him. "And keep your arms stiff; you're swinging them too much."

"They're just so long," Thorn said, grinning at their success.

Claire bit her lip. "And Anvil doesn't really smile, unless he's about to use his double-headed ax."

Thorn's black brows furrowed in a very un-Anvil-like show of confusion. "You better tell me everything you remember if this is going to work," he said.

They quickly pulled on the spare Forger tunics Claire had tucked into her Hollow Pack, and spent the next half hour practicing moving around like the Malchains. How Anvil came off as forbidding but really most of the time he was just thinking. How Aquila often teased Anvil, and how Anvil pretended to hate it, but Claire could secretly tell he enjoyed when Aquila, only a few inches taller than Claire, told him exactly what she thought.

"We should go soon," Thorn urged, and Claire knew he was right.

They deconstructed the ReflecTent and scraped apple mush from the bottom of their shoes before placing everything in the Hollow Pack except for the spyglass. They had done the math, and it would take about eight steps north and west to get to Fyrton in Claire's boots. At each new spot, Thorn would use the spyglass to make sure that their next step wouldn't send them to the bottom of a lake or into the side of a mountain.

"Ready?" Thorn asked. "Wait! Claire, your pencil!"

Oops. She reached into Aquila's white hair and slipped the leafy pencil into her pack. Her heart thumped. Already she'd made such a silly mistake. How could she pull off being Aquila? How would she be able to convince anyone to give her the Forgers' Hammer Tine if she couldn't remember such a simple thing? Maybe this was a bad idea. But there was no time to reconsider as Thorn had already grabbed for her hand and was counting down.

"Three . . . two . . . one . . ."

They stepped together.

Though Claire knew what to expect, her stomach still leaped as the world rushed at them. The journey was smoother, though, with Thorn wearing one of the boots. She didn't wobble so much. In about as much time as it took to sneeze twice, they were in a glade of a forest. Thorn held the spyglass up to his eye, adjusted the lens, then nodded in the next direction.

They stepped again.

They passed a field, two more harvested apple orchards, and another forest glade before the terrain started to look familiar. Claire's breath caught as they landed on the edge of a rusty red plain, a ring of small rocks looming in its center. Last time she'd been here, it had been night, but even in the early-morning sun, the Sorrowful Plains felt like a shadowed place. They stepped quickly away, taking an extra step east to avoid the Petrified Forest.

"Two more." Thorn huffed as they stood in a long-ago-abandoned Gemmer village at the edge of a lake, which Claire could tell had once been a quarry. His face looked pale, his legs shaking slightly as he took a deep breath.

"Do you want to take a quick break?" Claire asked. After all, she was just along for the ride, while he was responsible for making sure they didn't squash into a random farm wall.

He shook his head. "Only two more steps," he said, grim determination settling into the lines of Anvil's face. He twisted the spyglass and nodded west. "This way."

They stepped.

Everything was the same as it always was: a sudden jerk from behind the navel, a sense of sliding, but then, instead of feeling solid ground rise up to meet her sole, Claire felt her booted foot keep going, sinking through the earth with a loud *squelch*.

Dampness started to seep in through her trousers, and Claire sputtered as she tasted mud and something—there could be no other word for it—*greenish*.

Glancing down, she saw she was standing waist-deep in an earthy confection of water, leaves, and mud. They had arrived at Foggy Bottom swamp. Actually, only Thorn had arrived *at* Foggy Bottom, as his feet were both placed firmly on a large boulder that stuck out of the muck, while Claire had arrived *in* Foggy Bottom, her booted sole missing the boulder by inches.

"I'm so sorry," Thorn said, his worry making Anvil's movements surprisingly jittery. "There must have been a smudge on the spyglass that knocked me off course!"

"It's all right," Claire said, trying not to think what kind of swampy creatures could be lurking about. "Just get me out!" Anvil's strong arms reached for her, and a moment later, Thorn had pulled her out of the swamp and onto the rock next to him. Claire's toes stretched to soak in the heat of the sun on the boulder. It felt nice . . . until she realized she shouldn't be *able* to feel the boulder through the Seven League Boot.

Looking over her shoulder, she saw one last flash of red cowboy boot before Foggy Bottom swamp closed over it, swallowing it whole.

"Ah," Thorn said, one hand covering his mouth. "That's not . . . great." A muddy bubble from the swamp popped, as though in agreement.

Claire took a deep breath. "There's still one boot left. Maybe if I . . . ?" She gestured to his back. Thorn bent down, and Claire scrambled up. She was out of practice piggyback riding, but what other choice did they have?

Claire shook her arm to let the rest of the swamp muck wick away from her clothes, a useful side effect of wearing Spinner-made fabric. "I'm ready," she said.

Thorn stepped alone.

This time, the world didn't just rush at them; it sprinted. The colorful streaks smeared together, becoming the same gray as a pencil smudge. How could Thorn *see*? Was he even in control? Claire screamed, but the Boot yanked them away before she could hear the sound of it.

They were going too fast! They were going to splatter; she was sure of it! And then no one would know how to stop Queen Estelle! Sophie would never be *Sophie* again. And the worst part, Claire would never get to say—

Thump! Claire's grip on Thorn's shoulders broke as they crashed into a field.

She rolled, everything spinning until she finally came to a stop in front of a set of long, sharp claws. Copper claws.

Chimera claws.

Gasping, Claire looked up into the snarling face of a chimera, with a wolf's teeth and a cheetah's whiplike tail, all the green of an old penny. A frozen chimera. And as Claire gazed around, she saw they were in an entire field of such chimera, rusted still for nearly three hundred years. Which meant . . .

She stood cautiously and peered over the long yellow grass that reached her shoulders. Yes, there it was, in the shadow of Mount Rouge: the gold fence that spiked around Fyrton.

"Thorn," Claire breathed, "You did it! We're here!"

The only response was a groan, and Claire glanced over her shoulder. Thorn—or rather, Anvil—didn't look so great. His breathing was shallow and somehow, Claire thought she caught a glimpse of the shocking green yarn in the undertone of his cheeks. But before worry could engulf her the same way the swamp had claimed one of the Seven League Boots, she heard a jangle in the grass.

Either the chimera had suddenly come alive or . . .

"The crash came from this way!" an unfamiliar voice shouted.

"Forgers," Thorn rasped out. "They're coming!"

Claire had just enough time to tug the Seven League Boot from Thorn's foot and shove it deep into the mouth of the frozen chimera before the tall grass flattened to reveal a group of shield-wearing Forgers.

There were four of them in total, each one tall and blinding as the sun glinted off their breastplates and metal helmets and the swords on their hips. And the knives in their armguards. And the axes strapped across their backs.

This wasn't just a group of inspectors. This was a squadron of warriors. And by the time Claire had taken all this in, there was already a knife at her throat.

CHAPTER 15

Don't move," a boy's voice ordered from behind a visor. "As unauthorized trespassers, you are both now prisoners of the Fyrton Watch." Claire did as she was told, but her eyes strained, seeking out Thorn. From her periphery, she could just make out a sword under his chin, too. A blade to the throat, she was learning, was basically the equivalent of a Forger handshake. It was how she'd first met Sena, too. Thinking of Sena's stubborn bravery and Aquila's sharp wit, Claire took a deep breath. It was time to be a Forger.

"Good morning to you, too," she drawled in Aquila's voice. "Manners have certainly changed since I was young." She tilted her head toward Thorn. "Even my baby cousin Anvil has more courtesy. Which is saying something."

"I—" Claire's Forger stopped short, and there was a great

squeak as he lifted his visor to reveal a teenage boy with a crooked nose and round eyes.

"Rusted nails," he swore, clearly stunned, and Claire used his surprise to take a step back and away from his blade. "You're Aquila Malchain!" the warrior said. "You've returned!"

Claire nodded. "So it would appear."

"And you!" Thorn's Forger said, lowering her blade. "You're Anvil *Malchain*?"

Thorn jerked his head and stayed silent, exactly as the real Anvil would have done. He always chose his words as carefully as he selected his knives.

"Twenty-Third Legion, why have you stopped moving?" the fifth and final Forger demanded as she appeared from the yellowed grass. Like the others, she, too, was encased in armor and wore her weapons as easily as jewelry. Judging by the feathered black plume rising out of her helmet like smoke, Claire guessed she was the legion's leader.

"It's the *Malchains*, General Scorcha!" one of the Forgers said. "Anvil *and* Aquila!"

The Forger removed her helmet to reveal a woman about Anvil's age, with platinum-white hair cropped to just below her chin. Her face was pointed and small, like a cat's, but her arms were as muscled as Anvil's.

"Apologies," the general said. "It's been a long time since Fyrton has had the pleasure of your axes—" She broke off, and her eyes narrowed. "Where are your axes?"

Worry flickered through Claire. She knew that Anvil was

famous for wielding a double-headed ax with the blades shaped like bat wings, and she'd never seen Aquila without her two smaller axes crossed over her back. Claire had thought they would be able to buy some replacements in Fyrton before anyone noticed. She swallowed hard, hoping to keep the fear out of Aquila's voice. "Our axes were . . . What I'm trying to say is—"

"We were attacked," Thorn cut in with Anvil's deep baritone. "Ambushed by Queen Estelle."

His simple words set off an explosion. One of the Forgers slammed his metal-clad fist against a stationary chimera, while angry shouts rose from the others. Only General Scorcha seemed to remain calm, but even she let out a long, low hiss.

"We need to see Grandmaster Bolt," Thorn said. "He needs to send a warning to the other towns and grandmasters."

"You'll find all the Forger grandmasters taking their midday meal at Alkaline's Kettle," Scorcha said. "It's easiest to declare the War Council's decisions at that gossip house."

Thorn frowned. "A War Council's been called?"

"Yes." The general nodded. "As of last night, the Forger guild is officially at war against the fake Gemmer queen and all those who support her." Her eyes flicked to Claire. "We've already sent troops to Constellation Range. While everyone is at Hilltop Palace for Starfell, we will lay siege to Starscrape Citadel and cut off the Gemmers before they can rule again."

Claire bit her lip. The Citadel had its own protections, but there were so few Gemmers left! Only two hundred or so, and they would be up against thousands of Forgers. A metallic taste filled Claire's mouth. What would happen to Zuli and Lapis? To Carnelian? And friendly Scholar Pumus?

"All the more reason to talk to the grandmasters," Claire choked out.

General Scorcha nodded and gestured to Claire's Forger. He pulled out a bright-green flag and waved it in the direction of Fyrton's gates. A moment later, an answering green flag waved back. Scorcha stepped aside, holding back the tall yellow grass to clear a path for Thorn and Claire—or, more accurately, Anvil and Aquila.

"Welcome back," the general said. "Welcome home."

Fyrton was different than Claire remembered.

Last time, the city had been alive with the cheerful chink of hammers and the singsong of school bells. Now it echoed with the sound of marching boots. She watched wide-eyed as a squadron of men and women stalked by, shields on their forearms and swords gleaming at their hips. But not *only* swords. There were hammers, and maces, and spears, and strange curved knives.

The Forgers were preparing for war.

"Stop that," Thorn murmured to Claire, his voice a deep rumble.

"Stop what?" Claire asked. All she was doing was walking.

"Your eyes are all big," he said. "From what you told me

about Aquila, there's nothing that would surprise her—especially in Fyrton."

Thorn led the way, easily guiding them past the great walls of Phlogiston Academy, its hundred bell towers looming above them like judgmental lords. The great doors to the school were left open as apprentices hurried in and out, carrying bundles of kindling and buckets of water. Claire assumed that with war imminent, classes had been canceled. All hands would need to be free to keep the battle forges burning.

War. Battle. They were such short words, but the enormity of meaning behind them began to weigh on Claire: sorrow, sacrifice, and pain. Death. She just *had* to convince the Forgers to give Nadia their tine.

"Let's go faster," Claire whispered, and Thorn picked up the pace.

Steam billowed out from the hundreds of smithies and forges, making all the streets misty, even in the midmorning light. Figures carrying armloads of metal rods and pulling carts full of jangling helmets would appear from the haze and then vanish just as quickly. Suddenly, a shout came from somewhere down the hazy street: "Help!" A moment later, Claire could make out the drumbeat of hooves against cobblestones.

"Help!" the voice called again. "I need healers!"

Pedestrians scattered to the edges as the rider finally became visible. She galloped her horse down the middle of the street, all while balancing a large sack of flour slung across the saddle in front of her. Yanking on the reins, the woman flung herself off the horse's back before it had even come to a complete stop. The door of a nearby building slammed open, and Claire had just enough time to move out of the way as three healers rushed toward the horse and carefully pulled down the bag of flour.

Except . . .

It wasn't a bag of flour.

It was a man.

A boy, really, only a little bit older than Thorn. His dark-brown hair looked like a seaweed mop against the gray of his skin. Strange splotches clustered across his arms and face. It almost appeared as though someone had covered their hands in ash and then pressed their fingertips against his skin. He looked terrible, but the boy wasn't dead. He shivered violently as the healers bundled him up in a thick quilt. They slung him onto a stretcher and ran past Claire and Thorn and into the dark of the healers' building, but not before Claire caught a glimpse of the boy's eyes.

His *eyes*. She wrapped Aquila's arms around herself, trying to stop the cold that had suddenly shuddered through her. They'd had no *spark* to them. It was as though a wall of ice had been built between his thoughts and the world. He'd seemed trapped within himself. The passersby murmured to one another as they stepped back onto the street and resumed their business, but Claire couldn't get her feet to move.

"What—what happened to him?" Claire whispered. She hadn't been screaming, but for some reason, her throat felt raw.

"Wraith attack," Thorn said, his voice flat. "That's what untreated wraith-burn looks like."

Now Claire understood why the boy had been shivering. She'd faced wraiths before. Their long limbs and sticky shadows were what nightmares were carved from, and Claire had felt their cold seep into the pit of her stomach, wrinkles of her brain, and holes of her heart. Each time, though, she'd managed to get away from their grasp. Each time, Sophie had saved her. If Sophie hadn't been there . . . Now it was Claire who was violently shivering. She might have ended up like that boy. Or Nett's parents.

"She's sending a message," Thorn said. "If they don't give her the Hammer Tine, the wraiths will continue to attack." There was no need to say who the *she* was.

"The grandmasters," Claire said. "We need to talk to them. Now."

Thorn nodded and broke into a jog.

Alkaline's Kettle was at the far edge of town, where Fyrton's buildings butted up against Mount Rouge. Like the rest of the shops and taverns, it, too, had a hanging sign, this one a wrought-iron teakettle, with a swooping *A* in the center.

"Ready?" Thorn asked, and when Claire nodded, he pushed open the swinging doors.

Claire's first impression was of a hunting lodge. Vaulted wooden beams arched over several round tables, and servers bustled from table to table, taking orders and carrying silver platters piled high with tankards and steaming bowls. Large iron lanterns dangled from the ceiling, casting the diners in an orange glow, which was further emphasized by the reddish rock of the farthest wall. Half of Alkaline's Kettle was actually carved into the mountain, making use of its sturdy base.

Claire and Thorn slunk into rickety wooden chairs and pulled up to a small table. A single tin lantern with pinprick holes outlining the galloping shapes of unicorns sat at its center.

"Do you see any grandmasters?" Thorn asked, craning his neck to look around at the rest of the tavern's visitors. Claire, too, glanced around, trying to take note of people's sleeves. Guild members on the job had their rank sewn onto their clothes. A single ring on the left sleeve indicated an apprentice, while a single ring on both sleeves meant the wearer was a journeyman. Grandmaster Iris of Greenwood had had two white rings on each sleeve of her emerald robes, marking her as the most accomplished Tiller in Greenwood Village. But as Claire let her gaze slide from table to table, she didn't see anyone who wore the right rings. There was, however, an empty table on a dais, with settings placed for five.

"I don't think they're here yet," Claire said, careful to keep her voice low even though she didn't think that anyone could actually overhear them in the clamor of the tavern.

"Maybe they'll arrive soon," Thorn said, nodding toward the high table. He shifted uncomfortably. The small chair wasn't really made for someone of Anvil's bulk. "It's not quite lunchtime yet—"

"Order!" A small man with an elegantly waxed mustache and bulging triceps had suddenly appeared over Anvil's shoulder.

"Sorry?" Claire asked.

"Order. What's your order, ma'am?" the man barked. "There are mouths to feed, and it's not like meals are going to make themselves. Cornucopia Cauldrons are things of the past."

"The day's special," Thorn said quickly. "Two, please."

The server nodded briskly, plunked two copper mugs of water onto the table, and hurried off.

"Thor—I mean, Anvil," Claire said, leaning forward to resume their conversation. "That boy we saw, will he be all right?"

"I don't know." Thorn shook his head. "Sometimes people survive, and other times, they just kind of . . . *succumb*."

Claire lowered her gaze to the table, where the lantern projected unicorns on the wooden surface. If Estelle wore the united Crown of Arden and Claire failed to make Nadia a queen, then more people would fall victim to the wraiths. More people would die.

"Hey, don't worry," Thorn said as he patted her shoulder in a clumsy attempt at comfort. "One of the reasons historians think the wraiths increased so much after the Guild War is because there were no more unicorns to sweep them away. But remember! There *is* a unicorn out there now—and Estelle hasn't gotten it yet." He smiled, but Claire couldn't smile back.

A tiny, treacherous voice whispered in her mind: *If Sophie transforms completely into a unicorn, maybe she can protect everyone.*

No, Claire thought back stubbornly. *Sophie's useful even as a girl. I'll crown Nadia and Nadia will defeat Estelle. Problem solved, without any transformations . . . right?*

"There could be other ways to fight them," Claire said, looking up. "Something *more* than just sunlight and unicorns."

Thorn, who'd been taking a sip of water, made a face. "Maybe."

He placed the mug back down and scratched his chin. "We don't really know much about wraiths or how they came to be. They weren't always in Arden." He shrugged. "They might be like Spydens. A magical experiment gone very, very wrong."

Claire turned over his words. Magic was definitely beautiful, but it had its risks. Sena's parents, a Tiller and a Forger, had been experimenting with the seams of the world, and they had vanished without a trace.

"Cinders and smoke," a man's voice said from behind them. "I didn't believe what they're saying on the streets, but here you are: Anvil and Aquila Malchain."

Claire looked up to see a man who was roughly the size and shape of a boulder standing behind them. He wore a leather apron over what could have been a gray shirt, or a white shirt covered in soot. Wrapped around his considerable girth was a thick belt from which hung a handful of hammers as well as some clinking keys that were just as shiny as his bald head.

Claire recognized this man. The last she'd seen him, he'd locked her and her friends up for trespassing on his secret supply of black-market items. But—what was his name? The blank expression in Anvil's eyes told her that Thorn didn't remember, either. She thought it had been on the sign of his shop. *Something's Silverorium* . . . She had it!

"Scythe!" Claire said too loudly in her eagerness to spit it out. "How—how are you?"

"No need to be so formal with an old friend," Scythe said, pulling up an unused chair to squash himself between Thorn and Claire. "Edgar will be just fine. And I must say, it is good to see you, Aquila, considering that you swore never to return to Fyrton."

"Hmm," Claire said, stalling for something Aquila-like to say. She hadn't realized that it *would* be a surprise that Aquila had returned to Fyrton. In fact, there were a lot of things she didn't know about Aquila: her middle name, who her friends were—she didn't even know how old Aquila was! Just . . . *old*.

"Times . . . they change," Claire said feebly.

"What are you doing back?" Scythe asked, reaching for Claire's untouched tankard of water. The smell of smoke lingered on his shirtsleeve.

"We're waiting to speak to the grandmasters," Thorn said truthfully.

Scythe snorted into the tankard. "You'll be waiting awhile; didn't you hear who arrived at dawn? Axel."

A loud gasp erupted from Thorn, and Claire glared at him. Thorn quickly changed his gasp into a yawn.

"Pardon," he mumbled, and Claire was treated to a sight she thought she'd never see: Anvil's ears turning pink. Scythe stared at him quizzically as Thorn continued to ramble. "I'm just tired. Axel," he said with a pointed look at Claire, "is a *Grand* friend. One who writes *letters*."

Claire nodded ever so slightly to show she understood: Axel was a Royalist and a messenger. But why was the council of Forger grandmasters agreeing to meet with him if they had already decided to war against the queen?

Panic squeezed Claire's insides. Estelle already had the Gemmers' Stone Tine and the promise of the Oak Leaf Tine. Estelle might, for all Claire knew, even have the *real* Love Knot Tine. Perhaps Estelle had ordered her Royalists to replace the real one with a decoy, in order to doubly ensure someone like Claire couldn't foil her plans. And if Estelle hadn't, then who *was* the thief? And where had the stolen piece of crown gone? And— Wait a second.

Claire backtracked through her questions. Because if anyone would know where a stolen treasure had gone, it would be . . .

"Scythe, er, Edgar," Claire said, interrupting a rather uncomfortable interrogation as the silversmith probed Thorn for more information about what Anvil had been up to the last two months. "Has anything, I don't know, *regal* come across your shop recently?"

Claire held her breath. Scythe was the head of a thriving black market of dangerous, jumbled, or sometimes stolen magical artifacts, but she knew she was taking a risk mentioning his secret establishment. Scythe's expression, however, remained calm as he studied her.

"Interesting you should ask," he said, making Claire's heart leap. He knew something—she was sure of it! And her certainty only grew sharper as he pushed back his chair and said, "Perhaps this is a discussion that should happen someplace more private?"

After plunking down a few silver coins next to the lantern, Claire and Thorn followed Scythe out of Alkaline's Kettle and back into the maze of Fyrton. Claire wondered what the other Forgers thought when they saw the three of them— Scythe, Anvil, and Aquila—walking together. She knew they must make a formidable picture, so long as the Make-a-Face was still holding. Her fingers darted up to her chin, and she was relieved to feel it was still just a bit too round.

Soon they reached the familiar, enchanting quarter of Fyrton known as Silver Way. The silversmiths were hard at work, and the steam muted the bright reds and oranges of their forges so that everything, even the fires, seemed to be gilded in silver. But even the haze couldn't obscure Claire's growing excitement. The Love Knot Tine could be just a few yards away. She might be able to hold it in the next five minutes, and after that, they would convince the Forgers to support Nadia. By evening, she might have *half* the Crown of Arden—and Starfell was still two nights away!

When they reached the Silverorium, they waited a moment while Scythe fished the right key from his belt, and Claire had to sink her heels into the stoop to stop herself from bouncing up and down with impatience. Somehow, she didn't think Aquila would approve.

There was a click. Scythe pushed the door open and waved them inside his workshop. It was just as Claire remembered. Haphazard heaps of silver objects rose up to the ceiling. It was hard to tell how many objects were in his shop, exactly, because each polished item threw back a reflection of another polished treasure. Claire knew that somewhere in this forest of silver, there was a wardrobe that hid a secret room.

"Please remove your shoes and hats," Scythe said, coming in after them and pulling the door shut. Claire made to remove her shoes, but suddenly, she paused. Thorn had already noticed the problem.

"We're not wearing any hats," he rumbled in Anvil's deep voice.

"Really, now," Scythe said, and Claire turned to see the man's great bulk filling the entire doorframe. In one fist, he held a giant hammer, which he'd unhooked and now raised above his head. "You know my line of business. You were fools to think I wouldn't recognize illegal *jumbled* magic. Reveal yourselves, and I might let you live."

CHAPTER
16

Claire stood frozen as Scythe's hammer reflected a thousand times in the silver stacks, its blunt head gleaming in platters, helmets, flutes, and goblets. There was a grunt beside her, and in the next second, a new reflection joined the hammer: Anvil, struggling to tug the ax free from the strap on his back. Struggling in a way the *real* Anvil never would.

"I'd put that away if I were you," Scythe warned as Thorn, with one final grunt, freed the weapon from its holster and pulled it around to his chest. Thorn held it awkwardly, the entire ax trembling in his grip as though it were a twig in a wind and offering just about the same amount of protection. For one second, Claire thought she saw Scythe hesitate, but then he shook his head . . . and swung.

A loud *clang* reverberated throughout the workshop as the

hammer connected with the ax. The weapon flew from Thorn's hand, spinning wildly in the air until it hit a pile of coins. Claire threw her hands over her head as metal bits clattered down around them. But even in the din, Claire could hear Thorn's terrified yelp.

The hammer's blow had knocked Thorn to the floor, and though he still looked like Anvil, a red lump was protruding from his head where a wayward coin had smacked him. But that wasn't what made her breath catch in her throat. Scythe had stepped to loom over Thorn, and this time, his hammer wasn't aiming for Thorn's ax. It was aimed at his head.

"I'm giving you until three," Scythe growled. "Who. Are. You?"

"I-I'm . . . ," Thorn rasped, but he couldn't seem to get the words out.

"One," Scythe began. "Two . . ."

Claire couldn't look away. This was *her* fault! She'd been the one to say they should go to the Silverorium, though she knew how dangerous it was to cross the silversmith. Last time, she and Nett and Sena had ended up under a chain net. Last time, they'd almost lost their lives as Sena had looked for the stolen Unicorn Harp. Last time— Claire's thoughts caught, as though on a hook, as she remembered *what*, exactly, *had* happened last time.

"Three!" Scythe's hammer swooped down.

"*Nadia!*" Claire yelled. "IknowNadia!"

Thud.

At the last moment, Scythe's hammer had changed direction, shifting slightly to connect with the floorboards instead of Thorn's head.

"What did you say?" Scythe practically snarled as he lifted the hammer back to his shoulder, revealing a new dent in the hardwood floor. He stalked toward Claire.

"Nadia," Claire babbled. "I know Nadia and Cotton and Ravel and Woven Root!"

"What makes you think those names mean anything to me?" Scythe demanded as he tapped the hammer's head against his palm. It made a wet, hollow sound.

"B-b-because," Claire said, the letters tripping over her tongue as though they were trying to hide from his hammer, "Sena stole the Unicorn Harp to trade you for information about her parents. And you—you *told* her that her mom was somewhere near Constellation Range!"

"So?" Scythe sneered, but confidence surged through Claire. He was stalling. She *must* be right!

"So," Claire repeated, "Constellation Range is where Woven Root is. Or was," she added hastily. One of the ways the alchemist village managed to maintain its secrecy was by never staying in one place for too long.

Scythe studied her, silent. And then suddenly—he lunged!

Claire caught a glimpse of silver scissor blades in the second before Scythe grabbed Aquila's gray hair and pulled. Hard.

"Let go!" Claire shouted over Thorn's outraged cry, but it was no use. Scythe's strong fingers had managed to pinch the

Make-a-Face, and the enchanted cap, which had expanded and threaded its way across her body like a wet suit, protested the attempt at its sudden removal. Claire could feel the magic stretching across her, tension building like a pulled rubber band. The magic would either break, revealing her, or it would snap back against her.

She braced, ready for the recoil, but instead, there was a soft *snip*, and Scythe let go.

Without his hand, Claire stumbled forward. Helplessly, she tried to hold the unraveling halves of the Make-a-Face together, but yarn, Spyden silk, and river sand cascaded around her feet. And in the bulging sides of a knocked-over sugar bowl, Claire saw her own gray eyes and frizzy brown hair.

"*You!*" Scythe gasped. Claire tried to hide her own face, though it was way too late. "You're the girl who was with Sena. You're *Claire Martinson!*"

"Leave her alone!" Thorn said, and Claire looked to see Anvil brandishing a silver candlestick, even if his eyes didn't seem quite focused yet.

"Sit down before you hurt yourself, whoever you really are," Scythe growled, never taking his eyes from Claire. "I don't want to harm Apprentice Martinson. In fact," he said, neatly twirling his hammer and hooking it back onto his belt, "I've been looking for her."

Stunned, Claire felt her mouth drop open as a gazillion questions swarmed her, but all she could manage was a breathless, "*What?*"

Scythe shook his head. "Not yet. Not here." And with a meaningful look, he waved at them to follow him around the silver stacks to a familiar wardrobe.

"Sorry about the scissors," he said, keeping his voice low. "But I had to be certain because, well, you'll see." He opened the wardrobe and slid the false back silently open, then stepped aside.

At first, all Claire could make out was bare shelves and clusters of candles. They were of uneven lengths, so that the shadows they threw looked like a set of crooked teeth munching on the wall. But after a moment, she realized that in a dark part of the room sat two figures. Their backs were to the door, all their attention focused on the pile of keys in front of them. As Claire watched, one of them with tufted black hair held up a golden key. "How about this one?" he asked.

"Where did you get it?" a girl with fire-red hair asked, and when the boy pointed toward a smaller pile, the girl sighed irritably. "That's my 'already tested' pile!"

"Whoops," the boy said. "Sorry about that, but don't worry! The worst thing that can happen is that one day your nose itches and you forget you're wearing the gauntlet and accidentally break your nose."

"Not funny," the girl ground out. "*You* try having your hand permanently locked in a glove of gold! It's heavy! And— No, Gryphin. *No!*"

There was a squawk like a rusty hinge, and Claire caught a glimpse of candlelight on copper wings as a chimera about the size of a large drinking goblet pulled out of its dive. A silver key dangled in its talons, and the formerly neat clump of keys was now scattered across the floor. The girl let out an exasperated sigh while the boy scrambled after one still spinning on the hardwood.

Claire *knew* this boy and girl. But before she could say anything, a third figure melted out from the shadows. With an easy grace, the new figure snatched the chimera out of the air and plucked the key from its talon.

"Here you go, " she said, her ponytail swaying sassily as she handed the key to the redheaded girl and sternly addressed the boy. "Nett, back off of Sena." She paused and glanced toward the gauntlet-clad girl. "I think your jokes might be getting . . . *out of hand.*"

Sena Steele scowled while Nettle Green let out a gleeful whoop of laughter.

"Not funny," Sena huffed, which only made Nett laugh harder.

The second girl ducked her head to hide a smile, turning her face ever so slightly toward the door where Claire stood, flanked on either side by Scythe and a Make-a-Face Anvil. The second girl suddenly straightened. "Scythe, you're back! Did you manage to get the File Away? Or find out why *another* grandmaster meeting was called this morning? And—" She broke off with a gasp. "Wait . . . is that you, Anvil?! How did you—? But . . ." Her eyes finally landed on Claire. *"Clairina! "*

And then Sophie was running toward her with a fluid grace

that made Claire's breath catch. Or maybe that was how hard Sophie was now hugging her, squeezing her as though she would never let go. This was no Spyden silk illusion. Claire wrapped her arms around her sister. Her *human* sister. Sophie was here! In Fyrton! With Scythe!

And then.

Something barreled through Claire, pushing at her insides like helium in a balloon: an emotion. But she couldn't name it. Was it a stunning joy or a devouring fear?

Sophie was *here*. In Fyrton. *Away* from Woven Root.

The questions flooded Claire, each one clamoring, each one demanding an answer. But only one question could come first. Claire stepped out of Sophie's hug and looked up at her big sister. "Why are you following me?!"

Sophie blinked in surprise. "I— What?"

And the thing that had been pushing at Claire grew sharper, twisting in her gut, and suddenly, Claire realized it wasn't joy or fear. It was *fury*.

"Why are you following me?" Claire repeated, crossing her arms. "I told you I could do this! I told you to stay in Woven Root. Why don't you believe in me? You never *listen*!"

"Claire, I—"

"YOU NEED TO BE SAFE!" She was shouting now, ignoring Sena's and Nett's stunned faces. It didn't matter. She knew only that she had to make Sophie understand. That Sophie had to be safe. "I CAN *DO* THIS, SOPHIE! I DON'T NEED YOU TO DO THINGS FOR ME! YOU DON'T—"

"Claire!" Sophie said. Reaching out, she gripped both of Claire's shoulders. "Calm down! We're *not* following you. I *know* you can do things by yourself. We're here because of the unicorn!"

"I— *What?*" Now it was Claire's turn to blink in surprise.

"*The* unicorn!" Sophie repeated. "The one from the rock—he's been trapped!" She spoke fast, seeming to try to get the words out before Claire could recover from her shock and start yelling again. "The night you left, I had a dream— *more* than a dream, really. A message from the unicorn."

A strange mixture of awe and worry washed through Claire, sweeping away her fury and leaving only Sophie's incredible statement: *a message from the unicorn.*

"What?" Claire breathed again. "You—you spoke to the unicorn? Where is he?"

Now that it was clear Claire was done yelling, Sophie released her shoulders.

"Kind of. We share dreams," she said, with a quick glance to the two adult Forgers. She kept her voice low, and Claire understood Sophie was protecting the secret of her creeping change. "I'm able to see his dreams, and he can see mine. He doesn't really *talk*, but he shares his memories and feelings with me— feelings of being confined, but always by different things."

She raised her voice again to a regular volume and continued. "Sometimes it's metal, other times it's thread or stone or roots, which makes me believe that one of the guilds has him, but I'm not sure which one."

"We have some ideas though!" Nett piped up.

Sophie nodded and held up four fingers. "We know it's not the Gemmers, since you and me, Claire, were at Stonehaven and we would have definitely heard about it." She put down a finger. "And it's not the Tillers—we just spent a couple of days in Tanglevine, the biggest Tiller village, but the only things we found there were a few snapdragon bites and a nasty run-in with a Guarden Rose."

Over Sophie's shoulder, Claire saw Nett roll up his tunic sleeve to show off his arm, which was mottled black and blue and punctuated with thorn-prick-sized scabs.

"So," Sophie continued, now with only two fingers held up, "that left us with either the Forgers or Spinners. We were closer to Fyrton and also, since the Forgers have declared war on Estelle, it made sense to us that they would be the ones to keep a unicorn hidden—to use as a secret attack, or something. We snuck into Fyrton and then went to their treasury, but then—"

"But then that flying nuisance ruined it for us!" Sena said with a pointed glare, directed toward somewhere above Claire's head. Claire followed her gaze. Perched on the top of a tall, empty shelf, the chimera looked down at her with interest. It had the head and wings of a magpie and the body, tail, and hefty paws of a lion cub.

"What *is* that?" Thorn asked in Anvil's voice.

"Gryphin!" Nett piped up proudly as he rushed in to give Claire a hug. "Sena and I crafted him following the directions in some of the journals we found in Sena's parents' workshop. He's part lion and part magpie. He's meant to help us locate the unicorn, since magpies are good at finding shiny things, but he's been a bit . . . distractible."

Sena snorted. "That's an understatement. No, no, *no*, Gryphin!"

But it was too late. The little chimera had already launched himself off the shelf and was diving straight for Sena's hair. A second later, the copper creature careened into Sena's shoulder and promptly wrapped the Forger's long red braid around himself before closing his eyes. Gryphin appeared to be settling in for a nap.

Sophie's lips twitched while Sena scowled.

"He likes Sena best," Sophie explained. "Sena saved his life."

Claire's head whirled. Just a minute ago, she'd thought Scythe was going to kill her but now, incredibly, she was with her sister again, and Nett, and Sena, and she'd received the miraculous, wonderful news that the last unicorn, the unicorn she'd called from rock, the unicorn that had started a change in her sister, was alive.

Which meant there was still a chance Sophie could be *just* Sophie again.

Claire studied her sister. Sophie was wearing a black leather vest over a sweater of a purple so light it was almost gray— clothes appropriate for a Forger working near soot and hot flames. A disguise, then. A streak of white still gleamed in Sophie's dark hair, but other than that, nothing seemed to have changed since Claire last saw her. There was no telltale bump on her forehead, though if there had been, it might be hidden under her bangs.

As though Sophie could read her thoughts, she brushed away her fringe to reveal smooth skin.

"I'm *fine*, Claire," she said softly. "Seriously. And I feel good, better than good."

Claire reached out and hugged her sister again.

"I'm sorry for yelling," she mumbled into Sophie's shoulder. "I just missed you."

"Obviously." Sophie squeezed back. "But even though I know you can take care of yourself, don't do that again. You can't just *leave*."

A weak chuckle escaped Claire, and she let go. "I learned from the best."

"How dare you!" Sophie said with mock indignation, but her eyes sparkled. And even though questions still poked and prodded Claire, she felt lighter than she had in a long, long time. Sophie was here, and Claire now knew that together, they could do anything: Collect the tines. Save a unicorn. Go home.

"I don't get . . . what's happening," Thorn said, sounding slightly dizzy. Claire turned to look at him and saw that Anvil's eyes were as round as dinner plates as he stared at the copper chimera, and Claire remembered that he'd never been to Woven Root and, therefore, had never seen a chimera move until now. However many questions she had couldn't come close to Thorn's.

Sophie turned a dazzling smile on Thorn. "Anvil! I'm so glad you've been de-rubified! How did they fix you?"

"That's not Anvil Malchain," Scythe said as he finished bolting the seventh and final lock on the secret door. Sophie's smile slipped, and her eyes narrowed as she stared at Thorn. Under Sophie's gaze, Thorn seemed to collapse a bit. Even though Thorn still looked just like Anvil, as his ears sank toward his shoulders, Claire was suddenly reminded of the first time she'd met Thorn in Greenwood's stables.

"Is that . . . ?" Sophie paled. "Thorn?"

For a moment, Thorn didn't move. Then he nodded.

Gasps startled from Sophie and Nett, while there was a slight hiss of metal as Sena yanked Fireblood from its scabbard.

"Stop!" Claire said. "Give him a chance to explain."

Sena scowled. "But—"

"Put that away," Scythe ordered Sena, turning his back on the secured door. "No need to make a bloody mess in my wareroom." He tugged the scissors from his tool belt and handed them to Thorn. "Snip that illusion off, will you? The rest of you," he said, looking at Claire, Sophie, and Nett, "come over here and help me."

Scythe trudged to the back corner, knelt down, and pulled open a trapdoor Claire hadn't noticed. A secret room inside a secret room! Though as Claire peered closer, she saw it wasn't really a room at all but a tiny cellar stuffed with all kinds of dried food and travel provisions.

"Here," Scythe grunted as he pulled up a dusty picnic blanket and threw it at Claire. "Go spread that out. We don't have much time, by the sound of things, but stories and plans are always best with a full stomach."

Sophie took a corner of the blanket. Grinning at Claire, she added, "And with sisters."

CHAPTER
17

𝕴ifteen minutes and one self-boiling kettle later, Claire found herself sitting cross-legged on the edge of the blanket, holding a bit of cheese in her hand. Beside her, Nett was busy unwrapping the last of the biscuits while Thorn—returned to his usual blond-haired state—sat quietly across from Claire, occasionally sneaking a glance at Sophie. Seated next to Claire, Sophie was in the middle of recapping just *exactly* how a golden gauntlet had come to clamp onto Sena's hand.

"So," Sophie said with a toss of her white-streaked pony-tail, "we asked ourselves, 'Where would the Forgers hide something as rare and precious as a unicorn?' And that's when Nett suggested—"

"The Fyrton Vaults," Nett supplied.

Sophie shook her head emphatically. "Right. Because—"

"Because the Fyrton Vaults are the most secure place in all of Arden," Nett interrupted again as he reached for the kettle and poured in a packet of dried leaves. Immediately, the smell of new sketchbooks and sunshine filled the space. "They're hard to break into, and even harder to break out of, and full of dangerous decoy objects to protect the *real* treasures. They're a perfect place to hide something you don't want others to know about."

"Excuse me." Sophie raised an eyebrow. "Who's telling the story?!"

"Sorry," Nett said, sounding cheerful and not sorry at all as he poured the newly made tea into silver goblets and handed them around. Claire hid her smile behind the rim as she accepted hers.

"Go on, Sophie," she nudged. "What happened? How were you able to break into the treasury if it was unbreakable?"

Sophie's eyes darted to Thorn, who at that very moment had been staring at her. Quickly, he turned away, reached for the tin of walnuts—and promptly knocked them over onto the blanket. As he was scrambling, Sophie looked at Claire meaningfully.

"I have my ways."

Right. Ways. *Unicorn* ways.

One of the many magical abilities of unicorns was that they could open doors—any doors, including, it seemed, the ones set with the strongest of Forger locks.

"So we go inside," Sophie continued, ignoring the *plink* of walnuts as Thorn dropped them back into the tin. "But instead of finding a unicorn, all we found were piles of treasures. Mountains of it. And oh, Claire!" Sophie's eyes shined as she clasped her hands dramatically to her heart. "I wish you could have seen it. Some of those rooms—they looked like the illustrations from the storybook about Ali Baba and the Forty Thieves! Or the underground fairy world from the 'Twelve Dancing Princesses.' We saw golden tree branches with sapphire plums. *Actual* gold and *actual* sapphires!"

As Sophie continued to describe the many magical and fantastic things stowed in Fyrton's vaults, Claire felt memories settle around the picnic blanket. This felt just like all those times before, when Sophie had outlined which Experience they were about to do next. But those stories had all been carved from Sophie's imagination, and what her sister was describing now— a waterfall of steaming silver; gowns of woven platinum—was *real*. Sophie had actually seen and done what she was describing; these weren't just descriptions of a wish.

"Yes, yes," Sena slipped in while Sophie paused to take a breath. "We saw a lot of things—but no unicorn." The Forger girl was sitting on a stool next to a cluster of candlesticks and the brighter light of Nett's marimo, a mossy plant that grew in a ball that had once belonged to his mother, before she'd died in a wraith attack. In the bright light, Claire saw Sena's hand drift uselessly over Fireblood's hilt, her fingers locked in place by the golden gauntlet.

"And all those treasures," Sena continued, "were *shiny*,

which meant this one"—she jerked her head toward the high shelf where Gryphin was perched, happily lapping a saucer of vegetable oil—"couldn't keep his beak to himself."

"It was terrifying," Nett said, his brown eyes darkening for a moment. "Gryphin angered a suit of armor, and so Sena had to duel it to save his tail. But she slipped and accidentally grabbed onto the gauntlet, which immediately clamped onto her. After that, she couldn't touch anything that didn't belong to her without the gauntlet turning red-hot—you know, making her *caught red-handed*. But Sena did manage to rescue Gryphin."

"It wasn't worth it," Sena muttered as she glared up at the shelf.

"Ignore her," Nett said, taking a bite of biscuit. "She luffs Gryffffin."

"I do not!"

Nett swallowed. "Whatever you say," he said amicably, but as soon as Sena looked back at her hand, Nett mouthed, *she does*.

Realizing she was losing her audience, Sophie quickly summed up the rest of the tale. "We were a bit loud, but luckily, Scythe was already on the lookout for us and he was the one who found us trapped in the Hall of Mirrors. He got us out, and brought us back here to see if any of his keys could unlock the gauntlet. We figured out pretty quickly it probably wasn't going to work, and Scythe said that if Sena wanted to be able to use her sword hand again, the gold would have to be scraped off. He left us here to keep trying out the keys while he went to barter for a File Away, and then—well." Sophie shrugged. "He returned with you." She patted Claire's knee, then took a sip from her own goblet.

"Wow," Claire breathed. Her mind reeled with all the new information as well as bright images inspired by Sophie's tale. She longed for her set of oil pastels, so that she could try to capture them, the way she usually did at home. All those magical objects! And among them, maybe even the Hammer Tine.

She was just about to ask Sophie, Nett, and Sena if they had seen something that looked like the point of a crown, when Thorn spoke up.

"Sophie, would you please pass the sugar?"

But Sophie didn't seem to have heard him, and so Claire handed the bowl to Thorn, who accepted it with a small nod. Clutching her silver goblet, purple steam rising up from it, Claire couldn't help but stare at the shelves in the secret room.

Once, they'd been crowded with illegal magical objects, sagging under the weight of such things as chokers and mirrors that revealed the gazer's greatest weakness. But now the shelves were full of nothing but dust.

There was no Love Knot Tine here, stolen or otherwise.

"It's all been sold," Scythe said, answering Claire's unasked question as he stomped by her and toward Sena.

"All the black-market objects sold?" Claire repeated Scythe's words, surprised and also a bit uneasy. There had been so many of them!

"Guild tensions have been rising for some time now," Scythe said, and settled himself next to Sena. He was much larger than his three-legged stool, and it creaked under his weight. Hunching over, Scythe pulled out a large file and gestured for Sena to give him her hand.

"In dangerous times," Scythe said as he carefully cradled Sena's golden fingers and began to file the metal, "people seek dangerous solutions. Desperate ones—such as untested jumbled transformations made of dangerous substances like Spyden silk."

Thorn, who'd taken a quiet sip of his sugary tea, spluttered a bit at that. His ears, back to their normal large size, turned pink as he wiped his sleeve across his mouth. "Sir, how could you tell we weren't the Malchains?"

Scythe snorted and continued over the soft *scritch* of the file on gold. "Aside from the fact that Anvil looked terrified of his own ax? A few things. Like the fact Aquila hasn't called me by my first name since I once rented out a treasure she wasn't quite ready to part with—"

"You mean," Sena interrupted with a raised eyebrow, "you stole it and sold it."

"I prefer 'long-term rental,'" Scythe said. "Don't move while I'm doing this—you don't want me to accidentally file off a finger! The other giveaway was that Nadia told me about the Malchains' actual rubified condition." He shook his head. "Haven't heard directly from her in nearly ten years, and then two weeks ago, *he* showed up."

He nodded to the pocket on his leather apron. Claire was

confused at first, until she noticed the outline of an embroidered heron. So that was how: a Messaging Thread. The last time she'd seen one, a heron had unstitched itself from Sophie's hem and flown to seek Nadia for help.

"Nadia let me know a gaggle of children would probably attempt something foolish," Scythe continued. Sweat gleamed on his bald head and gold dust coated his hands. "She asked me to keep an eye out for them. Good thing, too," he said, the rhythmic *scratch* pausing for just a second as he looked up to glare at Nett and Sophie, "or someone else might have discovered you trapped in the treasury." The *scratch-scratch* resumed, and then—

"Aha!" Scythe suddenly said. There was one more scratch of metal on metal and then a sharp *clank* as the gauntlet fell to the floor. Sena's hand was free.

"Yes!" she said, wiggling her fingers, which looked fine, if a little pink. After a few more shakes, Sena wrapped her hand around Fireblood's hilt and gave it a few swings. Clearly she'd been practicing. The sword moved easily in a silver blur, reminding Claire of Lyric and the Spinner dancers and how easily they twirled their Starfell ribbons. Scythe, meanwhile, had picked up the golden glove and was weighing it carefully in his palm, already calculating its value. He placed it on an empty shelf and came to join the picnic.

"Nice work," Nett said, scooting over to make room for the burly Forger. "Though I admit I'll miss being able to use Sena's hand as a mirror to check for any boogers."

"Don't worry," Sena drawled, sheathing Fireblood at last

and joining them. "I can slice off your nose if you want. Save you the inconvenience."

Sophie and Thorn laughed, but Claire only smiled. Something still worried her. Something still didn't make sense. "Mr. Scythe, one of the rules of Woven Root is that no one can *leave* Woven Root. So how are you here?"

"I never said I was a member of Woven Root. I've never been," Scythe said as he picked up the last two biscuits. "But I've known Nadia since before even she learned of Woven Root, back when she went by Diana."

Claire nodded; she still wasn't entirely comfortable with Scythe, but she felt better knowing Nadia trusted him with her most precious treasure of all: Woven Root.

She looked at Sophie. She seemed relaxed. Sophie must trust Scythe, too.

"Mr. Scythe," Claire said, "are you able to send a message to Nadia?" And when he nodded, she took a deep breath. "Okay. Here's what we know."

Beginning with the Spyden's words, she told them all about her journey to Needle Pointe, the discovery that the Love Knot Tine was a fake, and how they needed to gather the four tines of the powerful Crown of Arden in order to make Nadia queen. Because only a queen could defeat a queen. And only then would they be able to stop Estelle.

Estelle, who wanted a unicorn's heart.

By the time Claire got to the end—with a few helpful insertions by Thorn and a few gazillion questions from Nett— Scythe had stood and started to pace. His legs were so long, however, that he needed to take only five steps to cross the entire length of the room.

"How did you know that the tine was fake?" Scythe growled, not angrily but in a focused way. Claire pulled the pencil out from behind her ear, and his brow lifted in amazement.

Next to her, she heard Sophie let out a soft "Wow."

"Give it to me," Scythe said, holding out his hand. "That looks like Charlotte Sagebrush's pencil! It's one of the most valuable treasures in all of Arden! Why, I bet it could fetch—"

"You're right," Claire agreed. "It is priceless." But instead of handing him the pencil, she tucked it back behind her ear. Scythe frowned, and Claire wondered what he would do, but then suddenly, from beyond the hidden door, they heard a sound: bells.

Sena shot upright, her eyes flicking to Scythe. "What are they saying?"

Scythe was already walking to the door. "It's muffled," he said gruffly. "I'll need to go out to hear the message properly. You," he said, pointing at Thorn, "come with me to keep watch." A second later, both Forger and Spinner disappeared.

"What's going on?" Sophie asked, setting down the cloth napkin she'd been folding into a blossom, as though she'd wanted to make something for the pencil's leaf.

"In a time of war," Sena explained, "if the Fyrton leaders need to get a message out quickly, they relay it through the bells." She shook her head, her brows furrowed. "Usually around this time of year, the bells would be tolling 'Unicorns in the Snow.'"

At Sophie's cocked eyebrow, Sena added, "It's a traditional Forger song for the Starfell holiday. On Starfell night, the newest class of apprentices get to ring the bells during the shower—supposedly to let the stars know not to fall on our roofs."

"But I'm guessing whatever we just heard wasn't 'Unicorns in the Snow,'" Sophie said, and when Sena shook her head again, Claire felt Sophie's warm breath on her shoulder as her sister sighed. Sophie was worried about the unicorn.

Claire looked around and lowered her voice. "Sophie," she said, "what's it like to share a dream with a unicorn?"

Sophie shook her head, and for a moment, Claire thought it seemed she'd shaken a mane. "It's hard to explain. It's definitely spectacular, but even then, that doesn't cover it. Maybe if there was a word for something that was strange and perfect and strong and gentle, that could be a start."

Sophie looked at Claire, and for a second Claire thought Sophie might be about to cry from the wonder of it all, but then she realized that the glitter in her eyes wasn't due to tears. No, Sophie's eyes, which had always been as warm and brown as maple syrup, now held the thinnest ring of moonlight silver around her pupils. It was faint, but it was there. Cold bloomed in the pit of Claire's stomach. What did it mean? How much longer did they have? And what if—?

But before she could finish that thought, she heard loud stomps as Scythe and Thorn burst back into the room.

"What is it?" Sophie asked, shooting to her feet and overturning her tin mug. A few drops of purple tea spotted the tablecloth. From above, Gryphin gave a startled "*Purr-kaaa*!" and flapped down to land heavily on Sena's shoulder.

"The Forger guild has agreed to a temporary truce," Scythe said, ignoring the tiny commotion around the chimera. "War is stopped for now, and the armies won't attack Stonehaven just yet, but they might decide to give Estelle the Hammer Tine after all. They'll hold off on their final decision until Starfell! And worse—I just saw a regiment led by Grandmaster Bolt and General Scorcha gallop out of the gates. The Hammer Tine is already on its way to her."

The pit in Claire's stomach was now so big, she thought it would swallow her whole.

Estelle had done it.

At Starfell, she would have all four tines. She would have the complete Crown of Arden and become so powerful that there would be no possibility of ever stealing it from her to crown Nadia. Estelle would win. And Sophie . . .

"Why?" Claire cried out, forgetting to keep quiet. "What changed the Forgers' minds?"

"Estelle got her proof," Thorn said. Ash seemed to have settled under his cheeks. "She has the unicorn."

"Did you know this?" Sophie asked, whirling on Thorn and speaking to him for the first time.

He shook his head, blond hair flying. "No," he croaked out. "I swear I didn't!"

"I believe him, Sophie," Claire said. She remembered how sickened he looked when he told her of the queen's plan to carve out the unicorn's heart. Now *she* felt sick. After the queen used the unicorn to convince the Forgers to give her their tine, Estelle would have no need for a *living* unicorn anymore . . .

"But it just doesn't make sense," Sophie said, shaking her head so vehemently that her ponytail brushed the tip of her nose. "In my dr— I mean, my information doesn't say the queen has him. His messages are images of the four guilds: locks, and reeds, and jewels—he's definitely been captured by one of the four guilds!"

But Nett, who'd been unusually silent, finally spoke. "Maybe he wasn't saying the captor is one of the guilds, Sophie," he said quietly. "Maybe your, uh, informant was trying to tell you he's at a place where all four guilds are gathered together. After all, the Royalists have members from all four guilds, right?" He glanced at Thorn for confirmation, and Thorn nodded. "And they will all be gathered at Hilltop Palace."

"Maybe . . . ," Sophie said, though she still sounded uncertain.

"There's only one thing to do, isn't there?" Sena said. "We have to save the unicorn. We have to free him from Estelle so she can't convince the Forgers to join her. We'll save the unicorn, and then the unicorn can help *us* convince the Forgers to give Nadia their tine. And then . . ." She shrugged. "Then we'll tackle getting the other three."

"But how will we get there in time?" Nett asked. "Starfell is tomorrow—how are we going to travel there without being captured ourselves?"

Claire remembered the one red Seven League Boot out there in the chimera's mouth, but even if they could retrieve it without being seen, there were too many of them to make the journey with one boot.

No one spoke. And then—

"Me," Thorn said, looking miserable. "You'll sneak in through me."

CHAPTER
18

The first few hours of traveling as prisoners of His Royal Highness Thorn Barley of Arden were surprisingly fun. Though the wooden cart and bony mare Scythe had procured for them were a far cry from Mom and Dad's car, it didn't feel too unlike going on a special weekend trip to the lake.

After Thorn's suggestion, they had spent the rest of the day and most of that night preparing for what was to come. When dawn had at last broken, Scythe had helped them ride out of Fyrton without any questions. Once they were on the road that led to Hilltop Palace, he'd handed the reins over to Thorn and clambered off the cart. The Forger would not be traveling with them to save the unicorn and collect the tines, but instead would be following his Messaging Threads to wherever Nadia and Woven Root were currently camped and would let her know the Spyden's words: *Only a queen can defeat a queen.*

But Scythe hadn't left them without some help. "If you encounter a Royalist, you can easily claim you're on a secret mission for Estelle," Scythe had said to Thorn, who would be riding up front while the others hid in the cart. "But if a Forger stops you, just flash this Fool's Gold coin." He'd explained that when it was in Thorn's pocket, the coin would be as smooth as a windless lake, but as soon as he showed it to a Forger, it would immediately etch the crest of the grandmaster the viewer happened to respect the most and lead them to believe Thorn was traveling with that particular grandmaster's permission.

"Fool's Gold helps ensure my business runs smoothly," Scythe had said after he'd pressed it into Thorn's palm. To which Sena had muttered, "And keeps treasures flowing into your shop." Thankfully, however, Scythe didn't seem to have heard her dry quip, and Claire had quickly swallowed back her smile. She'd *missed* Nett and Sena, her first friends in Arden, and the little copper chimera quickly found a large place in her heart.

"How did you do it?" Claire asked now as the cart's wheels trundled over grit and dirt. She stuck out a finger and gently petted the copper feathers. Gryphin made a sound midway between a chirp and a purr. Claire grinned.

"It was all Sena," Nett said, stretching out his own finger to scratch the base of his lion's tail. "She has a real talent for chimera."

"I'm all right, I guess," Sena said, looking uncharacteristically uncomfortable.

"All right?" Nett said, shaking his head. "You're way better than all right!" He turned to look at Claire, his brown eyes serious. "The Forgers in Woven Root say she's got a knack for metalwork they've never seen before."

"It's just because of my parents' journals," Sena explained, though she looked pleased and a little surprised at Nett's praise. "They're not, like, diaries of their innermost thoughts or anything. Just notes they took on their research, a few guesses." She shrugged. "Sometimes they have helpful shortcuts or a way of explaining things that just, I don't know, *chime*. Though," she said, her expression darkening, "if I can't find my parents, who cares if I discovered the fourth property of metal?"

"Don't worry," Nett said quickly, and Claire had the sense that they'd had this conversation a thousand times. "When we find the unicorn, he'll help us figure out what happened to your parents."

"Hmph," Sena said, but she reached for her Hollow Pack—identical to Claire's, only black leather instead of powder blue—and pulled out a dog-eared book with *Vol. MCMLXXXIX* stamped on it with rose-gold foil: one of the Steeles' many journals.

"Here," she said, tossing it to Claire. "Take a look if you want. I brought all their journals with me."

Ignoring Gryphin's clacking protests that she'd stopped petting him, Claire caught the book and flipped it open. It was filled with strange symbols and lots of scribbles that she supposed were letters. The handwriting was spiky, seeming to crackle and snap unexpectedly like a dry log. Squinting, Claire thought she could make out a familiar name.

"Does this say *Malchain*?" Claire asked, and when Sena nodded, curiosity trickled through her. "Why are the Malchains mentioned in your parents' journal? Did they know each other?"

"Not sure," Sena admitted as she pulled the end of her braid out of Gryphin's beak, "but that's not about Aquila and Anvil Malchain." She pointed to the scribble before it. "It says *Alloria* Malchain."

Claire frowned. "Have I heard that name before?"

"Yeah, you have," Sophie said, cracking open an eye. She was stuffed between Claire and the back corner of the cart, where she had leaned her head to try to take a cat nap. Apparently, sharing dreams with a unicorn wasn't the best way to get sleep. Purple crescents outlined Sophie's eyes, making her face seem narrower than it actually was and her freckles washed-out. Stifling a yawn, Sophie continued. "Alloria Malchain was the most talented Forger in Arden's history. She was the one who helped Martin and the unicorn craft the path between the well and the fireplace."

Sena frowned. "I didn't know that story."

Sophie nodded. "And she forged the Kompass that directs to the moontears."

The moontears. Claire's heart squeezed whenever she thought about the Great Unicorn Treasure that was now, most likely, hanging around Estelle's neck, waiting for the touch of a unicorn's horn to awaken them.

"Sophie," Claire said as a horrible thought stabbed her, "if

Estelle already has the last unicorn, do you think she's already woken the moontears?"

Sophie shook her head, "I don't *think* so. I kind of feel like, you know, *I* would know."

Maybe. And yet . . . But before panic could really set in, Nett gently tugged the book out from Claire's hands.

"I can't believe you can actually make sense of this, Sena," he said, holding the book so close to his nose that he was in danger of smudging the ink. "It might say *Alloria Malchain*, but honestly, it could also say 'Alchemical maturation' or even 'All of our mittens.'"

Sena snorted. "Why would my parents write about mittens?"

Nett shrugged. "Their fingers were cold? They were working on fireproof oven mitts? They were sharing knitting— No, stop!" Nett broke off with a yelp as Sena jabbed a finger in his ribs and began to tickle him. The commotion excited Gryphin, who immediately launched himself onto Nett's head and began flapping his copper wings, trilling happily.

"Quiet back there!" Thorn said from the front.

Nett protested, "But she—"

"That's enough," Thorn said firmly. Claire glanced at Sophie and saw her sister was already looking at her. They burst into giggles at the same time. It was nice to be with her best friends.

By noon, however, being royal prisoners was decidedly less fun. The bumps on the road added bruises to their bruises, and the laughter came a little less frequently. It had to.

As they drew closer to Hilltop Palace and the night of Starfell, the dirt roads began to fill with people eager to witness the return of Queen Estelle and, as Nett had whispered, experience Starfell the *proper* way for the first time in hundreds of years: in the complete dark, all sunlight tucked away. With a unicorn to protect them all, the citizens of Arden could watch the stars fall without fear of a wraith attack.

The lines of yellow sunlight that slipped through the wooden planks slowly faded away as the sun began to set. Finally, Claire felt the cart turn off the road. They rattled a few more feet before rolling to a stop. Peering out through a knothole in the cart's slats, Claire saw they had arrived at the edge of a forest.

"It's time," Thorn whispered back to them, and Claire pulled away from the knothole. The next several minutes were ones of bumping elbows and stubbed toes against the cart as the four of them pulled on the leather tunics that would mark them as Forger apprentices. When they were done, Thorn clambered to join them in the back of the cart and pulled out a thick coil of rope. Then he looped it around their ankles, knotting them together. Even though Claire had agreed to this plan, anxiety crept across her like a handful of ants. It was one thing to agree to be carried to your enemy tied up; it was another thing to actually do it.

"Everyone set?" Thorn asked. He'd already changed into what Claire thought of as his "princely" outfit: long, loose-fitting shirt with a tunic of royal blue embroidered with

Estelle's moon crest. He'd placed the thin circlet of gold back on his head, holding it in place with a few well-placed knots in his hair.

"Yes," Nett answered a touch too loudly, while Claire and Sena nodded. Sophie, however, kept her eyes fixed on her fingernails. Hurt flashed across Thorn's face, but he gave the group a weak smile and returned to the front of the carriage.

Poor Thorn. Claire had thought it before, but now she was certain: Sophie was purposefully ignoring him. She couldn't really blame Sophie. Out of all of them, Thorn had been closest to Sophie, which meant his lies must have stung her sister all the worse. And now they had to trust him to bring them to an even greater danger.

"Sophie," Claire said, her voice low, "maybe you should stay here, in the forest. If Estelle catches you . . . I mean, it's *your* heart she wants."

Sophie reached out and tucked a wayward curl behind Claire's ear. "Don't think about Estelle," she whispered. "Think about the unicorn instead." Delight danced across her face. "I've never met the unicorn in real life. I was unconscious when you released him from the rock."

Sophie wasn't scared at all! She was excited. Claire didn't know whether to be impressed or exasperated. And before she could make up her mind, there was the crack of reins, and the mare kicked up to a trot. They were on their way.

Sophie scooted over to whisper plans with Sena. Alone, Claire pressed her forehead to the side of the cart and peered out between the planks to watch as they burst out of the forest and into a small meadow flanked by a large hill.

Though a purple twilight streaked across the sky and shadows made everything hazy, she knew exactly what she'd find on that hill. The dark ruins of a castle. A forgotten garden, lush with moss and blossoms in the summer, and in the middle of that garden, beyond a wall of pillars and arches, there would be a well. A way home.

Claire pulled away from the plank. She couldn't think about that now.

As they crossed the meadow, Claire could make out the sounds of other travelers. The clanging shields of a marching Forger regiment, and above the beat of their marching, a thin melody—most likely Spinner singers practicing for their moment before the newly crowned queen. She wondered if Lyric would be wearing the same slippers Claire had sketched on with chalk.

As they clattered into the crumbling courtyard of Hilltop Palace, Nett took Claire's spot by the knothole.

"I see some Tillers I recognize from Greenwood and even Dampwood," he reported. "There are some Forgers in armor and Spinners in costume, but I don't think the Gemmers are here yet."

"Really?" Claire asked, and her spirits lifted slightly. She'd assumed that the Gemmer guild would want to support Queen Estelle, one of their own, but maybe they didn't want to make the mistakes of their ancestors. The Gemmers of the past had a nasty reputation, and rightfully so. They had made life unbearable for many Forgers and harmed the other guilds with their selfish demands.

Patterns form and stories repeat—that's what Estelle as Scholar Terra had said in Starscrape Citadel. But perhaps it was possible to *shift* the story. Break the pattern. Start again . . .

"Maybe the Gemmers are already inside," Sena suggested, and Claire's fragile hope sank back down. If history—like the story of the flute-playing princess who turned into a unicorn—was destined to happen again, then what did that mean for Sophie?

In the dark cart, she felt someone pat her knee. "We got this," Sophie whispered. Her voice was calm, serene, even, but instead of feeling better, Claire felt worse. She would have rather had Sophie tease her, like she would have done before they climbed up the fireplace. But now Sophie was a little *too* knowing. A little too watchful. A little too patient.

The unicorn, Claire repeated in her mind. *Free the unicorn, get the tines, defeat the queen . . . keep Sophie safe. Keep Sophie the same.*

"Halt!" a commanding voice ordered. "State your name and business."

"Prince Thorn, heir of Queen Estelle d'Astora," Claire heard Thorn reply, his tone bored. "I bring some unruly dissidents for Commander Jasper to keep a closer eye on."

Claire heard a commotion as the Royalist must have done a hasty bow. "My apologies, Your Royal Highness, for not recognizing you, but I'm afraid you'll need to leave your prisoners and come with me."

"Why?" Thorn asked as Claire buried her gasp in the crook of her arm. They couldn't be separated from Thorn! She wished she could see what was happening.

"Because," the Royalist said, "by Queen Estelle's command, you, Prince Thorn, are under arrest."

CHAPTER
19

$\mathcal{T}$horn laughed.

How he was able to, Claire wasn't sure, but he laughed as though there was absolutely nothing funnier in all the world than what the Royalist had just said: *Under arrest by order of Queen Estelle.*

Claire felt Sophie's fingernails dig into her leg, and in the dim light, she could see Sena's foot twitch, as though she was preparing to leap out of the cart and fight her way free.

"Is that so?" Thorn asked, his tone mild, as though he were arrested every day. "And may I know why, Flax?"

The Royalist—Flax, as Thorn had called him—clearly wasn't expecting this carefree response. "Y-you were commanded to safely escort the Love Knot Tine to the Hilltop tonight, my prince, but instead you disappeared, and the Love Knot Tine along with you."

"You mean," Thorn said, and Claire heard the soft rustle of fabric as Thorn must have reached into his coat's pocket, "*this* Love Knot Tine?"

Flax gasped, and Claire could imagine his surprise—it was the exact same surprise that had swallowed *her* up when they'd been in Scythe's secret room and Thorn had suggested they sneak into Hilltop Palace as his prisoners.

"How would that even work?" Claire had asked as she'd leaned against one of Scythe's empty shelves. "You disappeared from Needle Pointe, when you were supposed to be escorting the Love Knot Tine to the palace! Queen Estelle won't trust you."

And that's when Thorn had reached into his coat pocket—a special, Spinner-sewn one for secret things—and produced the fake Love Knot Tine. "After I saw you in the lobby, I grabbed the tine before the diamond branches could re-weave themselves. I'm sorry I didn't tell you sooner," Thorn had said to Claire as he handed the tine over to Nett for inspection. "When you told me it was fake, it didn't seem to matter whether I had it or not, but now I think it can come in handy."

Now, Claire could barely breathe as she pressed her ear to the wooden planks, straining to hear what Thorn would say next to the Royalist.

"The Love Knot Tine!" Flax said, sounding slightly awed. "You have it!"

"Of course I do," Thorn said, his words as pointed as a spindle. "And the Forgers I have in here"—there was a thump on the side of the cart—"are the very Forgers who have been harassing Needle Pointe. I caught them trying to steal the Love Knot, but as we're *trying* to get the Forgers to cooperate without a war, I thought it best to keep what happened to myself. Now let me in."

"Y-yes, Prince Thorn," the Royalist guard said, though he still sounded hesitant. "Do you mind, though, if I *see* your prisoners?"

There was a creak, and evening light suddenly filled the cart as Thorn opened the back and stood aside to let the guard peer in. Claire kept her head down, and she was aware of Sena tugging her own Forger's hood tighter around her bright red hair. But their Forger disguises must have worked, because a second later, the guard shut the cart without another look.

"My sincerest apologies, Your Royal Highness," Flax said. "I can take these prisoners while you go explain to Mira Fray, so she can let Her Majesty know. Mira is in the south wing."

"I will keep the prisoners with me, Flax," Thorn said so scornfully that, for a moment, Claire wondered if he was really acting. The Thorn she'd known would never be able to make his voice so cold, his tone so derisive. "No one is taking credit for capturing them other than me."

"That's not what I meant!" Flax cried out, but the rest of his words were lost in the crack of the reins, and the wheels lurched forward—they were in!

The next time the cart stopped, it was behind a crumbling wall, part of what might have once been the stables. "I have to go," Thorn said, looking anxious, his royal act dropped. "If Mira Fray doesn't see me and the Love Knot Tine soon, she'll know something is wrong. If the unicorn is anywhere, I would check the kitchens—they're next to the dungeons but still intact and a good place to hide something as big as a unicorn. The north wing, too." He tugged their knots free, and then he took off into the crowds.

"We should split up," Sophie said as they pulled Royalist cloaks over their Forger outfits. (A jumbled combination of Sophie's spinning skills along with a Grafting Draft in Nett's Hollow Pack had resulted in three exact duplicates of Claire's stolen Royalist cloak.) "We'll cover more ground that way. Claire, you come with me and—"

"That's not a good idea," Sena said, blunt as usual. When Sophie looked at her, the Forger explained. "I mean, Estelle is more interested in the two of you, right? You *definitely* look like sisters. You're more recognizable together."

Claire's heart sank. She'd just been reunited with Sophie, but she knew Sena was right. And from the disgruntled look on Sophie's face, Sophie knew it, too. She gave Claire a quick hug before nudging her toward Sena. Sophie and Nett then stepped into the crowd, heading toward the north wing, while she and Sena moved forward. They would need to cut through some of the bigger ruins in order to reach the old kitchens.

When Claire had first seen Hilltop Palace, she had been too shocked to take in its details—other than the fact that it must be in another world far away from Windemere Manor. Its walls still stood, forming corridors, but there was almost no roof. Claire had the vague sense of rattling inside the rib cage of a giant fossil. One turn and then another and then—

Sena stopped suddenly, and Claire almost smacked into her. "What's wrong?" she asked anxiously. "Is it Estelle?"

Sena stepped aside to reveal a wall of people. They stood, shoulder to shoulder, packing what Claire realized must be the ancient throne room. There seemed to be at least a thousand people, all crammed into the space, their curiosity stamping out any concerns about standing next to someone from another guild.

Tillers clustered together, their green tunics and robes matching the moss on rocks, while the Spinners, dazzling in their costumes of glitter and white, balanced on their toes, trying to see through the congregation. Only the Forgers stood apart, in obedient silver lines, still deciding if tonight would mark a celebration—or the start of a war.

"We need to cross," Sena said. "The old kitchens are on the other side, but there's no way we can make it—"

"*Prrip!*" Gryphin said, hidden in Sena's hood.

Sena stopped. "Oh," she said, sounding embarrassed that she hadn't thought of whatever Gryphin was saying sooner. "Right. Go on, then, Gryphin."

There was quick whirl of wind, and then Claire caught a

shimmer in the air before she completely lost track of the chimera in the darkening sky.

"Gryphin is going to scout for us," Sena whispered. "But come on, maybe if we stick to the edges, we can get closer."

Claire nodded. "Lead the way."

Careful to avoid treading on anyone's toes, they tried to pick their way through Tillers, Spinners, and Forgers. Claire still didn't see any Gemmers, even as they stepped around the tall pillars that had once held up the roof and the sapling trees that grew inside, roots breaking through the patches of flagstone floor that remained.

"Look up when you leap!" Claire heard a familiar voice bark out just as she scooted around a Tiller and saw a troupe of Spinner dancers. "Remember: eyes to the sky, you'll fly—eyes to the ground, you'll stay down. Lyric, are you paying attention?"

"Pardon, Director, just trying to capture the ambiance!" Lyric said, looking up from where she'd been scribbling on a piece of paper with her quill. "Would you say the crowd is more *humming* with excitement or *buzzing*?"

"All I know," the director said warningly, "is that if you don't put your notebook away in the next two seconds, you'll be trying to come up with words to describe the Dance of Ribbons from the wings, rather than performing."

Lyric hurriedly shoved her notebook into her bag, but not before hastily waving the pages so that the ink would dry. As she did, her bright eyes landed on Claire. She frowned. Her mouth opened, but Claire yanked on Sena's tunic, whirling them away into the crowd before Lyric could call out and ruin their cover.

Ducking behind a pillar, Sena and Claire stopped to catch their breath. After all this time, they'd managed only to cross about four yards, and they were no nearer to the front than they had been before.

"This is impossible," Claire said. "We'll never find the unicorn in time!" But at that moment, Sena's arm pushed down slightly, and Claire could just make out a copper gleam before he darted back into the safety of her hood. Gryphin had returned.

A series of chirps sounded, a cascade of fast and furious notes that made Sena's brows furrow as she tried to understand.

"Slow down," she growled quietly to the air, which answered back with a rusty meow. But the chirps did slow down, and Claire's heart began to beat faster as a fierce delight spread across Sena's face.

"Gryphin says there's a new hedge maze in the garden, and a bunch of Royalists are guarding it!" Sena said triumphantly. "The unicorn is probably at its center!"

"*Good* chimera," Claire whispered, and she thought she could hear the chink of metal as the creature must have started to proudly preen copper feathers. The sun had now fully set, but the voices around them had risen. It was only a couple of hours until the star shower would begin, but at least they knew now *where* the unicorn was trapped.

Claire took a deep breath. "We should go," she said to Sena. "We need to find Sophie and Nett—"

She broke off as she realized her words were alone in the complete and sudden silence that had fallen over the ruins. Claire turned back to face the front and saw a line of hooded Royalists walking across the dais, led by the tall, black-haired, spindly figure grasping an obsidian spear tight in his hand: Commander Jasper of Stonehaven.

Claire inhaled sharply. When she'd last seen him, he'd worn the uniform of a member of the Stonehaven Wraith Watch, but now he was in Royalist-blue robes, four rings of white sewn around both sleeves, which meant he was no longer Commander Jasper but *Grandmaster* Jasper.

There were other Royalists she recognized as well: a large man with a club she'd seen on the Sorrowful Plains, a woman with a wreath of woven leaves, and the hunched figure of an old man, with a single bushy eyebrow—Nett's grandfather, Francis Green. Each Royalist carried onto the dais an object that seemed to glow with an inner light: unicorn artifacts.

Claire caught a glimpse of a knife hewn from unicorn bone; a staff inlaid with a glimmer that could only be unicorn ivory; and a drum stretched tight with unicorn hide. There was more—oh, was there more. But Claire couldn't stand it any longer. She let her gaze unfocus as, one by one, the Royalists piled the artifacts on top of each other until all that could be made out was a gleaming mound.

Just when Claire thought the horrible parade would never

end, the last Royalist finally took the dais. Like the others, her cloak hood was down, so Claire could clearly see the ancient and water-thin features of Mira Fray. She took her place at the center of the stage. Beneath her robe, she wore a blue gown that fluttered, despite the fact that there was no breeze in the hall. The fringe and tassels on her dress undulated on their own accord.

Sophie. Claire needed to find Sophie!

But she couldn't move, couldn't breathe, as Mira Fray's voice rolled over the expectant crowd. "All hail the last queen."

Fray did not shout, but her voice was clear and strong, amplified, Claire guessed, by some sort of magic. "All hail the Lady of the Moon, the Guardian of the Guilds, the Sorceress of Stone, the Wrath of the Wraiths, and"—Fray gestured out somewhere beyond the crowd, toward the garden wall—"the Rider of Unicorns."

Fray fell silent, and for a moment, the entire crowed seemed as confused as Claire felt. And then, from a distance, Claire heard the quiet thunder of hoofbeats.

"The garden!" someone shouted. As though they were one creature, the guilds of Arden turned to face the forgotten garden, where a figure galloped toward them.

The rider wore silks of midnight navy, her skirts a billowing ocean over her horse's hide, white as sea-foam. For a second, Claire wondered how she could see the colors so well with the sun already set, but then she realized that the rider and horse racing toward them carried their own light: a clear diamond glow that emanated from the spiraling horn between the horse's ears.

Between the *unicorn's* ears.

Queen Estelle d'Astora had arrived.

CHAPTER
20

At first, Claire thought the roar she heard was simply the rush of blood in her ears. But even though she took deep breaths, the sound would not clear. Instead, it only got sharper until she realized what it was: an entire nation cheering.

An entire world celebrating. Crying. Laughing. Rejoicing.

An entire world—except for Claire and Sena.

Sena's fingernails sank into Claire's arm, and Claire was glad for the pain that cut through her dizziness. What was happening? Sophie had said the unicorn was *captured*, but Claire couldn't see any chains around the creature. And when the queen galloped down the aisle and dismounted at the front, the unicorn stayed put, as quiet and calm as a trained dog, while the crowd's euphoria rose higher and higher.

Starfell ribbons lay forgotten on the ground as Spinners

hugged one another. A Tiller father wiped at the corner of his eye before scooping his daughter onto his shoulders so she could see. Even the Forgers, who seemed more stunned than pleased, had left their weapons dangling harmlessly at their sides, their expressions hungry with hope. And from everywhere and everyone, Claire heard the same words repeating again and again and again: "the unicorn."

The unicorn.

The unicorn!

Claire looked at Sena, and the Forger's amber eyes were so round, she looked more owl than girl. Her lips moved, but Claire couldn't make out what she was saying until Sena leaned in and choked out, *"How?"*

Claire did not know. She did not know how the last unicorn had come to the queen. Or *why* he would allow the murderer of his herd on his back. Unless . . .

Unless Claire had gotten it wrong.

Come on, Sophie's voice groaned in her head. *You* know *what you heard in the Petrified Forest. Estelle* told *you herself that the only useful unicorn is a dead unicorn. Trust yourself!*

Estelle stood before the cheering crowd, letting their joy wash over her. Her gown, encrusted with blue sapphires so dark they were almost black, glittered in the torchlight. Her dark curls had been swept into a silver net, but her head was empty of a crown. She expected a coronation.

The queen held out her hand, and Jasper strode across the dais, his spear in one hand and a cane with a ram's head handle held in the other. Grandmaster Carnelian of Stone-haven's old cane. He presented it to Estelle with a flourish, and when she accepted it, he bowed low, once to her and once to the tranquil unicorn. Claire's thoughts continued to race, trying to find a reason—*any* reason—the unicorn would ally with Estelle, and she finally landed on "Mesmerization," which she whispered to Sena. "Like how Estelle tricked all of Stonehaven."

Sena grimaced. Unicorns were creatures of pure magic. If Estelle was so powerful that she could manage to bend even a unicorn to her will, then what chance did Claire, her friends, and Nadia have against Estelle? The only thing that slightly comforted Claire was the fact that the Spyden had said—

Claire breathed in sharply. The Spyden had said that only a queen *can* defeat a queen . . . not that she *would*.

"We need to break Estelle's control," Sena said harshly, unaware of the storm in Claire's mind. "How does she do it?"

"With—with a Mesmerization Opal," Claire said. "She's probably wearing one."

"Then, we need to get closer." Without waiting for Claire's agreement, Sena threw herself into the crowd, carving a path with her pointy elbows. But they weren't the only ones trying to reach the front. The crowd pressed forward, wanting to be closer to the promised queen. Closer to the unicorn. A chant broke out around them, swelling like a wave that would never break: "Long live the queen! Long live the queen!"

Finally, when Claire thought that the frenzied excitement

of the crowd might crush her, Estelle raised her hands. Her sleeves fell back to reveal pale wrists, and the entire cheering crowd immediately fell silent. At last, Estelle d'Astora addressed her court for the first time in three hundred years: "Welcome."

The single word hit Claire like an arrow, and she stumbled to a halt. Until now, Estelle had been far enough away that she could have been a stranger. But when the queen spoke, her voice, magically amplified, was both familiar and comforting. It sounded of sing-alongs in Starscrape Citadel, encouragement next to a crackling fire, and a warm chuckle when Claire had finally made a ruby spark. It was *Scholar Terra's* voice that resounded over Hilltop Palace.

"Welcome, Forgers; welcome, Tillers; welcome, Spinners; and welcome, Gemmers. Welcome," Estelle said, opening her arms to the crowd, "my dearest Royalists, who have never lost faith, and to all of my beloved Arden."

The crowd roared again, and the sound jolted Claire from her daze. She looked around for Sena—but the crowd had swallowed her whole. Claire was alone in a sea of hundreds that kept pushing forward, sweeping her nearer and nearer the unicorn and the queen, who had started to speak again.

"You know me, Arden, though we have never met," Estelle proclaimed. "You've spoken of me, sung of me, waited for me: the last queen of Arden who used the final drop of her power to spare Arden's last unicorn for a time when the world was ready. For a time of change. That time has come."

The crowd stayed quiet, breathless with excitement, loath to miss anything the queen might say.

"Tonight," Estelle repeated, raising the ram cane like a royal scepter, "I come to you not as a legend from another age but as a leader for this one. Tonight, the Crown of Arden will again be remade, and a new era shall begin. One of infinite possibilities, of wonder, of magic"—she placed her hand on the gleaming arched neck—"of unicorns!"

At that, the crowd thundered so loudly, Claire could feel the timbre of it in her bones. Spinners flung their ribbons into the sky while the night air burst with the scent of lilies and jasmine, roses and hyacinths. Spring flowers that shouldn't have been anywhere close to bloom. Even the Forgers rattled their shields in anticipation. With each new cheer, Claire felt their chances of persuading the Forgers to give them their tine slip away.

Where was Nett? And Sena? And Thorn?

Where is Sophie?

Claire stumbled forward. Only a single regiment of Forgers stood between her and the unicorn now, but they were trained soldiers, and there were no gaps between their shields to let Claire wiggle by. She would need to backtrack. Turning, she tried to slide through the crowd, using her shoulder to push.

Meanwhile, Estelle nodded at Fray, who stepped forward, the unicorn's horn casting a radiant glow on the old woman's face, but there was nothing that could take away the cruel, proud lines etched around her mouth. In her hands she held a pillow, on which sat a black arc: the Love Knot Tine. From where she stood, Claire could not tell if it was the fake tine Thorn had delivered or the true Spinners' tine. Either way, Fray placed it on a broken, waist-high pillar near the queen.

Another Royalist Claire didn't recognize stepped forward. He wore boots of birch bark and beneath his cloak, she could make out a tunic outlined by thorns. Excitement rustled through the Tillers in the crowd as the man, too, presented a cushion with another gleaming arc: the Oak Leaf Tine. It, too, was placed on the pillar.

Finally, Jasper stepped forward and added the Stone Tine to the collection.

At least two, and possibly three of the crown's four tines were within arm's reach of Estelle. She lacked only the Hammer Tine.

Claire's heart pounded. She needed to get to the front! She needed to break whatever Gemmer enchantment hobbled the unicorn.

"My dear Tillers and sweet Spinners, I thank you for your promised allegiance," Estelle said as Claire pushed her way forward. "And now our friends the Forgers shall unite the tines at last, and with the crown's new power, I shall be able to rid Arden of the wraiths—forever!"

The crowd let out a cheer again, but Claire noticed the Forgers remained quiet. They shifted slightly to reveal a man with a round girth and no-nonsense blond cut. He looked so similar to General Scorcha that Claire knew this Forger had to be related.

"Grandmaster Bolt," Estelle said, extending her hand as if she expected it to be kissed. "I am grateful for your allegiance."

"It's a bit early for that." Grandmaster Bolt snorted. "Before we pledge anything or crown anyone, the Forgers have questions—"

"Grandmaster Bolt," Fray cut in, her voice cool, "you see the unicorn, do you not? Each moment you delay, another wraith could attack an innocent!"

"And another Forger's blood could be turned to stone!" Grandmaster Bolt said firmly. He looked at Estelle, his gaze steady above his rather spectacular mustache, which made him look slightly like an armored walrus.

"We concede that you do appear to be the last queen of Arden, who ruled hundreds of years ago. However, for the last month, people of *all* guilds have been discovered frozen in their homes and in their fields, their blood turned to rubies by a rogue Gemmer. If that is not you, madame, then, who is it?"

There was a murmur of assent from the Forgers behind him. The grandmaster continued. "The Forger guild was not treated well by your family in the past, and now the Gemmers are again terrorizing us? Why should we trust you? Why should we give you the Forgers' Tine?"

Fray opened her mouth in anger, her lips contorted in fury, but Estelle held up her hand, silencing the old historian. "I planned for this to be my token of appreciation, but instead, I'll make it my promise to you." She clapped her hands. "Bring out Claire Martinson!"

What? Claire whirled around, expecting to find a cohort of

Royalists standing right behind her. Instead, there was only a cluster of Tillers, each one eager and expectant as they kept their eyes forward. Claire turned back just in time to see Thorn Barley, golden circlet gleaming, emerge from the darkened side of the dais. One fist was held over his heart, but the other held the end of a chain.

Claire choked on a scream. Tears—hot and furious—stormed her eyes as she realized *who* was on the other end of the chain: Sophie.

Thorn tugged, and Sophie stumbled. A white strip of cloth had been tied over her mouth, but the glare she threw at Estelle was as clear as a shout. She *loathed* her. And something had been done to Sophie's hair. Her ponytail no longer fell in an inky slick but poofed out, as though it had been curled to look like—

"This is Claire Martinson," Estelle lied to the crowd as she gestured to Sophie. The blue sapphires of the queen's dress caught the glow of the torchlight, giving each jewel an orange pupil that seemed to watch the courtyard hungrily.

"Don't be fooled by her youthful appearance. This Gemmer apprentice is a friend to the dangerous exile Sena Steele. She helped take the Unicorn Harp from the Tillers, and then, just a few days ago, she attempted to steal the Love Knot Tine. And just tonight, she almost succeeded in snatching these."

Estelle reached for the neckline of her dress and pulled out a chain. Four stones gleamed like stars caught on a hook: the moontears—the Great Unicorn Treasure, Arden's hope—dangled helplessly in the queen's ring-covered hands.

Murmurs broke out as the crowd realized what they were

looking at. Some dropped to their knees, overcome, while others shouted angrily at Sophie, furious that she would attempt something so heinous.

"Fortunately for Arden," Estelle said, tucking the moontears back under her neckline, "our beloved Prince Thorn caught her in the act and brought her to me!"

Claire told herself to breathe. Thorn *had* to be pretending to be on Estelle's side . . . right?

Then Thorn stepped back . . . and bowed low to Estelle.

For the second time that night, Claire thought she was going to throw up. And for a second time since she'd come to Arden, she knew she'd been a *fool* to trust Thorn Barley.

"Claire Martinson is responsible for the attacks on non-Gemmers!" Estelle lied easily. "And though she is of my guild, I vow this very moment that I shall never put Gemmers above any others. Grandmaster Jasper?"

Estelle beckoned Jasper to come toward her. Before he did, though, he checked the chains on Sophie's wrists. Claire expected Sophie to struggle, but instead she seemed to hardly notice him. All her attention was on the unicorn. The unicorn that stood still—and did nothing.

As soon as Jasper turned away from her, Sophie tilted her head and widened her eyes in a very familiar Look. It was the very same Look Sophie gave when she was trying to tell Claire something without Mom and Dad knowing. But now, she wasn't staring at Claire but across the dais, toward Thorn. Then, so quickly that Claire thought she might have made it up, Sophie nodded. A signal?

Before Claire could figure it out, Estelle had slipped a knife out from the ram's head cane. A long knife.

A *carving* knife.

"Kneel," Estelle commanded, and Sophie was pushed to her knees before the queen. Placing long gloved fingers under Sophie's chin, Estelle forced Sophie's face upward, exposing her neck and the bit of collarbone that bore a pale-pink star where the unicorn had touched her, just above her heart.

She needs a unicorn's heart, Thorn had told her. And now she would take it.

As Estelle raised the knife, Claire's breath caught. The queen's plan was as brilliant as it was cruel. Estelle would murder Sophie, right here, in front of everyone, blaming Sophie-as-Claire for the queen's own crimes while taking the unicorn heart she wanted—and *still* seeming to be the heroine of lore.

The knife began to press down, and it was as though it cut through the shock that had frozen Claire.

"NO!" Claire screamed, and with one last shove, she was through and onto the dais! "I AM CLAIRE MARTINSON!"

She'd surprised Estelle. Everyone turned to look at her. Everyone but Thorn. In the two seconds everyone turned to Claire, he'd started sprinting across the dais toward Sophie.

"Stop!" Estelle said, changing the direction of her knife to point it at Thorn. But he dodged it easily, knocking it out of the queen's hand as he ran past both her and Sophie. And that's when Claire realized his real target: the last unicorn.

There was a flash of silver in Thorn's hand: the scissors

Scythe had given him—the ones that could cut through anything. And then they were plunging into the unicorn's white mane. *Snip!*

A horrified wail rose from the crowd as bits of grit, Spyden silk, and unicorn mane slithered to the floor to reveal a plain gray horse.

Now Claire understood why the unicorn had seemed so still and tame. Now she understood why she'd found a Royalist cloak in the Spyden's cottage. The queen, too, had needed the rare silk to craft an illusion strong enough to trick the people of Arden—and to use as bait to lure Sophie to her. Sophie, the *true* last unicorn of Arden.

"Estelle lies!" Thorn shouted to all the guilds of Arden. "It's an illusion—all of it!"

"You," Estelle snarled, and she raised her ram's head cane high. "You vile, horrid little—" But she seemed too angry to finish her sentence as she sliced her arm through the air and the ram's head came hurtling down.

A sickening crack resounded through the throne room as the ram's head connected with bone and flesh. As Estelle pulled her arm back, the ram's horns glittered darkly red. Claire, however, had seen the horns up close and knew they were not inlaid with rubies. That was blood, reflecting in the torchlight.

But it wasn't Thorn's blood.

Thorn still stood, his face white as he looked down at the body of Francis Green crumpled at his feet, a dark stain sprouting from where the ram's horn had pierced the old man's heart.

CHAPTER
21

The stain on Francis's chest grew, sprawling and spreading across his tunic like a wild vine. As Claire watched, the bloody vine seemed to grip everyone on the hilltop, wrapping around their feet so that they could not move, wrapping around their tongues so they could not shout. She—and the Forgers, Tillers, Spinners, and Estelle—stood still, seemingly rooted to the ground, until a cry cut the dark.

"Grandfather!"

A dark shadow stumbled out from behind a pillar and sprinted up the grass-patch aisle to where Francis lay. A low, mournful sound rattled against Claire's skin, as though Nett's pain had become a living thing. The sound vibrated through Claire like the bass of an unadjusted speaker. It didn't seem human.

And then Claire realized: that sound—that wail—it wasn't human. And it wasn't coming from Nett but from beyond the garden wall.

Estelle understood a second before anyone else. "Royalists, at the ready!"

The foundation of the ruins shuddered a final time, and the crowd scattered to reveal an elderly woman gripping onto a lion chimera with her knees, as the Woven Root army sounded its golden trumpets and thundered into Hilltop Palace.

Claire's breath caught at the sight. When she'd left Woven Root, there had been only a handful of the beasts unfrozen. But it seemed that with Nett and Sena and the Steeles' journals, the alchemist handlers had brought life back into at least fifty of the creatures. Copper teeth, copper fangs, copper wings, all streamed through the throne room as easily as sunlight and just as bright. Here and there, though, Claire saw green patches that had not yet been polished, and one chimera—a wolf with a squirrel's tail—still had moss hanging from its snout. It had clearly been wakened only recently, and as Claire watched, she saw its bushy tail wag furiously in sheer delight.

From somewhere far above Claire's head, she heard an excited "*Purr-ka!*"

The guilds, however, had not seen a chimera move in hundreds of years, and they had just seen the last unicorn unravel in front of them.

They panicked.

Tillers' thorny vines suddenly raced up the columns while

Forgers unsheathed their many types of weapons. Meanwhile, the hair on Claire's neck rose as Spinners pulled at the static electricity in their heavy woolen vests. Metal clanged. Wood snapped. Whips cracked.

Chaos reigned.

It was impossible to tell who was doing what, who was fighting whom, and why. Was that a Tiller of Greenwood or a Tiller Royalist? Were those Forgers looking to escape or were they stalking the Spinners? And still, the only Gemmers Claire spotted aside from herself were Jasper and Estelle. What had happened to Stonehaven?

The horse reared, screaming its fright, before slamming down right where Sophie was—or had been. In the confusion, Sophie had disappeared. Her chains, however, lay on the dais.

Sophie. Claire had to get to Sophie!

Claire thrust her hand into her pocket and pulled out the budding pencil. But she didn't know what to do with it. In the roaring, scattered, terrified crowd, no one knew who their enemy was and who was their friend.

"Claire!" someone shouted. A woman's voice.

Claire whirled around and saw a massive lion chimera barreling toward her, Aunt Nadia's gray head peering over its ears. The mayor of Woven Root gave a sharp tug on its copper mane, and the chimera immediately clanged to a stop.

"Claire," Nadia repeated. She leaned down and gripped Claire's hand with her own. "You're safe!" She gave Claire's

hand a quick squeeze, then let go. Auntly duties fulfilled, she asked, "Where's the crown?"

"The tines were up there—" Claire gestured at the dais. "On a broken pillar!"

Nadia nodded sharply. "Get out of here!" she said, leaning forward against the chimera's neck to dodge a spinning dagger. "Go to Greenwood. We've planted Camouflora around it. You'll be safe there!" With that, the mayor dug her heels into the copper sides, and the lion chimera—which Claire had already thought was pretty fast—turned into a copper blur as Nadia charged toward the front.

Grit and dust trickled down from the ceiling, and a few stone blocks clattered near her feet. Claire looked up. The ruins were old, and one wayward Exploding Mulberry could make the entire structure collapse. More gravel fell in front of her, and this time, Claire realized that when the pebbles hit the ground, they didn't stop moving. They jumped and wiggled, like kernels in a frying pan. Frowning, she reached down to pick one up, but as her hand neared the earth, she yanked it back.

Something was wrong. Something was very, very wrong.

The ground—it was *warm*. And Claire felt a hum. But it didn't originate from her. It came from the earth itself. Magic was swelling beneath her feet. And she could feel its *thrum* spread out and sink down, deep . . .

and deeper . . .

and deeper into the earth.

"GET OUT OF HERE!" Claire screamed to nobody and

everybody as she leaped to her feet. She swayed as the hum rattled her knees. "OUT OF THE RUINS!"

But no one paid her any attention. They were too focused on their own battles. Claire began to run. As she sprinted past a group of huddled dancers hiding behind a fallen stone, she managed to scrape out, "It's going to collapse! Out!" She didn't wait for their response but kept running. "Get out! Get out! Get out!"

Her cry was picked up, and she could feel people—Forgers, Tillers, Spinners—begin to rush for the open entryway, the wooden doors long ago rotted away. They spilled out into the courtyard. And still, Claire could feel the hum beneath her feet.

"KEEP RUNNING!" Claire shouted. Around her, she was aware of others fleeing into the night. Her feet pounded the cobblestones of the courtyard as she aimed for the crumbling garden wall. But no matter how fast she moved, she couldn't seem to escape the *thrum* beneath her feet. The earth shuddered—

—Claire could picture what was happening: Estelle, inside, surrounded and protected by her Royalists, aided by the unicorn artifacts that would now be draped across her, raising the ram's head cane high and slamming it down—

—and the world cracked open.

Screams and thumps filled the air as fissures and trenches suddenly laced the garden. Whole trees disappeared as the ground opened up beneath. Claire fell and grasped at the grass as the ground undulated, as though it were a trampoline and not solid at all. From the new cracks in the earth, shadows darker than the night rose up like a black fog and, with them, a cold as bitter as hate: *wraiths*.

Their queen had called them, and they had obeyed.

The wraiths rose up from the newly formed fissures, and Claire realized for the first time that the cracks in the earth's surface weren't natural but followed straight lines and sharp edges. The queen had collapsed the tunnels that must have crisscrossed beneath Hilltop Palace, just as they crisscrossed beneath Starscrape Citadel and the Drowning Fortress—all built by Gemmer architects.

Claire had wondered once before where wraiths dwelled during the daylight hours, and here was the answer: under the earth, away from the sun, the only thing that wraiths feared, aside from a unicorn's horn.

But Sophie had no horn, and the sun was hours away.

The ground continued to tremble, and Claire knew she couldn't stand up yet. And so she began to crawl as fast as she could through the garden, twigs and pebbles jabbing into her knees and palms. Her breath came in fast white puffs as the air grew colder and colder. Wraiths spilled into the garden.

All around her, she was aware of others running, and she wished she could call out to them—to ask them if they were Sophie or Nett or Sena or Thorn or Lyric—but the cold had teeth, and it tore at her. Around her, shouts turned to sobs as the wraiths' cold carved away any memory of warmth or love from the people who couldn't outrun them.

From somewhere nearby, Claire could hear the rusty screech of the chimera as their metal joints froze. She could tell that the riders—those who had managed to stay on—were fumbling for their cotton nets of spun sunlight that could keep the beasts at bay. A few bright bursts broke the night, followed by the inhuman shriek of a wraith hit by a Mulchbomb. But the humans had been surprised, and there were too many wraiths: more than Claire had seen in the Drowning Fortress. More than she had seen on the Sorrowful Plains. And they kept coming.

Claire didn't know when she'd stopped crawling, but she suddenly realized she was face-first in the leaves. She tried to roll over, to look up at the bare branches of fruit trees, but she couldn't move. Her body was frozen, and soon, her mind would be, too. But . . . she was holding out longer than she had before. Now she was aware that though she was cold, the earth still felt warm beneath her, as though Estelle's magic had given it a fever. If only Claire could help heal it. If only she could stitch the fissures back together, maybe she could stop the never-ending swell of shadows.

But some things could not be fixed. Not even with magic.

With that knowledge, Claire cut herself adrift into a tattered darkness.

One without friends or hope.

One without sisters.

"THIS IS FOR MY GRANDFATHER!"

A hot shout cut through the drowning black, pinching Claire, urging her to wake up. To *fight*. She knew that voice. Her first friend in Arden, Nettle Green. *What*, she wanted to ask, *is he doing for Francis?*

And suddenly, the black beneath her eyelids was replaced with gold. Bright, shimmering gold. Claire opened her eyes and saw that the garden was on fire.

With a yelp, she squeezed her eyes shut again, but the image was seared onto her brain: the fruit trees, the overlarge leaves, the rosebushes, the autumn leaves coating the ground, everything was a golden glow—a *sun's* glow.

It wasn't fire. It was sunlight!

Her ears were suddenly warm again, and she could hear the hiss of wraiths in retreat, a sound like ice evaporating in extreme heat. A little more cautiously, she cracked open her eyes, and peering through her lashes, she saw the roiling shadows hissing in pain and tumbling over one another to flee the daylight and dive back into the bowels of the earth.

Sitting up, Claire brought her hand to her eyes, shielding herself from the brightness, even as she tried to look for its source. And there, in the center of all that golden glory, stood the black silhouette of Nettle Green, every inch of his five-foot frame fierce and determined as he pressed his palm against the trunk of a tree and asked if it would like to glow. If it would like to fight back against what had just disturbed its delicate root system and its home of thousands of years.

Nett's other hand was gripped by a girl whose long ponytail whipped in the wind like a victorious banner: Sophie. The garden's light streamed out from around her like a halo, radiating over the entire hilltop, making everything that was previously unseen visible. And though Sophie still looked like Sophie, Claire felt that maybe she was already more unicorn than girl. Someone who was pure magic and made all magic stronger.

Nett pulled back his hand, and slowly the sunlight trickled out of the plants, and the night's blue darkness settled over them all again. But now the chimera and their riders had recovered, and the alchemists had their nets ready. With triumphant shouts, they galloped at the remaining dregs of the wraiths, sweeping them away from the people who were slowly staggering to their feet.

Claire closed her eyes. She was so exhausted, she thought she might pass out right there.

"Claire!" She felt a tug on her shoulder, and looking up, she saw that Sophie was pulling at her. Nett and Sena were already streaking ahead. "We need to retreat. The wraiths might not be able to withstand sunlight, but the Royalists can."

Claire nodded, understanding what her sister was saying. She let Sophie yank her to her feet. And that's when she saw it.

She almost fell back down again. "Sophie," she croaked out. "The *well*."

The old stone well was no more. Smashed like a dropped cake, its stones lay on the ground like discarded crumbs.

"I know," Sophie said, and Claire could hear tears in her

words. "Later. We'll deal with it later." Her voice hitched. "We need to get to Greenwood."

Gripping hands, the Martinson sisters ran down the hill—alongside a torrent of terrified Tillers, Spinners, and Forgers—toward the lanterns that waved above a brand-new hedge. Panting, they surged through the leafy embrace and stepped into an Arden that would never be the same.

CHAPTER
22

Later, Claire would never quite remember how she came to be in the chaos of Greenwood's Hearing Hall. All she knew was that one moment, she was running through the newly planted Camouflora, and in the next, she was standing beside Sophie while people rushed about, shouting instructions and carrying in the wounded from the hilltop.

The Hearing Hall was a testament to Tiller talent, a building that had been grown instead of built. Tree trunks formed the walls of the space, and their branches arched upward and inward to form a leafy roof. Though most of the leaves in Arden had fallen, the branches of the Hearing Hall still retained their autumn splendor. It had been decorated for Starfell with garlands of paper stars draped from the ceiling, and the benches had been scooted to the sides to make room for round tables heaped with Tiller delicacies: powdered cookies in the shape of snowdrop flowers, sweet breads filled with jam, flaky spinach pies, and pitchers of sparkling chrysanthemum juice.

But no one was touching them.

Anxious children wearing festive star wreaths were herded out of the hall, while grown-ups turned benches into makeshift beds. Spinners frantically pulled out quilts for those shivering with wraith-burn, and Forgers hammered heat into coins before pressing them into hands blue with cold. Voices called for help, and footsteps pounded as healers from all guilds rushed to attend as many as they could, no matter the guild.

"What should we do?" Claire asked, stepping out of the way of a Tiller sprinting through with jars of an inky purple liquid. "And what happened to the tines?"

But Sophie didn't seem to have heard her. Her sister was standing on her toes, looking frantic. "Do you see Thorn anywhere?"

Claire's stomach dropped. She knew she'd seen Sena and Nett running in front of them, even if she didn't know where they were now, but Thorn . . . she hadn't seen him at all.

"If he's alive," Sophie said, spinning around, neck craned, "I'm going to *murder* him!"

"What, why?" Claire asked. Her index finger tapped nervously against the pencil she'd pulled out of her pocket. "He helped us, Sophie! You can't *still* be mad at him!"

"Oh yes I can," Sophie said. She looked left and right. "I'm beyond mad! I'm— *THORN!*"

Claire jumped and shifted slightly to see the gangly figure of Thorn Barley just entering the Hearing Hall. One arm was clutched to his chest, holding something tight, while his other hung strangely at his side, limp. Dirt streaked his face and his blond hair was matted with leaves. But as he turned in the direction of Sophie's voice, Claire thought that he had never looked more heroic.

And then Claire saw what Thorn was cradling in his unbroken arm: two tall points, one with an oak leaf stamped on it, while the other held a gemstone.

Two tines.

One half of the Crown of Arden.

Before Claire could fully register what she was seeing, she felt a draft against her arm, and she was suddenly aware of Sophie taking off, streaking across the hall. Thorn stood frozen, seemingly stunned, as Sophie charged him.

"HOW DARE YOU, THORN BARLEY!" Sophie was shouting. "OF ALL THE RECKLESS, ASH-BRAINED, GRAVEL-HEADED THINGS TO DO!"

Oh, no.

"Sophie, don't!" Claire called and broke into a run herself, chasing after her sister. Thorn was *definitely* going to need help managing Sophie in this temperament. Sophie wasn't slowing down, even as she got nearer to Thorn. Was she going to run him over?

But Thorn didn't move. He stood his ground, though Sophie was going to slam into him in three strides. He held out his unbroken arm with the tines in his hand and then—

Claire stumbled to a halt.

Sophie had flung her arms around Thorn and was kissing him. On the lips. Right there, in front of everyone!

And Thorn—he was kissing her back!

Claire, standing behind her sister, didn't know where to look.

"*Purr-ka*!" A soft weight landed on Claire's shoulder and Gryphin nestled next to her neck.

"I thought she hated him?" Claire whispered to Gryphin. The chimera just purred. And then, rising up onto his lion hindquarters, he stood on Claire's shoulder and let out a piercing screech.

Claire's ear rang, but Sophie and Thorn had broken apart at last. And Sophie—her cheeks pink but not nearly as pink as Thorn's ears—casually brushed a strand of hair out of her eyes and turned to face Claire and Gryphin. "Yes?"

Gryphin launched himself into the air, along with a series of chimes and whistles. While Sophie listened, Thorn held the tines out to Claire. "They're real, aren't they?" he asked, sounding surprisingly shy. "The tines?"

With trembling fingers, Claire accepted the two crown pieces. The tines looked as they had in the pencil's memory— the Gemmers' stone on one peak and the Tillers' oak leaf on the other. But more than looking right, they *sounded* right. Though the song was not as clear as it had been in the pencil's memory, it was still there, alive beneath her fingertips.

"Yes," Claire breathed. "Oh, Thorn—you did it!" Now all they needed was to convince the Forgers to give them the

Hammer Tine, and, of course, find the Love Knot Tine, but they were so much closer than before! "Sophie," Claire said, "look, it's— Sophie? What's wrong?"

The happiness that had lit Sophie's face only moments before had vanished, and Gryphin was already soaring out of the Hearing Hall.

"It's Francis," Sophie said shortly and broke into a jog. "We need to hurry." Claire immediately followed, holding the tines tight in her hands. Thorn stayed back, looking unsure if he was included in the "we," but Sophie paused and, reaching out, laced her fingers in his and pulled him to the great doors.

The three jogged into the night, following the gleam of moonlight reflecting off copper wings. Other than the thinnest of crescent moons, the night sky was still an inky black. The star shower had not yet begun.

They reached the cottage at the very edge of the forest just as a Tiller healer exited. The healer's face was grim, and Claire and Sophie didn't bother to ask what was wrong as they hurried inside.

Flames flickered in the fireplace, and someone had lit candles and set them on the long worktable that took up most of Francis's home. The straw pallets that had been Sena's and Nett's had been piled onto the grown-up-sized trundle bed, making it extra cushiony. Two heads, one black and one auburn, bent over it, but at the sound of Gryphin's wings, they looked toward the door.

Recent tears shimmered on Nett's cheek, while Sena's eyes were rimmed in red.

"Who is it?" a tired voice asked from somewhere beneath the pile of quilts and pillows.

"It's Sophie, Claire, and Thorn, Grandfather," Nett said. His eyes widened slightly. "And—is that half of the crown?" Both he and Sena looked ready to explode into questions, but at that moment, Francis began to cough, an ugly rasping that sounded like sandpaper across stone. Answers would have to wait.

"Ah." Francis sighed softly once the fit had subsided. "Come in, come in." The old Tiller was small against his pillows. His chest barely went up and down, and his skin seemed as fragile as tissue paper. But his eyes when he looked at them were still bright under his single bushy eyebrow.

"Hello, Mr. Francis," Claire whispered as they drew near.

"Just Francis," he corrected with a small smile. "No need to whisper, though."

Claire ducked her head, feeling shy and uncomfortable. To hide her awkwardness, she set the Oak Leaf Tine and Stone Tine among the broken bits of pottery and piles of soil on the worktable. Nett and Sena, meanwhile, scooted to make room for Sophie and Claire to join them on the bench that had been pulled up to the bedside. Sophie slid in, but Claire hung back, not really sure what to do. Sophie's face was composed, though. Without a word, she slipped her hand into Francis's, and the pinched look that had been on the old Tiller's face seemed to loosen just a bit.

"Martinson sisters," he said, "I've been thinking about you." He struggled to sit up against the pillow, but Sophie shook her head, the single white streak in her hair glittering like a tear.

"You need to rest," Sophie said firmly. "You need to get better."

Francis ignored her and pulled himself up anyway. "I have so many things to say, the first of which is that I'm sorry. From the depths of my heart, I apologize. I made a grave mistake."

At his words, Claire realized how tight she'd been holding herself. Anger, sadness, fear, hope, despair—all these emotions had been threading through her, and she'd gathered each bit, wrapping them into a tight ball that sat heavily on her chest. But at Francis's apology, it unraveled.

"Why did you do it?" Claire asked, unable to sit. "*Why* were you going to let the Royalists kill Sophie that night on the Sorrowful Plains?"

"I never thought they intended to kill her," Francis said, bringing his eyes away from Sophie's and to her. "But I am a foolish old man, who was so focused on making the past come back that I ignored what was happening in the present. I dreamed of the old days. Of when guilds could mix freely and my dear friend Mathieu wouldn't be condemned for falling in love with a brilliant and beautiful Forger and forced to abandon their bright daughter. Of a time when wraiths were few and wraith-made orphans even fewer, so that my son and daughter-in-law could have seen what a kind and clever soul their son has grown into."

Claire looked at Nett. The tip of his nose was red as tears

rolled down his cheeks. Sena wrapped an arm around his shoulder. Her eyelashes were wet.

"I dreamed," Francis continued, his eyes landing on Thorn, who had also remained standing, "of a time when no one was considered lacking. And"—his gaze flitted to Sophie—"of unicorns." He breathed in, and the breath seemed to rattle around his rib cage rather than in his lungs. Eyes still on Sophie, he said, "I'm not asking for your forgiveness. I'm only telling you my dream so that maybe you can keep fighting for it."

Another deep breath. "I look around at the five of you. And I *hope*. A Tiller with a Forger sister. A Forger with a Spinner friend. And a Gemmer, working to fix the mistakes of the past."

The certainty in Francis's voice was too much.

"But I *can't*," Claire said, her voice cracking. "We might have half of the Crown of Arden, but we still don't know where the *real* Love Knot Tine is and the Forgers seem unlikely to have *anyone* be their queen—legendary or otherwise!"

Claire wrapped her arms around herself as her overwhelming emotions and memories of the night threatened to burst out. "Meanwhile, Estelle has the Royalists, who believe her. She controls the wraiths. She has the moontears! And the unicorn I freed is trapped somewhere, and we can't find him!" The others looked at her, their expressions bleak, all except Francis.

"Nett, Sena, help me up," Francis said, pushing off the quilts. Clean dressings had been applied to his chest wound, the bandages seeming expertly wrapped by a Spinner of high level. "Come, take me outside."

"You—you want to garden now?" Nett asked, puzzled.

"You're not strong enough," Sena protested.

"I'm strong enough for this," Francis said, swinging a trousered leg over the bed's side and pulling on a thick green robe. "Will you help me or not?"

Using Nett, Sena, and, eventually, Thorn's good arm, Francis was able to hobble out of the candlelit cottage and into the night. When Sena and Nett asked him to sit on a quilt in the pumpkin patch, Francis shook his head. "No, take me to the north wall of the cottage."

Sena and Nett exchanged confused looks, but they did as they were told, and the group headed around the cabin. Still using his grandchildren for support, Francis leaned forward, examining the ivy that grew over the cottage and its wooden planks. After a moment, Francis plunged his hand into the leaves. First his wrist disappeared, and then his elbow, and then his entire arm. Claire blinked. She had no idea ivy could be so thick.

"What are you doing?" Sophie asked, curious.

Francis, panting heavily from even the simple act of standing, didn't have the breath to answer, so Nett did instead. "It's Concealing Ivy," he said. "It's a very loyal plant, passed down through generations. Anything hidden in its leaves can only be retrieved by a member of the family."

Francis huffed and puffed and then withdrew his hand. It was empty. "It's in there," he said, "I can feel it, but I'm afraid I need to sit. Nett, Sena, can you try?"

Sena shook her head. "But I'm not—"

"Hush, Sena," Francis said. "You are as much my grand-daughter as Nett is my grandson. Of course the Concealing Ivy will recognize you."

Sophie hurried to take Sena's place next to Francis. Nett plunged his hands into the leaves without a second thought, while Sena was more cautious. Claire saw the look of wonder on the Forger girl's face as her hand slipped in easily.

"What are we looking for?" Nett asked.

Francis opened his mouth, but only a wheeze came out.

"We'll find it," Sena said firmly. "You relax." Rolling up the sleeves of their Forger disguises, she and Nett got to work, while Thorn, Sophie, and Claire guided Francis to a grassy spot in his vegetable patch. Once settled, the old man managed a ragged "Thank you."

"I'm the one who should be thanking you," Thorn said, sitting down next to him. A leaf still clung to his hair. "You— you saved my life."

Francis managed a small smile. "Your grand would have *murdered* me if I had let anything happen to you." He grimaced, and the wrinkles of his face deepened. "Estelle is doing the opposite of what your grand, me, the Royalists dreamed of. The Royalists were a society dedicated to the *eradication* of wraiths. We thought that by waking the last queen of Arden, we would rid ourselves of the shadow scourge. Instead, they only seek to do her bidding."

He broke into a fit of coughs, the price for all his words.

For a little bit, they were all silent as they watched Sena and Nett pry deeper into the Concealing Ivy.

"How does Estelle do it?" Sophie asked suddenly, turning to Francis. "How does she control the wraiths?"

Francis was slow to answer, his breath shallower with every exhale, but at last he managed a few whispered words. "The queen promised to reunite the wraiths with the sun."

"Diamonds above!" Sophie's mouth dropped open and Thorn looked as sick as Claire felt. If the wraiths could withstand sunlight, then all of Arden was in danger. Everyone would soon look like that poor wraith-burned boy she'd seen in Fyrton. "How is she going to do that?" Sophie demanded.

"Not sure," Francis said. He was so quiet, Claire could hardly hear him above the rustling ivy leaves. "I think it has something to do with her want of a unicorn's heart."

"But why?" The question flew from Claire before she could stop it. "I don't get it. She's so terrible—what she wants is awful for everyone! Why do the Royalists still follow her?" Claire asked, and let her tone carry her other accusation. *Why did you?*

"Some because of fear," Francis said. "Others because of power. Once you've had a sip, it's hard to never thirst for it."

There was a sudden commotion at the cottage wall as Sena let out a small yelp. "Francis! Is it—?!"

Whatever Sena had found in the Concealing Ivy had left her speechless. A smile appeared on Francis's face as Sena slowly began to withdraw her arm from the ivy. At first, Claire thought that Sena was so happy that she was singing, but then she realized the girl's lips were closed, and the song was coming from the ivy. A familiar song, one she'd heard before in a pencil's sketched memory. A moment later, a bundle wrapped in rags broke loose from the leaves.

"Dogwood's bark," Nett gasped as Sena unwrapped the rags to reveal the ebony point of the Love Knot Tine. *"How?"*

Francis opened his mouth to speak, but a sputtering cough came out instead. Thorn ran inside to grab a soothing tincture from the bedside table, as well as a quilt. Together, the children tucked it around the old man.

"I think I know how," Claire said, at last taking the Love Knot Tine from Sena's hands. The same bursts of song echoed against her skin. Thinking of what Lyric had told her, Claire slowly pieced it together. "Some Royalists went to Needle Pointe a couple of weeks ago to check on the Love Knot Tine and build extra protections around it. Francis—you were one of the Royalists who went, right?"

He nodded, but Claire needed to be certain. "You were the Tiller who helped craft the jumbled Diamond Tree Vault, the one that could only be opened by the queen's hand? But you switched out the Love Knot Tine with the fake to delay Estelle in becoming even *more* powerful."

Francis nodded. His lips moved, and Claire leaned forward to make out the barely formed words. "I knew I had to stop what I had done," Francis said. "I knew I had to help."

At his words, Claire felt the last of her anger recede. But she didn't know what to say. What words would be enough.

So instead, she reached for his hand and squeezed, trying to convey all her emotion in that one little gesture. He squeezed back. Francis understood.

"I can fix this," Sophie said suddenly, loudly. "I can fix you!" She looked down at her hands. "I'm not sure how exactly, but I've healed Claire's ankle." She stopped as Francis shook his head.

"Sophia," he said, quiet as the moon. "Some things are beyond even unicorns."

Claire turned away from the pained expression on Sophie's face. And as she did, a flash momentarily illuminated the garden. A storm was rolling in. But then—

"Children," Francis whispered, "the sky!"

Claire looked up, expecting to see clouds, but instead she saw a clear canvas of dark, broken by a single burst of light. Then another. And another. And then a night that had only an hour ago been filled with screams now sang with starlight.

"Spectacular," Sophie breathed, seemingly unaware that the brightness of these falling stars matched the newly bright silver ring in her eyes, and Claire wondered for a moment how the queen's illusion could have ever fooled her. Unicorns weren't just horns and silky manes; they were creatures made of the same fire that burned in stars.

From somewhere up the path, Claire could hear far-off cheers, as all of Arden looked up. She didn't know how long she sat there, in a vegetable patch with her friends, the Love Knot

Tine in her hands. It could have been seconds. It could have been hours.

At some point, though, a breeze full of winter's promise brushed Claire, pulling her back to the earth. Only then did she realize that Nett and Sena were staring down at Francis, whose eyes remained fixed upon the stars he could no longer see.

Nett bowed his head, and Sena began to weep.

CHAPTER
23

The wind picked up. Claire's hair blew into her eyes, but she didn't bother to brush it or her tears away. Her arms felt too heavy to move, and her entire body ached, as though she had the flu. She wanted Mom. She wanted Dad. She wanted—

"Claire," Sophie said quietly. "Do you hear that?"

Claire dragged her eyes away from Sena and Nett, who'd remained huddled close to Francis. She wasn't sure how much time had passed, but the stars were still falling, and she sensed dawn was still an hour or two away.

"Hear what?" she asked, voice thick. But before Sophie could answer, Claire heard it, too.

Claiiire? Soooophie?

Someone was calling their names. Claire had the sudden memory of another time she and Sophie had been off alone.

Sophie had just climbed a few rungs on the ladder, her turquoise sneakers disappearing the moment before Dad poked his head into the gallery. Claire's heartbeat sped up. Could it be—?

"Claire! Sophie! Where are you?"

It wasn't Dad after all. Claire's heart returned to its normal rate as disappointment seeped in, even though she *knew* she was being foolish. After all, how would Dad find them in Arden with the old stone well destroyed? And what had happened on the other end, to the fireplace? Did it still exist at all?

"We're over here!" Sophie cut through the ever-darkening turn of Claire's thoughts. "Here!" She waved her arms in the direction of the fields, and a few seconds later, Lieutenant Ravel and his chimera, Serpio, came into view. Ravel was Nadia's second-in-command, and though he was a Spinner, he was a talented chimera keeper. Gryphin poked his head up, intrigued by the larger chimera, but he stayed where he was, wrapped around Sena's neck, as the rider lurched to a stop.

"You're all right!" Ravel said, his many loops and braids bouncing as he leaped off Serpio and ran over to them. "And Sena and Nett, too! Nadia's been so worried."

"Where is Aunt Nadia?" Sophie asked, wiping a bit of dirt from her palm onto her purple dress and standing up. "Is she all right?"

"She will be when she sees you," he said. Ravel's cloak billowed a bit in the wind and Claire caught a glimpse of his oakwood woven tunic, which doubled as warmth and protection, and the whip coiled on his hip. "If you're not hurt, she needs to see you in the Seed Cellar. She, Scythe, and the grandmasters are . . . are talking." By the way he said "talking," Claire knew he meant "arguing." "Nadia—*everyone*—has questions for you."

"Will they listen to *alchemists*?" Sophie asked sharply as Claire scrambled to her feet, brushing bits of leaves and twigs from her trousers.

Ravel grimaced. "They said they would, yes. I think we can thank the Camouflora for that. It's keeping everyone safe tonight from another attack." He gestured out to the fields, and Claire could just make out peaks of fabric and leaves. Woven Root was setting up their tents in a protective circle around Greenwood Village, settling as close to the Camouflora as possible to keep an eye on it. Here and there, Claire even saw a flash of copper as alchemists and their chimera patrolled the village borders.

Sophie nodded. "Yes, we'll come but . . ." She trailed off, looking in Sena and Nett's direction. Suddenly, Ravel seemed aware of the still quilt next to them.

"I'm so sorry," Ravel said, and though his words were simple, Claire could feel their honesty. Nett seemed to as well, because he nodded.

"Thank you," he said. "If you could just help us carry him back inside, we can go."

"You don't have to," Claire said gently. Nett looked wilted, as though he needed some sunshine and water. "Sophie and I can do it."

"We *do* have to," Sena said, and Claire was glad to hear fire in her friend's voice, even if her expression still seemed lost. "And you have to bring that"—she looked meaningfully at the rag-covered bundle still in Claire's arms—"and the others to Nadia. There's nothing more important."

The inside of the Seed Cellar looked like a snail's shell. Everything was gentle curves and circles, and the roots of the Hearing Hall directly above wove together to form a delicate lattice to stop the dirt ceiling from caving in on them. Here and there, roots dropped down to create sprawling chandeliers, with little tea-light candles perched comfortably in their bends and crooks. The overall effect was cozy—or it would have been, had the round table in the center of the cellar not been occupied by scowling adults.

"This is absurd!" Grandmaster Bolt was shouting as Claire and her friends followed Ravel into the room from the dirt stairs. "Why should we believe anything a group of outlaws says?" The Forger grandmasters seated closest to him all nodded, their eyes as hard as the silver breastplates they still wore.

"Because those alchemists—outlaws, as you call them—just saved all of you from crowning a fraudulent queen?" Scythe shot back. He looked even larger in the cramped curves of the cellar than he had in Fyrton. His hand was balled into a fist and his face was flushed, as though it was taking every ounce of will not to smack the table. "Stop being so stubborn, Bolt!"

"Scythe, please," Nadia said, rubbing her temples. Claire's great-aunt sat at the top of the table. She was a small woman, hardly taller than Claire herself, but Nadia's white hair fluffed out around her head, giving her a few more inches. Usually, she wore a haphazard wreath of leaves, wire, string, and gems, but tonight her wreath had been set aside in favor of the copper helmet that now rested by her elbow. Her expression seemed pained.

"And Grandmaster Bolt, there's no need to— Ah, children!" Nadia's face brightened as Ravel nudged Claire and her friends forward. "*They* can help explain! Grandmasters, my nieces, Sophia and Claire Martinson, and their friends Nettle Green and Sena Steele."

If Grandmaster Bolt had seemed angered before, now he looked furious. "We're supposed to believe the word of *Sena Steele*? The exile who not only illegally entered Fyrton *twice* but also stole the Tillers' Unicorn Harp?" He shook his head as the other Forgers around him murmured their disapproval. "The Grand Council proclaimed her guilty just last month! This is preposterous!"

A cat's hiss resounded through the room, and a few tea lights snuffed out as Gryphin, previously tucked beneath Sena's braid, launched himself at the Forger. It was only due to Scythe's lightning-quick reflexes that Grandmaster Bolt kept both eyes.

"What's preposterous, Bolt," Scythe said, trying to hold onto a squirming Gryphin, "is exiling a Forger with so much talent just because her father was a Tiller! It's just as preposterous as trying to lock up Sylvia Steele, one of the best locksmiths Arden has ever seen."

Sena snapped her fingers, and Gryphin instantly stilled, though his rounded ears lay flush against his head in a lion's sulk. He let out one last chirp, and Sena grinned.

"He says he's hungry, grandmaster," Sena said, her voice dangerously polite. "And that you look delicious."

Nett looked positively horrified at what his sister had said, but Claire felt relieved. Though Sena always projected unrelenting confidence, Claire knew that when it came to the Forger guild, she was as sensitive as one of Sophie's failed attempts at a soufflé. It seemed, however, that her training in Woven Root had soothed the sting of the Forger guild's rejection.

"Hmph," Grandmaster Bolt said, far from appeased. But his eyes had landed on something even more offensive than Sena Steele: Thorn Barley, who'd just managed to squeeze through the door and into the crowded room.

"What is the lackie princeling doing here?" Bolt demanded. "He could be spying for Estelle!"

"No one here is lacking anything except for manners," Sophie snapped, glaring at the grandmaster.

Bolt glared right back. "And I suppose you're going to tell us the same story Nadia and Scythe just did, a nonsense tale involving lost descendants of Prince Martin and a Spyden?"

"As a matter of fact, *I'm* not," Sophie said, grabbing Claire's hand and pulling her forward. "*She* will. She's the one who spoke to the Spyden, after all." She gestured to Claire. As all eyes turned to Claire, she once again felt as she did before at the Tiller Council: confused and woefully out of place.

"Sophie," Claire whispered urgently, "I'm not the story-teller—you are!"

"Go on, Claire," Sophie whispered. "I believe in you."

Scythe pushed back his wooden chair and, standing up, gestured for Claire to take his spot next to Nadia. Reluctantly, Claire slid in and took her place at the circular table, while Sophie, Nett, Sena, and Thorn scooted so that they stood right behind her. Looking around, she realized she recognized many faces: the director of Needle Pointe, Grandmaster Bolt, General Scorcha, and Grandmaster Iris, as well as a few other Tillers, and alchemists from Woven Root. But still . . .

"Where are the Gemmers?" Claire asked.

"An *excellent* question," a Tiller grandmaster with squinty eyes piped up.

Nadia hastily spoke over her. "They're fine, Claire, for now." She pushed an untouched plate of snowdrop cookies toward Claire. They were shaped just like the little springtime flowers that sprang up in a unicorn's hoofprints, but there was no way Claire could eat, not when it felt like her stomach was doing the polka.

"According to my scouts," Nadia continued, "shortly after you left Stonehaven, Jasper challenged Carnelian for the grandmastership. Jasper lost, though the Gemmering he threw at Carnelian was destructive enough to break Estelle's Mesmerization on all of Stonehaven. Estelle, however, is *furious* that the Gemmers won't join her, and so she's sealed them behind the Everless Wall. Anyone currently in there can't get out—and no one can get in." A troubled expression darted across Aunt Nadia's face. "Supplies, we suspect, are low."

"I've had enough of Gemmers," Grandmaster Bolt growled, and the sound was so bearlike, Claire wondered for a second if it hadn't come from the etched bear on his breastplate. "And I've almost had enough of this conversation, too. Scythe claims Nadia needs to be crowned, but with three of the four tines most likely destroyed in the magical earthquake, that question appears moot."

"Actually," Sophie said, and Claire felt the warm press of her sister's hands on her shoulders, "it's not. Claire?"

As carefully as though she were unwrapping a precious oil painting, Claire pulled the rags away from the bundle she held. Gasps filled the pine-scented space as the Spinners' Love Knot, Tillers' Oak Leaf, and Gemmers' Stone tines glittered in the chandelier's tea lights.

Bolt seemed at a loss for words, his mustache framing a round O of surprise. Reaching behind his breastplate, he pulled out the fourth and final tine: the Hammer. But he did not put it with the others. He gripped it in his vice-like fist.

"All right," the Spinner director said, tilting his head at Claire. His splendid white velvet doublet and matching cape had somehow managed to survive the queen's attack unscathed, but his white-blonde hair still looked a bit like an exploded firework. "You have our attention. I would like to hear what this girl has to say because, if I'm not so mistaken, she and I have met before, yes?" He raised an eyebrow at her. "In the Historium?"

"Er, yes," Claire said with a blush. "That's right."

"Then tell, why do we need to crown Nadia?"

Nerves swept through her again, but Sophie placed a hand on her shoulder, and it felt for a moment like Sophie had adjusted her sails, keeping Claire upright. They were *so close* to completing the Crown of Arden! Just one more explanation, and Nadia could become queen.

The pressure pushed on Claire's stomach, but the fire crackled as though it were cheering her on. Claire took a deep breath and began. "I had never seen a ladder in a fireplace . . ."

Slowly, she told them everything, the truth behind Queen Estelle and her brother, Prince Martin, and who she, Sophie, and Nadia were to him. She told her story, all of it, letting the secrets unspool from her. With each one she cast off, she felt lighter. She only held one thing back: that Sophie was a unicorn.

Finally, she told them about her arrival in Needle Pointe and how the Spyden had told her that the only way to stop Estelle was with another queen, and what Estelle wanted: to make her wraith army able to withstand the sun.

Horrified gasps erupted around the table.

"If we are going to stop Estelle and the wraiths from taking over," Claire said, raising her voice and keeping her eyes on the tines, which in the candlelight seemed more like broken off bits of darkest seawater than points on a crown, "Nadia *must* be made queen."

Silence filled the Seed Cellar, and Claire wondered if she had done enough.

"One thing I don't understand, though," a Tiller grandmaster said slowly. "Is why it must be *Nadia* who is crowned. Why can't it be, for instance, me? Or General Scorcha or Grandmaster Bobbin?"

"I, well," Claire said, flustered. She'd been so focused on *what* she must do, she hadn't given much thought to the *why*. So she said the first thing that came to her mind. "Because Nadia is the oldest d'Astora. She's the heir!"

Immediately, Claire knew she'd said something wrong. The Grandmasters began to whisper among themselves, and the sound was like angry hornets.

"A fancy name and royal blood is not a good enough reason," Grandmaster Bolt snarled.

"But they were when Estelle showed up?" Sophie demanded. Her fingers, which she'd been resting on Claire's shoulders, now dug into Claire's skin with a painful squeeze.

Bolt looked down at Sophie with distaste. "We *asked* Estelle to prove herself. *She* promised us a unicorn."

Sophie opened her mouth and for one terrible moment, Claire thought Sophie was going to do something brave and foolish and very, very rash. But then, she looked at Claire and took a deep breath. "But Mayor Nadia *has* proven herself," Sophie said, her voice quiet. "Unlike the rest of you, Mayor Nadia has led a coalition of jumbled magic peacefully for *years*."

"And," Nett said, his usually bright voice dark with annoyance, "she's overseen magic the likes of which hasn't been seen since the days of King Anders the First!"

"Under her leadership, the chimera are even waking up again," Sena pointed out.

The murmurs around them grew, and Claire sucked in her breath. Had they done it? Did everyone believe them?

"You're very convincing," the director said, looking at Claire. "A talented storyteller, for a Gemmer . . . but we have no reason to believe you." He reached across the table and plucked the Love Knot Tine from the middle of it. To Claire's dismay, more heads nodded in the cellar. For once, the Forgers, Tillers, and Spinners were all in agreement—and they were all in agreement against *her*, her friends, and Nadia.

General Scorcha nodded. "We have no need of queens, or royal blood." She stood up from the table, her head narrowly missing a chandelier root. "Whatever strangeness is afoot, the Forgers will face it as Forgers always do: alone. We'll leave as soon as the sun rises and the wraiths clear."

Grandmaster Bolt put the Hammer Tine back beneath his breastplate, and then the grandmasters from the other guilds stood up as well. A Tiller Grandmaster picked up the Oak Leaf Tine. Now only one tine gleamed on the table.

"No, wait!" Claire said, her voice lost among the scraping

of the chairs as the tines seemed to blow away as easily as dry leaves. Tears pricked her eyes. "*Please!* You can debate this matter until the moon falls out of the sky, but it doesn't change what is true. Believe us or not, ignore us or not, it doesn't change the Spyden's words. *Only a queen can defeat a queen.* Without a queen of our own, we will lose, because Estelle *is* from the legends. She *does* control the wraiths. And she *will* attack again."

The grandmasters paused, and Sophie stepped forward. "Will you give yourselves a chance to save your home?" she demanded. "You've already lost magic! You've already lost unicorns. Do you want to lose Arden forever?"

Claire knew they had heard her sister. She was right *there*! But it was as though Sophie was painted with Invis-Ability and the Forgers were wearing Lyric's earmuff braids. The guilds continued to march out of the cellar and Claire—Claire had failed to convince them. She stared at the empty spot next to the snowdrop cookies where three of the tines had gleamed only moments ago.

"It's all right, girls," Nadia whispered. "You tried. And who knows? Perhaps the Spyden's words have another way of coming true."

But Claire wasn't listening. She kept staring at the plate of flower-shaped cookies as a memory surfaced. A memory of white blossoms growing among the autumn leaves, right below strands of silver caught in a higher bush.

"Grandmasters!" Claire called out one final time. Her heart pounded furiously in her chest. "What if we showed you the last unicorn—the one from Unicorn Rock, not a Spyden silk illusion—would you believe us then? Would you crown Nadia?"

Grandmaster Bolt and General Scorcha exchanged a Look. "If you can show us a real, true unicorn—proof of your story," the general said, "then, yes. The Forgers will pledge our tine to Nadia."

"The Spinners, too," the director added thoughtfully, and the Tillers joined in a chorus of quiet agreement.

"By daybreak, then," General Scorcha said with a sharp nod. "If you can bring and show us the real unicorn by daybreak, we'll crown Nadia. Otherwise, we leave for our war, got it?"

"But dawn's only an hour away!" Sophie protested.

"Then, you best get moving," General Scorcha said and marched toward the dirt stairs and out of the cellar.

As soon as the grandmasters had cleared out of the cellar, Sophie whirled on Claire.

"What are you thinking?" she asked, worry scrunching up her face. "Do you actually know where the unicorn is?"

Claire shook her head, but she wasn't sure if Sophie saw, as she had already grabbed the Stone Tine and was running to the stairs. "I don't," she called back. "But I think I know where the unicorn *was*. Come on, follow me! We don't have much time."

CHAPTER
24

"All right," Nett said as they hurried into their Woven Root tent, constructed only a few feet away from the Hearing Hall. "Spill. What do you mean you know where the unicorn *was*?"

With a twist of his marimo, he sent its pearly light across the room, revealing four swinging hammocks, a tree stump table, and a beautiful rug with fringe that changed color with the seasons. The light also illuminated the confused expression on Sena's face and the shocked one on Sophie's.

The two of them and Nett had followed Claire out of the Seed Cellar, but Nadia and Thorn had remained, so that the alchemists could ask him questions about Estelle and her followers. Without a fully forged crown and the support of the guilds, they would need to scrape for every advantage.

"We have to go," Claire said, opening up her Hollow

Pack and throwing in a spare blanket. It was definitely getting colder at night. She also grabbed a warmer pair of boots and a few loose sheets of paper. The Stone Tine was a heavy weight in her tunic pocket.

"Hang on," Sophie said, gently placing her hand on top of the bag. "Before you put everything in your pack, tell us what you're thinking. Where do you think the unicorn was?"

"*Woven Root,*" Claire said, triumphantly. "I mean, where Woven Root *was*, when we first found Nadia and the others!"

She expected her friends to cheer, but instead, they only looked at her worriedly.

"Claire," Sophie said, in an overly gentle voice, as though she were pretending to be Mom. "A unicorn wasn't in Woven Root."

Claire let her pack slide to the floor. She knew there would be no way to make Sophie budge until she understood.

"There *was*," Claire said, putting every ounce of confidence she could into her voice. "Do you remember the night we tried to break into the chimera stable and escape?"

Sophie and Nett nodded. Sena didn't, however, as she'd spent that particular night in the cells of Drowning Fortress, waiting for her execution, not knowing that they were on their way to rescue her.

"It was the Tiller snowdrop cookies that reminded me," Claire said, taking care to say her words clearly even though she wanted to shout them as fast as she could and then ride off on a chimera to the old campsite. "When we were sneaking out, I saw snowdrops under a bush, right under some unicorn mane that had gotten stuck in the branches."

"Claire," Sophie groaned, burying her face in her palms, though her fingers couldn't hide her pink cheeks. "I already confessed that I made up the unicorn following us. You *know* that. The 'mane' was just the silver thread from my Gemmer dress to, you know . . ." She hesitated. "Convince you."

Claire shook her head so hard that she could feel her bun wobble. "No, Mayor Nadia burned our Grand Test dresses, remember? They were completely ruined from our escape from the Citadel!"

Sophie looked as though someone had slipped ice down her neck. "You mean . . . the mane was real?"

"Yes!" Claire said triumphantly. At last, Sophie was listening! "I think if we go back to the old campsite, we'll find more clues. We just need some chimera or a few pairs of Seven League Boots, and we can go right now!" She took a deep breath, flushed by her discovery. Even though she'd been standing still, she felt like she'd just ran the mile at Field Day. But unlike the end of a race, no one was cheering. Instead, Sophie was biting her lip.

"I'm not trying to be a pain," Sophie said apologetically, "but . . ." she shrugged helplessly. "I can *see* the unicorn in my dreams, and I know he's not at Woven Root."

Her words were like an anchor, and Claire, who had felt like she'd been flying for the last few minutes, plummeted back to reality. A reality where Queen Estelle still had all the power, the Crown of Arden would never be reforged, and an old stone well could never be fixed.

"Claire," Nett said suddenly. "Do you still have the mane?"

"No—yes!" Claire said. "I think I do!" She reached into her Hollow Pack, and after a little bit of ruffling, found it attached to a clean pair of socks. Meanwhile, Nett went rummaging through Nadia's Spinner supplies and returned with a small wooden frame: a loom.

He pressed it into Sophie's hands. "Go on, then," he said. "Do it!"

Sophie frowned. "Do what?"

Nett blinked in surprise. "Spin! You're still a Spinner, aren't you? Do what Spinners do. *Weave* the tale out from the mane; ask it where it's been, what it's seen."

"She's not a Spyden, Nett," Claire said, his words uncomfortably reminding her of the encounter with the beast.

"No," Nett agreed. "But she *is* a unicorn. Go on, Sophie, just try!"

Stubborn lines set in around Sophie's mouth, but as she looked at Nett—eyes still red-rimmed from crying—she seemed to reconsider. "All right," she said. "I'll try."

They all took a seat on a few overlarge petal-stuffed cushions surrounding the tree-stump table. Sophie took the gleaming strand of unicorn mane and began to weave it, over and under the weft threads. Over and under. Over and under. The unicorn mane began to shimmer. To shine.

Sophie yanked her hand back. "It's working," she said, sounding awed. "Look!"

The unicorn thread began to weave itself through the loom, shuttling back and forth, and as it did, it left behind pictures: two girls in the center of a ring of rocks, a unicorn rearing over them.

"That's the Sorrowful Plains," Sophie whispered, eyes fixed on the weaving thread. "That's us!"

The next image was the unicorn galloping, but the thread's color dimmed, and the creature looked more gray than white. A few circular dots trailed behind the unicorn. Sophie gasped, and leaned so close over the tapestry that the tips of her ponytail brushed it. "The unicorn—he was injured after he helped us! And so he went looking for a place where he could be safe and heal."

She pointed at the next image that was emerging on the loom. "He sought out—"

"Woven Root!" Claire exclaimed triumphantly, not needing her sister to decode the image of tents surrounded by flowers. Besides, *she* already knew the unicorn had been there.

"Yes!" Sophie said. "The only place left in Arden where magic still sounded and tasted like it did when he was a colt. The only place where jumbled magic was allowed to thrive."

Claire jumped as Sena suddenly yelped. The weaving continued, and this time, two figures were woven next to the unicorn: a woman with a sword on her hip, and a man holding a wooden hammer. The tapestry had adjusted itself to give them both bright red hair.

"Those are my *parents*," Sena breathed. "The unicorn! He went to my parents!"

"He did," Sophie confirmed, her hand reaching out to touch the tapestry. "Your parents were the cleverest Alchemists in Woven Root. They managed to fake Mathieu's execution and break Sylvia out of an unbreakable prison and stay hidden for all these years. The unicorn knew that if anyone could keep him safe and hidden, it was them."

Claire stared at the magical tapestry, at the mane-woven figures of Sylvia, Mathieu and the unicorn. And then, suddenly, the weaving stopped, leaving the figures incomplete.

It was as though all the magic inside the mane had been used up. Like a flame that had reached the end of its wick.

Sophie reached out a finger to give the tapestry a nudge, but the weaving did not resume. She looked back up at them, her eyes so wide it was easy to see the ring of silver. "That's it," she said. "That's the end of the story."

"But what happened next?" Nett demanded. "You can't just stop a story in the middle! Where are they now?"

"I think I know," Sena said. She jumped up and ran over to her hammock, then proceeded to pour her parents' journals from her Hollow Pack. She frantically sifted through them. Grabbing one, she hurried back to the others. "My parents' experiments with the seams didn't work because they were missing an essential piece: a unicorn."

She flipped the journal open to a page with lots of words and an illustration of unicorns. Tapping the picture, she explained, "The lore around unicorns is mysterious, but it is common knowledge that they can open any door."

"So," Claire said, her heart pounding. "Does that mean the unicorn is in our world?"

"Any world!" Sena beamed. Then she seemed to realize what she said, and the smile slipped off. "But we have no way of knowing where."

"Wait a second," Sophie whispered. "Wait a second! Wait a second!" She leaped to her feet, and Claire was momentarily reminded of a time when Sophie had excitedly come up with a brand-new way of playing checkers, one that involved all the pieces of their Monopoly set plus a gold coin Dad had brought back from his trip to Canada.

"All this time," Sophie said, "I thought the unicorn was showing me metal, rock, thread, and plants to tell me that one of the guilds had trapped him. But that wasn't what he was saying at all—he was giving me a *map*. Metal, plant, thread, stone. We need to jumble all our magics together, along with a unicorn—if we want to find him. We need a Tiller," she said, pointing to Nett, "a Gemmer, and a Forger"—she nodded at Claire, then Sena—"and," she placed a hand on her own chest, "me: a Spinner-slash-unicorn."

"I don't follow," Sena said, sitting back down on the petal-pouf with a frustrated crunch. "My parents are a Tiller and a Forger—I doubt a Spinner or Gemmer helped them."

"Exactly!" Sophie said. "They only had *half* the guilds and a unicorn, which was enough to get into the seams of the world, but wasn't strong enough magic to get them back into this one—or into another."

Sena's face whitened. "You're saying they're trapped *between* worlds?"

Between worlds. Claire had thought a lot about the fireplace and chimney in Windemere and the well in Arden, but she never really thought about that long, dark space where only the ladder seemed to exist. It terrified her.

"But why did the unicorn make them go there?" Sena cried.

"Because," Sophie said, turning to look out the tent's window where even now they could hear the Tillers and Spinners preparing to depart. "It wasn't safe for him to be in Arden yet. Until the guilds are willing to work together to defeat Estelle, it is too dangerous for him. And so, he went to a place that could only be reached when the four guilds were reunited."

Reunited. Like the four tines of Arden needed to be.

"It's almost dawn!" Claire said. The guilds would soon be gone, along with their tines and their only chance to defeat Queen Estelle. "What do we do now?"

"Do?" Sena's amber eyes glittered, but Claire couldn't tell if it was with fear or excitement. "We're going to open the seams of the world. We're going to get them back."

They scrambled around the tent collecting items while Sena ordered them about, as though she had taken notes from General Scorcha. And as Nett, Sophie, and Claire worked on their assignments, Sena pored over her parents' journals, occasionally reading out loud some of the more interesting passages:

"Magic is in the material, but what makes up the material? The elements of the universe: earth, fire, water, and air. . . . The Way Between is the place where one possibility ends and another begins . . ."

"What does that mean?" Nett called from his place in the center of the tent. He was tying vines around three large branches, lashing them together to form the outline of a freestanding doorway.

"Shush," Sena commanded, and continued reading. "The few travelers who have managed to safely traverse the Way Between and arrive in other worlds brought back stories of strange and most wondrous magics: of horseless wagons made of steel, and hand-sized, block-shaped wands that can contain entire libraries, sing on command, and make communication across vast distances. They are called 'fohnes.'"

"*Phones*?" Claire looked up from where she'd been placing geode bookends from Aunt Nadia's desk around the base of Nett's doorway, hoping it would help keep the wood upright. "Like—*cell* phones? And cars?" She'd never thought that there was magic in her own world before, and from the expression on Sophie's face, she could tell her sister was mulling it over. Maybe there was magic, only it was called by another name.

Sena shrugged and flipped the page. "I don't know anything about selling the 'fohnes.'"

Finally, the doorway was complete.

Taking a step back to eye their handiwork, Claire winced. It looked rickety and a bit silly, a door leading to nowhere. Sena had informed them that they didn't only need to open the seams, they needed to make sure that the unicorn and the Steeles would be able to find the door—it had to act as a beacon, a kind of lighthouse, as well.

Now that he'd finished lashing the frame together, Nett coaxed moss over the wooden rails, explaining that moss was a guiding plant, usually growing on the north side of trees, which helped Tiller journeymen locate themselves. Then, he and Sena had used the top of Nadia's wooden desk to create the *actual* door. It hung on the doorframe with two copper hinges forged, with Gryphin's permission, from two of the chimera's molted feathers. Sena had heated a third copper piece and shaped it into a tiny bell that was now strung on top of the door.

With a small flick, Sena set the bell chiming, a gentle, high note that made the hair on the back of Claire's neck stand up in a *good* way. She could imagine the sound soaring through the door, seeking out Mathieu and Sylvia. Calling them home. Then, Sena tugged on the handle—a loop of ribbons Sophie had braided together. As she was the one who would be opening the seams, Nett and Sena had thought the handle should be made of the material Sophie was most comfortable with.

Still, the overall effect was . . . haphazard.

"Sena," Claire said cautiously, not wanting to hurt the Forger's feelings and knowing they were short on time, "are you *sure* we don't need to make a well?"

Sena nodded, her red braid swinging as she pulled on the ribbon handle to make sure its knots were tight. "In all their notes, my parents keep underlining that there is never just one way to do something. I think we need to play to our strengths. And I've never made a well before, have you?"

"No," Claire admitted. "But that's another thing. According to Anvil, the well was made by a Gemmer, Forger, and unicorn. There were no Spinners or Tillers, so maybe we're wrong."

"Is that so?" Nett crossed his arm and cocked a black eyebrow at her. "And what, exactly, was that ladder made of that got you safely through? Wood! Of course there was a Tiller who helped. And I bet there's some unknown, unnamed Spinner who helped pull it all together. If there's anything we've learned with the Royalists and Queen Estelle, it's that sometimes, the history that's passed down is wrong."

Peering around the doorframe, Sena stared at her foster brother in disbelief. "Nett, are you sure you're feeling all right? You love your historians!"

"Timor the Verbose is a great read, it's true," Nett protested as he gave his marimo a little pat. They still needed its light, but the dark outside was lifting. The sun would rise soon. Sena seemed to have noticed the same thing.

"Claire," she beckoned, "it's your turn."

Claire nodded and stood in front of the door. With a deep breath, she tugged her pencil out from behind her ear. Her job was to make sure Sena's parents and the unicorn would recognize *this* seam as an opening to Arden.

And so, she set her pencil to the smooth wood of the door, and began to draw.

The Rhona and the Tayrn flourished under her pencil, and soon mountains and fields unrolled beside it, along with scenes of Spinners rowing in their narrowboats, Tillers tending apple orchards, Forgers bending over flames, and Gemmers standing in a citadel's tower, looking out over a wall they could not cross. Soon, the door was covered with a map of Arden—its towns and its people and its creatures.

Claire made a few more quick lines, adding a wyvern wrapping around Mount Rouge. She let its tail drop down to tickle the image of a sleeping Gryphin in chimera fields. The little copper creature perched on Sena's shoulder crooned appreciatively as Claire lifted her pencil away.

"There," she said, collapsing on the petal-pouf nearby to let the others take a closer look. "Done." She felt a bit dizzy, but she wasn't sure if that was the nerves or just the result of a long day followed by an even longer night.

"This is spectacular," Sophie said, "But . . ."

Claire straightened up. "But what? Did I mess up the map?"

Sophie shook her head. "No, not at all! But while this is the Arden Sena's parents know, I don't know if the unicorn will recognize *this* as his home. I've seen bits of what life used to be like—memories of racing the wind in Spinner sails and long afternoons in Tiller gardens, helping people with the more tricky crops. Forgers even used to make shiny golden rings for the unicorn foals to play with. And this—" she gestured at the door, "doesn't even have a single unicorn on it."

"I can fix that!" Claire said, rising to her feet. She was still tired, but Sophie's words had ignited her imagination. "I'll try again. I'll draw you a world *full* of unicorns."

As Sophie began to share, Claire drew the unicorn's dreams on the door—dreams of long-legged foals sleeping on meadows, of cold sea spray flying off his mane, of a family of sisters and brothers who knew each star by name and every shadow on the moon.

Sophie spoke with longing in her voice, and Claire let the longing seep into her work on the door. Claire knew the feeling well.

This *needed* to work. They *had* to open the seams. The unicorn *must* return to Arden.

Suddenly, it was like someone had turned up the volume on Claire's senses. The air became sweet. The textured grain of the door stood out in sharp relief. An unexpected certainty swept through her. And then—

She stumbled back, away from the door. From the round eyes of her friends, she knew they heard it too. Because even though nothing seemed to have changed in the tent, there was a sound coming from *behind* the door. An endless, deafening hum. A vibration of rock scraping across rock, strings disturbing the air, metal bending, green things growing. The sound of the winds of the worlds racing across the mouth of a chimney.

The copper bell chimed as the door began to shake. Flecks of moss flew off and the hinges groaned in protest.

"Open it!" Sena said. "Sophie—open it before it collapses!"

"Not yet!" Sophie said, the silver in her eyes seeming to shine brighter than ever. "They're not there yet—and if I open it too soon, I'm scared we'll get trapped in the seams!"

The door shook harder.

The wind behind it whipped, and its rush filled Claire's ears with a rhythmic drumming. No, not a drumming—hoofbeats!

Sophie reached for the door, but Claire grabbed her sister's other hand. A wave of dizziness washed over her as the world warped, but she wasn't about to let her sister get lost between worlds. Behind her, she felt Nett grab her other hand, and knew that Sena must be holding on as well.

"We got you, Sophie!" Claire yelled above the noise. Sophie's hands clasped around the ribbon handle—and opened the seams of the world.

Time seemed to slow and bend on itself. Claire caught a glimpse of her sister's face as she stepped back to make room. Sophie looked like an extended breath, poised on the edge of leaping, staring at something in the distance. Then—

The unicorn returned to Arden.

She was aware of chaos, of shouts, and cracking as the doorway disintegrated into nothing, but when Claire looked at the unicorn, all of it fell away.

He was serene power. Calming strength. Known purpose.

And as he turned his great head toward them, she saw entire galaxies in his eyes, and the tip of his glorious horn spiraled into a sharp point. It radiated with the strength of the sun that was now rising.

"They need you outside," Sophie croaked, tears of joy streaming down her face.

Faster than Claire could blink, the unicorn was gone.

But the tent's flap remained gusted open, revealing the sunrise breaking over Greenwood Village. In the pink light, Claire could see Spinners and Forgers trudging toward the boundary of the Camouflora that was just beginning to open to let them out of the village, but suddenly, the guild members stopped and turned toward something bright and wondrous galloping toward them—toward Nadia.

"Mama! *Papa*!"

Claire turned to look back. Where the door had once been, three figures had sunk to their knees, hugging each other tight. Sena's shoulders shook with sobs as Sylvia, a woman with hair even brighter than Sena's, and Mathieu, his smile too big for even his russet beard to hide, hugged their daughter tight to them, looking as though they would never let go.

Claire looked away, wanting to give the newly found family privacy. And she also needed to ask the unicorn a question—so many questions!

She made to move out of the tent, but the dizziness she'd felt earlier swung back in, and suddenly, Claire found herself falling, tumbling toward Nadia's plush carpet.

"Claire? *Claire!*"

She heard someone calling her name. Sophie. Maybe Nett.

"What's wrong with her?"

She was on the ground, and could feel someone grasping her arm. Then she heard words, full of fear, reply: *"Slug soot, that's a Spyden's bite! How long has she had it? Claire, hold on!"*

But Claire had already let go.

CHAPTER
25

Claire woke to constellations painted on a stone ceiling—strangely *familiar* constellations that reminded her of the tower bedroom she and Sophie had shared at Starscrape Citadel. But Greenwood was at least two weeks' journey from Stonehaven. So she couldn't be at the Citadel unless . . . Had she slept for two weeks? Startled, she tried to sit up.

"Hold up there, no need to be in a stitch," said the warm and friendly voice of Aunt Nadia. Her aunt's face broke into a smile. "Everyone will be very glad to see you're awake."

"Claire!" Nett popped his head over. "About time!"

"Nett!" Claire said. This was all getting more and more confusing. "What are you doing in Stonehaven? Where's Sophie? Where's the unicorn?"

Nett shook his head. "I thought I asked a lot of questions."

Leaning against the pillows, Claire saw she was indeed back in their room, but with some adjustments. A few chairs had been pulled up around her bed, along with crumpled blankets. "Sophie and Sena and her parents have been checking on you, though I came in so they could help with the war preparations," Nadia explained as she followed Claire's gaze.

"War?" Claire asked. "How long have I been asleep?" She was worried. Magic had never before exhausted her so much.

"Not so long," Nett said, coming to stand next to her. "Especially when you consider the fact that you let *Spyden* venom fester in your blood for days! Why didn't you tell anyone that a Spyden bit you? The poison is slow-acting, but if not removed, it starts shutting everything down."

Claire shook her head. "It didn't hurt anymore, so I didn't know!"

Nett shook his head incredulously. "Well, you're fine now, Nadia made sure of that. Anyway, after we freed the Steeles and the unicorn from the Way Between, you passed out for the entire day, and now it's nearing midnight."

"Of the same day?" Claire asked incredulously. "But how did we get here so quickly? And are all the guilds with us? What did the grandmasters say? Where are the tines?"

Nett came to sit next to Claire. "It's the unicorn," he said. "With him around, everything is just . . . *more*." He shook his head, seemingly at a loss for words, which, considering it was Nett, was something. "The chimera move twice as fast and the

Spinners' cloaks can catch even the tiniest breeze, as though they were great gales."

"And then there's the jumbled magic," Nadia added. "As non–Woven Root people are realizing, the combination of crafts can lead to incredible innovations, like Ten League Horseshoes."

Nett nodded. "As soon as the guilds saw the unicorn, there could be no mistaking what we had told them. They ended up listening to Nadia pretty snappily, especially after the unicorn galloped to her."

"Where's the unicorn now?" Claire asked. The wonder of it all still hung with her, even though it did really feel like a dream, between the mist and now being in Stonehaven.

"Around," Nett said, waving his hand vaguely. "He kind of appears and then reappears as needed. Celina Cerebella once wrote that unicorns were more fact than matter, which means, of course—"

"Nettle, hush," Nadia said. "You're just confusing her more! *I'll* explain."

And so Claire settled back in her pillows and let her great-aunt make sense of it all for her.

When the unicorn had arrived at dawn, the Tillers, Spinners, and Forgers had quickly come to believe what Nadia, Claire, and her friends had shared. And all agreed on one thing: it was essential to protect the unicorn, especially if Estelle's goal was to make the wraiths able to withstand sunlight by some use of his heart.

Messages of all natures had been sent throughout Arden, informing the many villages and towns to up their wraith protections, while all those who had been at Hilltop Palace and fled to Greenwood would now make up the unicorn's escort and guard at Starscrape Citadel, the only place big enough and secure enough to house them all.

"But what about the Everless Wall?" Claire interjected. "I thought Queen Estelle did something to it so that it wouldn't let anyone out or in!"

"That's true," Nett said. "But Estelle hadn't counted on the Forger Blades working in tandem with Tiller Roots and Spinner Ropes. The entrance revealed itself pretty quickly."

The goal, Nadia continued to explain to Claire, who could hardly believe her ears, was to draw out Queen Estelle, away from everyone else and have her meet . . . Queen Nadia.

"Queen Nadia!" Claire said, surprised and delighted. "You've been crowned!"

"Not yet," Nadia said.

Claire's delight faltered. "But we did it! And everyone's here! Why haven't—" she stopped as Nadia held her hand.

"We've been waiting for the last tine." Nadia stared meaningfully at Claire.

"I—*oh*!" Heat rose in Claire's cheeks as she remembered how she'd taken the Stone Tine from the Seed Cellar. "It's in my pocket."

"And that pocket," Nadia said with a slight smile, "happens to be a Lock-it Pocket, which as you know—"

"Means only the person who puts the thing in can take it out," Claire said, quickly slipping her hand into her tunic's pocket to pull out the Stone Tine.

As one, Nadia, Claire, and Nett stared down at the crown's point. It was as smooth as night on water, and just as mysterious.

"Yes," Nadia said quietly, her expert eye taking in the treasured artifact. "That is, indeed, the Gemmers' tine."

"Take it!" Claire said, holding it out to Nadia. "Join it with the others! Go be queen!"

But Nadia tucked Claire's fingers gently back over it. "The other three tines are being reforged at this very moment. It's been difficult and delicate work to combine the tines, and has taken up the whole day and night, but they should be ready for you now." She stood up. "If you're feeling up for it, would you do me the very great honor of bringing it to them now? I need to watch over the more complicated jumbled magic we're adding to the wall."

"I'm fine!" Claire said, swinging her legs over the bed. It wasn't a lie. The room *hardly* spun at all. She pressed the precious bit of metal to her heart once. Its thin song flowed into her. "Where is it being reforged?"

After Nadia gave her directions, she and Nett—who wanted to help with some preamble training—left Claire so that she could change into fresh clothes.

After peeling off her dirt-streaked Forger shirt, Claire quickly pulled on a thick woolen tunic in a soft red, tugged on some goat-hair boots, slung her Hollow Pack across her shoulder, and tucked her pencil behind her ear. Last, she checked to make sure the Stone Tine was secure in the front pocket of her bag. She was ready. But before she hurried out, a gleam caught her eye. Next to the standing wardrobe was a silver breastplate, and a note:

Light as a petal but strong as steel, please wear this with our gratitude. It will never rust but do make sure to run a polishing rag over it now and again.
—Mathieu and Sylvia

Grinning, Claire snapped the breastplate over her clothes. There was a slight clanging as the metal adjusted to her, contracting itself ever so slightly so that it was a perfect fit. Glimpsing herself in the polished stone mirror that stood next to the wardrobe, Claire caught her breath.

She didn't just look brave. She looked fearless.

And she *felt* fearless.

All her friends were here, with her. Sophie was safe. The guilds, for the first time in three hundred years, were working together. The unicorn had returned. And soon enough, Nadia would be crowned queen.

She ran out the door and stepped into the hallway—and almost stopped in her tracks.

Starscrape Citadel was a large and sprawling complex, and while it was home to a few hundred Gemmers, it had never felt even close to full. Tonight, however, it was full to bursting. For the first time, noise rang out in every section of the marble hallways. Claire had to dodge and duck Forgers adding sun steel to the tips of the Spinner nets, while outside through the windows, Claire could see Tillers coaxing as much foliage as they could: roses, vines, mosses—anything that could help protect them from the wraiths. Gemmers raced up and down the corridors, carrying polished Gemglows and guiding the new arrivals through the labyrinth Citadel. As she watched, she saw kindly Master Pumus lead a group of Gemmer and Forger journeymen, bows slung over their shoulders, in the direction of the armory.

From what Nadia had shared, Claire knew that they did not expect Estelle's attack until tomorrow night. News of the unicorn's return and the Everless Wall opening again had probably reached the Royalists by now, but grandmasters and generals didn't think she would have had time to react. Tomorrow, too, would be safe—until sunset, at least.

"She won't attack without her wraiths," Nadia had said with confidence. "Especially not now, when she knows we have *two* unicorns with us."

Claire hoped her aunt was right.

She ran by a few classrooms and saw that while the apprentices weren't allowed outside, many of them were crouched over Lode Arrows and Mulchbombs, making sure that the watch would be well equipped whenever the queen attacked. Another turn and she passed a courtyard filled with Spinners and Gemmers being led in sword drills by Sylvia and Sena

Steele. At another door, she recognized the pearly light of Nett's marimo trickling out, and as she hurried past, she saw he was busy teaching a bunch of Gemmer preambles how to water plants *properly*. "Everyone should be able to do this," he was saying. "Even if you're not a Tiller. Happy plants equal more sunlight equal no wraiths, got it?"

Soon, Claire found herself in a dark courtyard lit by Gemglows, where a makeshift forge had been built. She recognized the large figure of Scythe looming over the anvil. With each swing of his hammer, he sent orange sparks into the night sky, which illuminated the other figures standing around him, assisting: Grandmaster Carnelian, Mathieu Steele, and, to her utmost astonishment, Mistress Weft. With a look of great concentration, she used a silk fan to direct wind currents to specific parts of the blaze, adjusting the fire's heat.

"Elaina! Er, I mean, Claire! "

Surprised, Claire turned to see Lyric rush at her, her many braids flying out behind her. With a squeal, Lyric wrapped her arms around Claire's waist. She still wore bits and pieces of her white Starfell costume, but a Forger's warm leather coat had been thrown over her shoulders. "I can't believe what you've been up to! Your stories even make our Spyden adventure seem tame. How did you—"

"That's enough, Lyric," Mistress Weft called, looking up. Smoke had tinged her ruffled apron gray, and though she looked weary, she didn't seem mad that Claire had lied to her. "Hello, Princess Claire. Did you bring the Stone Tine?"

Claire nodded and pulled the tine from her pack.

Grandmaster Carnelian smiled at Claire. He seemed thinner than before, and now he sat in a wheeled chair with tourmaline spokes—the consequence of his great battle with Jasper and the ensuing days of seige by Estelle. His eyes flashed as he accepted the Stone Tine.

With expert fingers, he examined the piece of crown. "Are the flames hot enough, Scythe?"

"Yes, sir," the Forger called back.

Carnelian rolled his chair toward the flame. "Then let's finish this and go after that miserable, mesmerizing manipulator. Now please, everyone stand back!"

Claire did, and she watched as the Grandmaster of Stonehaven used his glassblowing instruments to manipulate the tine in the heat. Its edges warped, looking almost molten. With a look of great concentration, he slipped the tine into its place.

"Water!" Scythe called, and Mathieu hurried forward with a wooden bucket. A second later, there was a hiss and enough steam for Claire to wonder for a second if they were back in Silver Way.

The four adults collapsed on a nearby bench, clearly spent.

Scythe gestured for Claire to move to the bucket. There, at the bottom, sparkled the Crown of Arden, each of its tines submerged beneath the water.

The most powerful object ever crafted, capable of twisting rivers and moving mountains—reforged, once more.

Claire plunged her hand into the water and grasped the Crown of Arden. It was whole in her hand and she felt a warm flush of triumph race through her, but as she lifted it from the water, she began to frown.

The song, it was there, but it was still so *quiet*. Claire had thought that when the tines were connected, they would be as loud as they had been in the pencil's memory.

"Go on, then," Grandmaster Carnelian said. "Bring it to Nadia. Hurry!"

Clare tried to shake her uncomfortable feeling loose. She had the Crown of Arden. In just a few minutes, her aunt would officially be queen.

"I'm not sure where Nadia is," Claire admitted. "She said she would be on the wall, but I don't know where."

"Here!" Lyric said, and she pulled out her ball of yarn. She tied a knot around Claire's finger and the string began to gleam. Lyric made one last twist then said, "The B.P.S. should take you straight to Mayor Nadia. I mean, the almost-queen! Oh, this is so exciting!" She threw her arms around Claire, giving her a spontaneous squeeze.

"Thank you," Claire said, trying to smile, but something was pushing on her. Something about the crown and Lyric . . . but she couldn't think *what*.

And so, she let the B.P.S. drop from her hand and began to jog after the gleaming golden thread and back into the Citadel. Following the B.P.S., Claire found herself in a part of the Citadel she'd never been in before. While she could still hear the clamor of Starscrape's preparations, no one seemed to be working over here. The only things she saw were goat-chewed signs proclaiming the following corridors off-limits—for good reason, too, Claire was sure. Bits of the Citadel were always in danger of crumbling off the mountain.

She wondered if the B.P.S. was really working. After all, Nadia had said she would be outside, overseeing the jumbled magic. She clutched the Crown of Arden so tight, she could feel the Love Knot pressing into her palms.

Claire was about to turn around and head back when a pearly glow caught her eye. The marimo? But she knew Nett was in the classroom. Which meant . . .

The unicorn.

And suddenly, she realized what had bugged her. Why the crown's song wasn't as clear as it should be. Lyric had said the Crown of Arden had been *blessed by unicorns*.

Before it could be truly whole again—could sing again—the unicorn needed to set his horn upon it!

Claire turned left, ignoring both the B.P.S., which continued to roll right, as well as the signs that read Forbidden. There was no more room in her for rules, not when her question had grown so big. She had to speak to the unicorn and make him listen to her. Make him understand what he'd done when he'd transformed the wish into Sophie's heart and turn her back into only a human girl, and nothing else.

Claire broke into a run.

But she always just missed the unicorn, catching only a glimpse of white as he rounded another corner. Her breath came loud and fast, and her first steps echoed heavily. She reached the next corner, then stopped. Two corridors branched in front of her, one left and one right . . . but neither held the glow of the unicorn. Holding her breath, she tried to make out the delicate clip of hooves on stone, but all she heard was a slight rustle to her right, behind a closed wooden door. She pushed it open.

"Claire?"

"Sophie!" Claire stepped inside. It was a small room for the Citadel, and aside from two sapphire Gemglows in one corner and a looming statue of someone Claire thought might be King Anders, there was just Sophie here. No unicorn—well, not a four-legged one.

Sophie gasped as she saw what was in Claire's hand. "The Crown of Arden! It's been remade!"

"Yes," Claire said. "I need to give it to Nadia but I'm looking for the unicorn first. What are you doing here?"

Sophie made a face. "Nadia didn't tell anyone about my, um, condition, but she did tell them that Queen Estelle would be targeting me, as the oldest Martinson girl. So everyone's roots and spectacles and whatnot have all been on me. Hovering—and you know how I hate hovering!"

Claire did.

Sophie shook her head. "I needed to go someplace where I could just be . . ." she trailed off and finished with "*be.*" She waved her arm around them. "So here I am."

"Which is where?" Claire asked, pulling out her pink marble to take a better look. Its rosy light mixed with the sapphires' blue, washing everything in lavender. The room was octagonal in shape, and the ceiling arched into a dome above them. Claire realized they had to be in one of the many squat little towers that ran the edge of the precipice, one of the towers long ago abandoned by the Gemmers as superfluous and left to collapse. No wonder there had been so many Forbidden signs.

"I've never been here before," she said, and her eyes fell to the floor. Among the marble flagstones sparkled a mosaic of a unicorn. Its hooves were lifted proudly, and its spiraling horn glittered in the light. It seemed to have been set with bits of opal shards and diamond dust.

"I don't think many people have," Sophie said. "I discovered it when you were taking your Gemmer lessons— Don't give me that look! I wasn't snooping. A goat got stuck down here. Anyway," Sophie said, giving a dignified tug to the narrow sleeve of her gown, "it just seemed like a place I could be alone and, you know, try to do magic." She nodded toward the statue's base, where Claire could just make out a pile of loose jewels as well as some books, remnants of a time when Sophie didn't know she was a Spinner or what the unicorn had done to her.

"It's a pretty place," Claire said, moving farther away from the entrance to stand next to her sister.

"It's even more beautiful in the daytime. The stained glass is amazing."

Claire hadn't noticed the windows in the dark, but now she saw that all the walls except for the one she'd entered from had a large stained glass window. But without the sun, it was hard to see their images.

"What do they show?" she asked.

"Unicorns, mostly," Sophie said with a small smile. "Come look." Picking up the Gemglows, Sophie moved closer and Claire followed. The windows did show unicorns—unicorns in gardens, next to rivers, on cliffs, under waterfalls—but that wasn't all. They also showed humans, men and women and children in jewel-toned cloaks and with smiling faces, standing peacefully with the unicorns.

"This one's my favorite," Sophie said, nodding to an image of a unicorn approaching a girl in a sunset meadow. She'd pulled her ponytail to the top of her head. Now she let go, and it slid easily back into place. As easily, Claire thought with sudden panic, as Sophie had slid into Arden.

"I also like this one, too." Sophie pointed to the border. "Do you see how the page boy is pretending to be a unicorn with a pine cone? That's *totally* something I would— Hey." She broke off as she turned to look at Claire. "Is something wrong?"

Claire wasn't sure what to say. For a moment, she stood quietly, the sounds of the war preparation outside nothing more than a distant growl.

"There are creatures out there that are after you. Estelle is after you," Claire said at last. "Aren't you scared? Even a little?"

"Me?" Sophie let out a small laugh, and it was so unexpected, Claire almost jumped. "Clairina, I'm scared of *everything*. I'm scared of *losing* everything. But I've lived with that fear since long before I was in the center of a magical war."

Her illness. If Sophie did turn back into just a girl, would that mean . . . would she still be sick? Magic couldn't fix everything. Was she destined to lose her sister either way?

"Sophie, I—" Claire stopped talking. In the darkness next to her feet, she caught a glimpse of skirting movement. She gripped the crown tighter as the hair on the back of her neck prickled. Beetles?

But as she held up her pink marble, Claire saw what it was. The tiny tiles that had once been a unicorn in the mosaic were scurrying over one another, running away into the corners of the room, leaving behind a large hole in the middle of the floor, between the sisters and the exit. In the Gemglow light, she could make out a spiraling staircase descending into the ground.

Sophie grabbed Claire and pulled her down behind the statue of King Anders. Claire quickly put out the marble's light and extinguished the Gemglows just as she saw the tip of an obsidian spear rise up from the ground, followed by the spindly frame of Jasper. But he wasn't alone. As soon as he stepped out off the stairs, more followed: Mira Fray and the other Royalists.

Sophie slapped her hand over Claire's mouth before she could scream. Helpless, Claire watched as the Royalists poured into the Citadel. She gripped the crown close to her heart and wriggled her pencil out from behind her ear. Why had she delayed? If she had just gone straight to Nadia, Nadia would be queen now, and they would stand a chance! Bile rose in the back of her throat.

They—she, Sophie, Nadia, Carnelian, the grandmasters, everyone—had been so *foolish*! *Beyond* naive to think they knew all the secret tunnels and passageways of Starscrape Citadel. Zuli and Lapis's parents knew many of the passages, but not all. Estelle, on the other hand, had summered here, her parents alive and able to pass on the secrets of the castle.

The Royalists—about twenty in all—circled the opening as a final figure emerged from the depths: Queen Estelle d'Astora.

Without Scholar Terra's spectacles she seemed younger but no less monstrous—after all, only monsters would wear what she was wearing.

On first glance, her ebony gown seemed more suitable for ballrooms than for battle. But when she shifted, Claire heard the clink of gems and saw rainbows ripple across the hundreds of Mesmerizing Opals that had been sewn to her skirt. Claire immediately looked away, not wanting the stones to catch her mind and put her under Estelle's persuasion. But a moment later, she wished she had lost herself in the dreamy control of the gems, because what she saw next was worse.

Much, much worse.

The necklace around her throat was not of pearls but of teeth. Unicorn teeth, collected from long-ago battlefields. The breastplate she wore over sleeves slashed with gold was ghostly white and much thinner than the metal Claire had seen the Forgers hammer. It took her one breath more to realize that the overlocking links weren't metal at all but shards of bone. Next to her, she heard Sophie swallow hard.

Estelle had guessed—had known—they wouldn't expect

her onslaught until tomorrow night. Or expect her to infiltrate the castle so close to dawn. She would sneak in, kill the unicorn, and use its heart to make her wraiths withstand the sun, and then she would attack Starscrape in the bright light of day, when absolutely no one would be ready.

Claire wanted to turn her head and bury her eyes in Sophie's shoulder. But she was a Gemmer—maybe she could stop them from leaving this room. A tight pinch on the inside of her knee made her look at Sophie. Her sister shook her head ever so slightly. *Don't risk the crown. Wait.* So Claire did.

Estelle didn't say a word; she only nodded once, and the Royalists' blue cloaks rustled slightly as they streamed out of the room ahead of her, like an announcing procession. In just a few seconds, Claire and Sophie would be alone, and then they could figure out the next step.

But as Estelle neared the door, she slowed, then stopped. "I know you're in here, little unicorn," she breathed. Claire and Sophie had only a second to react before Estelle whirled around and slammed the ram's head cane into the statue of King Anders.

CHAPTER
26

The statue fragmented, sending shards of stone flying in all directions. The rocks should have knocked Claire unconscious, but Sophie had guessed—had *known* a moment before—and pushed Claire to the ground, rolling them away safely before Estelle struck.

Winded, Claire gasped for breath even as she tried to scramble to her feet. She still gripped the crown tight, but fumbled for her pencil. It had been knocked from her fingers and she couldn't see it anywhere. She looked around, but all she could see were bits of rock, a few wooden splinters, and a torn leaf.

Claire almost choked. Her pencil—it had been crushed! But there was no time to mourn.

"Don't move," Estelle ordered and hit the flagstone floor

with the cane. Claire suddenly felt her legs grow heavy—heavy as rock. Claire tried to call out to Sophie, but even her tongue felt heavy now. It was as though gravity had increased, and the stone heart of the world wanted to pull her into itself, like a magnet.

Claire fell prone, her cheek flat against the flagstones and her legs and arms seemingly cemented to the earth. A moment later, Sophie, too, collapsed, sprawling next to her.

They were trapped.

Queen Estelle's hideous gown whispered as it moved across the floor, and the sound only stopped when she reached Claire and plucked the Crown of Arden from her hands.

"Thank you," Estelle said, "for preparing this for me." And then she raised the four-pointed crown—the crown that made its wearer's magic even more powerful—and set it on her brow.

It was over.

Finished.

Done.

Even if anyone *did* come to help them, it was too late. Estelle, adorned in unicorn artifacts, wore the Crown of Arden.

Estelle was queen again . . . and Nadia would *never* be crowned.

The remade queen of Arden closed her eyes and breathed in, as though smelling something sweet: Victory. Triumph. Absolute power. A terrible grin spread across the queen's face.

With the last of her strength, Claire struggled against the earth's pull, lifting her head just enough to turn it the other way. Her gaze locked on Sophie, who was already looking at her. Sophie's littlest finger twitched.

A pinky promise.

A sister's promise.

A promise to be with her, until the very end.

Except . . . a pearly light softly filtered in.

Estelle turned around, the gems on her gown clinking.

"You," she breathed.

The unicorn had arrived.

Unable to see clearly at first, Claire could still hear the chime of diamond hooves striking the floor. The unicorn didn't charge forward, like he had that night on the Sorrowful Plains. Instead, he approached steadily, deliberately, until at last, he moved into Claire's field of vision.

The queen leveled the ram's head at his chest, but still the unicorn did not falter. One step, and then another, and then he was toe to hoof with the queen, the deadly cane an inch from his chest.

An inch from his heart.

Strange shadows flitted across the queen's face in the glow of the unicorn's horn. The last queen and the last unicorn stood across from each other, still as the monoliths they'd once been. And then—

I remember you. The unicorn's voice did not sound in Claire's ears or even in her head but in the same place she heard magic's hum. He spoke not with words but with memories. Chubby hands wrapping in his mane as the little princess pulled herself up to take her first step. Round cheeks, tear-streaked, pressed against his neck as she cried over a skinned knee. The memories shifted and settled into a story.

✳

A girl Claire's age stood at a white marble crypt, her mother's name freshly engraved across it. Her little brother stood beside her, eyes solemn beneath his crop of curls. When the unicorn took a step toward them, the girl turned fierce gray eyes on him. "Go away," she shouted. "You didn't save her!" The unicorn did as she requested, knowing grieving hearts needed time to heal and that one day she might come to understand not everyone needed saving.

✳

Death was in Arden. Another graveyard, another funeral: the girl-turned-woman grieved as they now laid her father the king to rest in his grave. That night, the woman stormed at her younger brother, telling him it had to be done. It was the only way. If they didn't, they would keep losing family. Keep losing friends. The Gemmers were losing too much.

The brother refused and instead called the unicorn with the crystal flute, and together, both creatures fled into the night.

✳

The next time he saw her, she wore the Crown of Arden and led a hunt. She was happy. The legends had been right: anyone who killed a unicorn did live forever. Her armies were undefeated. Her most loyal soldiers now immortal and incapable of leaving her like her parents had done. The unicorn sorrowed. The humans did not yet know the cost.

The unicorn watched as the rumors began to spread: of Gemmer soldiers disappearing overnight. Of whole regiments retreating from the sun. And at the same time, of new and terrible creatures appearing in Arden, monsters as twisted and terrible as the crime they had committed.

The unicorn watched the queen rage fearfully in the night, scrubbing at shadowed spots on her hands that would not come off, no matter how many elixirs and antidotes she tried. The potions and vast amount of unicorn artifacts she wore only slowed down her transformation, but they would not stop it. Each week, she had to add a new ring to her finger, to hide the skin that seemed to have turned into melted shadow.

The unicorn watched from the Needles as Estelle traveled to the Spydens, and one told her how she could stop from turning into a wraith: she needed an exchange of hearts. So the queen decided that she would change out her heart for the most powerful one of all: a unicorn's heart.

She would live forever. Rule forever. She would walk in sunlight again.

The unicorn watched as the Spyden shared another truth

with Estelle: "When the last unicorn with crystal horn is extinguished, the wraiths will no longer have anything to fear, not even the sun." They would be able to step into the daylight.

"No more of these half steps and potions," Estelle crooned to her former Gemmer army. "We will find the last unicorn. I will take its heart to keep my human form, and when the last light ebbs from his crystal horn, you, my darling wraiths, will move in the daylight once more." The shadows swarmed her, but the unicorn knew that the queen did not feel their cold. She was already frozen, even as she promised to reunite them with the sun. "The last unicorn still gallops the Sorrowful Plains, and I will ride tonight."

She was so focused on her wraiths that again she did not see the unicorn watching her through the branches of the petrified trees or notice him gallop off into the night in search of the lost prince.

✳

Though her body still felt too heavy, Claire's mind raced.

Arden legend promised that anyone who killed a unicorn would live forever.

Three hundred years ago, the Gemmers hunted unicorns to extinction. Three hundred years ago, wraiths swarmed Arden. The wraiths did not appear in Arden *after* the unicorns had died out. They appeared in Arden *because* the unicorns had been killed.

The unicorn hunters would live forever, but not as humans—as wraiths.

Which meant Queen Estelle, huntress of unicorns, had also been cursed, her transformation into a shadow only slowed down by the powerful magic of the unicorn artifacts she wielded.

But . . . surely Claire had seen Terra in daylight? Yet, as she combed through her memories, she realized she'd never seen Terra in the morning or afternoon. She'd only ever seen the woman in the evenings, after sunset, and always in the protection of walls or tunnels.

Estelle d'Astora was a wraith.

And her brother, Prince Martin, had known—and with this knowledge, he'd chosen to transform both unicorn and queen into the monoliths on the Sorrowful Plains. But why?

Claire glanced at Sophie . . . and saw the answer. And its urgency and clarity pulled Claire out of her own swirl of emotions as the unicorn again addressed the queen.

I remember, the unicorn seemed to be saying to Estelle. *Do you?*

"I remember how you lied," Estelle snarled. "You and your kin *tricked* us with those stories of immortality! And you— you stole Martin away from me!" She raised the ram's head cane.

"No!" The word scraped against Claire's tongue.

Estelle looked at her in surprise. "Your magic has grown considerably to resist my enchantment," she said, and for a moment she sounded like Scholar Terra, and that gave Claire strength.

She might not be able to reason with Estelle, Hunter of

Unicorns, but maybe, just maybe, she could with Scholar Terra, her friend. Her teacher.

Maybe Claire could reason with the little princess who'd loved the duck pond that Claire had glimpsed in the pencil's sketch.

The big sister Martin had come back for.

"Martin never abandoned you," Claire said. "He *loved* you!"

Scorn filled every line of Estelle's face. "Martin *trapped* me," Estelle snarled. "He turned me to stone. For three hundred years, I was helpless on the Sorrowful Plains. Alone."

"But you were never alone," Sophie said, her voice thin as she tried to speak around whatever Estelle was doing to them. "The unicorn never left you. He stood by you, watching you all this time. For *three hundred years*."

"Because he was too weak to complete the craft without doing so," Estelle snapped. "Unicorns are useless alive. Unwilling to help. He took Martin away from me, and my little brother left me all alone, like everyone else."

"No," Claire said. She suddenly felt Sophie's hand in hers, and the weight in her limbs began to lighten. "Martin didn't abandon you. He *loved* you," she repeated. "You were turning into a wraith! He turned you into stone to *slow down* the transformation. To give you time to find an antidote that wouldn't cost you the rest of yourself. Like you, he couldn't bear to lose anyone else, especially not his big sister, who used to take him to feed the ducks in the pond."

The queen and the unicorn were still.

"Martin never gave up on you," Sophie said in such a

knowing voice that Claire couldn't help but remember she was an older sister talking to an older sister. "He *never* forgot you. How could he? You're his sister. He missed you."

Sophie took a deep breath, as though trying to rein in her emotions. She squeezed Claire's hand tighter. "He told stories of Arden to his children, encouraged them to seek out the wonderful land of his stories, so that when someone—our aunt Diana, Nadia—at last found the way back, she wouldn't be scared to venture in. He wanted us to come. He wanted us to wake you and give you another chance!"

The unicorn stayed still, his neck nobly arched, but Claire could feel his approval in the warmth of his dark eyes, ringed by silver.

"You're lying," Estelle whispered, but her hand twitched. Claire held her breath. She could see how much Estelle wanted to believe Sophie and Claire. How much she *hoped* it was true.

At first, Claire thought it was only the expression on Estelle's face that had changed, but then she realized that it was more than just her expression—it was her face, her skin, her body. She seemed to be shrinking, her skin turning thin and wrinkled as she began to age in front of them. The immortality of a wraith seemed to be draining from her with each passing second as another year was added to her. In just a minute more, she would be dust.

The earth, which had been hugging Claire to itself, loosened its hold. Hope fizzed through her. Had she and Sophie done it? Had they managed to defeat Estelle after all?

Suddenly, the unicorn reared up, shrieking in pain.

Claire didn't understand, but then she saw a thin red streak across the unicorn's flank—and heard an obsidian-tipped spear clatter against a wall. She turned her head to see Jasper standing in the doorway.

"Your Majesty!" he yelled, running forward. "The unicorn! Take its heart. Stop your Shadowing!" But before he could utter another word, the diamond hooves slammed back down on the ground, and the unicorn kicked back—connecting with Jasper's chest. The former commander of Stonehaven flew against the wall and slumped down, knocked unconscious.

But the damage was done.

The unicorn sank to his knees, his glorious horn drifting toward the ground next to Estelle, who still held the ram's head cane. Estelle's black hair was now brittle white, her skin so cracked that it reminded Claire of fissures in the desert. She looked all of her more than three hundred years, but her eyes—gray as Dad's, gray as Claire's—were the same. And her hands still clutched the ram's head cane.

"No!" Claire said, terrified. Estelle was going to take the unicorn's heart! Suddenly, Claire found she could move freely again. She leaped to her feet and reached to grab the cane away, but she was too late. Estelle had already lowered it to the unicorn's streak of red. The blood no longer glistened, it gleamed. Like rubies.

Claire faltered. Estelle was not trying to harvest the unicorn's heart for a last chance at immortality. Estelle was trying to heal the unicorn.

But she was fading too fast.

They both were.

The queen and the unicorn looked as though they were eroding away, like rock beneath a waterfall for a millennium—all in five seconds.

"The sun," Claire thought she heard Estelle whisper into the unicorn's ear, and with the last of his strength, the unicorn lifted his horn to Estelle's heart.

Together, he seemed to say.

Wishing stars and wishing hearts can't be all that different, can they? Sena had once said, not so very long ago. Claire knew, from tales and life, that sometimes a heart could contain a wish so big, it was capable of changing everything.

The chamber was filled with a sudden rush of wind, throwing dirt and dust into the air. Coughing, Claire squeezed her eyes shut as she tried to stumble closer to the unicorn, but she tripped, sprawling onto the floor.

The breeze settled as quickly as it had come.

All was silent.

All was still.

Jasper must have regained consciousness and fled, because he was gone, and it was only Claire and Sophie in the octagonal chamber.

No queen. No unicorn.

Except there, where the last queen and the last unicorn had stood, in the middle of the broken rocks and stones, grew two flowers: a single snowdrop and a morning glory, the first flower that greeted the sun each morning.

And, encircling them both, the Crown of Arden.

Coughing, Sophie staggered over and sat down next to the blossoms. "Claire," she said, her voice sounding hoarse, "the Spyden was *right*. Your Spyden and the one in the unicorn's memory!"

"What do you mean?" Claire asked, coming to sink down beside her sister. She was so tired, she thought she might sleep for the rest of her life. "The Spyden told me only a queen could defeat a queen, and Nadia isn't here—and she wasn't crowned!"

Sophie's fingers skimmed the petals, stark white against the crown's ebony. "But a queen *did* defeat a queen. Queen Estelle was defeated by . . . Queen Estelle." Her sister looked up, and Claire saw a veil of tears over her eyes. "All this time, all those *years*, Estelle thought that the only thing that would prevent her from turning completely into a wraith was if she had a new heart. A unicorn's heart. But all she needed was a *change* of heart. A moment when she, at last, decided to break her own pattern."

Bewilderment pressed on Claire, pushing her forehead into a frown and the corners of her mouth down. It seemed impossible, improbable, but Sophie knew things. Still . . . "She did terrible things," Claire said fiercely. "She wanted horrible things. That doesn't erase it."

"It doesn't," Sophie agreed. "And Arden won't forget. But her story won't end entirely in shadow."

"Hmm," Claire said. She wanted to make sure that

whenever a *new* poem was written about the last queen of Arden, it would contain all the correct details. And she knew just the Spinner she could trust who would take down Claire's every word. A ray of light tumbled through the stained glass. Sometime during the struggle, dawn had broken.

"We need to go tell—tell everyone," Sophie said, looking exhausted by the thought.

Claire nodded, but her attention had snagged on something: a bit of gleam in the grit.

"Sophie, look," she said. The moontears, whole and perfect, lay just a few feet away. With a strangled cheer, Sophie shot to her feet and put the moontears around her neck. But Claire didn't feel like cheering. Estelle was gone, the moontears retrieved, but something still felt . . . wrong.

And suddenly, she realized what it was. "Sophie, it's *dawn*!" The unicorn's memory of the Spyden came back to her.

"So?" Sophie asked as Claire scrambled for her Hollow Pack and grabbed the spyglass.

When the last unicorn with crystal horn is extinguished the wraiths will no longer have anything to fear, not even the sun.

Claire hurried to the window and peered out with the spyglass. All across Arden, she could make out pockets of shadows, like billowing smoke. But it was not smoke. Horror gripped Claire in its jaws.

"Estelle's warning," Claire croaked out. " 'When the last unicorn with crystal horn is gone'—oh, Sophie! It *happened*."

The sun had risen, but the wraiths remained.

CHAPTER
27

Claire and Sophie sprinted out of the stained-glass chamber and clattered into the hallway. Slipping a bit on the marble floors, they sprinted down the corridor and toward the "Forbidden" sign that Claire had previously ignored. In the growing sunlight, she realized she *did* actually recognize this portion of the Citadel. If she and Sophie were to continue down that way, they would reach a spiraling staircase that descended deep into a large cavern filled with stone statues of warriors: the Memorial of the Missing, a remembrance for all the Gemmers whose bodies had never been recovered in the Guild War.

"This way!" Sophie called over her shoulder as they tore down another hallway. Sophie had somehow found the tail end of the abandoned B.P.S. and was frantically winding the yarn as they retraced their steps. Claire, meanwhile, had her hands full with the Crown of Arden.

Even though it hadn't been blessed by a unicorn's horn and still did not sing the way it had in the pencil's memory, the crown remained a powerful example of jumbled magic. And with the approaching onslaught of sunlight-immune wraiths, Claire knew the guilds would need every last bit of help. But the crown was heavy, and that in combination with her Hollow Pack slowed her down. Up ahead, Sophie was already turning the corner—

"Ah!"

"Sophie!" Claire cried as her sister's shout echoed down the stone hallway. Fear pushed her legs faster. Had the Royalists come back for Estelle and caught Sophie instead? With one last gasp of breath, Claire flung herself around the corner . . . and saw familiar faces.

"Claire!" Zuli said, the Gemmer apprentice's tight curls bouncing with joy. "It's so good to see you!"

"You mean, it's great to see her!" Zuli's twin brother, Lapis said.

"Stupendous," Zuli shot back.

Behind the Gemmer twins stood Nett, Sena, and Thorn, all panting heavily.

"Slug soot," Nett wheezed, "I'm so glad we found you! We thought the Royalists might have gotten you—"

"There was an infiltration!" Sena jumped in. "But this preamble"—she reached behind Thorn and pulled Lyric into view—"sounded the alarm and they were caught pretty quickly. That's when Nadia and everyone realized that you two had disappeared, along with the Crown of Arden."

"We thought you might have been kidnapped!" Thorn said, his voice tight. "But Lyric found me and told me she thought you were still somewhere inside Starscrape. She described it for us—"

"—and we guessed where you were," Lapis finished.

"How did you do that?" Claire asked Lyric.

Lyric looked a bit sheepish. "When I lent you the B.P.S., I also kind of slipped a Snitch Stitch into your pocket. I overheard you describing stained glass windows and I heard the arrival of the Royalists. That's how I was able to warn everyone in time. I'm sorry!" she added quickly as Claire reached into her cloak pocket and pulled out a thin red string. "I *know* you're not supposed to eavesdrop, but you just disappeared last time, and I wanted to make sure I could find you again!"

Next to her, Sophie made a muffled sound somewhere between a snort and laugh. Claire shot her sister a look and Sophie pulled herself together. "That's all right, Lyric," she said. "I'm sure Claire understands. But where is Nadia now? We need to talk to her right away!"

"She was planning to ride out of Starscrape to look for the two of you," Nett replied, worry in his eyes.

"No!" Claire gasped and dumped the crown into Zuli's arms to pull out her spyglass again. She half-ran, half-stumbled to a narrow window. With an expert click, she slid open the instrument and held it up to her eye, searching for any flash of chimera that might have been sent out on a search mission.

Meanwhile, she heard Sophie telling the others what had just happened—and what was coming for them.

"But if sunlight doesn't work, we're utterly defenseless!" Nett cried. "Nothing we have will protect us. Fighting wraiths like that will be like trying to fight a hurricane, punch a tornado, or hug a wildfire: Futile. Deadly. The elements will always win. The most we can hope for is to survive—to *just* survive one more day and the next and the next! It'll be an unending storm!"

"But magic is always stronger surrounded by other magic," Sena, always stubborn, pointed out. "With all the guilds together—and the crown!—maybe we'll be all right."

At that moment, Claire spotted Nadia, and relief rushed through her. She was still on the Wall. She was still safe. But that's where Claire's relief ended.

Because as she turned the spyglass beyond Starscrape Mountain, she could see dark clouds roiling across the land: wraiths. They were closer than they had been only a few minutes ago. Much, much closer. The wraiths were swarming toward Constellation Range and Starscrape Citadel, where they still thought they might find their queen.

She snapped the spyglass shut and whirled around just as Thorn spoke.

"But there's just not enough magic left in Arden to face them," he said softly. "We need unicorns."

Sophie lifted her chin, and as she did, the four moontears at her throat winked. Claire wished that the unicorn had managed to wake them with his horn before he'd left, and she could feel her heart breaking.

"We still need to try," Sophie said.

They all took off at a sprint.

If only there were more moontears, more unicorns, more *magic.* They would need an entire sky of falling stars—like Starfell—for that wish to come true.

Wishing stars and wishing hearts can't be all that different, can they?

As she ran, Claire felt like she was trying to solve a puzzle painted by the Impressionists. A painting made up of millions of little dots that finally, if you stood far away, made a beautiful whole. For three hundred years, the guilds had been their own dots and taken with them their own sayings and traditions.

The Spinners celebrated Starfell by dancing with ribbons to imitate unicorn manes and tails as they ran up the mountains to meet the stars. But the Forgers celebrated something else—the finding of unicorns in the snow. Claire's heart was pounding now. Maybe even unicorns in *mountain* snow. The Tillers celebrated the coming of winter with a cookie named after a springtime flower, but it was also a flower that bloomed in a unicorn's steps. And the Gemmers—Claire looked around— they lived on *Star*scrape mountain.

She stopped running, while the others sprinted ahead. All except Sophie, who immediately fell back. "Claire? Are you okay?"

"Yes," Claire said, her heart racing as she remembered the dazzling display of falling stars from just the night before. "I know where there are more moontears!"

"What?" Sophie gasped, her hand flying to the necklace. "What do you mean?"

The answer to everything was right *there*, in all the tales and traditions of Arden. Individually, the guilds' customs seemed like fun ways to celebrate, but together they wove a greater tapestry. A greater meaning. A truth that had been lost as the guilds drifted apart.

"Moontears," Claire said, barely able to get out the words. "They're falling stars that landed in the mountaintops!" She felt like laughing. She'd even thought that the stars had made it look like the moon was crying last night.

"Every year," Claire hurried to explain, "the unicorns would run up the mountains to greet the stars—that's what the Spinners say. But I bet it wasn't just to greet them, but to *waken* the new moontears that had landed in the mountain snow. And no one ever realized that's where moontears came from; because there were so many unicorns, it was impossible to know that more had been added to the herd."

Sophie gasped. "That means—that means there *could* be thousands of moontears, collecting under the snow for the last three hundred years. But I can't awaken them!"

"That's all right," Claire said, because she knew that it was. "Moontears are the Great Unicorn Treasure! They're still incredibly powerful. If we can bring more down to Stonehaven, they will make *all* our magic stronger! Arden might stand a chance against the wraiths!"

"Hey, what's going on?" Zuli and Lapis ran back to them, while the others sprinted ahead, calling out for the grandmasters to gather and for someone to get Nadia right away.

"We need to get out of the Citadel," Sophie said. "Without the grown-ups knowing—No, Claire!" She held up a hand to stop Claire midprotest. "They won't let us leave the walls, especially once they know about the wraiths and the sunlight!"

Sophie was right.

"We know a way," Lapis whispered, as a Tiller journeyman sprinted down the hall, calling for reinforcements. "But are you sure you need to? Maybe the Crown of Arden will be enough."

Claire shook her head. "It doesn't sound right, but—oh!"

She broke off. Because for the first time since they'd left the stained-glass chamber, she listened, really listened. A song emanated from the crown—one as clear and strong as there had been in the pencil's memory.

"It's been singing this whole time," Zuli said, looking down at the gleaming black circle "and it only got louder and louder the more we talked."

Claire gaped. Maybe the Crown of Arden wasn't a powerful tool after all. Maybe all it really was, was a measuring tool: a way to gauge the bond between guilds. When the bond was weak, the crown was quiet and magic seemed less plentiful. But as the relationship between guilds strengthened—as they bonded, planned, helped, and forged friendships—the crown's song and Arden's magic was at its most powerful.

The true strength of a leader wasn't found in some crown, but in the strength of their people. The true crown of Arden . . . was the guilds themselves. And from the way Sophie had just gasped, Claire knew her sister had figured it out, too. Claire looked at Sophie and nodded.

"Yes," Sophie said, her voice strong and full of hope. "We still need to leave. There's no time to explain! We need to move fast, before the wraiths arrive, or else it will be too late. Can you show us the way?"

"Come on," the twins said at the same time. "Follow us."

With Zuli and Lapis's help, the Martinson sisters slipped out of the Citadel using one of the secret entrances that was no longer manned by Gemmers.

All hands were now outside, helping to fortify the Everless Wall against the oncoming onslaught of shadow.

Starscrape Mountain was tall, but it wasn't the tallest mountain of Constellation Range, far from it. There were taller peaks—peaks that were always capped in white—one of which they could reach if they just followed a goat-trodden dirt path up for a mile.

The way was steep, and the air was thin, but both girls ran their hardest. Claire knew if they could make it to the peak and bring back moontears, it might be enough.

It had to be.

But.

Each breath Claire took felt like a knife to her lungs. She paused a moment to catch her breath. She shielded her eyes, but the jagged peak didn't seem any closer than it had before. How much longer did they have until the wraiths reached Stonehaven? She fumbled for her cloak pocket and pulled out the spyglass and directed it at Starscrape Mountain. From here, the Citadel looked like an upside-down teacup, one of the porcelain ones she'd once helped Dad pack away. Something precious and beautiful and easily shattered.

She pulled the spyglass back a bit, then stopped. There was no need to refocus it.

The wraiths were already there—at the base of Starscrape Mountain! Which meant— Claire bit back a scream as she swept the spyglass over the rest of Arden.

Wherever she looked, there was evidence of wraith-burn. Entire towns and villages were full of shivering, gray-skinned people. And still it wasn't enough for the wraiths, who continued their march on Starscrape Mountain, to finish what they believed to be their queen's last wish: destroy the last unicorn.

Destroy Sophie.

But Stonehaven—and all of Claire's dearest friends—would be destroyed first.

"We can make it," Claire said, collapsing the spyglass with a *snap* so that the instrument seemed to agree with her. "Come on!"

She began to run, but almost immediately, she slipped. The path, which had only been wet before, was now icy as the wraiths drew nearer. Only then did Claire realize she didn't hear the crunch of gravel behind her. "Sophie?"

Her sister hadn't moved. Her back to Claire, she was still looking down onto the frosting swoop of the Citadel's topmost turret. Though Claire couldn't see Sophie's face, she could see the taut lines of her body as she held perfectly still, her entire being focused on their friends below. She was so quiet, Claire wondered for a second if her sister had forgotten how to breathe. Only her ponytail, dark with its Milky Way streak, held any movement.

"Sophie!' Claire said, the word coming out with a puff of white. "We need to move, now!"

"We're not going to make it," Sophie said softly, back still turned. "Not unless . . ."

And at last, Sophie looked up and back at Claire. Her dark eyes seemed too large for her narrow face, and the silver ringing them seemed to catch Claire like a hook. Now Claire was the one who could hardly breathe.

"Claire?" Sophie asked, her entire body a question.

Claire couldn't speak, even though she knew the answer— *had* known it a long, long time, since even before they'd ever climbed up a ladder, back when she'd tried her hardest to ignore her parents' late-night whispers behind the bedroom door. Back when she'd purposefully overlooked the fact that Mom and Dad had taken off work for an entire summer, not just to clean out his aunt's manor but so that they could spend a last summer with both their daughters.

Claire had known the answer even when she sought out the Spyden, and she had been secretly relieved to have to change her question at the last moment. Because even though she'd known the answer, she had been too cowardly to have it confirmed. Even now, she couldn't speak it out loud.

There were some things even magic could not change.

Claire met Sophie's eyes and nodded.

Fumbling, Sophie set the moontears on a twisted stump. They gleamed in the morning sun. They had each grown to be the size of a river stone, fitting comfortably in her palm. Faint pink stars had started to appear in the lightly purpled moontears, stars that did not look unlike the little pink scar situated at Sophie's collarbone.

Sophie looked up. "Claire—are you *sure*?"

Claire knew she could take it back. One word and she could stop it all. But she knew what was needed: *a change of heart*. So instead, she said, "I'll be all right." The truth had never hurt so much.

"I love you, Clairina," Sophie whispered; then she smiled her wild smile, showing all her teeth. Sophie began to run, and Claire tore after her, even though this time, she knew she would never catch up.

Sophie moved faster and faster, her stride lengthening, stretching. She seemed to loosen like long hair released from a ponytail, unspooling like a silver ribbon, unfurling like a blossom, strengthening like tempered steel, and sparkling—sparkling, sparkling, sparkling—like a jewel.

Like a star.

Like a sun.

With a cry, Claire fell back, flinging her arms up and over her watering eyes, as the world turned blinding white.

For a moment, nothing seemed to exist. It was as though the light had swept away the entire world along with Claire's five senses. But somewhere in that infinite vastness, Claire heard the tiniest of sounds: a hum. Slowly at first and then quickly, the hum elongated and rounded into a note and then into a melody that found its way into the heart-shaped hole in Claire's chest . . . and filled it.

Joy—swift as the winds, deep as the seas, bright as all the suns in all the skies in all the worlds—engulfed Claire in a warm embrace. And with the joy came courage.

Slowly, Claire lowered her arms from her face. The light was still there, but this time, Claire refused to look away. Letting the tears stream down her cheeks, she focused on the brilliant haze. Though she had to squint, she thought she could make out the arch of a neck, a ripple of mane, and then—

A spiraling horn—clear as sunlight—dipping down to brush the moontears.

The melody burst into a harmony.

Claire laughed in delighted wonder as she caught a glimpse of five horns and five flowing tails before they galloped up the mountain, moving so fast that they seemed to be only streaks of light. They looked like shooting stars in reverse, and Claire questioned how she and all of Arden hadn't realized sooner what the unicorns truly were: wishes come to life.

And then they were gone, vanished somewhere into the jagged peaks and clear blue sky. The only things the unicorns left behind were a mess of hoofprints stamped in the mud and a single purple ribbon.

Claire swooped down to pick it up. The mud easily slipped off the Woven Root material, and she quickly wound it around her pencil before placing it into her cloak pocket. The spark of joy remained in Claire, though its warmth was less without the unicorns' song. In fact, everything was colder. Much, much colder.

The wraiths.

Anxiously, Claire scanned the jagged peaks again. There was still no sign of the unicorns, only snow and the blue dome of the sky.

But wait. Claire frowned. The glare of the sunlight on snow had intensified, and the snow line seemed closer than before. And then she heard it: a rumbling. The sound of not one unicorn, or five, or even a hundred—but *thousands*.

They galloped from the peaks, spilling down the mountainsides as though an evening sky had been tipped over. They poured out over the rocks like infinite rain.

A herd of unicorns.

A blessing of unicorns.

An avalanche of unicorns.

They were a blizzard of flowing tails and whipping manes, a flurry of diamond hooves and dark-jeweled eyes. Crystal horns as sharp as the points on a crescent moon and as brilliant as ice on fire pointed upward to the stars they'd come from.

They were a storm of starlight.

Stunned by the glory, Claire couldn't move—or take her eyes off the unicorn in the front. This unicorn galloped with the graceful sway of the magnolia blossoms outside their shared bedroom window. Of dance parties in the living room. Of the millions upon millions of everyday moments that made up their lives as sisters.

Without stopping her gallop (and probably not without a little bit of magic), the unicorn bowed her head, and Claire wove her hands into the mane and heaved herself up onto the unicorn's back. The scent of watermelon hit Claire. A summertime smell.

I promised not to leave you behind again.

A grin broke across Claire's face. This wasn't a faded memory or a guess at what her sister might say—it *was* Sophie.

Hang tight! Sophie said, her voice chime-like around the edges, and Claire did.

Claire had ridden a wyvern, escaped on a chimera, and flown through the clouds with a cloak, but none of it had prepared her for what it was like to ride a unicorn. A unicorn wasn't like riding the wind. It was *becoming* the wind. A lightness filled her, and she felt she might float away if she was not tethered by the tresses of unicorn mane wrapped across her fingers. All around her, the unicorns surged forward, their diamond hooves pounding out Arden's heartbeat as they galloped down the mountains to where the wraiths had already begun their attack.

CHAPTER
28

Starscrape Citadel had been swallowed by shadows. Skeletal shadows that howled, tore, and raged. Shadows so thick that Claire wondered if she was not looking at creatures but instead a hole, a void, a nothingness.

And yet.

Here and there, there was a flash of white marble. The Everless Wall still stood, helped along by the most ancient oaks' strength woven with the hardness of steel. Helped along by the magics of each guild, from each preamble to the wisest grandmaster.

"We're coming!" Claire shouted, even though she knew she was too far away for anyone to hear. "Hold on!" She leaned low over the unicorn's neck. The silvery mane whipped back, tickling her nose. Any moment, the unicorns' magic would make all the guilds' magic stronger.

Any moment, the magic in Mulchbombs and Sunlight Ropes and Sun Swords would be able to cut into the shadows, stronger and more powerful than ever before. A tiny seed of light suddenly flitted from a tower. Claire was still too far away to see, but the unicorn could, and she pressed into Claire's heart the vision of a bird, woven from the mossy fuzz of a marimo, shining with a pearly light, its beak edged with sword steel that could glow in the night and cut back the wraiths.

Nett's marimo, shaped by Thorn and edged with Fireblood's tip.

For a moment—a single, magnificent moment—the little bird withstood the storm. But just before Claire could let out a ragged cheer, she saw the wings of light bend, and the bit of alchemy was sucked into the vortex of shadows.

Gone.

Swallowed whole.

The wraiths were space without light, swallowing it, devouring it, like the black holes that lurked in space, eating stars.

"Stop!" Claire screamed out to the unicorns. "Go back!" But the unicorns galloped forward. Once, Claire had seen a single unicorn sweep away a plain of these monsters with a swoop of his horn, but now . . . Claire imagined another unicorn, shoulders as large as boulders, with a blue sheen to her creamy coat, charging at the solid shadows, only to be blown out like a spark.

Claire tugged at the unicorn's mane. "Please! You have to tell them to turn around! It's not working!"

It wasn't unicorns who defeated the Wraith Queen.

"What?" Claire shouted, confused, but the unicorns surged with them, brighter than sun on snow—a burning brilliance that should have blinded Claire but, somehow, made her see everything. *Remember* everything.

✳

Her first evening with Terra, after a day of disappointments, Claire thought that maybe she'd run out of magic. "Magic never runs out," Terra had told her. "It's always there, in the material. Magic is really about seeing, about finding the possibilities."

✳

An evening Claire should have been practicing but instead chose to follow Sophie down a forbidden set of stairs to a chamber full of red-stone warriors. An army, they'd thought. But no. Jasper had said it was a memorial—one that commemorated all the Gemmers whose bodies were never recovered from the battlefield.

And now Claire understood why those Gemmers' bodies had never been recovered.

They had never died.

✳

"A changing of hearts," Sophie had said. "Estelle saved herself."

✳

Claire knew what needed to be done.

"Let me down!" Claire shouted, and the unicorn beneath her swiftly dropped to her knees. Claire flung herself off and hit the ground, rolling to the edge so she wouldn't be trampled.

Without the unicorn's touch, the wraiths' cold prickled against her skin, but she was not afraid. Claire was loved by a unicorn, and she knew, somehow, that she would never again be in danger of a wraith's touch. And with that knowledge in her mind, Claire threw herself onto her hands and knees and plunged her hands into the earth—into Arden.

She gasped.

Magic—hot and fresh—bubbled, trilled, surged, and sang at her fingertips.

The hum that had first scared Claire in the chimney had become a familiar friend, but now it was gone, and in its place was a symphony: a concerto of tectonic plates, chiming gemstones, and warbling pebbles. The magic of Arden spoke to her, singing a story of all the possibilities of Arden—how the smidgen of clay near her thumb could be crafted into a perfect grail, how the boulder a few yards away could shoulder the weight of a new and airy palace on a hilltop, how the wyverns hidden in the heart of the mountains were ready to return.

But Arden was made up of *more* than just rock. The unicorns' song and the rush of renewed magic seemed to momentarily blur the boundaries among the guilds of magic, and Claire could hear, only slightly less clearly, the clarion call of metal running through the soil, the green *thrum* of roots twisting between metals and minerals as it made a gentle promise to nurture the fibers that could be spun into warmth and protection.

Metal was in stone was in green was in cloth.

With the return of the unicorns, Arden *itself* had awakened, and it joined in the unicorns' song, telling a story of all that Arden had been, was now, and could be—something brighter and stronger than any one of them could have ever possibly imagined.

Claire had an entire world of magic at her fingertips. Arden's fate was in her hands. Her heart skipped a beat. There was no way she could do this! It was too much!

The unicorn next to her reared up, a silver scythe against a blue sky. *Don't be afraid!* she proclaimed. *You are not alone!* Four diamond hooves stomped back on the earth, and the unicorn who had been a girl lowered her head to let her crystal horn rest on Claire's shoulder. And all across Constellation Range, the unicorns continued their gallop toward the Citadel's peak.

The symphony of magic swelled.

Claire, the unicorns sang, *change the world!*

And pushed by unicorn song, Claire did.

With her fingertips, Claire found a tendril of heat sent up from the world's heart, a delicate breath that wove in and out of underground pools, coaxing life into even the deepest and darkest places, where nothing should have been able to exist.

You can do it, Claire. You've already done this before. An image of the Sand Dolphin leaped into her mind.

Claire smiled. "You mean *we* can do it."

After all, Sophie had always made the world around Claire come alive. Sophie had always sparked Claire's courage. Sophie had always been a unicorn.

And they would always be sisters.

Together, the sisters of Arden urged the tendril of heat—of magic multiplied by a thousand unicorns—toward the Citadel. With the crystal horn on her shoulder, Claire could feel the magic twisting and turning as it made its way through the ground to Starscrape Citadel and then underneath it.

It moved faster and faster, spreading like roots as it passed under one chamber of craftsmen, and Claire could hear Tiller call to Spinner call to Forger call to Gemmer to help one another against the fury of wraiths. But that wasn't where the magic needed to go. Instead, it flowed past them and down deeper and farther to another chamber, one that could be reached only by a spiraling staircase that had been roped off, marked as forbidden. And as the magic moved, it gathered strength, swelling like a wave, and then—

Thunder rolled out over the peak as the Everless Wall collapsed.

Claire's ragged breath caught in her chest.

The wraiths had broken through. Arden's last defense was now only a ring of dust.

Not just dust, the unicorn said with a gentle prod. *Look.*

Claire fumbled once more for her spyglass and brought it to her eye. Something moved within the clouds. Giants.

Statues.

Claire let out a joyful shout as row after row of red-stone warriors shrugged out of the dust and surrounded the Citadel in a protective circle, forming a barrier between the wraiths and the people.

The Memorial of the Missing had awakened.

Or, as Claire had realized, the memorial of all those Gemmers who'd gone on a unicorn hunt and whose choices had twisted them beyond any human recognition, corrupting them into shadow. The only thing left of their humanity was the memorial sculpted by the loving hands of those Gemmers who were left behind, with no knowledge of what had happened to their friends and family members. The sculptors from three hundred years ago who, at the direction of Prince Martin, who'd been a friend to unicorns, had preserved the best aspects of those hunters so that they, too, might have a chance to feel sunlight again.

The wraiths, confused, shifted back, away from the strange marching statues, but the unicorns charged forward. Their horns brimmed with light, illuminating the wraiths' former selves carved into the stone.

But one unicorn did not go forward. She stayed behind with Claire, and they watched together from the higher peak as the white ring of unicorns rushed toward a red-stone band to squeeze out the dark shadows between, a circle of darkness that grew thinner and thinner as the unicorns' light grew stronger.

For a moment, Claire thought she could hear a bubble of laughter—of joyful recognition, of reunion with a long-lost friend—as the wraiths saw and remembered who they had been and could be again.

A changing of hearts.

Then again, maybe it wasn't laughter at all but only the chime of diamond hooves on rock.

Still, Claire was sure of one thing: the dark was lifting. Slowly at first, but then like a thunderstorm giving way to rain and then a gentle patter, it lessened until it was nothing at all. The shadows were gone, replaced by misty rainbows that hung over the mountaintop.

Estelle's promise, at last, had been fulfilled.

The wraiths had been reunited with the sun.

The stone statues, their mission done, settled back into their stationary state, though they remained circling Starscrape Citadel, replacing the Everless Wall that had separated the Gemmers from the rest of Arden for three hundred years. A new kind of memorial, one not of loss but of being found again.

"Where are the unicorns going?" Claire cried out. They had not stopped running. Instead, they were streaming down the mountains, flowing like rivers into the rest of Arden.

Do not fear, her unicorn said. *We are here to stay. We will seek out all those suffering from wraith-burn and will heal them.*

She stood behind Claire, and Claire was aware of her solid warmth as she leaned back into the creature. The unicorn lowered her head and rested it on Claire's shoulder. Again, Claire felt joy and courage flow through her, but this time, they were tempered by something else, which made the emotions less fierce and more soft—comfortable, even. Peaceful.

Claire turned and threw her arms around the unicorn's arched neck. "We did it," Claire whispered fiercely into the mane. "We did it."

"*Purr-ka*!" At the sound of the familiar chirp, Claire let go of the unicorn and looked up. Gryphin was soaring in the air, making dizzying loops, as though marking the spot where Claire stood. Claire looked down the path to see people spilling out of the Citadel.

Claire brought the spyglass to her eye. Spinners danced with Tillers while Forgers dropped their weapons and stared in awe at the flick of tails rushing down the mountains. Gemmers, meanwhile, stood in family groups, a little bit shy as they studied the new wall. Adjusting the lens slightly, Claire saw the spotted face of a Tiller scribe chatting animatedly with a Forger apprentice who wore pigtails, while next to them, she saw the familiar face of Master Pumus bending down to help a Spinner collect the ribbons she'd thrown into the air in celebration.

But it wasn't until Claire turned the spyglass onto the path leading upward, toward the higher peaks, that she found who she was looking for. A grin broke across her face as she realized Gryphin had been successful in relaying his message.

"It's Nett and Sena! And Thorn!" Claire said. "They're running toward us! And so is Kleo! And Lyric and Lapis and— and *everyone*!"

Grandmaster Carnelian rode Lixoon, while Mathieu and Sylvia carefully led the chimera up the narrow path. And behind them, finally, Aunt Nadia!

She was slow, however, and Claire worried that her aunt was injured, but then she saw she was helping a smaller woman with thick gray hair and rosy cheeks make her way up the path. And behind them walked Mistress Weft and Scythe, each one holding the arm of a taller man across their shoulder. The man moved stiffly, as though he'd forgotten how legs were supposed to work, but the double-headed battle-ax across his back gleamed as bright as ever.

"It's Anvil and Aquila!" Claire shouted, lowering the spyglass in delighted surprise. "But how?"

When we asked stones to move, you also asked the rock in other things to waken, too. Everyone Estelle rubified should be back to who they were, a little stiff but otherwise all right.

"We're here!" Claire called, waving her arms at them. She could see Sena's red head and Nett's black one break away from the group as they broke into a run. "We're safe! We're—"

But Claire stopped as a sudden chill hit her back. Suddenly, it felt like a cloud had come between the sun and her. The unicorn had drawn away.

I can't face them. Not yet.

"But—"

Claire's protest was cut off as Nett and Sena finally appeared, followed by all the others. And in the next second, many hands were reaching for Claire, pulling her in tight. And Claire let herself be enveloped by warm hugs, which made it easy to hide the few tears that dripped down her cheeks, as silent as the unicorn who had already slipped away.

CHAPTER
29

When Sophie had first gone to the hospital, Claire had gotten used to days with no answers . . . but that didn't mean she liked it. And so now she knew enough to keep busy, and with Aunt Nadia's inauguration only two weeks away, there were plenty of things that needed to be done.

It had been one month since the unicorns' return to Arden. And in the time since, the four guilds of Arden had met at Drowning Fortress to discuss a new way of living. A new structure of how Arden could be: a republic.

Every grandmaster from every guild had been considered, but at the end of three long days of discussions and deliberations, the vote had been unanimous: Nadia Martinson would be Arden's first Prime Minister.

"I didn't vote for you because you're a d'Astora,"

Grandmaster Bolt had boomed from his boat when the results became clear. "I voted for you because of how equally you've treated the members of Woven Root."

"And here I thought it would be my chimera-riding skills," Nadia had murmured, loud enough for Claire, the Malchains, and the Steeles to hear, but no one else.

Aquila had shrugged, adjusting the weight of her twin battle-axes. "That's why *I* voted for you."

Aquila and Anvil had completely recovered from the weeks of rubification, and Nadia had selected them to join her personal guard. Not everyone was pleased with the changes in Arden, though most of the Royalists like Mira Fray had been caught and were currently being held in Drowning Fortress awaiting their trial, the Grand Council of Arden couldn't be sure they had caught all of Estelle's most loyal followers. In fact, they knew they hadn't.

Commander Jasper had not yet been found. Anvil suspected he had sailed across the Sparkling Sea, and had at least reached the Sunrise Isles by now.

"But there will be time for us to worry about that," Anvil had told Claire as she had spent one afternoon helping him scrub moss off a lynx-squirrel chimera they had found on the edge of the Sorrowful Plains and Petrified Forest. For the inauguration, Nadia had wanted an entire regiment of the copper beasts behind her. Once the lynx-squirrel was properly shiny, Anvil rode it over to the alchemists so they could awaken the beast.

And luckily, the alchemists weren't far away from Aquila's

cabin—at least, for now. Woven Root had set up camp in the Sorrowful Plains, the only place big enough to hold the vast crowds they were expecting to witness Nadia's Vow.

Though the alchemists were no longer outlaws, many of them couldn't imagine setting up stationary homes. Besides, Nadia herself had said that she wanted Woven Root to keep traveling. That way, she would be able to spend equal time with all the guilds' many towns, villages, and cities. Not one corner of Arden would be overlooked on her watch. As soon as the inauguration celebrations were over, Nadia had plans to move Woven Root to Starscrape Mountain.

"If ever a place needed some love and care," she'd said with an arched brow, "it's that dilapidated castle." Maps had been spread over her desk, and Claire had been helping her update the villages with all their most current names.

"I don't know," Claire had said as she blotted ink from her paint brush. She'd just finished adding "Spyden's Lair" to a currently empty bay near the Sparkling Sea. "I think you just want an excuse to look at their mosaics and art collection."

"Their collection is impressive," Nadia had agreed. "I must admit, I'm looking forward to exploring all those forbidden corridors and secret passageways. Imagine what treasures might be hidden there!"

But Claire had chosen not to imagine.

It was too hard without Sophie by her side.

Sophie.

Claire had seen many unicorns in recent days, racing one another across far-off hills, free and unrestricted. But she knew, with a sister's intuition, that none of the sparkling creatures she saw were Sophie. She hadn't seen her sister since she'd slipped away on Starscrape Mountain.

"I . . . I think she's just busy," Claire said when Nett and Sena had asked last week at dinner. And it was true. Arden had been without unicorns for three hundred years, and everything needed their attention.

"She'll return when she's ready," Sena said sympathetically. The girl had become less sharp with the return of her parents. The Steeles had moved into Francis's old cottage and had, of course, already asked Nadia's and the Grand Council's permission to officially adopt Nett. Claire had spent many cozy winter evenings with them, enjoying the warmth of a family. But most of the time, she stayed with Nadia in her Woven Root tent.

Thorn, like Claire, had chosen to stay within the Woven Root community, and Nadia had offered to train him to be her scribe. It wasn't very heroic, but Thorn seemed to take to the work happily, and Claire often saw him carrying armloads of tapestries and scrolls from tent to tent, helping with all of the guilds' matters.

She and Thorn didn't talk much about what they had lost, but sometimes, Thorn would share a funny tidbit about her sister or Claire would surprise him with something Sophie once said.

They were just waiting.

One week before Nadia's inauguration, Claire found herself hauling home a collection of diamond bits that needed to be polished into Gemglows. They were a gift to Nadia from Stonehaven, and Zuli and Lapis had been very specific over dinner about how hard they'd worked to make sure all the pieces were the same size. It was a generous gift, only Claire wished it wasn't quite so heavy—or so big.

As she wove between the tents that seemed to multiply overnight, Claire calculated where she would put this particular gift. Next to the racks of Flying Cloaks from Needle Pointe? By the vat of Swamp Berry cordial from the Tillers of Foggy Bottom? Or maybe, Claire thought, she could move the jumbled tapestry of golden thread and silk that had come from Mistress Weft, Kleo, and Lyric, and which depicted a life-sized portrait of Nadia herself.

Claire was still problem-solving when she rounded the last row of tents to arrive at Nadia's many-quartered Pavilion. To her surprise, the tent was lit. Nadia must have finished her meetings early! She usually didn't get home until well past midnight.

Claire walked in and set the diamond bits down with a soft *clink*.

"Aunt Nadia?" she called, but her aunt didn't respond. And then—

"Hi, Clairina."

Every hair on Claire's neck rose. She knew that voice. And it sounded . . . totally normal, though maybe a bit more bell-like at the edges. She whipped around to see Sophie—two-legged, two-armed, ponytailed Sophie—standing in front of her.

"Sophie!" She threw her arms around her sister's neck and felt her sister squeeze her back. Claire broke the hug. "You're *you*! But are you still a—?"

"I'm still a unicorn," Sophie said, "yes, but this is how I feel the most comfortable. After all, girls and unicorns aren't that different, really."

And Claire could see it was true. While Sophie looked almost the same, down to the freckles on her nose, there were two things impossible not to notice: the ring of silver in her eyes and a pale-pink scar on her forehead, one that perfectly matched the pale-pink star on Sophie's collarbone.

But those were small things and easily explained away in the world of Windemere Manor.

"You can come home after all, Sophie!" Claire practically squealed, sounding more like Lyric than her usual self. Quickly she began to think of all the ways they could conceal Sophie's new—and there was no other word for it—sparkle.

"Maybe Mom will let you get contacts, to explain your eyes, and you can grow your bangs out a little more to make sure the star is covered. Though," she said with grin, "you can start wearing a unicorn headband to school and . . ." She trailed off.

Sophie wasn't jumping in to agree or make a joke or laugh or say *of course*.

Because there was no *of course*.

And in the moment before Sophie took a breath and opened her mouth, Claire held up her hand.

"Please," she said, sadly. She felt a tear leak out and she hastily wiped it away. "Don't say it—not yet."

Sophie reached out and squeezed Claire's hand. Her touch held the echo of the great, magical song that bubbled throughout Arden, and though Claire's heart still felt heavy, it didn't feel as though it would crush her anymore.

Taking a cool, calming breath, Claire managed to sound somewhat normal as she asked, "So, are you going to tell me where you've been?"

"Actually," Sophie said with a grin, "I can show you."

"Show me?" Claire asked, surprised. "Show me what?" But at that moment, she heard a slight rustling, and she turned to see that since she'd left the tent that afternoon, another silk corridor had been added, leading to a newly woven apartment.

"Well," Sophie said, moving toward the new cloth door, "I had a *sense*, when I was on the mountaintop, that perhaps you, me, and Nadia weren't the only, uh, *travelers* in Arden. And so I followed my sense, and I listened, catching wind of a tale of two travelers who appeared the morning of Starfell, and carried with them the strangest rucksacks ever to be seen in Arden. Unfortunately, the travelers ran into some trouble—chased by Royalists, took a few wrong turns, ended up in an inescapable labyrinth, etcetera—but before they did get stuck, these travelers were inquiring about a pair of missing children. Missing *daughters*, actually."

With a small flourish, Sophie pulled back the curtain, to reveal—

A man, with round glasses that looked not Arden-made, and a woman, whose curly hair had been pulled into a top-knot on her head.

"Dad!" Claire yelled. "Mom!" And then she was flying across the room, throwing herself into her parents' arms.

"Claire! *Claire!*" They wrapped her up tight, and Sophie too, a tangle of happy tears and laughter and questions and love.

The Martinson family had been reunited, once more.

CHAPTER
30

The day of Nadia Martinson's inauguration broke bright and clear and cold—though Claire felt warm in her many-layered gown of rose pink, sky blue, and gold. It could have been the strands of heat that had been woven into it, courtesy of jumbled Spinner and Forger magics. But then again, it could have been the pride she felt as she watched as Nadia greeted the four grandmasters who stepped into the center of the ring of stones that had once surrounded Queen and Unicorn Rocks.

Next to her, Nett practically bounced on his toes.

"I told you to wear your thicker cloak, but no," Sena grumbled out of the side of her mouth. Sena's red hair had been pinned into delicate coronet braids, but her golden armor with a growling griffin on the breastplate declared strength and respect. (And the *real* Gryphin, lounging across her shoulders, would make sure Sena got it.) Sena Steele looked like a heroic knight, and the only thing missing was a sword. Since Sena had lost Fireblood in the Battle of the Wraiths, she'd been unable to find a blade that felt, in her own words, "hers."

"I'm not cold." Nett did a double jounce. "I'm excited!"

He, too, was dressed up for the occasion. His pine-green sweater brought out the flecks of hazel in his eyes and his leather boots had been trimmed in shiny holly leaves, and here and there, shiny golden acorns: gifts from Sylvia and Mathieu.

Sena grimaced. "Still, stop it. Everyone can *see* you."

That was true. As one of a few people allowed inside the ring of rocks during the Vow, they were clearly visible. But she was pretty sure all eyes were on Nadia, who was about to make her pledge to the guilds and become Arden's first ever Prime Minister.

"My dearest Arden, I vow," Nadia said, looking out over the Sorrowful Plains, which had been transformed into a field of candy-colored silk tents, leafy Tiller dwellings, Forger Reflec-Tents, and Gemmer-made gazebos, "to water all things green. I vow to mend all tears. I vow to polish all that may rust. I vow to move mountains."

The crowds cheered, and four figures moved into the ring of rocks where Nadia stood—the same place Unicorn Rock and Queen Rock had loomed for all those years.

Grandmaster Bolt, the Spinner director, Grandmaster Carnelian, and the newly reinstated Grandmaster Iris of Greenwood stepped forward with the crown.

"The guilds of Arden accept your words, and bind them to you for the next five years," the director said. "As our thanks to you, for your promise, will you accept the Crown of Arden?"

Claire held her breath as Nadia shook her head. "No," she said, startling a gasp from all, even the shining regiments of chimera riders who stood proudly with their mounts. "I have no need of it. While magic exists in all things—in all worlds—" she said with a significant look at Claire, "it is people who bring it out. Who are responsible for wielding it, who live and die, love and grow and change. Magic may be in the material, but we are the ones who put the magic there."

She paused, then smiled. "Besides, I've been told the magic of this Crown is to let the monarch know how united the guilds feel, but we have no need of it now, when we are blessed by unicorns." She gestured toward the edges of the Sorrowful Plains.

As one, the crowd and Claire and Nett and Sena turned to look. Surrounding the Sorrowful Plains like pearls bordering a music box stood Arden's unicorns. They had come to witness this new and exciting change in Arden's history. They had come to give their blessing, and their gifts sank into the land, making the snow whiter, the cloaks brighter, and the hope inside Claire's chest almost unbearably sweet.

"Instead," Nadia continued, her voice magically amplified to roll across the great open space, "I choose to gift the Crown of Arden to the unicorns, as a thank-you and a promise that from now, they shall be cherished and protected by all the guilds."

At that, the crowd parted slightly and Sophie appeared,

dressed in a flowing gown of white silk and lavender gauze, and trailing silver ivy. Her hair fell in shining black waves to the small of her back, the white streak still clearly visible. She moved with a grace unusual to a girl but common among unicorns, and Claire felt her breath catch slightly. But as Sophie drew nearer, Claire was relieved to see her smile was still the same. Still Sophie.

Nadia bowed to Sophie and presented the Crown. Sophie took it with an elegant nod. "We thank you for this gift," Sophie said. "And we will hold you to your vow. The unicorns, too, have a gift for Arden. Gifts," she stressed to the crowd, "*not* artifacts. Nettle Green, will you come forward?"

Nett immediately stopped fidgeting. He looked as surprised as Claire felt. Sophie hadn't told them there were going to be Unicorn Gifts!

He stepped forward while Sophie reached into her gown's pocket and produced a fuzzy little plant, perfectly round and glowing with a pearly light.

Nett gasped. "It's a marimo!"

"It's *your* marimo!" Sophie corrected with a smile. "In thanks for your boundless curiosity that helped our return, we unicorns healed the plant that was your mother's. It's the same but changed. It will never run out of sunlight. May it always light your way . . . and the darkest corners of the library."

Nett's smile was so bright Claire wouldn't have been surprised if he'd started to glow, too.

"Sena Steele," Sophie called, and a bemused Sena clunked forward . . . as did her parents. Extended between the older Steeles hung a gleaming sword, its pommel in the shape of an arched unicorn head.

As Sena grasped it and drew the blade into the air, Sophie spoke: "The unicorns gift this blade to you, Sena, for your fierce loyalty and even fiercer heart."

Sena gave it a few practice swishes. "Thank you," she whispered, her voice tight with emotion. "It's beautiful."

Sophie leaned forward, and lowering her voice, spoke so only the four of them could hear, "The same starfire that the crown was forged from makes the core of this sword. Listen to it, so you can always know who deserves your loyalty."

Sena nodded. "Its name is Clearcut," she said, and, cradling the sword like a small puppy, she stepped back to stand next to Claire.

"And finally," Sophie said, "Claire Martinson."

"Me?" Claire asked, surprised.

"Well," Sophie amended, lowering her voice slightly. "This one's from me, really." She reached behind her ear and tugged a pencil from her dark hair.

Claire gasped. It was *her* pencil. Though last time she'd seen it, it had been nothing more than a few splinters. Though it was a little shorter and the blossom was gone, as she took it she could still feel the familiar spark of the letterstone. And on the side, so tiny it was hardly even a fleck, was a little leaf.

It was whole, and it would grow again.

Sophie smiled at her and raised her voice. "The unicorns thank you, Claire Martinson, for your courage. You are brave beyond all measure and by all definitions. Use this pencil as you continue to explore worlds and magic."

Claire felt tears prickle at her eyes, but she wouldn't let them fall. Not yet. So instead, she chose to be joyful, and she hugged her sister and then Mom and Dad, who'd stepped forward too, beaming.

The unicorns reared, their crystal horns throwing rainbows into the air. The Guilds of Arden cheered, long and loud, and Claire felt as though a star had risen in her heart. And when the sisters broke apart, Nadia raised her hands and grinned.

"And now," she called, "we celebrate!"

The banquet was a feast to remember. Claire sat with her friends on one end of a long table piled with savory Forger pies, grilled river fish from the Spinners, and buttery Tiller pastries. (The Gemmers had been happy to leave their thin lentil stews in the mountaintops.) Nestled next to Sophie, she laughed and joked with her friends and family. At one point, Thorn slid away to get them all more hot apple cider, and Claire took advantage of the opportunity.

"I'm still really confused," she confessed. "You were so *mean* to Thorn in Fyrton and during the cart ride. I thought you were mad at him?"

Sophie shook her head. It was still strange to see her hair, dark and loose, tumbling past her shoulders. The only time Claire had ever really seen Sophie with her hair down was when they played mermaids on the beach.

"I wasn't mad at him, not at all," Sophie said. Sophie still sounded like Sophie, but she'd become more formal in the past week. "I just didn't know how to tell him that I wasn't . . . that I was becoming a unicorn. And until I knew what that really meant, I didn't think it would be fair to, you know . . ." She fluttered her hand, as though that were any explanation, and for the first time, Claire saw a pink blush color her sister's nose.

"Lead him on?" Sena asked, grinning slyly across the embroidered tablecloth.

"Yes, fine, if you want to call it that."

Claire smiled. "I feel a little bad. At Estelle's coronation, for a second, I thought that he actually had switched sides. Again."

"It was my plan, to get captured," Sophie admitted. "The crowds were so thick, and the only way I could think of getting to the unicorn in time to talk with him was if Estelle called me to the stage herself." She wrinkled her nose. "I suspected that the unicorn wasn't *the* unicorn. Thorn did something funny to my hair, though, to try to look like yours. But your curls are so beautiful, there was no way he could manage to replicate them in such little time."

Self-consciously, Claire tugged on a curl and looked down

at the peacocks embroidered on the tablecloth. They strutted about, congregating around fallen crumbs, though their thread beaks didn't need them for nourishment. For a moment, everything felt perfect.

Golden trees from Fyrton's Vaults had been pulled up, the metal lightly heated to keep everyone warm even on the cold night. Gemglows had been strung, crisscrossing the sky and bathing everyone in diamond light. Meanwhile, Tillers had planted special winter roses that, paired with a bit of Spinner string, plinked melodically during the courses.

This was better than perfect.

It was *right*.

And she would enjoy it while it lasted.

The celebration continued long into the night, and Claire could not remember ever being so happy. She beamed as she watched her parents relax in Arden. Mom chatted happily with Mistress Weft, and Dad had a deep conversation with a very enthusiastic Aquila. He nodded as he listened carefully, while at the same time he was careful to avoid the pointed heads of her battle-axes as she turned animatedly to address the small crowd gathered around them—Spinners, Tillers, and even a Gemmer journeyman Claire recognized from her time at Stonehaven.

Later, Claire listened to the Malchains discuss plans for one of Nadia's other ideas: an Academy of Magic, where all four guilds could learn together for the first time in more than three hundred years. Claire also asked the Steeles questions about the family's plans to travel through Arden, revitalizing the frozen chimera wherever they came across them, and she could see how excited Nett was at the thought of the new books and knowledge they were sure to encounter.

Her friends had bright new futures, and Claire was sad she wouldn't be able to see them. Because Claire and her parents had decided that right after the inauguration, when all the guilds and unicorns were still gathered, would be the best and safest time for them to travel into the seams of the world and back to Windemere.

Home. She missed it. And she was curious about the magic Nadia had mentioned—the magic in all worlds. Even so, as the morning birds began to chirp, she wasn't quite ready when Nadia came to gather the Martinsons and their friends for their final goodbye. She led them to a private spot behind Aquila's cottage where a doorframe of silver, oak, ribbon, and rock had been constructed. The door itself had been left blank, waiting for Claire's pencil.

"Promise you won't forget to water your pencil," Nett said, the tip of his nose bright red.

"I already promised," Claire said, but she promised again as she hugged her very first friend in Arden tight. "And you, don't forget your promise."

Nett laughed. "I promise to make you two inches taller in all my historical accounts." He turned away to make his farewell to Claire's parents, who had fascinated him with their stories of the other world. Next, Claire found Sena, and was shocked to see the older girl had already burst into tears, a distressed Gryphin flying away to avoid the wetness and potential rust.

"Sena," Claire said, somewhat delightedly, "You're going all 'moss soft' on me!"

"I can't help it," Sena grumbled, wiping away her tears with the back of her hand. "Don't tell Nett."

Finally, the others seemed to drift away to let the sisters speak to each other.

"Sophie, are you *sure* you can't come back with us?"

"Claire," Sophie said, "I don't think I *can* go down the well or through your drawing, and even if I could, I wouldn't." She took a deep breath. "I belong here. Arden needs me."

"*I* need you!"

Sophie smiled sadly. "You don't, not really. You know me just as well as you know yourself." That much was true. Even apart, Claire couldn't help but hear Sophie's voice—her advice, her teasing, her love—wherever she may go. Sophie would never be gone from Claire, not really.

But even so, she reached out for Sophie's hand and gripped it hard.

"There is magic in our world," Claire said, thinking of Sylvia and Mathieu's journals and Nadia's speech. "Aunt Nadia said it was all around us." She fumbled, trying to think of how best to articulate what she was feeling, needing to say her tenuous thought to make it whole and permanent. "Sophie, unicorns are *magic*, right?"

Sophie nodded ever so slightly. "And magic," she said, reaching out to squeeze Claire's hand, "is *every*where. If you know how to look for it."

They were both quiet a moment, watching the inauguration banners fluttering from Woven Root's tents, and letting thoughts drift in and out.

"Sophie?" Claire said, her voice breaking. "I'm going to miss you."

"Me too," Sophie said, her voice thick. "I love being your sister." She let go of Claire's hand and held out her arms, and Claire threw herself into them. The tears came freely.

They stood like that, the sisters of Arden, for a time. It could have been for a season; it could have been the time of Windemere or the time of Arden, but she felt as though they had stepped outside it, and they were just themselves.

Something warm nudged the backs of Claire's knees, and she saw Gryphin had settled by her feet, and then she saw something else. Startled, she broke into laughter. All around them, where Sophie's tears had fallen, were snowdrops.

And somewhere inside, Claire felt her sorrow break. She giggled and wiped her nose. "Imagine what people would think at school if you cried flowers everywhere!"

Sophie chuckled, dabbed at her eyes with a sleeve. "You're going to have the most amazing Experiences."

"Me?" Claire laughed. "You're a unicorn!"

A smile as wide as the horizon and as bright as the dawn now breaking across the plains appeared on Sophie's face. "I didn't say that *I* wasn't going to have amazing Experiences! There is so much to see and do and explore."

They returned to the others, and there was one more round of hugs and promises to remember forever.

"You'll take care of her?" Dad said, keeping his arms around his oldest daughter but looking at Aunt Nadia.

The new Prime Minister of Arden smiled. "I think it's more like Sophie will be taking care of me—of all of us, really."

"We love you, Sophie," Mom said, her eyes sparkling. Then it was Claire's turn.

"Will . . . will I see you again?"

"Unicorns know a lot of things," Sophie said, "but we don't know the future. I *can* tell you, though, that you'll dream of me. Often. And when you have a sudden inspiration to draw something, it'll be me, sharing my adventures with you. And I do know that this goodbye won't be forever."

"But it's not going to be the same, is it?"

Sophie didn't say anything, but she didn't have to. Claire knew she already had the answer. One more hug, tight and fierce and short, and then Claire let her sister go.

Taking a deep breath, Claire turned away, and she did not look back again. She had a new quest, her own quest, and she would make sure to enjoy every moment of it. Behind her, hundreds of hooves pounded across the plain, and then a moment later, the air was full of song as all the unicorns of Arden were home at last.

Claire pulled her pencil from behind her ear and set the tip to the door. Last time she'd sketched everything she loved about Arden, but now it was time to remember everything she loved about her own world. With the weight of Mom's and Dad's hands on her shoulders and the magic of unicorns in the air, Claire drew her own way home.

EPILOGUE

She'd grown since the first day she and her family had arrived at Windemere Manor. Last summer, the fireplace's mantel had loomed overhead, but now Claire was eye level with it. Well, *almost* eye level.

After everything that happened, Mom and Dad had changed their mind about selling Windemere Manor. It would take two years for the house to be properly rebuilt from the strange flames that had torn through the mansion. But it was a historic home, and there were societies that were willing to help them cover the costs of fixing the damage from the fire that had begun, somehow, in the art gallery on the first floor. Everything would be rebuilt—even the fireplace's chimney.

It had been a strange fire, everyone agreed on that, but

nothing had befuddled the fire department more than the hearth of the fireplace. It wasn't scorched but warped. As though the stone had been melted and reformed. As though it had survived an earthquake—though no earthquakes had been recorded *here* for a very long time. Claire let her hands run over the mantel's carvings of forest animals among foliage. And here and there, she'd discovered, a carved image of a hammer, a gemstone, an oak leaf, and a love knot.

She would always be searching for magic in this world.

"Claire! It's time to go!"

"In a minute, Mom!" she called back. Outside, she could hear Dad rev the engine. They were heading home to their small house, two hours away, but they would be back next weekend. Like Claire, her parents preferred to be here. She hurried down the length of the gallery, empty now but for a few footprints.

As she reached the double doors, Claire turned back to look one more time at the room.

Though none of the windows was open, a wind sighed through the gallery, soft as Spyden silk and light as a unicorn. A wind that seemed brushed with the sights and smells of possible worlds. Claire closed her eyes. For a second, she thought she felt a tug at her bushy ponytail, and her hand drifted to the purple ribbon wrapped around her curls. She would see her sister again—she was sure of it. And in the meantime, what other worlds were out there?

Her fingers tingled. She was ready to capture the image that had just blossomed in her mind, one of a unicorn, her head high, crystal horn gleaming, as she raced the wind to her next Experience. Smiling, Claire closed the double doors and tugged her pencil free.

Its leaf was still green.

ACKNOWLEDGMENTS

In a strange twist of fate, quests sometimes begin at the end. The very first thing I knew about Claire and Sophie's story was how it would conclude. Though I knew the destination, I needed the creativity, thoughtfulness, and patience of many people to light the way. And so, it seems right to end this trilogy by thanking the people who were with me from the very beginning.

Tremendous thanks is due to the guiding stars at Glasstown Entertainment: Lexa Hillyer, Laura Parker, Rebecca Kuss, Emily Berge-Thielmann, and Lynley Bird. A special thanks to Rebecca, for her endless enthusiasm, keen eyes, and passion for children's literature—Sophie and Claire are lucky to have you venture into these pages. Thank you, too, to Stephen Barbara, a literary agent with a unicorn's talent to open previously unimagined doors, and to the rest of Inkwell Management, in particular Lyndsey Blessing, Sharon Chudnow, Emma Gougeon, and Alexis Hurley.

I owe an avalanche of thanks and gratitude to my editor Sarah Shumway. Without her support, wise words, sharp insights, and encouragement, this book would simply not exist. She made it possible to travel through the hazy Way Between and into Arden. Thank you to the rest of the Way-Makers at Bloomsbury, both in the US & UK: Cindy Loh, Lucy Mackay-Sim, Annette Pollert-Morgan, Claire Stetzer, Valentina Rice, Erica Barmash, Phoebe Dyer, Lily Yengle, Alona Fryman, Teresa Sarmiento, Faye Bi, Courtney Griffin, Erica Loberg, Beth Eller, Nick Sweeney, Veronica Gonzalez, Jasmine Miranda, Stacy Abrams, Katharine Wiencke, Juliette Rechatin, Maia Fjord, Stephanie Amster, Laura Main Ellen, Cesca Hopwood, Grace Ball, and Namra Amir. And an extra thank you to Melissa Kavonic, Oona "Oona-corn" Patrick, Donna Mark, John Candell, and Claire Henry, who deserve an entire night's sky of wishing stars for the incredible amount of effort and kindness they showed this book. And last but not least, thank you to Nicholas Church, who moved mountains and founded a brand-new, fifth guild: the Time-Maker guild, which can spin days from seconds. *Thank you!* And of course, much appreciation to artists Vivienne To and Matt Saunders for the beautiful covers that provided so much inspiration for these final pages. And speaking of inspiration . . .

Unicorns are wonder. They are hope. They are love. They

are all those cheesy things that we only call cheesy because we're too intimidated to acknowledge that they are the forces that shape our world—and us. And so I want to thank the authors whom I've never met but who directed me to wonder: Beverly Cleary, Shannon Hale, Madeleine L'Engle, Gail Carson Levine, L. M. Montgomery, and Tamora Pierce.

Thank you, too, to the friends and family who continued to ask "what happens next?" and made me imagine bigger: Sarah Jane Abbott, Melissa Albert, Medea Asatiani, Rhoda Belleza, Lizzy Mason, Brigid Kemmerer, Kristina Pérez, Matthew Richman, Tara Sonin Schlesinger, Catherine Waters, and Alexa Wejko, as well as to Liz Silva, D. J. Silva, Molly Silva, Katie Blacquier, Charlotte Blacquier, Eliza Blacquier, Caroline Spector, Alice Spector, and Sean Spector. Special thanks to Tara, Mimi, and Brigid, whose insights and feedback were both invaluable and necessary to gallop forward.

I wish I had the words to properly thank my parents, Marguerite and Zoltán Benko, and my siblings, Gabriella and Matthias Benko, for all their love while I spun, grew, forged, and sculpted ideas into novels. They see the very messiest moments of creating—and they still like me anyway. In particular, thank you to Papa, who took phone calls at all hours of the day and night, and always had the answer. And from the whole of my heart, thank you to Andrej Ficnar, who braved sinks full of dishes, emergency chocolate runs, and weekends of typing. You're the best partner in this world and in all worlds.

And finally, thank you to *you*—for sticking by Claire and Sophie and Arden until the end. It's been the joy of my heart to write these books, and though this tale is over for now, I hope you keep questing for unicorns. I promise: they're out there, and if you look, you will find them.